Gold Dust Grimoire

THE CHTHONIANS BOOK 1

BILLIE NICKS

Book Cover by Erin Grisham with art by Amanda Desilets (@art_by_adsilets)

First edition December 2024

Dedication

To all the other kids out there who were obsessed with Greek mythology and Fleetwood Mac (the Venn diagram for this is pretty much a circle in case you were wondering) and wanted nothing more than to write down their fantastical dreams, which just so happened to include unhinged smut. Follow those dreams—you'll end up somewhere magical.

Content Warning

Although Gold Dust Grimoire is the *lightest* of the stories in The Chthonians, it still has fairly dark themes. The way a reader experiences content is extremely personal, and everyone's sensitivity to triggers are different. If you adhere to the "this is a shopping list," no triggers approach, then by all means, proceed!

I do want to provide a list of triggers that you may find within Gold Dust Grimoire for those that are sensitive to specific content issues. These are definitely spoilers so, if you're concerned with that and don't need the trigger warnings, please flip the page now! Within Gold Dust Grimoire, you'll find the below spoilers:

- Abduction/Kidnapping
- Child Abandonment
- Child Abuse/Endangerment
- Forced Sterilization
- Genocide
- Hallucinations (discussions of auditory and visual)
- Mass Murder

- Matricide
- Spree Killing
- Explicit Sexual Scenes (including BDSM-style sequences)

These are intended as a **guide only**. I've done my absolute best to ensure that you have the information you need to make an informed decision about whether you read Gold Dust Grimoire, but, ultimately, cannot be held responsible for your personal views or triggers. Please be mindful of your mental health!

Translations

Cole is our very favorite filthy-mouthed Cajun babe, but that does mean he uses some French here and there. To support your reading experience, I've included the below translations as a guide for Cold Dust Grimoire. The words "*ma*" or "*mon*" mean my. When used in combination with the nouns below, th ey mean "my [translation of word from the list]."

- *Allons-y* – Let's go!
- *Amour* – Love
- *Ange* Angel
- *Bel(le)* – Beautiful
- *Cher(ie)* – Dear/Darling (Cajun endearment)
- *Couyon* – Crazy person/Fool (Cajun endearment or insult, dependent upon who it's directed to)
- *Déesse* – Goddess
- *Fille* – Girl

- *Jaloux/Jalouse* – Jealous
- *Mais* – But
- *Ma putain d'épouse* – My fucking wife
- *Ouais* – Yes (Cajun informal)
- *Petit(e)* – Little
- *Piké twa* – Fuck you (Creole insult used by some Cajuns)
- *Sorcière* – Witch
- *Nonc* – Uncle
- *Villaine fille* – Bad girl

For once, I can honestly thank my brain for retaining years of French and my weird interest in unique dialects. So... thanks, brain! You did good this time.

Playlist

Arsonist's Lullabye Hozier

Bad Moon Rising (Cover) Mourning Ritual, Peter Dreimanis

Bad Ritual Timber Timbre

Darker Still Parkway Drive

Everybody Wants to Rule the World Lorde

Gold Dust Woman Fleetwood Mac

Him & I G-Eazy, Halsey

I Walk the Line Halsey

Last Dance Butcher Babies

Let the World Burn Chris Grey

Lucky Ones Lana del Rey

Persephone in the Garden Aidoneus

Pleasure ††† (Crosses)

Something in the Air Steelfeather

Sparks Parkway Drive

Sugar Sleep Token

Type III Bear McCreary, Rufus Wainwright

Until Eternity Blackbriar

Witch Which Florence + the Machine

Part 1

Only at the End May The Witches Ride

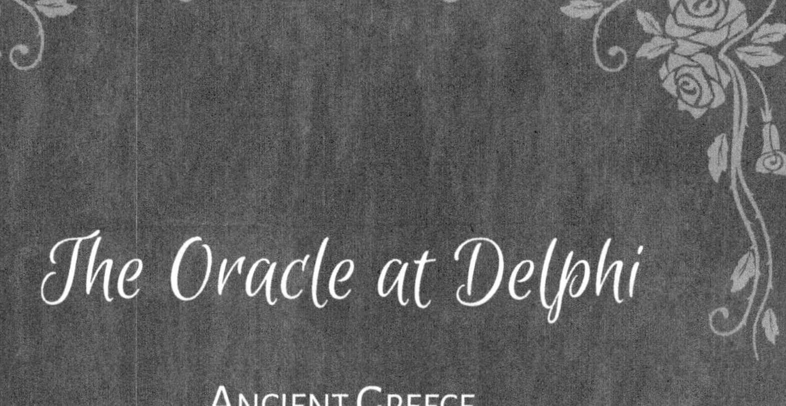

The Oracle at Delphi

Ancient Greece

Only at the end may the witches ride,
When men embrace hate,
Evil has spread across the land,
And the old gods, once lost, have returned.
Although it may seem all is lost,
A witch's choice may render the world anew,
The wrongs of men set to rights,
The darkness lifted,
And justice served.
A new world empowered under ours,
When two take the crown.

Salem, Massachusetts, United States

May 1693

Deep in the woods surrounding Salem, women waited as the smell of burnt flesh grew stronger. They knew this day was coming, had watched patiently as trial after trial occurred. Rarely had the villagers actually caught what they sought—a witch. A sister of the witches who now watched from the shadows.

It seemed that smell never truly dissipated anymore. Although it was not their only means of execution since man knew all too well how to kill their compatriots, it was the most grotesque and had certainly become a local favorite since the villagers began hunting the devil's mistresses—their less-than-complimentary term for witches. That malodorous smoke wound its tendrils through the forests, their homes warded against physical intruders such as the villagers who wished them harm but not against the foul reminder of their crimes against humanity. In its own way, that smell had become a ghostlike reminder of their coven's sacrifice, surrounding them with its wraithlike embrace, symbolizing mankind's failures and hatred.

This was not the first time the witches had watched. They had watched as their sister, Sara, was presented before a tribunal. During the farce of a trial, where young women clutched their heads and feigned possession, screaming and wailing, they watched while their sister was sentenced to death and then as she was surrounded with firewood and set alight. She could have easily escaped, had been taught the means to shift her surroundings to transport herself through space as a child. But to escape would expose her sisters, those same sisters who watched now, and condemned her own family to her fate. Their beliefs said that Sara would be reborn, first in nature then in flesh, as they all would upon their natural death. For witches, at least at present, were mortal. They were subject to the emotions of humanity. The witches of the world were not allowed to react upon their emotions, though, requiring logic and facts to substantiate their actions. Thus, as their sister burned, they observed, bound by their oath, reeling in society's betrayal.

The youngest among them, a small blond child called Amelie, cried silently as the desiccated remains of Sara's corpse were abandoned on her funeral pyre. Young Amelie stared at her elders, begging them to stop this, to converge upon the villagers. Celestine, the High Priestess of the Salem coven, sighed and patted Amelie on the head before gesturing to the witches to gather around her. Once they did, Celestine whispered to them of their task, the procedures of the overwhelming burden with which they were tasked. Each coven bore the burden of ensuring the harmony and equality of their unique area; as a global collective, however, the witches were responsible for the harmony and equality of the world. Now, on this cloudy May day, the Salem coven's time had come to restore equilibrium.

Celestine donned her tiara of bone and draped herself in a mantle of pure starlight. Her sisters had drawn sigils and glyphs in blood down their forearms and across their face, representations of the power of the covens. In the dreary light, the symbols glowed. If fate were on their side, the witches' mere appearance would shock the villagers into submission, recanting their ways and restoring balance to the region. If not, the witches would be forced to sow death and their own form of judgment to bring harmony to the area once more.

The women mounted their horses in one graceful movement. With Celestine leading the charge, those of an appropriate age raced their mounts out of the protective covering of the wood to the edge of the village, a short but exhilarating jaunt for both witch and horse. They came to a coordinated stop at the northernmost corner of the village, where a small wood cabin and a dirty child greeted them. Their path also put them in direct view of the village chapel, the square in front of which bore the scorched evidence of their most recent executions, and a sizable gathering of the people of Salem.

One woman noticed the witches gathered, screamed, her hand extended and shaking. The people of the square slowly turned, eyes growing wide as they did so. The witches knew their appearance was unreal, ghastly yet ethereal. Celestine's mount, a pale peridot-colored horse, the death's tiara she wore upon her head, the skeletal mounts of the others... all told, they appeared an army of death. This army waited as Celestine extended her arm in an accusatory point, invoking ancient words of admonition, informing the villagers of their punishment if they chose to continue their ways.

As one, the people knelt, dropping whatever they held to lay their arms above their heads. Celestine demanded the leader of the people acknowledge the warning and recant their ways. Shaking with fear, the pastor, the village's moral compass, rose to his feet, fear present in his eyes, and accepted her terms. Celestine accepted his terms, and as she turned, inscribed the sigil for memory in the air in front of her, imbuing it with her will. Although the people would forget the witches' existence thanks to her spell, they would recall their acceptance of a higher being's bargain: the villagers' continued existence for the cessation of the witch trials.

As the witches rode back to the forest, shrouded in fog created by the talented water witches to the edge of the group, many of the villagers shook their heads as if waking from a dream. Some looked to the charred remains of their most recent victim and vomited, now sickened by the death in front of them as a result of their agreement.

The only person who remembered the so-called goddesses attempted to share her experience with the others. Nobody believed her, and she was ultimately ostracized, cast from the village but not burned as a witch because of the villager's promise to the deities. Rumor had it she scribed a tale of her experiences and the vast power that she witnessed, of the goddess on the pale horse. The witches heard tell of this woman, searched for her, but never found her. They could never determine why their spell of forgetting did not work completely, but eventually as the older generation aged and died, the villager who remembered became a legend. Never substantiated, never located, and, ultimately, never believed in.

Until he came to power.

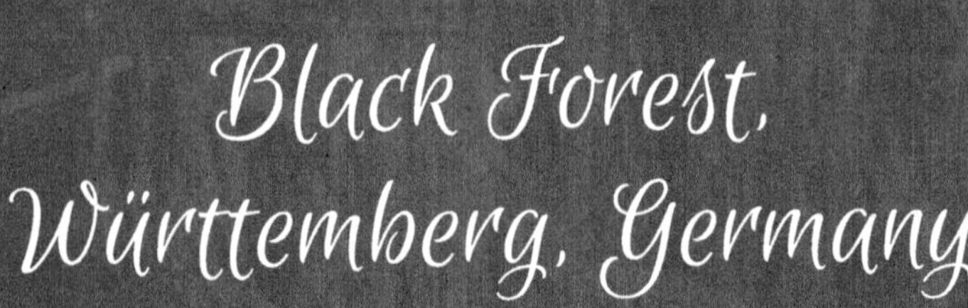

Black Forest, Württemberg, Germany

March 1933

An unremarkable man in spectacles entered the forest, grasping a tattered journal in his sweating hand. The grimy pages detailing unfathomable magics had inspired his journey into the vast forest.

According to the journal, goddesses could be found in the woods, the forests, the jungles, the unoccupied overgrown area of the woods. Well, the pages only referenced the one experience in the United States, but the power-obsessed Heinrich Himmler disregarded the argument favoring Americans out of turn. If these goddesses existed in one forest in America—barely tolerable as a nation—then of course, they had to exist in the Motherland as well. Which had led him in search of the powers beyond his comprehension that he could funnel into his own exploits. The historical account was extremely specific, however: the deities were female. Himmler firmly believed that he must wrest control of this power from these women as the only appropriate caretakers for power of this magnitude must be Aryan men, preferably the top researchers of his *Ahnenerbe*.

He had been walking for hours, the trees and vines above him growing into tangled shapes that blocked out the sun. Around him, he could hear the skittering of creatures best left in the shadows, but before him... before him, he could see lights and fires, twinkling with the force of a thousand stars, illuminating the area with incomprehensible force given the depths of the forest in which he found himself.

As he walked into the well-lit area, he noticed house after house built into and around the trees, even up into the canopy, moss and ivy intertwining in bizarre, almost symbolic patterns on the walls of each residence. In fact... he leaned closer. The symbols glowed with their own light, illuminating the wooden walls. The closer he got to them, the brighter they burned.

From the west, he heard a deep, rhythmic chanting. He followed the forest stars to a medium size clearing filled with dozens of women of varying heights, ages, and coloring. In the center stood a woman in a cloak of midnight, jet black hair tangling around her shoulders, catching in the hood of her cloak, whipping around her as a mysterious and inexplicable wind swept through the gathering. As he gazed upon her, Himmler whispered, "So beautiful. So impure."

The woman whirled to face him. Himmler would give her one chance to relinquish the power that she clearly held. But the wretch seemed ungrateful when he told her this, informing him in no uncertain terms that she would not relinquish the power. The woman stalked toward him, her eyes alight in fury as she prophesied a future for the Third Reich that was so bleak he could barely breathe.

"We see the future that you and your *Führer* promise. We see the suffering and death of generations at your hands. We see the intended destruction of this realm at your hands. We cannot move against you until these visions have come to pass, but, know that once they do, we will act swiftly and without mercy. Now leave this place and never return. You will see us soon on the battlefields of your own making."

Himmler opened his mouth to argue, to insist that they empower him. Before he could even speak, a tornado wrenched him from where he stood, flinging him with incredible violence far from their gathering, battering him into unconsciousness.

When he woke, he was sprawled on the ground at the precise point where he had entered the forest. His men surrounded him. Himmler rose, swaying as he straightened uncertainly. He glared at the trees, at the ridiculous waste of firepower that he must now expend because these *vile creatures* had forced him to do so. He shifted his gaze to his men, uttering the words that would shift the power, allowing for years of atrocities and genocide to occur: "burn it down." On Himmler's orders, his men took torches to the Black Forest, the fire spreading uncontrollably through the trees.

The *Schutzstaffel*, commonly known as the SS, were feared throughout Europe. They spread like an interminable, rabid plague, kidnapping and murdering inhabitants suspected of ascribing to particular races, ethnicities, religions, sexual orientations, and lifestyles, devastating the relics representing those people's history and faith. The first sign of their power, however, was to raze the forest with fire.

When they did, the people of the occupied village swore the forest tried to fight back, at first seeming to reject the fire before finally succumbing to its wrath. As the trees bowed and crackled under the overwhelming heat, crumbling to ash, those nearby were certain they heard screaming from the forest's depths.

By 1935, the European covens were decimated. Their African and Russian counterparts attempted to rally and provide aid, but it was difficult for them to leave their homes as all but the coven elders were tied to the land. To abandon their area, the witches had to separate themselves from their home, a process that required time and no small amount of effort. Once they finally managed to sever their ties to their region and arrive on the scene, their magic was exhausted. Ultimately, they too were wiped out by the SS as each coven required a source of power, and the SS was monopolizing the resources of the continent.

As entire covens across the globe were annihilated, the remaining witches felt the loss. Each drew power not just from their element and their land, but from the collective as well. Their ability to carry out their universal duty suffered, and eventually witches became a thing of the past, present only in limited pockets across the world, impacting only their small regions.

But with each new generation, witches are reborn. As their population swells once more, each coven believes that their collective power may someday be required to equalize and unify the world... by destroying it.

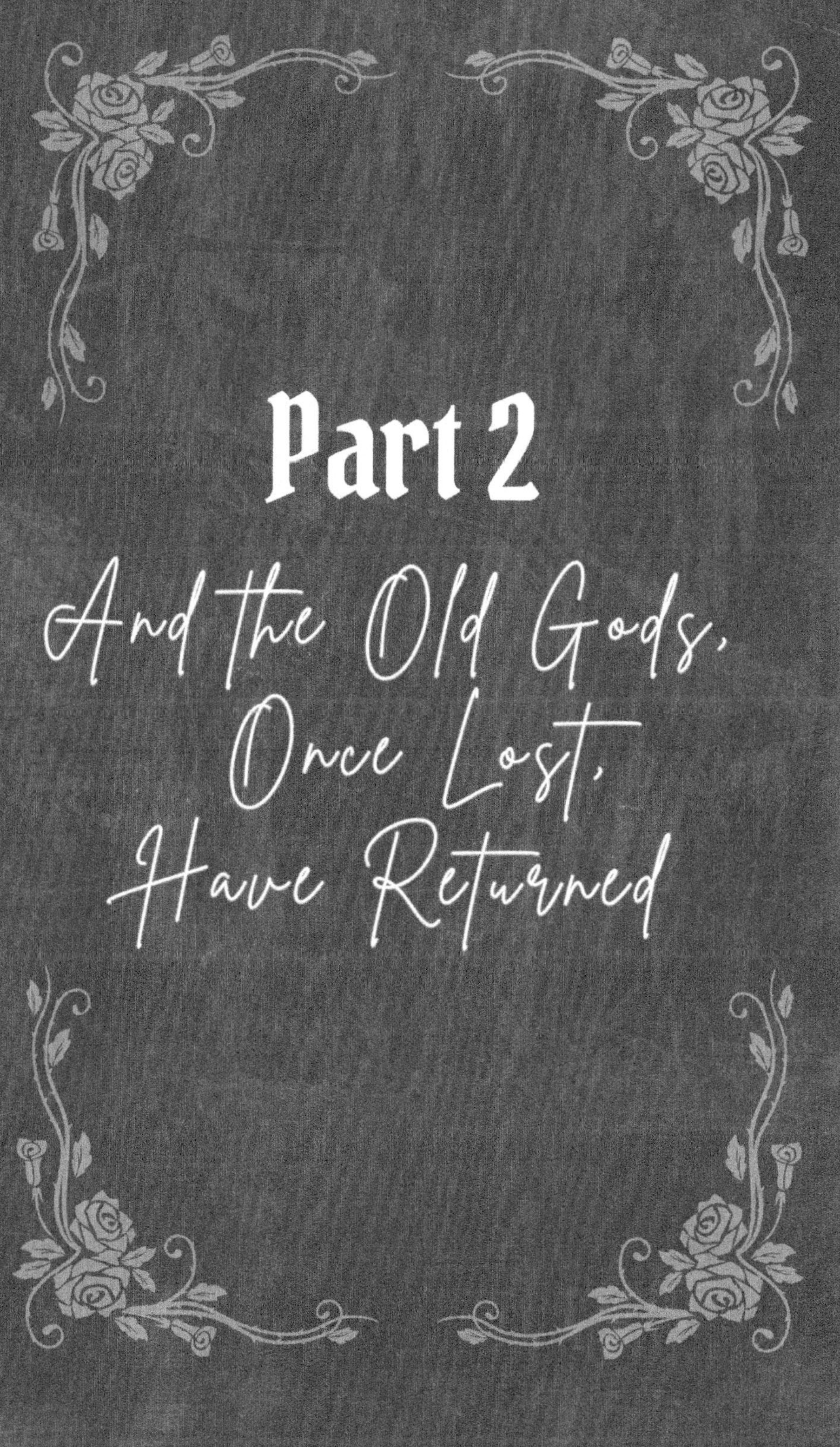
Part 2
And the Old Gods, Once Lost, Have Returned

Chapter 1

It is a fact universally acknowledged that a parent who suspects their daughter is a witch will send her into the woods to remove the danger she presents to society. Less of a fact, actually, more of a little acknowledged tradition. It started in the early days of Ireland, widely thought to be the birthplace of the first witch in some year lost to history, where a family who believed their young daughter was possessed by the devil sent her into a nearby forest. She was never seen again.

As whispers passed across villages, across provinces, across countries, of children born with mystical powers, the isolated incidences of abandonment became far more prevalent. Parents would send their young children, typically only four to five years of age, into the mountains or forests, never to be seen again.

As the world became more enlightened, the tradition continued, although it did evolve with the times and the unique cultures of the area. Women from families known to be bearers of witches cloistered themselves during late pregnancy, hidden from the world in case their daughter was born with powers, and they were forced to abandon their daughter. The age of children left to the wilderness grew younger and younger with some truly desperate parents leaving infants at the edge of the trees within their first month of life.

Most children never returned after their parents abandoned them, and they were never found. Those who knew of the tradition believed that they died, especially the newborns. No corpses were ever found, though, no remains ever spotted. And, with the children gone just as quickly as they appeared, it became easier as the tradition grew more ingrained in society to pretend they never existed.

There were a rare few who came back within days. Usually when this happened, the parents would open the door to their infant, swaddled and sleeping, on their stoop. The toddlers and older children who were returned were often found sleeping in their own bed or standing confused at their parents' door. If the parents chose to abandon the returned child at the forest once more, they would find their daughter once more under their care by noon the following day. The general thought became that, if a child was returned from the forest, she did not possess mystical powers.

Several parents attempted to abandon their male children at the forest. They were returned to the parents within hours. The forest did not accept male children.

Sometimes, the parents thought they saw their daughters standing at the edge of the forest, clothes rippling and hair blowing in a breeze they could not feel. Each time, they looked closer. Each time, there was no one there.

Chapter 2

October 21, 1991

Barataria, Lousiana

It was these legends that drove Luanne and Desmond Dyeus out of their home in Barataria, Louisiana, Luanne clutching their two-year-old baby girl, Evangeline, as she sprinted from the house.

Desmond following, finally catching up to Luanne and curling his arm around her shoulders before shifting their baby girl into his arms away from his sobbing wife. Giving him a grateful look, Luanne swiped her tears away with the back of her hand and stared over her left shoulder at their house. A lone hallway light shone through their front window, revealing curtains that were burnt to a crisp, shattered glass on the floor, and charring along the back wall of the living room.

Luanne slid in the driver's side of their beat-up old Jeep, turning over the car engine and cranking up the air conditioning to combat the mid-autumn heat and humidity. Desmond dropped into the passenger seat and buckled his seatbelt, all one handed as he cradled their toddler to his chest. "She's just a baby, Lu. It was an accident. It had to be." His wife glanced at him before turning her attention back to the road. "She was upset, weren't you sweet girl," he cooed down at their daughter, who wriggled happily in his arms even as Luanne sped down Privateer Boulevard so quickly that the houses and trees around them blurred.

"I know, Des," she choked out, toggling the right turn signal. "But we're just... we're just not equipped to handle this. I don't think we can do this with a daughter who's... who's like this."

"This isn't right. For Christ's sake, she's our *daughter*, Lu. We can't abandon her! I don't care what you think she may or may not be, she's still our child, no matter what." Desmond lifted his gaze from his beautiful daughter to his wife, whose elegant face bore a wild expression and tear stains. "How can you think this is okay?"

"This is what a good parent would do!" Luanne clenched her hands so tightly around the wheel that her knuckles turned white. Her voice rose in the small car. "This is something we need to do for her safety. We can't raise her like this; we're not equipped for it. She'll be better in the forest. Safer!"

Desmond took a moment to get himself under control before responding, drawing on every de-escalation course he had taken in his career as a therapist to try and talk down his wife. "Tell me again why we're doing this. I've never even heard of this forest bullshit; it just seems like a good way for our baby girl to get eaten by an alligator rather than a way for her to be raised by somebody who can protect her." Evangeline rested her small fists on his chest, her grey eyes suddenly serious in her chubby toddler face. "*We* can protect her. Why would we ever leave her to anybody else?"

Luanne breathed in deeply, her response terse when it finally came. "It's an old story that my mother used to tell me—" she started before falling silent. The forest seemed like an answer, the only answer, to Luanne. Over many generations, her Creole family had passed down stories of kids in the family, strange daughters who were unstable and problematic, whose instability had led to property damage and physical injury. So the stories went, these children vanished, never to be seen again. During one drunken episode, her mother confided to Luanne that she remembered a terse family drive through the night to a forest filled with shadows that seemingly had eyes and more movement than shadows usually did; Luanne's grandmother left the car with an infant before returning to the car empty-handed, driving away as a baby's wails pierced the night behind them. The memory of that experience terrorized Luanne's mother; the story haunted Luanne herself, often flavoring her own dreams throughout her life. She never expected to use that nightmarish knowledge, never once thought that it might come in useful.

One late night in February 1989, Luanne gave birth to a tiny baby girl. Over the next three months, she kept seeing bizarre things out of the corner of her vision, anomalies that resolved when she directed her attention to them, which she chalked up to the fatigue of having a newborn. After five months of this oddness, she woke to her daughter's screams and the house rattling on its very foundation, lightning striking close enough that the windows shook. She shrugged it off as another oddity, rocked her daughter back to sleep, and sank into a deep sleep herself.

Three weeks later, Desmond awoke to their daughter's laughing and babbling. He rushed over to her crib, ever the doting father. She kept pointing and nonsensically babbling to the darkest corner of the room, a corner filled with shadows that looked like a human figure. Unsettled, Desmond pulled a chair next to the crib, uncertain why except maybe to protect her from the shadows, an absurd thought if ever there was one, and dozed off, one arm resting on the rail.

After that, Luanne and Desmond experienced regular nightly abnormalities. Sometimes, it was the noise of something crashing as if it had fallen from a great height; other times, it was finding their six-month-old daughter, only in the very beginning stages of crawling, sleeping cozily between them in their bed when neither of them had moved her. Terrible storms that didn't show on any radar and weren't reported on by any news station blew open their windows and doors after midnight. They would wake up in the morning to shattered glass on the floor or, worst-case scenario, an outside door knocked off its hinges and dented, resting on the other side of the hall from the frame in which it ordinarily sat.

The tall trees surrounding their house grew three times faster than any in the neighborhood, the long limbs reaching towards and crowding the structure. Desmond cut back the trees every week, but they grew back even more quickly than before. It was completely normal to find branches punched through their windows or vines curling in, around, and underneath their doors. Strangely enough, the trespassing flora and fauna only ever seemed to go towards Evangeline's room.

Spontaneous fires occurred regularly in their house. They blamed it on their gas stove, an old radiator, anything that used electricity and wasn't in particularly good shape. Although they weren't wealthy by any stretch of the imagination, they invested in new appliances and, in a bout of paranoia, stocked every room in their three-bedroom home with a fire extinguisher. Small fires continued to break out, irregularly situated within the house but consistent. Luanne even called in the top electrician in the area to investigate their wiring. No dice.

It wasn't until Evangeline's first birthday that Luanne and Desmond began recognizing that the bizarre occurrences took place during their daughter's emotional occurrences. They could directly tie her laughter, crying, screaming, or speech to specific incidents, although they never sought to hazard a guess whether her emotions caused the incident or whether the incident incited the emotion. Then one night in June 1990, they heard their small baby girl cackling from her spot in her high chair. On the heels of her laughter, their back door started shaking in its frame. Evangeline's voice rose into a screech and, seconds later, the door's glass window erupted, a sharp crack of noise before shards of glass flew into the room just as a branch the width of Desmond himself came hurtling in towards their daughter. He leapt in front of it, desperately trying to get to his daughter, but the branch flicked him away into the wall. From his spot crumpled against the wall, he watched the limb stop just in front of the baby chair where his daughter was making grabby hands at it, babbling eloquently to the tree as only toddlers could do. He'd sustained three fractured ribs that night.

The incidents continued with ever-increasing intensity. By unspoken agreement, Desmond and Luanne settled into sleep rotations, where one of them would sleep and the other would watch their baby girl and put out any sudden fires before they could burn down the house.

Several times, Luanne brought up the forest as a way to solve their problems, but it always ended in arguments. Desmond was born and raised in New York and had never once heard of abandoning one's child to the wilderness. He thought it was utterly absurd, even if their daughter was magical, mystical, or whatever designation Luanne felt the need to assign to the abilities. Luanne felt alone and terrified, completely incapable of caring for or raising a child with uncanny abilities that felt wrong. Abnormal. Unstable. Their arguments grew more and more frequent as Luanne pushed the issue after each incident. He finally threatened to divorce her and take away their daughter for good. She loved him deeply, though, so she promised that she wouldn't take their daughter to the forest without his consent.

Until tonight. A week passed between incidents, but then, Evangeline started shrieking. In the far corner of the living room, a fire exploded into existence, working its way rapidly up the wall. A second blaze wove its way around the curtains. Both Desmond and Luanne grabbed fire extinguishers while their daughter continued to merrily scream, lightbulbs exploding and cracks splintering the walls.

After finally extinguishing the fire, Luanne turned to check on their daughter, who just stared at her, head tilted eerily to the side, normally grey eyes now the color of molten gold. At the sight, Luanne screamed and burst into tears, snatching her daughter—was this even her child? was it a demon?—and sprinting from the house, holding the infant that she refused to call hers in her arms so tightly that it almost certainly must have hurt Evangeline.

Desmond tried to calm Luanne as she raced to the Jeep, as they got in the car... but alas, she wasn't listening to reason, seemed incapable of even hearing his words to her, as if she wasn't even connected to this world anymore.

Now, as Luanne drove recklessly towards the nature preserve, the silence grew between them, slowly filling the car, the only interruptions Desmond's continued attempts to sway his wife, his comforting murmurs to Evangeline, and the inconsistent chime of the turn signal. Their life was slowly falling apart,

Luanne's threatened abandonment of their infant daughter an albatross around his neck. His wife didn't even seem to hear him, kept mumbling to herself in French. He couldn't understand everything she said, but the word "*diable*" kept coming up, which seemed like a pretty damning indication of his wife's mental state at the moment.

Luanne slammed on the brakes on the nonexistent shoulder, sliding them to a stop in the mud caused by the recent rains. Desmond glanced at her, bracing himself to fling the door open and sprint like hell away from the car with Evangeline in his arms. He would be damned if he let Luanne just fucking abandon their baby girl like this. It wasn't going to happen. Although there weren't any road lights in the area, the preserve visitor center wasn't too far from here. He was pretty sure that, if he could get to the visitor center and break in, the Jefferson Parish Sheriff's Office would send uniformed officers who could help him. Somehow.

Before he could even open the door, though, Luanne turned to him, her eyes shining and manic, tear tracks dried on her face. He opened his mouth—one last try to convince his wife not to do this, he supposed—but before he could say a word, she suddenly seized their daughter from his arms, shoved open the car door, and darted away.

He leapt from the car, running at full speed behind her, just behind her. "Luanne, stop it!" he shouted. "Fucking stop! You can't do this!" He was gaining ground on her, but somehow, she seemed further away than ever. "Luanne!" he shouted again, his tone pleading. Not above begging to protect his baby girl. "Please don't do this! We're a team; we can protect her. We can't abandon her!"

Ahead of him—must be fifty yards at least, how did she get so far away—Luanne took a sharp turn into the wetlands. He sprinted at a parallel, hoping to cut her off, but instead he sank his foot into a moldering log and went sprawling. From the ground, he shouted his wife's name once more as he turned his foot sharply this way and that to extricate himself. What felt like hours later but was probably only seconds, he ripped his foot from the rotten log. He heard something tear and a burning pain in his calf but couldn't care less, even as he felt something wet—probably blood—soaking his sock. Unsteadily, he shoved himself to his feet, limping towards the last place he had seen his wife. No sign of her; the wetlands and velvet night concealed her as surely as they did the alligators and snakes that lived here. He turned wildly, looking for any clue, and stopped abruptly.

In the humid mist of the night, a shadowy figure with six red embers glowing around the height where eyes would sit in a human face stood only feet away from him among the trees. He couldn't make out what it was, but chills ran down Desmond's spine as he stared in horror; this couldn't be real. He mustered up the courage to call "hello," but as quickly as the shadowy figure appeared, it vanished, leaving him alone and more scared for his family then ever.

He roamed the perimeter of the preserve for hours, calling for his daughter and wife. He searched for so long that the sun rose, the Preserve employees who staffed the Visitor Center arriving for their shift, only to find a distraught man covered in mud and blood, shouting desperately, weeping as if his heart was broken.

Two deputies with the Jefferson County Sheriff's Department came around 9:00 am to take Desmond to the station. He was drenched in blood and rambling wildly, begging them to find his wife and daughter while the deputies marched him to their car. As they drove away, Desmond turned back for one last look. Nothing there but a group of women, seemingly part of the fog, and not a one of them his Luanne or their Evangeline.

Three days later, they found the body of a petite woman with strawberry-blonde hair dressed in tattered clothing and missing one shoe, not far from where the Preserve staff found Desmond that fateful morning. The Sheriff's Department easily identified her as Luanne Devereaux-Dyeus.

Between the blood on his person, the outlandish claims Desmond made about a magical daughter, the intense fights with Luanne that Desmond admitted to, and his honesty about chasing his wife and baby daughter through the preserve, it was the easiest double homicide trial that the Parish had ever seen. They had Luanne's body; the absence of the daughter's body was clear evidence to the District Attorney and the jury that, in Luanne's crazed run from her husband, their daughter had been lost to the forest and most likely became 'gator food.

Desmond's last sight of Luanne was the photos displayed during the trial. Of his daughter... he never saw her again.

Chapter 3

Evie

Barataria Preserve, Marrero, Louisiana

Evie shifted back into the brush, resting her back against one of the towering live oaks circled around her like sentinels. Across the marsh, two alligators wrestled desperately over what looked like it had once been a bobcat, although it was missing one too many limbs to be fully recognizable as such. Above the fray, a bird warbled a tune pitched to carry far to potential mates. She smiled as the song made its way down to her. Just another day in the forest, the only home that she had ever known. She loved the beautiful area, but this sunken section was her favorite. She could sit here for hours just seeing the animals go about their lives, feeling the humid wind blow across her damp skin, and generally existing in the quiet ambience of the trees.

After watching the sun lower slowly into the horizon, lighting the sky in majestic shades of pink and orange, Evie stood, spreading her arms wide as the moon rose high into the sky, feeling it tug on her spirit in a loving, familiar way. At the best guess of the coven elders, she was a lunar hedge witch whose powers were fed by the moon and most powerful on plant life. Even standing here, though, she knew there was more to it than that. Because as much as she could feel the moon tugging at her, she also felt something else lingering underneath its pull. Something darker and more deadly. The coven elders never quite understood it, couldn't interpret what else fed into her magic, so they never explored it. And a small part of her always felt neglected because of it.

Evie knew she was lucky, though. She lived in a beautiful area that fed her magic, she had received extensive training in the craft from the coven elders who also ensured that the younger witches were safe, and she was surrounded by her sisters, women who ranged in ability, appearance, and age but were bonded by magic and love. Even still, it was hard not to feel inadequate when it seemed that her magic was limited to casting under a moonlit sky upon the vegetation that grew in abundance in her family's home, especially when she knew deep down that she was capable of so much more. Shaking her head, she forced a smile, embracing the feel of the moonlight surrounding her.

"Rise, my pretties," she mumbled under her breath to the nascent Chanterelle mushrooms she could feel under the soil's surface, careful not to draw the attention of the two 'gators who, after ingesting their dinner, had nodded into a sleeplike state that didn't fool her in the least. She knew if she moved too quickly or spoke too loudly or, Hecate help her, even breathed too audibly, the grumpy beasts would swing into action faster than she could summon the vegetation to her aid. Although the trees would surely rush to assist her, her conscience couldn't bear any damage to the beautiful live oaks that had been here long before she entered this world and that would be there long after she departed her mortal coil for the afterlife.

Around her feet, the Chanterelle mushrooms blossomed quickly, spreading their wrinkled yellow faces to the sky. She knelt gently and ran her fingers lovingly over their now-bulbous heads that stood almost to her knees. "Good babies." The mushrooms shivered in response, although whether at her words or her gentle touch, she couldn't have said. She talked to the plants, even though she knew they couldn't talk back... mostly. Every now and again, they would respond as if they recognized her words or her voice or... something about her. It wouldn't be the first time something happened around her that she couldn't explain, but Evie was rational enough to know that it was more likely her magical connection to the plants rather than any speech-based capacity that these lifeforms may have. She shrugged as she tugged open the bag at her hip, filling the interior with enough of the large mushrooms to supplement the coven's meals for the next few days. The root balls she left for later summoning.

She glanced at the 'gators one last time before darting the other direction, back towards her coven. Behind her, they lurched into action with all the power she had predicted, but, by the time they lumbered their way over to her fresh grove of Chanterelles, she was long gone.

As she raced through the trees, she thought of what lay ahead. Her coven was her family, a gathering of sisters who loved and supported one another desperately. She had been away for longer than usual, exploring the depths of the forest that they called home. It wasn't the longest she had been gone, but it was far longer than she needed to travel to the mushroom grove. Now, looking back, she wasn't sure why she had stayed away for so long. It was like the moons blended together and time had passed, seemingly without her noticing it. The elders would blame it on the restlessness she had been feeling for months, and they probably wouldn't be wrong. Each time she explored outside of the warded safety of the coven's clearing into the forest beyond, she stayed away a little longer and found it a bit harder to return. It felt like she was looking for something. Or someone? Maybe the holder of the green eyes and that deep voice that haunted her? She snorted and shook her head. No. Those were just a dream or a vision. They weren't real.

Evie came to a stop at the edge of a clearing where, despite being buried in the deepest part of the forest, light still radiated. Directly in front of her was the bayou that constituted her family's home. The area was lit by floating orbs, which illuminated the expansive area, their colors dictated by the collective emotional health of the group. Right now, they were vibrant white, which made the bayou appear as if it were full day, even though the sun had only just risen after her long trek home. Legend had it that they could go dark, either by extinguishing or turning darker colors, but Evie and her coven dismissed that idea out of turn. At least in the Barataria Coven, no one had ever seen anything darker than a velvet blue mimicking the night sky.

The witches' homes were grouped by power, and each witch had their own unit, customized in design to their wishes. The red witches who drew their power from fire ringed the common eating area directly in front of Evie; among its other benefits, this area boasted the coven's firepit. The shamanic witches lived almost immediately to her left, the only occupants in that direction since they required as much quiet as possible due to their type of spell casting. The voodoo practitioners who drew their power from the loa—the spirits who came before them—lived tucked into the back right of the bayou. Finally, the hedge witches, almost all of whom drew their power from the earth itself, occupied the quarters surrounding the edges of the large clearing so they were closest to the oaks and cypresses, their homes built into the very trees that towered over the coven's sprawling clearing. Evie herself lived among the hedge witches, even though her source of power was the moon, a unique, even unusual, point from which to draw one's magic among her coven.

The Spanish moss draping the stately trees on either side of her swayed towards her, lightly brushing the side of her neck in greeting. She grinned up at the beautiful trees. They were as much a part of her family as her sisters and far less inclined to personal dramatics. Speaking of which... Evie ducked behind one of the trees as she heard the coven elders' voices echo across to her. Although she was thrilled to be back, she was also soaked in sweat and disheveled from her run through the forest. On her way home, she had rescued a frog that appeared to have taken up residence in her wild auburn curls. The coven elders emphasized the importance of finding beauty beneath surface appearance, but, even still, she was sure that they would frown over her intense dishabille.

She danced through the shadows, passing her fingers through the sunbeams that snuck through the trees above her. The light dappled her fingers and made them look sun-soaked golden rather than her usual ivory. As she finally drew near to her unit, she looked up and felt her heart contract with pride. She spent years making her home a reflection of herself and her unique powers, starting with its location. Unlike the other witch's dwellings, hers was nestled in the forest's canopy, raised high off the ground and surrounded by the leaves, which, in their attempts to get closer to her, even formed the floor of her home. When she lay down at night, she could see the moon's beams from her bed as she gazed up through the barricade of cypress limbs that offered her protection from the elements most days but parted on clear nights.

Raising her arm, she summoned a nearby tree limb to her feet. She stepped carefully on to the thickest point of the branch; with a twitch of her fingertips, she magicked the branch into the air. It rose quickly at her bidding, and she repeated the process, creating a moving staircase that finally deposited her at the foot of her home. She removed the frog from her curls, nestling him safely into the lush foliage forming the house's entrance. He croaked at her before disappearing among the leaves. As she stepped over the soft floor, she shed her clothes, uncaring as to who may look in and see her. Although she understood that houses outside the forest contained walls intended to maintain privacy, the coven believed in no such boundaries. For starters, the witches were part of the forest; they drew power from it and were one with it, so walls created an unnecessary barrier.

More importantly, though, members of the coven had no secrets from one another and were utterly entangled in each other's lives. No privacy was needed when you shared your lives that closely with others. Nudity and sexuality were celebrated, the witch's form in all its appearances cherished. Although they called one another sisters, it was a term of endearment; most of them bore no blood relation to each other. Many of her sisters had even found their life mates among the coven. The coven members reveled in those connections and saw no need to cloister it away behind walls and doors. Love in all its forms was a joyful event for them.

Evie paused as she drew on a light dress that brushed the tops of her thighs. She was no stranger to relationships and adored sex, but she knew she had never been in love. For a brief time, she had even lived with Marie, a beautiful coven member with deep olive skin, beautiful black hair, and a quick smile. While their flame had burned intensely, their sex passionate, it went out all too easily. Partially because they shared no interests other than sex. And partially because… something had always felt off. Evie had never felt fully herself; at the oddest times, she felt her heart tug and her stomach sink as if something was *deeply wrong*. Sometimes, before the moon fell and the sun rose, she heard a low, gravelly voice calling her, rich emerald eyes staring at her, through her. She felt like she was betraying this phantom that did not, could not, exist. So she and Marie separated with little fanfare, and she returned to her home in the trees, fantasizing about a rich voice and jewel-like eyes that only she could see.

Although it was bright outside, she desperately needed sleep. She hadn't slept much during her foraging trip, and she felt every second of the lost rest. She crawled into bed, drawing her velvety soft blankets to her chin. Sensing her exhaustion, the limbs overhead shuddered as they drew closed, blocking the sun's rays as her eyelids slid shut. While she lay quiet in the semi-darkness of her home, she could almost hear that baritone voice saying her name.

Chapter 4

Cole

Central Business District, New Orleans, Louisiana

"Evangeline?" Cole Aidoneus squinted at the top sheet of paper in the manila folder his uncle had just handed him. It was a missing persons report filed by Desmond Dyeus for his daughter, Evangeline Cora Dyeus, after the New Orleans Police Department took him into custody for the suspected murder of his wife and daughter. Filed in October 1991, he could see from a quick skim that it gave barely enough details for him to figure out just why exactly his uncle thought this was relevant. He glanced up at his uncle, eyebrows raised then, unable to resist, dropped his eyes to keep reading, even though, like every born-and-raised New Orleanian, he knew the basics of the story. Hell, it was practically an urban legend in the city more than thirty years later. Wife abducts daughter, husband chases down wife, wife's corpse found the next day, daughter missing and never seen again.

But the report in front of him laid out a much grimmer story. After almost two years of disturbing events around the house, the wife abducted the daughter with plans to dump her in the nature preserve because the child began displaying unnatural abilities... Jesus Christ. That was fucked up. But it seemed farfetched that the missing daughter was the one they were looking for, given that, best anyone could tell, she was dead. "Evangeline Dyeus? You serious?"

Charles, the stoic man who raised him after his parents died when he was young, leveled his gaze at Cole. "She matches all of the descriptors that Essi gave us, down to the grey eyes." At Cole's eye roll, he countered quickly, "We know your feelings on the Moirai, but we have no reason to doubt their reading of the lifelines —"

Cole cut off his uncle. "Nobody's seen this girl since she went missing in 1991, Charlie. Even if she's still alive—and that's a big if since nobody has seen her in *three decades*—are we really going to say that she's the key based on her fucking eye color when she was an infant? That's absurd, especially since kids' eye colors can change as they grow up."

Well used to Cole's sarcasm and assertive nature, Charles continued mildly, "If you had let me finish, you would know that it's not just the eye color, although children's eyes colors don't just change willy nilly." He raised his hand and began counting off items. "It's her birthdate—February 01, which, as you well know, falls right in the middle of Imbolc." One finger went up. "It's the fact that her family name is Dyeus, well known as one of Zeus' many names." He raised a second finger. "It's the types of abilities she showed, based on her father's statement. Spontaneous decay in everything except plant life, control over plants, pyrokinesis, telekinetic powers, just to name a few. And, yes, it's her grey eyes too. All of that aligns with what Clo and Essi told us, and you know it." Third, fourth, and fifth fingers all raised.

Cole scowled at his uncle, shoving a hand through his black hair. At 35 years old, he was the founder of Elysian Counseling, a boutique law firm with offices in many major U.S. cities, and the heir apparent to the Underworld; he wasn't used to not knowing all the facts. In fact, if he had to sort his dislikes, he was fairly certain that "lack of knowledge" and "lack of control" would top the list. He liked to think he had all the time in the world to find the key to his kingdom, but the Moirai, the group of fates tasked with providing guidance to his family in their rule—*and the most annoying group of women in New Orleans,* he thought uncharitably—recently signaled that was not the case. Time was no longer on his side. Which meant he had to find her. Now.

It was almost poetic if you thought about it. He had avoided marriage like the plague for almost two decades, skirted romantic attachment like it was a contest. When he needed a woman, it was easy enough to find one. He had two long-term casual hook ups, Lucy and Aimee, that he could call if he couldn't find a suitable single woman—and sometimes not so single, he wasn't too picky—out on the town. Now, at 35, he had to take a wife just so he could save the fucking world and claim his throne and wasn't that just a kick in the balls. And not just any wife. He had to take his "fated wife." Persephone reincarnated.

Fucking absurd. He knew magic existed, had more than enough of it himself, but it was still hard to believe that he was the fated Hades and that, somewhere out there, was his fated Persephone, and the two of them were responsible for stopping the apocalypse. Not only that, but they would be bound to each other for a literal eternity after they claimed their rightful seats as the royals of the Underworld. He snorted audibly at that, causing Charles to jump in the cushy chair he had settled into after skewering Cole with logic.

"Are you ready to accept that I and the Moirai know what we're talking about?" Charles stood and walked to Cole's desk, nudging the folder sitting atop all the other piles of paper. "That we aren't just trying to trap you in a marriage?"

"Fine." Cole steepled his fingers under his chin. His thoughts raced as he started planning. "Are we assuming she's a witch then? Seems the most likely option." The old legends demanded that a parent abandon their female daughters who displayed magical powers to the forest. He would have bet money that was a myth started by coven elders to sow fear, but Luanne Dyeus appeared to believe it, so much so that she had been prepared to dump her two-year-old daughter in a nature preserve filled with 'gators and other predators.

Charles inclined his head. "It makes the most sense. We've heard tell of a coven that lives in the Jean Lafitte Preserve, but we've never been able to confirm their existence. Even the Moirai can't tell us anything about it."

Cole dropped a hand, tapping his fingers against the desktop. That was... troubling. The Moirai's powers were comprehensive. If they couldn't see a lifeline, beginning, middle, and end, something was amiss. Only intense power to rival the Morai's could block their sight. He grumbled, knowing that there was only one solution. Shit. He hated hiking in Louisiana—it was too humid for it to be anything but horrible. "Sometimes the best answers are the old-school ones, Charlie, you know that."

His uncle's brow furrowed as he shook his head emphatically. "Cole, it could be unsafe. We can't see into the forest. We don't know what's there, and you could get injured before you find her and settle into your immortality."

"There's nothing for it, Charlie." Cole checked his watch, thumbing his mouse to wake up his computer when he saw he was about to run late for a call with a local casino. "I need to find her. As much as I hate listening to those creepy ass women, I do actually pay attention to the Moirai, especially when they tell me that our time is running short. If y'all think Evangeline is alive and the right girl—" He sighed deeply. "—And Essi can't see any lifelines in the forest, then the only option is for me to go looking around over there for Evangeline."

He clicked into the call conference link, where he saw he was still waiting on the business owner. "I'll be careful. You taught me well, Uncle Charlie. I know what I'm doing. I know how to use my magic." A chime sounded as the business owner admitted him to the virtual conference room, and Charles began to leave the room. "If she's there, I'll find her."

His office door closed softly behind Charles. "Good morning, Mr. Boudreaux. I understand you're interested in reincorporating your company in Delaware. Tell me a bit more about your concerns." As his client rambled—something about corporate shields and potential criminal liability, neither of which were a wholly accurate description of the law—Cole's eyes caught on a sharp corner jutting out from beneath the stack of papers in the folder. Flipping through the papers in the folder, he finally came to an old Polaroid photo about halfway through. In it was a small child, red-haired and beaming at whoever was holding the camera from her seat in her father's arms. In her chubby face sat big grey eyes, too serious for any child's face. Familiarity burst through Cole. He knew those eyes, would have known them anywhere. He had seen them every night in his dreams since he was twelve.

Chapter 5

Evie

Barataria Preserve, Marrero, Louisiana

"WHEN DID YOU GET HOME?"

Evie jerked awake at the screech that filled her usually peaceful home. She cracked her eyes open just a smidge to peer at the feral gnome currently shrieking at her. Namely, one of her younger sisters, Sandrine, a beautiful, elfin girl with ebony skin and beautiful braids. Without moving, she threw the first thing to hand—one of the Chanterelle mushrooms as it so happened—at her sister blindly and tugged the blanket over her face. She wanted to go back to sleep and not just because she was still exhausted. For the first time in her life, she had dreamed of the man that went with the voice, had even seen blurry details of the face surrounding the stunning eyes that watched over her. "No," she groaned. "Civilized witches are sleeping!"

"Don't be silly! You're not asleep, otherwise you wouldn't be talking!" The blanket covering her shifted wildly as Sandrine jumped onto the bed, lunging at her older sister. "But that doesn't matter because you're back! When did you get home?!" Sandrine demanded, wrapping her arms around Evie's neck. "I missed you so much! It was so dull around here with just the coven mothers to boss me around!"

Evie hugged her sister back, her arms crooked at an awkward angle around Sandrine's small shoulders. "I missed you too, little sparrow, but you had the entire coven here to keep you company." She struggled to a seated position. "And I'm sure you had much more fun here then you would have had with me trying to avoid the 'gators." Pinching Sandrine's upper arm, she disentangled herself from the embrace, pushing her tangled hair out of her face and rubbing the sleep from her eyes. "Wait." She tilted her head. "How did you get up here?" Her home's height didn't lend itself to spontaneous visits, particularly from young witches new to their power.

Sandrine bounced a bit. "I wanted to surprise you! I've been working with Elder Hesteia while you've been gone. I can fly now!" At Evie's raised eyebrows, she corrected herself quickly. "Well, I can summon smoke from the fires to carry me. But that's pretty much flying! The smoke doesn't even dissipate anymore, so I'm not even falling that often."

Evie couldn't help herself; she burst into laughter at Sandrine's earnest defense of her soaring into the skies on a cloud of smoke. "Of course it's flying, Sandrine. You're able to rise into the sky with nothing holding you but smoke. Flying doesn't have to be with wings. Technically, I could fly by asking the trees to gather me in their branches and tossing me as hard as they could." Wincing, she chuckled before acknowledging, "But that would then become a *very* uncontrolled fall."

Sandrine threw herself from the bed, grabbing Evie's hand and dragging her forward. "I can even summon fire now!" She started to snap her fingers, presumably to show Evie her newly developed pyromancy, but Evie lunged forward to grab her wrist, nodding at the extremely flammable leaves now quivering in fear around them. "I'm sorry, Evie," Sandrine said, looking chastened. She knelt and petted the leaves at her feet gently, chanting softly, "I'm sorry, trees. I didn't mean to scare you."

"It's fine." Evie got out of bed, urging the branches above them to clear so she could see where the sun fell in the sky. "They know you didn't mean anything by it. You were just excited." It appeared to be midday, the sun sitting high in the sky. "If you want to show me anything Hesteia taught you, we should probably do that near one of the swamps or the trees might think you have it out for them."

"I did want to go exploring," Sandrine admitted in a low tone.

"Ah, I see." Hiding a smile behind her hand, Evie fixed her with a level gaze. "So today's visit wasn't entirely without a secret objective, then?"

Sandrine pouted guiltily. "But I did want to see you!"

Evie dropped her hand, allowing her smile to blossom in plain view. "You're fine, little sparrow. I've barely been home for a day, and I'm already getting restless. Some exploring may be just what I need." A memory tickled at the edges of her consciousness, something as she had fallen asleep. That voice saying something about... an angel? Was the voice the reason for her restlessness?

Pausing as she ushered Sandrine out the entryway, she considered. Ever since she was young, she had heard a male voice in the air around her, speaking randomly. It was never directly to her, more around her than anything else, and always the same voice. Deep and sensual with a rolling, melodic accent that never failed to send shivers through her body. Even with all the love she had for her coven and her sisters, the voice made her feel like she wanted more from her life than what she had right now.

So it definitely wouldn't be the first time that low, intense voice had caused her to go adventuring. No one in her coven could hear it; she had asked many times. So, although her coven believed the voice may be a spiritual guide or one of the many pantheonic gods speaking to her, she still saw the looks they exchanged when she asked about a voice no one else could hear. As if she needed another reason to be isolated from the coven, something she had experienced all too often during her life. With her distinct powers, including the darker source that no one understood and everyone was scared to explore, and the annual spell casting she had to take part in, she knew all too well what it was like to feel like she was both a beloved part of the coven and not quite a part of it. The voice that no one could hear—not to mention the emerald eyes that no one could see—was just another thing to ostracize her.

When she felt overwhelmed, she often found herself leaving for days on end, running deep into the forest. Whether she was running to the voice or away from it or just seeking an escape from the constant feeling of other-ness she had when she was with her sisters, she couldn't say with any certainty. All she knew was that the voice and those eyes, regardless of whether they belonged to a real person or not, were as much a part of her as her auburn hair. And after her dream last night...

Evie was jerked from her reveries by a quick screech and a thud. Looking to her left, she saw... no Sandrine. Racing to the entrance, she peered over the edge; at the foot of the tree, Sandrine lay in an uninjured pile.

"I'm okay," she shouted up to Evie, waving happily from where she was sprawled on the ground.

Evie snorted before summoning the trees to her aid, descending quickly to the forest floor. "I hear patience can be a good thing," she snarked at her sister, extending a hand to help Sandrine to her feet. Sandrine rolled her eyes but took her extended hand. "Where did you want to explore?" Evie asked. She scanned the grounds quickly. Apparently, no one saw Sandrine fall, and no one saw Evie, so it was now or never. If they waited much longer, they would be surrounded by their coven, and they would never escape then. "We could go look at the new Chanterelle gathering that I established while I was gone?"

Sandrine wrinkled her nose. "Eww, no, I don't want to go look at your *fungus*." She sneered the word "fungus" as if it had personally offended her. "I want to go see the birds! The loud ones that shout at the alligators."

There weren't many areas of the forest where they could find "the loud birds that shouted at the gators," but Evie knew of one such place not too far from the clearing. "Fine," she permitted, lightly pushing Sandrine in the direction beyond the tree housing her home. "We need to go that way. Stay close to me. Can't have you getting snatched as a bayou beastie's dinner."

As they left the clearing and passed through the wards that protected the boundaries from intruders, Evie felt able to breathe again. Her little sister yanking at her hand, pulling her in the wrong direction. The January winds whistling through the trees... her world felt almost perfect.

After a few hours' worth of traipsing through the forest, made longer by Sandrine's short legs and uncanny ability to get distracted by everything, they were closing in on the area in the forest where the grackles usually swarmed. For the first time, though, the forest was quiet, empty of the bird's undignified shrieking. In its place, Evie heard discordant noises that she had never heard before. Clanging metal, loud voices bellowing, a roaring sound she couldn't quite place. Through the tree line, she saw yellow blobs moving and... emptiness. Pure barrenness where the birds usually gathered. The hair along the back of Evie's neck prickled and not from the perspiration caused by the natural Louisiana humidity. Something was wrong.

I need to get Sandrine away from here. Now.

Sandrine started towards the trees, face crinkled in confusion, but Evie grabbed her hand, drawing her back. No way in the realms was she letting her young sister near that. "You know what? This isn't even the best place to see the birds." She tried to mask her unease but, based on Sandrine's skeptical expression, failed miserably. "I've got an even better place where we can see the grackles and get some dinner."

"What's the matter with here?" Sandrine asked, her little brow furrowed in confusion. "This is the best place to see them." She pulled at Evie's hand, managing to move them just a little bit towards the area beyond the tree line. "C'mon, Evie!"

Evie's gaze remained locked on the blurry yellow shape. "Sandrine," she said quietly.

From behind them, a shout sounded, and Sandrine froze. They were too far away to know what the voice said but close enough to know that it was male. All coven members identified as women, but they did have a few members who were transitioning with the assistance of the coven elders and support of their sisters, so both Evie and Sandrine knew what a masculine voice sounded like. But they had never heard one so unhappy, and it made them both aggressively uncomfortable.

Evie's skin crawled as she heard more voices join in before loud whistles echoed back to them, and her hand tightened on Sandrine's. *We need to go.* "Sandrine," she repeated, a bit more loudly this time.

Sandrine turned towards Evie, her eyes wide, concern crossing her face as the sounds grew louder, though they were still distant. They could even hear what Evie suspected was a horn, having only read of them.

A loud screeching started, the sound grating and scraping. "Evie, I want to go home," Sandrine whispered.

Evie nodded gratefully. "That's fine, little sparrow. We can see the grackles another day. Let's go home." Resting her hands on her sister's small shoulders, she turned her back in the direction of the coven's clearing, casting one last look over her shoulder before setting a quick pace home.

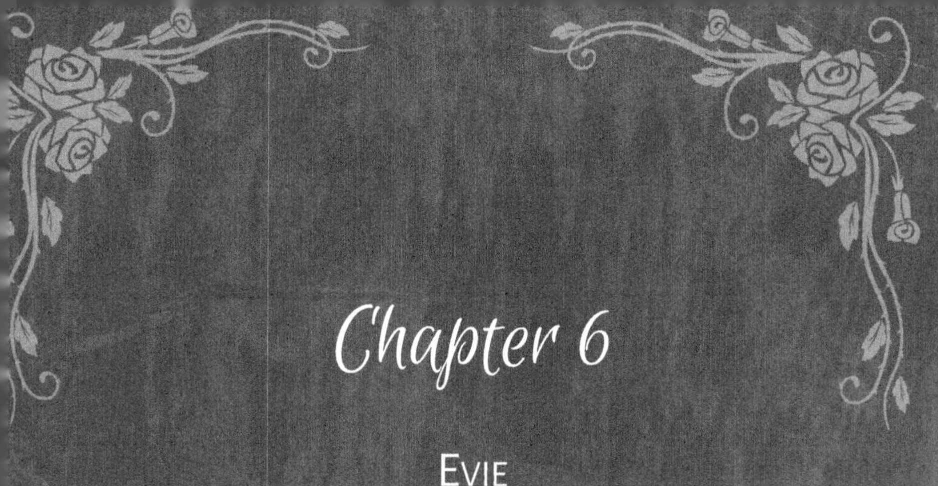

Chapter 6

Evie

Barataria Preserve, Marrero, Louisiana

Their trip back to the clearing was uneventful, which gave Evie plenty of time to think about what they had heard. She didn't visit the area all that often—couldn't even actually remember the last time she had gone there—but whatever was going on now hadn't been around then. This was new, and it felt *wrong*.

"Evie?" Sandrine's timid voice broke into Evie's grim thoughts as they passed over the bayou using a mostly intact log.

"Yeah, little sparrow?" She hated the fear she heard in Sandrine's tone, would do anything to keep her from being afraid of anything. No matter how unrealistic that goal may be.

Sandrine was quiet for long enough that Evie thought her sister may have forgotten what she was going to say. They had gone about half a mile before Sandrine spoke again, her voice wavering. "What was that? What were the noises? And those little yellow dots? It was... " She trailed off, walked a bit further, then finished her thought. "It was scary."

Evie looked to the heavens for guidance, but the evening sky gave her no answers. From a distance, she saw the trees circling their home, the slight waver in the air that marked the protective spells around it. She glanced over at her sister, wishing that the question had come about fifteen minutes later when she could pass it to the coven elders who were far better at handling scared children than she was. "I don't know. I wish I did so I could tell you everything was going to be okay, but... " She spread her hands wide and shrugged. "I really don't know what exactly we heard out there."

"Are we safe?" Sandrine whispered.

"Of course it's safe in here," Evie responded emphatically. She knew the answer to that, at least. "Just don't wander too far from the wards and don't go back there on your own, and I'm sure everything will be fine." A small smile tipped up the corners of her mouth, and she reached over and sneakily pinched Sandrine, who let out a small giggle. "So no exploring on your own, okay?"

"Fine." Sandrine rolled her eyes, her mood lifting just in time for them to arrive at the wards.

Evie, more familiar with the workings of the spell than Sandrine, drew the inverted runes for entry—a golden spiral and an all-seeing eye. It was the only way to enter their forest home.

A small blur rushed at them. "Girls!"

"Oh no," Sandrine murmured as Cassandra, the coven's seer, came to a stop in front of them. "We're in trouble now!"

Evie nodded, not missing how Sandrine was wrapped in a warm hug from the prophetess while Cassandra stopped just far enough away from Evie that she wouldn't accidentally touch her. Evie knew why; Cassandra suffered horrific visions any time she touched Evie but never remembered anything other than one ominous phrase. *A lovely death. A deathly love*. Cassandra's recovery was so intense that, after a particularly bad vision, she just never came close to Evie again. Just because she knew and understood why Cassandra kept her distance, though, didn't make it any easier. It was yet another glaring example of how isolated she was from the coven, had always been.

"Where have the two of you been?" Cassandra's gaze darted between the two of them. "I had a vision of danger and screams, and the two of you were standing in the middle of it all. We've been worried sick."

"We?" Evie asked, just as one of the coven elders, a red witch named Hesteia, came striding over to them from the tables where many of their sisters were sitting. A long sigh escaped her lips, quiet enough that only Sandrine heard it and cast her a confused look over the sound. Evie shook her head, silencing any questions that Sandrine may have. "Good evening, Hesteia."

"Evie, my darling," Hesteia remarked, a warm, low chuckle emerging from her. "I should have known you were the one getting our sweet Sandrine into trouble."

Evie wrinkled her nose at the elder, a reluctant smile forming at Hesteia's laughter.

"We didn't do anything, elder Hesteia, I promise!" Sandrine blurted out.

A snort escaped the elder just before Hesteia bit down on her lower lip, smothering her laughter before it could bubble out. "I'm sure you didn't, little love," she responded, running her hand over Sandrine's hair. "But I'm also certain your sister recognizes that any future nothings should be isolated to the daytime when she has you with her, isn't that right, Evie?"

Evie nodded slightly. "Of course." She tried not to take Sandrine with her when she went wandering because she never knew when she would be home. While it was fun to take her sisters with her sometimes, they usually weren't prepared for Evie's nomadic tendencies general restlessness. "Only during the day for future nothings."

"Well, now that that's settled." Hesteia shooed Sandrine towards the tables. "Go get something to eat, little one. You too, Cassandra." As Sandrine darted away, Cassandra following behind, Hesteia stepped closer to Evie. "Did anything happen? Cassandra has been worried sick."

Now would be the time to tell Hesteia what they had seen. What they'd heard. Evie opened her mouth, ready to share everything, but found herself saying instead, "No, everything was fine. Just took Sandrine to see the birds."

Hesteia looked down at her for a long moment, brow furrowed. Then, as if she had gotten an answer to a question she hadn't actually asked, she nodded. "Well, off you go then, Evie. Go get some dinner."

"I think I'm just going to go back to sleep." Evie shrugged. "Sandrine woke me up after only a few hours of rest, so I'm still feeling kind of tired."

Hesteia nodded. "Then go rest, sweet girl." Reaching out a hand, she pushed Evie's hair behind her shoulder. "We're glad to have you home after your time away. We've missed you."

Evie kissed Hesteia lightly on the cheek. "I missed you all as well. Blessed be, Hesteia." Without another word, Hesteia's murmured, "blessed be" in her ears, she walked along the back of their clearing. Animated voices from the witches gathered around the fire filtered to her, but she ignored the sound, summoning the trees to lift her to her home.

Once she walked in through the entrance, she tugged off her shift dress and dropped it to the floor before crawling into her bed, tugging the blankets up to her chin. She dozed off to the sight of a pair of emerald green eyes looking down at her.

Chapter 7

Evie

Barataria Preserve, Marrero, Louisiana

Evie jolted awake for the second time in as many days, her heart racing. Above her, the new moon shone through the parted branches. Her breath came fast, labored. Something woke her. What was it?

Out of the silence, she heard the low, baritone voice bark right next to her ear, "What the fuck do you think you're doing?" She screeched and fell from her bed, scrambling away from the unexpected noise. Around her, the crickets maintained their high-pitched song. No one stirred, save for the members quietly conducting their séance below, far from her tree. Nothing indicated that this was anything other than her standard experience of the voice. No one else could hear him.

But she knew he was real. Knew it the same way she knew that her hair was red, that she was too short, and that her source of magic was the moon. She rubbed her eyes, desperately trying to remember what woke her. It wasn't his shout; she was awake when she heard that. It was a dream. A dream of a man...

she struggled to capture the memory, but it eluded her. Clenching her fists, she stared at the moon, restless even thought her heart rate began to slow.

Since she couldn't remember her dream, she turned back to the odd noises she and Sandrine had heard beyond the trees earlier in the day. At the time, she had Sandrine with her, and there was no way she would risk her young sister by investigating the sounds. Now, though, she wanted to see what they were. She had never heard anything like that. The forest wasn't quiet by any stretch of the imagination, but the cacophony from the other side of the trees was... different. Angry, almost. She had so many questions, was so intrigued by the mystery it presented. The more she thought about it, poked at the memory, the more restless she became until her legs were twitching with the need to stand up and move.

This wasn't like her. Yes, she liked adventure, loved to explore the forest, but she never felt that she *had* to leave, to escape her beloved home. Even as she told herself this, she bolted to her feet, grabbing her discarded dress from the floor and pulling it over her head as she crossed to the entry. *I shouldn't do this*, she thought as she summoned the tree limbs to take her to the forest floor. *This is reckless*, she admonished herself as she descended, her short gown flapping around her thighs at the speed with which she was lighting from limb to limb. *Something could happen, and then who would care for the coven*, she scolded as she found her feet firmly on the ground. Of all her rogue considerations, this last one was the only one that caused her to pause.

Without sounding boastful, she knew her magic source made her the strongest among the coven, despite her own insecurity aout her powers. Even the elders admitted it, while also murmuring that she lacked control over her abilities and her temperament. If something happened to her, if she were unable to return, the coven may be unsafe. She and the other members were raised on stories of the death dealers, odd, dark shadowy figures who hunted witches. She was fairly certain that the stories were just myths to scare young witches, and her sisters weren't in danger, but it worried her even still.

She shook her head, dismissing panicked thoughts of dangerous people descending upon the clearing. It seemed extremely unlikely, bordering on ridiculous, that danger was waiting around the corner. She was jumping at shadows, scared of a boogeyman that probably didn't even exist. With an enthusiastic nod, she strode past the wards and, laughing, ran into the forest.

The moon lit her way, igniting her with happiness as she darted through the trees towards where she and Sandrine had traveled. Spanish moss drifted toward her, drawn by her magic, while the withered leaves, shriveled and dead from the dry winter, burst into vibrant green life as she dashed over them. Without Sandrine, she made the trip much more quickly—even after a detour to resurrect a field of dead giant blue irises—and it wasn't long before she came upon the tree line.

Evie came to a screeching halt less than twenty feet from the trees. Unlike before, it was deceptively quiet with only a dull hum indicating that anything might be amiss. Forcing herself to breathe, knowing she was probably being overly curious or dramatic, she crept towards the trees. She was light on her feet, barely making a sound as edged closer to where the noise had come from. Finally, after what felt like hours but was probably less than a minute, Evie reached the tree line and rested her hand on the live oak nearest her. Through her touch, she felt the tree's unease, sensed the wrongness of this whole place. She peeked her head around her arboreal sentinel, and her heart froze in her chest. *What happened???* She couldn't breathe, couldn't begin to fathom the sight before her.

The forest was just... gone. Trees were uprooted; the ground was violently overturned as far as she could see. Probably the work of the yellow machines that dotted the area. Blood pounded in her ears as she snapped her head from side to side, horrified and overwhelmed. She stepped into the clearing, further away from the healthy trees and into the valley of the death before her. Tree roots slithered along the ground towards her, drawn by her magic.

She wandered through the ruins of the forest; not even in her wildest nightmares could she have imagined this devastation. Dazed, she stared at the apocalyptic scene before her. "What happened?" she murmured, barely aware that she was speaking.

Although she couldn't hear her own voice over her shock, she could pinpoint the exact moment her blood began to hum, almost purring beneath her skin.

Goosebumps dimpled her flesh, and her body practically vibrated, her nipples pebbling under her short dress. Confused, she looked around. There was no reason for her body to be reacting to a mass casualty in this way, but she couldn't deny that she was more aroused than she had ever been in her life.

While she was spontaneous—the coven elders preferred to describe her as impulsive—even she didn't feel comfortable giving herself some much-needed relief in a wide-open clearing where any layperson could see her. She grumbled, knowing there was nothing she could do to help these poor felled trees, and pivoted, intending to race to the tree line. There, she could lift herself into the canopy and slide a hand between her legs, so she could quickly give herself a release. Halfway to the tree line, she heard a heartbeat. Not her own. Another person's.

She paused. Turned slowly. Not far from her stood a man with dark hair and eyes that were such a piercing green she could see it even in the darkness and from a distance. She knew those eyes. Almost before she could give her feet permission, she sauntered toward him, her body still on fire, until she was only a few feet away. Definitely closer than she should be. *But*, she couldn't help musing, *not nearly close enough.*

The man reached a hand out. Those intense eyes, emeralds shining under the light of her beloved moon, searched her face, and, without a single doubt in her mind, she knew this was the man who haunted her. She needed to hear him talk, more badly than she had ever needed anything, but she couldn't convince her mouth to open, to say words. Fortunately, her mystery man didn't seem to have that problem.

He twined a strand of her hair around his finger before opening his mouth. In a rolling baritone that nearly knocked her off her feet, he said one word. "Evangeline?"

Chapter 8

Cole

Central Business District, New Orleans, Louisiana

Cole clicked the end call button in the videoconferencing software, pinching the bridge of his nose in irritation. Calls like that made him want to walk into Canal Street traffic at rush hour or consider retiring at thirty-five. He already had more money than he could ever need or spend, even if his fated wife only believed in shopping 'til she dropped, and each passing day made him question his commitment to career. His clients just seemed to get more brainless with every damn day, and his satisfaction with his job plummeted whenever someone helped him discover the new lows of their stupidity. Times like these, he hated the advent of the internet with a fiery passion; there was just something deeply satisfying about slamming a phone back into the cradle or smashing a physical button to end a call when the person on the other end was that fucking moronic. Somehow, it just lost the effect when he was clicking a mouse button.

It had been a stupendously shitty day. Charles' unsolicited visit and Cole's realization that he had to go trampling through a forest—probably at midnight because he had hearings and calls until well after the sun set—to find a wife he didn't want to claim a mythological throne that would fuck up his entire lifestyle were just the beginning. Chief Executive Officers of multi-billion dollar companies were calling him every hour, acting like the world was going to end if he didn't answer a question he had already addressed. The number of times he had muttered, "Stop breaking the law, asshole," under his breath was, at last count, somewhere around the 200 mark. He got sideswiped by a bike messenger on his way to lunch. His most recent hookup, a barista named Lila (or was it Lana?) had thrown a stapler at his head after he set boundaries with her, namely that it was not okay for her to tell his paralegal to do anything, much less request that she clear his calendar so he could see his girlfriend, a role Lacey (maybe it was Laura?) most assuredly did not hold. Not to mention, the coffee shop had fucked up his standard order, which was a black coffee, the easiest option they had available on their fancy ass menu. He realized that last thing was more annoying than anything else, but dammit, it counted after the day he'd had.

On top of it all, he was still working at 2:00 am. His cell vibrated on the desk as if to prove that this was not his fucking day. Rolling his eyes in frustration, he tapped the answer button, picking up the phone and walking into the private bathroom of his office where he had spare clothes stashed. "Yes?" he snapped, not caring who was on the other end. As luck would have it, it was the owner of a local casino chain, a man so sleazy that he made politicians look genuine. The man got out about two words before Cole realized that there was no way he was getting out of this call without telling his client to fuck off if he didn't hang up now. "Listen," he broke into his client's ramblings, something about questionable conduct with a minor. "Go ahead and call the office in the morning to get a meeting set up."

The man stammered in rage, but the phone call was disconnected before he even finished threatening to take his business elsewhere.

Apparently, he was in the "piss off clients" stage of his day. He glanced down just in time to see the client's name pop up on his screen. With a swipe of his thumb, he declined the call and pulled up his text message chain with his business partner.

Just pissed off Landry. Your turn to deal with him.

After clicking send, he toed off his oxfords and pulled off his suit jacket, letting out a loud sigh of relief as he draped it over the bathroom vanity. *Finally able to get comfortable.* His black dress shirt and suit pants met the same fate. He had just pulled on a pair of jeans and was tugging a soft long-sleeve Henley over his head when his phone vibrated on the vanity. As soon as his head popped through the shirt's neck, Cole picked up his cell.

The fuck did you do this time?

Cole chuckled, his thumbs flying over the keyboard as he typed up his response.

At 2:00 in the morning? I hung up on him while he was trying to tell me it's not statutory rape if the girl looks like she's in her twenties.

Silence followed by a straightforward response.

Fuck my life.

Cole's chuckle grew into a full-blown laugh of happiness that he wouldn't be the one handling Landry's bullshit as he pulled on a pair of tattered Converses that he refused to get rid of because they were perfectly broken in. When his phone vibrated again, showing Landry's name on the screen, he declined the call and powered down his cell, stuffing it and his wallet in his back pocket and heading towards the garage. On his way out of the office, a clean, modern-looking space that occupied the top two floors of one of the tallest skyscrapers in the CBD, he passed through the empty hallways into a dark, open-concept room lined with windows. The lights of New Orleans lit up the area around him, vibrant reds and pinks and whites of the city's night life radiating in through the thick glass.

He stopped in his tracks and glanced out at the city he had been born and raised in. His mother and father had fallen on the poor side of middle class and were too proud to accept money from his uncle, who wanted nothing more than to help them out, especially once they had Cole. Despite their tight budget, they made sure that he had wanted for nothing, adoring and spoiling their only son. Their small cottage in Gentilly, which seemed so grand after they moved out of their Tremé shotgun house when Cole was three, had been filled with love and warmth. It was an area where the neighbors all knew each other, and it wasn't unusual for people to head out to their porches after dinner and share whatever leftovers they had with Ava and Noah Aidoneus' little boy. His mother taught him her native French on that porch; his father educated him on the importance of community in that old house. They never let him forget his roots, though, taking him back to their old stomping grounds in Tremé so he could grow up knowing the friends they were so close to that they were practically family. Through it all, he fell in love with New Orleans. No matter how far he traveled for work, he always came back to the city that had his heart.

Watching the bustle of the French Quarter nightlife just a few blocks away from the darkness of his firm's offices, Cole realized just how far he had come from being that little boy to the man he was today. He stuffed his hands in his pockets and strode to the elevator. During the short ride to the garage, he wondered whether his parents would be proud of who he was today. They died when he was so young. As he got into his car and toggled in the address to a small town with a good entrance to the preserve and parking, a small niggling thought told him that they would probably be proud of what he had accomplished professionally and for New Orleans but not so much with his romantic life. Cole and his best friend had built a multi-billion dollar business through sheer grit and perseverance. He gave back to the community, volunteering his time whenever he could and donating to causes that helped people. But he had never wanted to settle down with any one woman, instead jumping from casual hookups to one-night stands and back again. He liked sex. Fucking sue him. Deep down, though, he knew why he had never pursued anybody long term.

It was his dream girl. The girl he started dreaming about when he was a preteen, a petite thing with big eyes and wild hair. She kept him company and made him feel normal, had become one of his best friends through every conversation they had while he slept. At the time, he had a crush on her because he was a young boy, and she was cute and looked to be his age. Then one dream, she showed up, and she had filled out into a woman that knocked him on his ass.

Big grey eyes that looked lavender in the right light, auburn curls that would look incredible wrapped around his fist, beautiful curves that drove him crazy. She was everything he ever wanted, and the worst part was that she didn't fucking exist. So he fucked a path through New Orleans and everywhere else he went, enjoying himself while he fantasized about his dream woman and reminded himself that she didn't exist outside of his head.

Or at least he though she didn't. Until he looked down at that folder Charles handed him and saw that little girl's eyes, the same stormy eyes that he had seen for most of his life. But the missing Dyeus girl couldn't be his dream girl. She couldn't. Right?

His musings kept him occupied as he followed the GPS directions, thankful that traffic was light because he was more or less on autopilot at this point. Even as the lights of the parkway flickered over his head, he felt certain that this would be a fool's errand, doing his best to keep himself from getting too hopeful. Nothing to see, no fated wife to find, no coven to track. No dream girl who was actually real. Just a waste of time that he could otherwise be using to sleep since he had to be awake and in meetings in... he winced as he glanced at his watch. Six hours.

As soon as he drove up to the construction site that marked the closest point to the preserve with easy parking, though, his world went off its axis. The blood was pounding in his veins, hot and fast as goosebumps raised along the entirety of his body. He was somehow both too hot *and* too cold simultaneously. His heart was trying to beat out of his chest. His skin felt two sizes too small. *What the fuck is this?* He pushed the car's power button, the barely audible buzz of the electric engine cutting off, and swung his long legs out, cracking his back as he raised to his full 6'5" stature. Outside, the wind whistled through the night, the humidity making the chill feel even more brittle. He felt a bit like a serial killer just standing at an inactive construction site in the middle of the night. Actually. Amend that to "pervert" because the tension he had felt in the car had ratcheted up to excitement, which his body interpreted as arousal, the second he got out. And now he was fully erect while chilling in the middle of a dark construction site at 2:30 am. *Fucking great.*

He stepped forward cautiously. Was there an exposed electric line somewhere? Some form of radiation? A massive environmental accident was one of the only things that could explain the fact that he was now harder than he had ever been in his life when there was nobody around. He moved deeper into the construction site, centering himself as he began drawing on the magic deep inside of him, preparing to cast a searcher spell to find the Barataria Coven within the forest. His source of power was death; there was plenty here with the uprooted trees and animal corpses littering the area, so his magic flowed easily.

Wait. His eyes popped open. Somebody was here. He could feel them, skirting the edges of his magic. They were *powerful*, the heft of their own magic floating on the air around him, teasing his heated skin. Cole looked around as he walked further into the site, closer to the tree line. He couldn't see anybody, but he wanted—no, he *needed*—to see this person. Where were they?

A squirrel darted in front of him, chittering softly as it raced towards the trees. "Good call, buddy," he muttered to it softly. "Nothing here for you but death." Chuckling at his terrible joke, he followed its progress towards the forest but froze before he could see the rest of its journey.

In front of him stood a petite woman, pale as the moonlight that surrounded her, wearing a sheer white dress that barely covered her mouthwatering curves. Her big eyes, such an intense grey they were almost purple, observed him warily. Auburn curls tangled around her slim shoulders. The vibrations he had felt in the car, the sense of arousal that even now was crawling all over his skin, all of it was coming from her. From this absolute fucking vision in front of him.

She has to be a hallucination, he thought madly. A hallucination brought on by lack of sleep, stress, too much caffeine, something, because it was too much to believe that the woman he had only seen in his dreams —some of them extremely pornographic—was standing in front of him. This theory conveniently ignored the fact that he had never once shown so much as a hint of mental illness, but he was perfectly fine accepting that lapse in logic.

He had never told anyone besides his uncle and his best friend about his dream woman, although he supposed he should have. His family had been searching for his fated wife since his birth. The woman who appeared to him in dreams for most of his life could maybe, just maybe, be a clue to that little mystery. He couldn't bear to share her with anyone, though; she was his and his alone. Nobody else deserved to know about his dream woman: what she sounded like, what she looked like, what she felt like, what she *tasted* like.

In the minute it took his brain to cycle through his rapid-fire thoughts, she crossed the divide between them gracefully but quickly, coming to a halt less than five feet away from him. He couldn't stop himself. He had to touch her, see if she was real. Lifting his arm, he was surprised to see that his hand wasn't shaking. It felt like it should be because everything inside of him was screaming in excitement.

She watched him without fear. Gods, she looked like a mythological warrior in the darkness. Absently, he noted that she wasn't wearing shoes. It felt like that wasn't a good idea, but he couldn't think clearly enough to figure out why. *Doesn't matter.*

He wrapped a strand of her thick hair around his ring finger. It was silky against his skin, softer than he had expected given that he was almost sure she lived in the forest. He drew her closer, using only his grip on that one auburn curl. In an instant, a single breath, he knew who this was. He had to confirm, though. He cleared his throat, but it made no difference. When he spoke, his voice still sounded like he had recently taken up gargling gravel. Didn't matter. She could still hear him as that one earth-shattering word left his mouth. "Evangeline?"

Chapter 9

Evie

Barataria Preserve, Marrero, Louisiana

Holy mother of witches, he was so beautiful that it almost hurt to look at him. Ebony hair, high cheekbones with a sharp chin, lightly tanned skin, those piercing green eyes lit with intensity and fire. He was so tall that she was all but looking straight up, his tall, lean frame dwarfing her. Even as he drew her towards him, one hand in her hair, she knew she could stop this at any time, but she didn't want to. The scent of smoky mint wrapped around her, and it smelled like home. His eyes were locked on hers, and, suddenly, she couldn't breathe. Could barely even think.

She needed to think, though. He had asked her a question, not that she could remember what it was. What she did remember was that voice. She had heard it countless times before in her life. So hearing it for real? Gods, she needed to hear it again, but the only way for her to do that was for her to open her cursed mouth and freaking speak. That's how conversations worked. Only it felt like the connection between her brain and her mouth had been severed as her body settled against his, his hand still in her hair, the other hand now settled low on her back, practically grabbing her ass.

"Evangeline?" he repeated, unraveling his finger from her hair before cupping her cheek in his hand, his thumb rubbing absently along her face.

She flushed at his touch, heat crawling down her spine, and she couldn't help but rest her face against his palm. A low rumble sounded in his chest, and she pressed closer into him, wanting nothing more than to feel that vibration against her body.

His thumb traced along her cheekbone. "*Un petit ange*," he murmured, so low that she wasn't actually sure he even meant to say it aloud.

Finally, her mouth received her brain's order to speak. "Evie," she corrected hoarsely. Her voice cracked on her own name as it fell from her mouth, but she couldn't even blame herself for that. She had never felt like this before. There was fire under her skin, and her magic positively purred at the feeling of his body against hers, power seeping uncontrollably from her pores.

Around them, the devastated forest clearing shifted, tree roots coming to life and shoving their reformed roots into the ground, rising back to their original stance as if a giant hand had lifted them and put everything to rights.

At the center of it all, unaware of the chaos around them, she and her mystery man stood, staring deep into one another's eyes. She needed to know his name more than she needed her next breath. "Who are you?"

Chapter 10

Cole

Barataria Preserve, Marrero, Louisiana

Her voice was soothing and melodic, the notes of it jarringly familiar to him after all the years she haunted his dreams. Sometime in the last few minutes, they had ended up wrapped around each other, his hand all but resting on her ass, her hands clutching his biceps tightly. He heard noise around them but didn't know what was causing it, couldn't be bothered to figure out what it was. Dangerous considering who he was, who he was starting to believe she was, and the enemies they would both have because of it. He didn't care, though. The only sound he wanted to hear was her exquisite voice.

He cleared his throat. Again. "My name is Cole," he said, his eyes darting across her face, taking in every elegant inch of her. "And I think I've been looking for you."

Canting her head to the side, she lifted one brownish-red eyebrow in surprise. "Oh? And why would you be doing that, Cole? I haven't found that many people looking for strangers at night are doing so out of the goodness of their hearts."

The sound of his name on her tongue, even in disbelief, absolutely destroyed him. Surreal. That's what this whole thing was. Surreal. He was standing at a construction site in the dead of night, the woman of his dreams pressed against him, and she had decided to debate his apparent prospective serial killer status. He chuckled, overwhelmed by the strength of his reaction to her. He wanted to crawl inside of her and never leave. He needed to hear her say his damn name in every tone at every volume. "Well, I don't know about any malicious intent, but pretty little things who come out of the woods in see-through dresses generally can't throw stones at the men who spend their nights at construction sites." As if he made a habit of this. Fuck, he was an idiot.

She nuzzled her face against his chest. Goddamn, just that one small gesture had him grinding his hips against her. "Why were you looking for me, Cole?" she asked again.

Although he wasn't particularly familiar with the workings of long-term, romantic relationships, he didn't really think he could tell this ethereal sprite of a woman that not only had he dreamed about her for more than twenty years but that he also believed she may be the fated reincarnation of a goddess with whom he would rule the Underworld to stop an apocalypse. That felt like it may be a mood killer. Also, and he didn't remember the ancient texts too clearly, but he was fairly certain that the witches play a role in the exact world-ending event he was trying to stop. So if the angel in front of him was both the reincarnate and a witch... He almost groaned at his inability to recall the actual witches' prophecy. This was what he got for ignoring his uncle, the Moirai, his advisors, really anybody associated with the effort to put him on the throne, when they lectured him. Since he couldn't remember his lectures and he knew that confessing that he was here to take her home with him was a bad damn idea, he skirted the question, giving her a half truth. "I had a feeling you might be here."

He felt her gasp before she said softly, "I've seen you almost all my life." Reaching up, she touched his face gently. "But never your face. I always wondered what you looked like." Her fingers paused on his right cheek before combing back into his hair. "So much better than I ever imagined."

Her whispered words, the tender touch stroking along his face, the look of awe in her beautiful eyes, all of it triggered something primal, something deeply possessive, in him. Whether or not this was actually Evangeline Dyeus, whether or not she was Persephone reincarnated, she was *his*. That being said, he would bet his entire empire that she was his fated wife. Between the magic pulsing between them, their lifelong interactions with each other, this immediate recognition, there were too many signs that she was meant to be with him. He couldn't let her go back to the forest for a multitude of reasons, and most of them had absolutely nothing to do with the hazy memory of the witches' role in the apocalypse. He just... he needed her with him.

"Come with me," he murmured, grazing her cheek with his fingertips before sliding his hand down to her own, tangling his fingers in between hers. Electricity surged between them, and her eyes dilated with lust. Jesus fucking Christ. He needed to get them back to his home before he did something stupid like stripping his dream woman down and fucking her in the middle of a construction site. "Please, Angel, come home with me." He gripped her hand a little tighter, turning to escort her back to his car. For the second time that night, he froze at the sight that greeted him.

What had once been an empty construction site littered with the decrepit remains of trees and torn-up earth had been reclaimed by the forest. After time had frozen when he saw her but before he had turned to take her to his car, the upturned trees had somehow rerooted and stood themselves tall once more. Newly formed vines ran across the ground, and vibrant flowers positively exploded everywhere around them. It was as if none of the construction had ever happened. About thirty feet away, he could actually see one of the yellow diggers pinned into a tree as if the tree had grown into and around the vehicle. He suspected that, if he looked around for the rest of the equipment, he would find that they were subject to a similar reclamation. This would have taken so much magic and should have been loud as a tornado. But, despite being in the eye of what must have been an intense magical storm, neither of them had noticed a thing.

Chapter II

Evie

Barataria Preserve, Marrero, Louisiana

As her mystery man—no, she corrected herself, her *Cole*—gaped at the suddenly reformed forest around them, Evie almost felt like the Earth started turning again. Without those fiery emerald eyes on her, holding her hostage in their depths, she could breathe, her lungs finally taking in air once more. She was shocked at the forest's reclamation since she had never executed magic on that astronomical a scale, but it was what she had almost agreed to while wrapped in his arms that actually froze the blood in her veins. That pet name said in his raspy voice, that spike of lust she knew they both felt when he touched her, almost had her agreeing to go with him. To leave the forest. Her family. Her *home*.

"I can't go with you," she responded, tugging at her hand. "I just met you. And this place is my home. My family is here. I'm not leaving." She pulled at her hand again, knowing if she could get herself free of his touch that maybe the world would go back to normal again. Her palm rasped against his, and, for a second, she thought she was about to go free.

But then his fingers tightened around hers, and Cole turned back to her. And there went her oxygen once more in the face of his too bright eyes and beautiful features. "Angel, you said it yourself; I've been with you all your life. You can trust me." She opened her mouth, and he shook his head at her. "So trust me when I tell you that you need to come home with me. If you stay, you could be in danger. I won't leave you here and," he paused, glancing around him, his face crinkling in amusement before he finished, "I was not made for camping."

If she thought he was incredible when he was serious, he was even more astounding in happiness. Holy Crone Mother, his smile practically stopped her heart; she wanted to see more of it. Then his words trickled into her consciousness, and she frowned as she considered them. They didn't make sense. She steeled her backbone and argued, "Why would I be in danger if I stayed in the place where I've spent my entire life? Outside of meeting a random man trying to abduct me from my home in the middle of the night—" she gave him a pointed stare. "—I haven't really faced a lot of surprising and dangerous situations here. What danger could I be in if I just stayed home?"

His eyebrows raised in shock. "Evangeline—" "Evie," she corrected, smirking as he rolled his eyes at her. "Fine. Evie. The forest is not the danger. It's the people who are going to come looking for you now that I've found you."

If she was confused before, she was upside down now. "Wait. Now that you've found me? You were actually looking for me? Also. What people? Why would they be looking for me? And, again, what does you finding me have to do with anything?" Her voice rose angrily on the last question.

Cole scraped one long-fingered hand through his hair, and Evie tried not to get distracted at the thought of what those hands could undoubtedly do to her body. *Focus, Evie. It's time to focus.* She heard him mumble something that sounded suspiciously like, "of course she had to be stubborn," before he raised his voice to an audible level. "Evie, you just raised an entire fucking forest from a construction site. Rerooted centuries old trees, grew vines and flowers from nothing. Picked up machines that weigh at least a hundred tons. Have you ever done that before?"

He knew. He knew she had magic. How? The elders always made it sound like the general population's belief in magic had died out long ago. Were they wrong? Or were they lying to protect the coven? It wouldn't be the first time they had done something dangerous in the name of safety. She sputtered, wanting desperately to deny her magic and this sudden exercise of power on an exponential level, but she found herself fully unable to lie to Cole. "No. No, I've never used magic on that level." Her voice was quiet as she stared around them at the reclaimed land. "I didn't know I could."

Nodding emphatically, he pushed further, crowding back into her space. "Do you know why you were able to do that?" At the subtle shake of her head, his gaze lit up with victory and what looked like pride.

"Cole, I can't leave my home," she rasped, and his victorious look vanished, the corners of his mouth turning down in a small scowl. Even though he looked irritated, he couldn't seem to stop touching her. One hand wrapped around the back of her neck, tugging her into the warmth of his body, while the other ran down her side. She shivered as he brushed the side of her breast, and she felt more than heard the groan that rumbled from his chest. "I'm safe here." Although she wouldn't leave with him, she couldn't just let him go. She had to see him again. "But you could come back? Just because I'm not going with you doesn't mean that this is the last time we have to see each other." Gods, she needed this to not be the last time she ever saw him.

He didn't respond, his fingers continuing their steady agonizing pace down the length of her body. His eyes were steady on hers.

She suspected he was trying to distract her and, although she hated to admit it, it was working. "Cole," she sighed as he shifted the hand on her neck to cup the back of her head. "Please... " She didn't even know what she was asking for, but she knew she needed him more badly than she had ever wanted anything.

His touch may have started out as a distraction, but it had taken on a life of its own. And it wasn't just affecting her. Cole seemed to have lost the thread of their conversation just as thoroughly as she had. "Just one taste," he mumbled to himself, and then his mouth was on hers.

She melted against him as he slid his tongue along her lips, parting hers. Seizing her by the waist, he lifted her from the ground, pressing her body along the length of his. A throaty moan rolled out of her, the sound muffled under his sensual assault.

Cole nipped her lower lip aggressively before devouring her mouth desperately, his tongue twining sensuously along her own as one hand gripped her ass. His entire body was shaking at the intensity... no, that must be her because he was strong and stable under the legs that she had wound around his waist.

No. She wasn't shaking. Evie pulled back, confused. It took them both a moment to realize that it wasn't them shaking but the very ground beneath them. What was happening? The rumble grew louder, the earth's shaking intensified, and, from outside the regrown section of forest, she could hear screams and high-pitched sounds. *What the hell is happening?*

Without a word, Cole turned on his heels, arms holding her tight where she was still wrapped around his waist, and sprinted for the tree line.

"What are you doing?" Evie panicked, shoving at his chest. "Put me down!"

He barely spared her a glance, his long legs eating up the distance to where the final trees stood between them and the outside world. When he spoke, his voice was terse. "We need to get the fuck out of here. Something's wrong, and I need to keep you safe, Angel."

Although that name in his voice nearly did her in, she wasn't going to cave. He still needed to put her down. He didn't get to tell her what to do, and he definitely wasn't deciding where she lived. "Cole," she started sternly. "Put me down. Now. My magic is here." Only partially true since she drew her magic from the moon; it was just easier for her when there was plenty of fauna and flora around. He didn't need to know the details right now, though. Not as he was trying to kidnap her from her home. "My family is here. My life is here. And I'm not fucking leaving just because you ordered me to." Her voice rested heavily, sarcastically, on the word "ordered," letting her would-be abductor know exactly what she thought about his plan. When he refused to drop her, she slowly gathered magic to her, drawing from the moon's rays and whatever that dark power was, the one that lived deep inside her and had been trying to get out since she saw him. She gave him one last warning before she unleashed her wrath on him. "Cole. I mean it. Put me down. Right. Now."

He maintained his hold on her, and her temper redlined. Her lust transformed into rage, and she felt like she could level mountains in her anger. "How dare you try and take me from my home without my consent?" she hissed, drawing the vines from the forest floor to wrap around his lower body, their firm hold forcing him to a stop.

His grip on her upper thighs stayed firm, though, even as he swore violently at her, the forest, the vines, and somebody called the Moirai.

The trees around them bent inwards, those nearest to them extending towards Cole. He grimaced in pain and rage as their thick limbs squirmed in between his torso and Evie, forcing distance between them. His hold loosened just a bit, and the branches pushed more firmly against her stomach. She wiggled and, finally, felt his hand slip on her right thigh. With a firm press of her hands against his chest, she shoved backwards, her legs sliding down his hips towards the ground.

Just as she felt the toes of one foot graze the forest floor, Cole growled, a deep, almost inhuman sound, and his eyes flamed a deep radioactive blue, erasing all traces of the familiar green. The limbs between the two of them decayed, bark flaking rapidly until they turned to dust falling away in the January wind. She gaped as the vines were subject to the same treatment, and his hand locked around the leg that had escaped, wrapping it back around his waist impatiently. Snapping her gaze back to his face, she saw a crown of blue fire so dark it was almost black sitting on his head as he stared down at her imperiously, no trace of the man who had been lost for her just moments before in his glowing eyes.

"You shouldn't have tried to get away from me." He continued his march toward the treeline; her heart plummeted with each step. The further they got, the less chance of escape she had. Although she had never been outside of the forest, she felt almost certain that wherever Cole lived didn't have trees, vines, and other greenery to summon to her aid. "You should have come with me voluntarily." He leaned down and whispered in a voice raw with emotion, "No one, no force in the Underworld or on Olympus, not even you, powerful little witch, can separate us. You're fucking mine, Angel." And with a firm press of his lips to her cheek, he took the final step past the trees, and she left the safety of her home for the first time in memory.

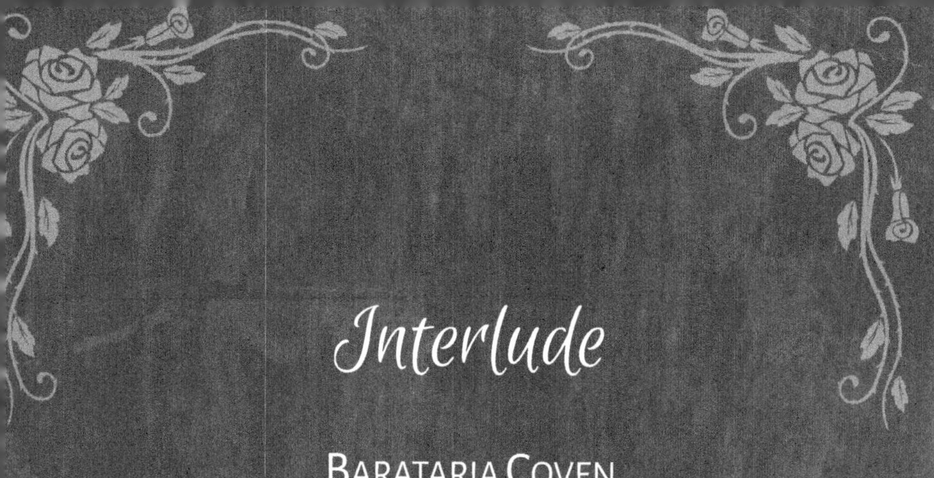

Interlude

Barataria Coven

Barataria Preserve, Marrero, Louisiana

Hesteia, a red witch and one of the Barataria Coven elders, stared deep into the fire before her, its flames reflecting in her dark eyes. The smoke that rose above it drifted towards her, stroking her face tenderly. Her love, Thea, sat beside her and clutched her hand in silence. Their home was never quiet; too many people bustled about, too much magic buzzed in the air, for the clearing to ever be truly quiet. Yet tonight, all was hushed. Coven members still milled around, but they were subdued, and it felt like there was a filmy layer over the world. In an effort to discover why, she was reading the flames, trying to see if there was some danger to the coven. Unfortunately, they remained empty of any hint.

A low rumbling reached her ears. She tilted her head, confused, just as the ground under her feet started to shake, and the trees began swaying around her. New Orleans wasn't a hotbed for earthquakes. Unlike in California, the Barataria Coven didn't need to concern themselves too much with the possibility. But it seemed like the time for one was finally here because the shaking became more violent, a deadly roaring filling the air.

The unsettling quiet over the clearing broke as witches screamed, women of all ages flooding the common area. A young witch near the fire stumbled to her knees and, no matter how hard she tried, couldn't get to her feet, eventually just curling into a ball on the ground. Pans clattered to the floor, books fell from their perches, familiars squawked and hissed and howled at the sound of trees in the clearing cracking and splitting. It was pandemonium, all underlined by that ghastly, rumbling sound.

Adelaide, the oldest coven elder and a shamanic witch, raced out of her underground home, eyes wild as she scanned the clearing before her gaze locked on Hesteia by the fire twenty feet away. "What's happening, Hesteia?" A high-pitched scream rose as a tree collapsed not far from them, and Bernadette, a young voodoo practitioner, sprinted past them to see if anybody had been injured. "I've never seen an earthquake as bad as this in all my years. It can't be natural!" A small slip of a child tried to get past where Adelaide was standing, but she grabbed the back of the witch's clothing, shooing her down into the linked caverns where the shamanic witches lived. "No, baby girl, go back to the caves where it's safe."

Hesteia shook her head, her box braids bouncing. "I don't know—"

Thea spoke over her wife, her low voice carrying. "It's not natural," she confirmed. Touching Hesteia's shoulder to capture her attention, she gestured to the fire.

Hesteia turned and gaped. From the fire rose two pillars of flame in the shape of a man and woman. The flames intertwined, merged into one, before a crown emerged in their place. The fiery portents vanished just as quickly as they appeared, and, as soon as they did, the violent shaking and rumbling stopped immediately.

Flame reading was more art than science and, oftentimes, infuriatingly vague rather than helpful. Hesteia leaned into her partner for reassurance, Thea's hand wrapping around her shoulders comfortingly. "Thea, what was that?" As Thea shook her head, her shoulders fell. "I've felt earthquakes. This was different.

This was peculiar and dangerous, and whatever was in the flames... that was the cause of it. A man and a woman and a crown." She shook her head impatiently. "Cursed flame reading. Would have helped if it shared names or features or anything of use. At this point, I might as well just try haruspicy for as much good as the fire did us." Beside her, Thea chuckled quietly as they rose to assist the coven with cleaning up the devastation from the earthquake.

All around them, they saw the impacts of it. Several dwellings had collapsed, and at least one house was crushed by a felled tree. Gaping cracks now extended along the soil, brackish water slowly filling the holes. On the other side of the clearing, a small area had developed a conelike formation out of silt and sand with water pouring from it. Everywhere they looked was just more chaos, although, fortunately, it seemed like nobody was severely injured.

Bernadette returned to them, a shattered teacup clutched in one of her hands, the other arm draped around Sandrine's slim shoulders. Sandrine was leaning her weight into her sister's side; the young witch appeared to be limping, and blood oozed from a shallow cut on her cheek. She was crying silently.

Hesteia wrapped her arms around Sandrine's shoulders in a comforting hug. "No need to cry, little one," she whispered. "We're all alright. Just some minor clean up needed." That may be an understatement, but she needed to keep everyone, including the younger witches in her charge, calm.

Sandrine shook her head so hard her braids whipped against her cheeks. "It's not that," she replied urgently. "I can't find Evie. I was going to find her for spellcasting under the moon—she promised we could tonight—and she's not home. I don't know where she is, and I'm scared something happened to her. She's never broken a promise to me before." More tears tracked down her face. "I don't know where she is, Elder Hesteia!"

Hesteia glanced back over her shoulder at Thea, whose eyes were almost comically wide at that unexpected bit of information. "It's okay, darling. We'll find her. I'm sure she's just out foraging. You know that Evie sometimes loses track of time while she's roaming." Withdrawing her arms from around Sandrine's neck, she turned her attention to Bernadette. "Etty, could you please take Sandrine to the healers? We don't want that cut getting infected."

Bernadette escorted Sandrine to the healers clustered at the center of the clearing, leaving Hesteia and Thea to themselves, thoughtful as disorder roared around them. They were both too scared to raise the very real question that plagued them. Eventually, though, Thea broke the silence. "What if the woman in the fire is Evie?"

"It's possible. We don't know much about her." Hesteia thought back to when she and the other coven elders found Evie. A little over two years old, she had been covered in blood, her mother's broken corpse laying not far from her. The coven had been cautious in taking in the blood-stained infant, and the Witches' Council itself became involved in the decision, especially after Evie showed mind-boggling powers of life... and death. She could raise a field of flowers in seconds; she could decay the flesh and bone from someone's body just as quickly. No one understood her unique abilities, but they certainly respected and feared them.

The coven had spent years trying to understand Evie's past and power through any means possible, including by some methods imposed by the Witches' Council themselves. Hesteia had tried to flame read Evie's past many times. Every effort failed. Cassandra, the coven's seer, even attempted to prophecy Evie's future once; her body contorted as she screamed, "a lovely death, a deathly love" over and over. After Cassandra had calmed, she fell into a weeks-long coma and remembered none of it upon her waking. Nothing, magical or otherwise, answered their questions so, whenever Evie asked, they simply played dumb and redirected the conversation.

So, yes, Evie was an anomaly. Even so, she loved the coven deeply, caring for every one of them. "What if she finally came into her power? The way we found her was so odd; we knew she must be intended for great and powerful things."

Thea wound flames around her arms, a sign she was thinking deeply. "What if this is a portent of the end, my love? Unnatural earthquakes? A couple and a fiery crown? These are not standard seer fare, and you know it." She lowered her voice to avoid being overheard, even though the panic around them made that unlikely. "What if we're meant to ride to Evie? Leave the forest and carry the end of days to this world."

"But the prophecy states that we will know for certain, no doubt whatsoever." Hesteia bit her lip. "Supposedly, the old gods' return will signal that we must ride." A thought occurred to her. "What if Evie is an old god? We found her in blood. She has unparalleled powers of life and death. There are gods that meet that description."

Thea nibbled on her lower lip, clearly wanting to disagree but not able to. "It's certainly not the most far-fetched theory you've ever had," she said, briefly nestling her head into Hesteia's shoulder, thanking the gods that her wife hadn't been injured in the unnatural earthquake. "We should reach out to the other covens in the morning after we put everything to rights and make sure everyone is alright. Maybe we could subtly ask whether any of them know anything about why this may have happened. After the devastation of the witches in the mid-1900s, we lost so much of our oral history. Maybe a coven somewhere has a writing that would explain some of this." She lifted her head slightly to look at her wife.

Hesteia nodded slowly, her braids brushing slightly across Thea's skin. "That sounds fine," she answered distractedly, gaze locked on a limping witch across the clearing.

Thea tugged slightly on one of Hesteia's braids, a small smile sliding across her face when her wife turned to her with a disgruntled look on her face. "Hessie, my love," she said, using the playful nickname that her poised, elegant wife hated to love. "We'll get to the bottom of this. We'll write to the other covens and see if they experienced the same issues. Figure out if there's any reason other than the prophecy that this might have happened." She doubted it, but she knew the feelings of their coven, a loving group that avoided violence at all costs and believed that the prophecy was more metaphorical than literal. "It will be alright, darling."

Hesteia didn't move, but her face softened slightly. "You're right," she finally responded.

"Of course I'm right." Thea grasped Hesteia's hand. "Now shall we go make sure everyone is healthy and has a place to rest until we can magic their homes back into being?"

Hesteia let Thea draw her around the clearing, checking in with each witch, all while she planned the letter they would distribute to the other covens.

Chapter 12

Cole

New Orleans, Louisiana

Cole's thoughts were absolute chaos. He had no real memory of the walk back to his car and didn't remember dropping Evie into his car or even starting the drive back to his home. His mind was simply cycling between panic at the idea that his Angel had tried to get away from him and an intense need to make sure she never left his side again.

They were halfway back to New Orleans before his vision cleared of blue flame. It happened so suddenly that he was disoriented, his rational mind racing to catch up. He couldn't have said with certainty where they were even after having driven this route only two hours before. Two utterly life-changing hours.

Last thing he remembered, he had the fiery little witch in his arms, his lips on hers, the world shaking around them. He had begged her to come home with him. A little voice in the back of his brain corrected him: *Less begged. More ordered.* After that, he remembered exactly nothing. It had been a long time since his death magic, unstable in his human body until the prophecy was fulfilled, had overtaken him. In fact... he didn't think he had ever lost control like that. He couldn't recall actually losing consciousness in a magically induced blackout before.

At that thought, he glanced over at the passenger seat where an exquisite ball of rage sat glaring at him. Apparently, in his power-induced dissociation, he had the good sense to bind Evie and place wards over key pressure points to keep her from using her own magic against him. *Smart*, he thought, flinching slightly as her furious eyes bored into his own. Thank the gods for his car's self-driving function and the empty roads; he couldn't tear his gaze away from her.

She was absolutely exquisite in her rage. Her intense grey eyes flickered molten gold at the power thrumming under her skin. The wards he had place flared shimmers of light around them like fireworks as she tried to break free of his magic. Her tattoo—*was that a... snake in a field of flowers?* he mused—positively writhed along her arm in a way that was *definitely* mystical, and her disheveled curls floated around her, courtesy of the wind her intense magic was raising in the car. It was unnerving as hell.

Cole had never seen anything so perfect in his human life.

"You know the wards I placed don't stop you from speaking, right? You're able to talk." He forced his attention back to the road, trying to play it cool. Like he didn't want to swivel back to her and just watch her, safety be damned.

Even not looking at her, he could see her sneer. "Oh, I'm allowed to talk? How very gracious of you," she hissed. "You going to listen to me this time if I do speak? Or just throw me over your shoulder and steal me from my fucking home again?"

Was that what he had done? Fuck. While he didn't have a ton of sustained, nonsexual experience with women, he knew that abducting them wasn't the way to their heart... although it had worked beautifully for his ancestor. Probably not a great role model, even though he had inherited that particular ancestor's magic, memories, and throne. He scraped a hand over the now-long-past-5:00 stubble on his face. He should apologize. Right? He opened his mouth, but the vengeful little hellcat was still going.

"How fucking dare you?" Her voice rose slightly. Beside him, the wards on her luminous skin almost blinded him as her magic tried desperately to find a weak link to attack him. Gods, she was strong. "Who do you think you *are*? We've never interfered with humans, not once, never endangered your kind. You took me from my home without *any* reason! You touched what you had absolutely no right to lay a hand on. This is an act of war against the witches and trust me when I say: you won't win that one, you absolute dumbass."

His lips curled into a feral grin. "Oh, Angel, you didn't seem to mind me touching you back there." Her jaw dropped in shock—or rage, who knew with the witch beside him—her full lips parting, and fuck him if that wasn't the sexiest thing he had seen in a long time. "In fact, you seemed perfectly thrilled when I did finally touch you." *Why are you baiting her?* "In fact, you begged me for more. So don't try to make out like I forced myself on you, little witch. You loved every single fucking second of being in my arms, and, if we'd had a few more seconds before that earthquake, I would have been able to feel just how wet you were for me. And, to one of your other points because the rest were bullshit, I took you with me because you're mine." He felt the growl, the overwhelming emphasis, he put on that last word, but he couldn't control it. "We stay together. There's no 'war' upon the witches, nothing except me keeping you safe and with me."

She shivered at his words, eyes drifting out of focus a bit as she mouthed the word, "mine" as if she couldn't believe that had just come out of his mouth. Honestly, he couldn't believe he had said it to her, but now that it was out and her face was lit with desire, he couldn't bring himself to regret it. He could work with lust, get this perfect angel completely addicted to what he could give her. He needed her to crave him, to desire them. To want to stay. They would be ruling together for eternity, and there was no backing out once they had sealed their bond and accepted their role as king and queen of the underworld. He needed her to choose to take that step with him in spite of what he was sure was a full life with her coven.

"That earthquake was weird though, right?" It just slipped from his lips. He wanted to talk to her, hear her melodic voice when it wasn't filled with rage.

Evie looked at him like he was crazy. Hell, maybe he was—she was magically bound in his front seat after he took her from her home. After a few moments of silence, though, she shocked the hell out of him by answering in a calm voice. "I don't know what it was. I thought you were shaking at first. I've gone through a few earthquakes before, but none of them ever felt like that." She shrugged. "It felt like something below us was... waking up." After catching sight of his questioning glance, she backtracked. "I don't know. It just felt like it was coming from the depths of the earth, so much deeper than anything I've ever felt."

Well, that certainly spawned a thought. What if the earthquake was the underworld awakening to welcome its deities home? A nice little confirmation from their realm that Evie was his queen? After feeling the world shake around him when he saw her, figuratively at first followed by a very extreme literally, he didn't really give a shit whether she actually was the reincarnate the Moirai had prophesied; she was his regardless, and he would force a square peg into a round hole just to keep her if she wasn't. He winced. So much more like his ancestor than he ever anticipated. Fucking yikes.

Sinking into his thoughts, Cole barely noticed the scenery around them shifting from the more rural areas surrounding her forest home to the bright city skyline. Having been born and raised in New Orleans—one of the rare few to claim that title—he thought it was the most incredible city in the world. That was doubly true at night when the sky positively glowed with the brightly colored lights of the city. When he was a child, Charles told him that the astronauts could see New Orleans from the space. His seven-year-old self absorbed that tidbit as absolute gospel rather than recognizing it as a desperate uncle trying to console his young nephew after the unexpected death of both of his parents. And even though 35-year-old Cole, a—mostly—rational man who had founded a well-respected, internationally recognized law firm and owned a historic home in the sought-after Garden District, was fairly certain that factoid was false, a little part of him still wanted to believe it. There was nothing more magnificent than this city.

Except the witch sitting next to him. Her big eyes took in everything as they exited the freeway, their grey shade reflecting the hue of every light they passed. Although it would be faster to go down any other street, he found himself driving leisurely down St. Charles, wanting to see her react to the sights.

Traffic was at a standstill, even at almost 4:30 am, so he took the chance to stare unashamedly at her as she discovered New Orleans, swiveling back and forth to look out of every window in the car. The bright lights illuminating the many hotels along the roadway painted her face, bathing her features in the neon colors and intense lights of the city. To their right, the historic Pontchartrain Hotel rose majestically; she gaped through the car's clear roof at the old-fashioned building. He could tell by her excited squint and small bounce in her seat that she loved the vibrant neon lights of the bars and restaurants. Watched her pretty, little mouth purse into a moue of disapproval at the deadened grass in the neutral ground by the streetcar.

And he couldn't get enough of her sounds. She chuckled at a group of women swaying with all the drunken swagger of Captain Jack Sparrow, gasped in excitement at the streetcar rattling alongside them, cooed over a squashed-face French bulldog leading its owner down the street. Each sound she made just forced him to realize, for the umpteenth time this evening, that he was in so far over his head with her. He had never had all that much interest in a specific woman, much less this intense, all-encompassing response, before. They had only kissed, for fuck's sake, and his dick thought that any noise of excitement she made was for it alone.

As they made their way further down St. Charles, the hotels and bars slowly transitioned into apartments and condos with the odd fast-food restaurant to break things up. Cole wasn't sure what her living situation in the preserve had been, but he would bet that it was distinctly different from the old-money homes and more modern rental living currently surrounding the car.

Slowly, she turned her head towards him, making eye contact with him for the first time since entering the city. "What are all of these places?" she asked quietly. "I know what the words mean, but I've not seen them used in some of these ways before."

Cole tilted his head. It must have been hellish for her to admit she didn't know something. In the two hours since they had met, he had been aroused, furious, possessive—not that he wanted to think too much about that one—and confused; most of all, he had been impressed. If he had thought about it before meeting Evie, he probably would have guessed that a forest witch would be overwhelmed, scared even, at being... removed—his brain still shied away from the word "abducted" to describe what he had done—from her home and brought into a bustling city. But she wasn't.

At no point did she even appear to be slightly scared. Of him or of anything else surrounding them. She had seemed *livid*, amused, turned on as fuck, but, even as the hits kept coming, she took them in stride. For her to break her silence and admit she didn't know something, despite what seemed like an overwhelming and fiery intelligence, it must have taken a shit ton of backbone.

"They're apartments," he responded before adding, "where people live," just in case she didn't know.

She eyed him frostily. "I know what an apartment is. Just in case you didn't notice, I'm not actually stupid."

He chuckled. God, she was a smart-ass. Exactly his type, if he was being honest. "I don't know what the schooling system in a forest looks like. You could be illiterate for all I know." Even though he'd seen her reading the signs by the road, the road names, hell, even the information on the car's touch screen. *Why the fuck are you baiting her, you moron?* he berated himself for the second time that night.

Her back stiffened instantly, and the wards went practically supernova from the massive influx of power that rippled from her skin at his words. "Excuse you?" she snapped. "You think I'm illiterate? I would wager that our education is a touch better than your human schooling. Especially given that our education is free from the political whims of hateful and bigoted humans, thank you *very* fucking much."

She raised a good point about the impact of politics upon schooling—and he wanted to unpack that with her later and see even more of how her brain worked—but he had to address the elephant in the room. His humanity. He knew she wasn't ready for the whole truth—he was barely ready for the whole truth of their relationship, and he had been aware of it for a lot longer—but she needed to be made aware of who he was. "That's the second time you've called me human, Evie. Do it again, and my feelings might get hurt."

"Are you not? Human, then?" She extended her hand to touch him, possibly read him, even though he didn't know if she possessed that ability, but the wards forced her hand away. "I know that there are humans who can use magic, so I just assumed you were one." At his slight head shake, she became more lively, her eyes sparkling in excitement, the fury of earlier forgotten in the face of new knowledge. "I've read stories of magical beings who appear human living in the human world. Are you one of them? What are you? Am I allowed to ask that? Feels like I shouldn't, but I really want to know!" She was all but bouncing in her seat as she fired questions at him.

What could he tell her that wouldn't be too much? The Moirai and Charles had never covered how to tell his fated wife that she was, in fact, his fated wife. No, they just babbled about duty and honor and ancient texts. Honestly, he had tuned most of it out after a while. Now that he had Evie in his car, he was regretting never asking them about what to do when he actually *found* the reincarnate.

He toggled the signal to turn left onto Seventh Street, waiting for traffic to slow enough to turn. During that time, he thought his way through a response, finally saying, "I'm the reincarnate of the god Hades." That felt like a concise way to address her question, but, even as he complimented himself on side-stepping the potential implications, she dug into what could only be charitably described as a cross-examination. Having conducted a few of them himself, he knew what to look for.

"I'm sorry... you're the reincarnation of a god? Don't think too highly of yourself at all, do you? What, did you get the keys to the kingdom along with it? All the powers, too, I'm assuming... " She trailed off as he pulled on to his street.

Cole knew, without a doubt, that it wasn't the astonishingly over-the-top homes surrounding his comparably modest 1860s Greek revival home that caught her attention. He knew it the same way that he knew he drew his magic from death. That he would commit murder before letting the wide-eyed little witchling sitting next to him out of his grasp. That they were responsible for reviving the Underworld and saving the human world. He knew wholeheartedly that it was the cemetery sitting directly across from his house—Lafeyette No. 1

to be precise—and the death that wafted from it that was causing the wards to thrum against her skin. Power filled the car, and, for the first time that night, her eyes took on a deep, neon blue hue rather than their usual violet-flecked grey or the molten gold that characterized her magic. He sucked in a breath. He knew that color, saw it every time he himself drew on death or the grave to spell cast. Only death magic cast that hyper-pigmented blue.

Interesting. His Angel drew power from death, as well. Not unexpected, especially if she was actually his Persephone, but a happy confirmation that her own magic wouldn't be impacted when—if, he corrected himself, knowing she had a choice, no matter how much he hated that fact—they descended to the Underworld.

As he guided the car into the driveway leading to the behind-house parking that had been a major draw, he noticed her chest rising and falling rapidly. Irregularly. He clocked a quick peek at her face. Pupils dilated, eyes soft and unfocused. Goosebumps raised along the pale flesh of her shoulders. Under her thin-as-fuck dress, which he'd tried to ignore since they had gotten in the car, her nipples were raised. Just like at the construction site, the sharp sting of magic surrounded them, arousing in its intensity. She was needy as hell. Desperate for something that he would kill to give her. He nearly groaned at the sight. But she wasn't ready for him. He had abducted her from her home less than two hours before. It would be better for them both if they just. Got. Out. Of. The. Damn. Car.

But he couldn't seem to make his legs move or his hand push the button to open the car door. Instead, he reached toward her, sweeping her curls back over her delicate ear. "Angel," he murmured. "I need you to chill. I don't think either one of us wants our first time together to be in a car."

Her gaze caught on his, sending shivers down his spine. That unearthly blue... he was losing his fucking mind seeing her draw upon the very source that fueled his own magic. "Angel." A warning note in his voice this time. He drew her closer, unable to stop himself. "Evie, I need you to get out of the car right now."

Voice throaty, she murmured, "I don't think I can. I'm not sure I can even move."

His final thread of control snapped.

With a savage curse, he pulled her across the console into his lap, loosing every ward controlling her magic. The car flooded with the rich scent of her power as he took her lips aggressively, nibbling, biting, before soothing away the sting with slow licks. He groaned when she opened to him, meeting his tongue with hers.

She straddled his hips, grinding down over his dick. Gods, she felt so good already, but he needed more. So much more. He needed to touch the silken skin of her thighs, lick her sweet nipples, get absolutely lost in her perfect pussy... with his tongue, his fingers, his cock. He didn't particularly care which part of him was inside her, just so long as he was bringing her pleasure. She moaned deeply when he traced his fingers over her, only now realizing that apparently women who lived in the forest didn't wear underwear.

Fucking hell, that was hot. "Dirty little witch," he growled into her ear, biting down gently on the lobe. "If I'd known you were bare under there, I would have pulled over sooner, so I could find out exactly how good you taste." His fingers slid over her clit, and she moaned, a low tortured sound that went straight to his dick. "Fuck, Angel, you're drenched for me."

She tunneled her hands into his hair, dragged his head back to center so she could look into his eyes. "Cole, please, I need this. I need you. Right now."

Their lips met again violently, messily this time. He wanted to eat her alive, lick her until she came, and then drape her toned legs over his arms and fuck her until morning. Tomorrow morning, preferably, since the sun was close to coming up on today. He would cancel every single fucking meeting he had, sell his whole goddamned firm, if it meant that he could stay inside her all fucking day.

Just as Cole was about to throw her into the backseat and eat her out until she screamed his name so loud she woke the neighbors, he heard a slamming sound.

His witch didn't even react. He knew he needed to respond to the unexpected noise, make sure they were—she was—safe, but she was writhing over him, bearing down on him so hard that he could feel her soaking wet core dampening his jeans. Fuck, she was perfect. *I can't leave her like this*, he thought, working one finger into her pussy. She was dripping for him, and it wasn't long before he worked a second finger in alongside the first, crooking them so he hit the sensitive nerves along her interior wall with the pads of his fingers while his palm worked her rigid clit.

Her moans were coming closer together, and all he could smell, see, and hear was her. She was everything. A threat could walk right up to the car, fully charged and ready to magically torch them, and there was a 99% chance that Cole wouldn't notice until the spell had been cast.

Her back was arching, and he could feel little tremors starting to pulse along his fingers. Gods, she was going to absolutely annihilate him when he actually got inside of her, could feel her tightening around his cock. "C'mon, I know you need to come, *mon bel ange, je sais que tu le veux.*" She had him turned upside down, lapsing into the French he had learned before he could even speak English.

She was moaning his name—and didn't that just make him want to rip his jeans off and sink into her, car or no—her entire body tensing just as he heard somebody say, "Hey, Cole, buddy, everything okay?"

She let out a sharp scream, her body writhing, beautiful as she came on his fingers, chanting *his fucking name* like a goddamn prayer. He turned to bare his teeth at the voice that dared get anywhere near his Angel while she came apart for him. He would rip them a-fucking-part with his bare hands, but only after he licked her taste off his fingers.

And around them, for the second time that night, the world shook once more.

Chapter 13

Evie

Garden District, New Orleans, Louisiana

Evie couldn't breathe. Everything fell away except for the sensation of Cole's fingers plunging inside her, his palm rubbing along her clit. Cole's name fell from her lips as she came, her body arching in his lap. Holy Hecate, she couldn't remember her own name. This man—her visions made flesh—was the only thing she could see, the lone person in her world.

Magic churned around them, tendrils dragging longingly across her skin, leaving raised flesh behind. At the prickling feeling, she screamed her way into another, even more intense orgasm before even coming down from her first one, clenching down on Cole's fingers *hard* as he continued to thrust into her. Fucking gods, she felt like she was on fire.

She could hear Cole snarling words beneath her. Not that she was processing a word of it, although she did hear, "What the fuck do you want," and something that sounded a lot like, "I'll rip your soul from your body and put it in Tartarus if you don't walk away right fucking now." They flowed over her like water, but all she could take in, all she could comprehend, were his brilliant green eyes staring into her own, holding her gaze just as firmly as the arm wrapped around her waist clutched her to his chest.

Slowly, Evie regained her ability to think, just in time to hear Cole whisper into her ear, "God, Angel, you're so fucking perfect," as he slid his fingers from her and raised them to his lips, his tongue flicking out to lick her taste from them. "Delicious. Can't wait to taste you right from the source."

Shivers raced through her at the sight of this incredible man, taking in the sight of her like he was starving for it, and she melted against him, snuggling her nose into his neck. Inhaling deeply, she caught a deep whiff of his scent: smoke and mint. He smelled like wintergreen burning in a campfire. Absolutely overwhelming and completely world changing. She would give up everything just to smell that scent for the rest of her natural life. He smelled like... home.

Home. That one word shook her, considering that Cole had just abducted her from her home. While she was nestled in his arms, though, feeling like her spinal cord had liquified from his touch, breathing him in, she just couldn't quite bring herself to care. In the light of morning, she would probably be humiliated, angry even, at how quickly she broke in his arms, how easily he had dismantled her, but right now, she was cozy and half asleep. He felt right.

He nuzzled her head, kissing her hair gently. His chest rumbled beneath her. "Let's get you to bed." Her eyes blinked shut then opened slowly as he swung them both out of the car, lifting her easily in his arms and rising to his full height. As he carried her from the car into the small backyard, she caught a glimpse of white stone walls and gleaming windows. Her head dropped back to his chest, her eyes slowly sliding shut. The last thing she saw before she fell into a deep, dream-filled sleep was a tattoo of a snake with floral scales running the length of his collarbone.

Chapter 14

She flinched as the sounds of battle rose around her. It was odd, though; she wasn't scared. She was . . . furious? Furious and holding a sword, wielding the weapon with fury.

Around her, the world was desolate, shaded in deep browns and yellows with an army of what she knew to be shades encroaching upon her. There was no plant life for her to draw upon, no sign of any living vegetation anywhere nearby. She couldn't feel anything alive here. No moon for her to source power from since the sun was blazing overhead.

Gods, though, she could feel the death here. While it wasn't her main source of power, it would do. She drew deeply upon the death surrounding her, supercharging herself before releasing a shock wave that tore the shades surrounding her into shreds. From behind her came a deep chuckle, one that made her heart beat faster. She turned, dropping the tip of the bloody sword at her side to the ground so as not to impale the man now standing behind her.

Her husband watched her fondly, a smile on his sharp face and snark on his lips. "Well done, my love. Impressive. A bit theatrical, but it did get the job done." Backlit by the sun, his ebony hair appeared tinged with blue, and his green eyes sparkled like jewels.

Smirking, she tossed her head. "Theatrical it may be, but they need to be afraid of at least one of us. You've gone soft in your old age, Aidoneus." She stalked towards him, poking at his muscular chest.

He seized her finger gently and pulled her into his body, one arm around her waist, one hand cupping the base of her neck, before dropping a kiss to her forehead. "May Olympus save anyone who disrespects the queen," he murmured. An inside joke for her ears only.

Her smirk softened into a smile at their call-and-response phrase, developed during their unusual courtship. "And may the Underworld forgive their souls because her king will not." They had taken on the mantle of king and queen of the underworld in the last decade, accepted their role even though they were both very much mortal. There was nothing for it, though. They had to do it.

Following Aidoneus' and his two brothers' successful efforts to overthrow the murderous despot, Cronus, and the rest of his Titan army, the human world had been overrun by shades. Human souls naturally crowded the Underworld after death, but there was little organization there, save Tartarus, the endless void where the worst of the worst fell. As soon as Aidoneus escorted the Titans to Tartarus, the human souls already in the Underworld panicked at the evil they brought and fled the unguarded realm of death to the human world where they became shades, slowly but surely destroying everything in the plane they once resided in. The dead were not meant to occupy the human world, and the world made that known as it fell into decay.

Before he took on the title of Hades, lord of the Underworld, though, he had been simply Aidoneus. Her wonderful man, tortured by a father he hated, surrounded by brothers he tolerated, and utterly alone in the world.

She herself had been raised by an overprotective single parent; Aidoneus took her away from the prison her mother created for her, one where she had no choice, no freedom. He changed her life with his unwavering love and support; she loved him all the more for it, knowing that she didn't deserve any of this incredible man's adoration. When it came time for him to take up the mantle of his birth ruling the Underworld, the choice to stay with him—to stand beside him—was an easy one. He asked for her hand in marriage and made her his queen. Despite their power and the asinine titles they were forced to bear to separate themselves from the destructive royal duties with which they were charged, he was simply her Aidoneus, and she was his Kore.

He sighed, lifting her into his arms and resting his forehead against hers. "I'm sorry, little Kore. I fear that this journey is far less than the adventure I promised you." His magic flared against hers, and she felt the prickles of arousal. Their passion was combustible, always just under the surface anytime they were near one another. Ever since she bound her life to his, accepted a piece of his magic, though, it felt like their bodies were on fire anytime they were in each other's vicinity. Their magic—their very souls—called to one another.

Now was not the time, though. His eyes were filled with despair; she knew he thought that she would walk away at some point. The bloodshed and risk of death were constant. Out here, the shades were free. They were desperate to maintain that freedom.

She cupped his chin, forcing his gaze to hers. "Aidoneus," she spoke sharply, forcefully. "I knew what I was getting into from the beginning. I knew it wouldn't be easy. But I will not do this life without you. You are my everything, and I would rather live this life with you in battle than have peace without you by my side." He opened his mouth, likely to argue if she knew her husband, but she covered his mouth with her fingers. "This was my choice, my love, and I would make it again in any lifetime. In every lifetime." She forced a smile. "Now stop arguing. You're absolute rubbish at it, and it makes me feel bad for you."

Try as he might, he couldn't stop his lips from twitching at her imperious tone. "Well, if my queen orders it, I must obey." Around them, the wind howled through the barren wasteland left behind by the shades.

"Damn right, you must." She traced his lips with her thumb, moaning softly when he brushed her outer thigh with his thumb. "My love, I think it's time for bed, don't you?"

The sun beat down on them, illuminating the earth around them just as effectively it did her ulterior motive to get her beautiful husband into a safe place where she could strip away his clothing and have her wicked way with him. Aidoneus' lips lost their battle against his mirth, revealing a brilliant smile that still took her breath away. "Insatiable little flower. You would think I wasn't inside of you just hours ago making you scream my name so loudly you scared the—" His voice cut off suddenly, and she glanced up.

A blade stuck through the center of his throat. Blood poured from his pierced throat, dripped from the corner of his lips, and she could hear his gasping breaths through the hole. She shrieked in pain and fear and fury as he—

Evie

Garden District, New Orleans, Louisiana

Evie woke to the sound of screaming and a calming baritone.

"Hey, it's okay, you're okay," she heard as if from a great distance. "C'mon, breathe for me, Angel." She took a choked breath in, barely able to fill her lungs. "That's right, sweetheart, just keep breathing. In and out." As the voice became clearer, her breaths came more easily. "You're doing good, Angel, so good. Now, when you're ready, go ahead and try to open your eyes. It will help if you can see the world around you."

It took a few more minutes of breathing and soothing touches before she felt comfortable enough to blink her eyes open. The first thing she saw were concerned green eyes. She lurched upwards, looking for blood, any sense of injury. The last time she'd seen green eyes that color, the man had been dying in her arms.

In her dream, Evie realized, slowly taking in her surroundings. The last time she had seen eyes that color was in her dream. Now, though, she was curled in

Cole's lap, wrapped in his arms, protected, warm, and surrounded by his smoky scent. After several greedy breaths tinged with the smell of him, she began to calm. Whatever the dream had been—memory, prophecy, dreamcasting—it had no place here.

As her pulse slowed, details she missed when she woke up filtered into her consciousness. For starters, Cole was nude from the waist up. Although she had seen the male form in books, she hadn't seen one in real life, and the pictures didn't make it seem any more appealing than a woman's body. She hadn't thought anything of it beyond that since they had no men in the coven, and a woman could satisfy her needs just as effectively as a man, if not more so. She didn't see all the fuss about whose body pleasured you when men's bodies weren't anything of note.

But that was before last night in the car. Before she saw Cole shirtless. Early morning light radiated in through the curtains—she was almost certain that was what they were called, given that coven houses bore no windows—illuminating his lean chest and chiseled features. Within seconds of taking in the sight of him like this, Evie immediately understood the intrigue. With a hum of interest, she rested a single hand on his chest, just to see what he felt like. His skin was softer than she expected, but the muscles underneath lent it a roughness, a hardness, that she didn't expect. His heart beat steadily under her palm, even though above her, his breathing began to grow choppy.

"You good?" Cole asked, his voice raspy. She nodded, but he grasped her chin between his fingers, forcing her head up and her gaze to his. "Words, Angel. I need to hear you say you're okay. You woke up screaming—and not in a good way—so I gotta hear your voice because you scared the shit out of me."

She nodded again, pairing it with a quiet, "I'm fine. I just... it was an odd dream, that's all."

"You want to talk about it?" At her slow head shake, he tightened his arms and rested his chin against her hair. "We probably have a few other things to talk about, though, huh?"

His question kicked the dust off her memories from the night before. The construction site. The forest's overwhelming shift from complete death and destruction to vitality and thriving, green life. The earthquake. His incredible intensity as he brought her to the most phenomenal orgasm of her life. Him threatening somebody? Her breath caught when she remembered one of the more significant events that took place, something she was shocked was so far down her list. *The abduction*. Despite her desperate need to interrogate him on everything, she decided to start with the biggest one. "I'm assuming you're referencing when you took me from my home without my consent?"

His head popped up quickly, and he blanched. "So *starting* with the elephant in the room, then, huh? Just going straight for the jugular." At her level stare, he scraped one hand down his face. "Yeah, okay."

She pushed out of his arms, and he let her go reluctantly. "I'll start. You need to take me back home." That was good. She sounded sincere. Stern even. Not like she couldn't stop looking at him—the absolute steady whole of him—after all these years of just having bits and pieces.

He was already shaking his head emphatically before she got the whole sentence out. "I can't do that. You're not safe there." She glared at him. "I promise, I'm not lying. You need to stay with me. The world became extremely dangerous for you when we found each other."

"You know I'm a fairly powerful witch, right? Who has somehow managed to survive a decent amount of my life without you?"

He scoffed. "Okay, I'll give you that you've been safe so far. But you haven't actually been without me, have you, baby?" Her eyes widened slightly before she could stop then, and a smug grin spread over his handsome face. "You said you've seen me most of your life. How was it? In dreams?"

She was going to try to direct the conversation back to the point or lie, really she was, but the memory of her nightmare, the dream woman's overwhelming heartbreak as the man who looked so similar to Cole bled over her, shoved the truth out of her mouth before she could stop it. "I heard your voice. All the time. Sometimes, you would just be murmuring, other times I could hear every word you were saying. Nobody else in the coven could hear you but me, and it was only ever your voice."

"Anything else?" he prodded.

In for a penny... might as well tell her whole truth. "Your eyes." Said eyes squinted down at her, and she clarified. "I saw your eyes everywhere and have since I was young, long before I ever heard your voice. I actually thought you were a forest spirit for the longest time, but your eyes followed me too closely, no matter where I was, so it had to be something else. Nobody else could see you, though, so, before I started hearing your voice, the coven elders thought I might actually be mad. Fortunately, you started talking to me soon after."

He tilted his head in confusion. "Why would they be concerned about eyes no one else could see but not voices no one else could hear? Out here in the human world, they get pretty alarmed about either. And they get *really* upset when they happen simultaneously."

She shrugged delicately. His eyes immediately lowered to her bare chest at the movement and stayed there. "I couldn't tell you. I have some theories, but the coven never spoke too much about it after I started hearing your voice, so it was a moot point." Pausing, she considered his overly familiar behavior, his references to finding her. "How did you recognize me? Why do you know me?"

A deep sigh met her question. He didn't want to answer, and he stayed silent long enough that she thought he wasn't going to answer. Finally, after a few minutes, his voice rumbled from his chest. "I dreamed about you."

"Only one."

Cole shook his head. "No." The answer sounded like it was ripped from his chest.

"How many times then?"

Another long pause. "Too many times to count."

Evie's jaw dropped, and she almost forgot how to speak. She didn't know how long she had stared at him for when she finally pulled her thoughts together enough to ask, "For how long?"

"Since I knew it was weird for one person to keep reappearing in my dreams and aging as time went by." A slight chuckle escaped him. "I was 12, I think, the first time you showed up. You were about my age, maybe a little younger, and you told me you were looking for me. I woke up and thought I made you up. I told my uncle about you, but he said it was just a dream. But you kept coming back, and each time, you were a little older. By the time I was in high school, you were all I thought about. I fantasized about you all the time. I tried to sleep just so I could see you more often. It got bad enough that Charlie put me through a sleep study." A short burst of laughter escaped his mouth. "I was so gone for you. Fuck, I saw your face when I lost my virginity. I couldn't even tell you who I had sex with that first time because all I could think about was you."

Her heart pounded at the raw need in his voice. His honesty made her want to share her own truths: that she had made herself come more times than she could count to the sound of him, to the point that just hearing his voice made her wet. But she couldn't quite bring herself to do it.

Cole lifted his gaze to hers, almost as if he could hear her thoughts. "Tell me I wasn't alone in all of this. Tell me it wasn't just me going crazy over here, that you thought of me too. All I've wanted my entire fucking life is to have you in my bed, Angel." He didn't wait for her response. His eyes went slightly wild as he wrapped a hand around her waist, tugging her towards him and rolling her to her back. With a possessive growl, he dropped down and nipped at her lower lip, sucking it into his mouth to alleviate the sting of his bite before releasing it with a pop. He rose to his elbows, raw hunger etched in his face as he said. "And now that you're here, I'm not ever letting you go."

Chapter 15

Cole

Garden District, New Orleans, Louisiana

Cole finally had his dream woman in his arms, was settled in between her legs where he could feel the heat of her against him. In some dim part of his mind, he was afraid that he would wake up, alone with a hand on his cock, two pumps away from coming at the dream of his desperate, little Angel writhing beneath him and screaming his name. It wouldn't be the first time he'd woken to that hollow disappointment, only to fuck his fist quickly and angrily because he was too close to coming not to finish but furious that his woman wasn't actually beneath him.

He wasn't creative enough to fantasize all of the little details of her, though. The reality of Evie in his bed was so much better than any dream could ever be. She was naked because there was no fucking way his woman was sleeping next to him wearing clothes; he couldn't bring himself to feel guilty about that caveman impulse in the slightest because the sight of her pale skin and red hair against his black sheets was awe-inspiring. His bedding was a stupidly high thread count—courtesy of the interior designer who decorated the house who had desperately tried to get into the very same sheets—so the soft fabric draped around her curvy hips like silk. "So perfect," he muttered, grasping her hair and tugging slightly.

She gasped, kicking her head back, exposing her throat to him.

"Such a good fucking girl," he rasped against her throat. Under his lips, he felt her pulse kick desperately. Did his little witch have a praise kink? *I could only be so lucky.*

Would he grow less unhinged for her with them? She hadn't left his eyesight in hours; he had been touching her for most of that time. Even still, Cole couldn't get enough of her, which was slightly alarming. He slowly moved down her body, kissing and touching every inch of her he could get his mouth and hands on.

Cole came to her breasts—so perfectly sized for his hands—and pulled back to look. Decades of dreaming, years of fantasy, didn't come close to this perfection, he concluded as he ran his thumb over her nipple. "Tell me what you want, Angel," he growled at her. "I need to touch you as much as you need me to."

She whimpered, wrapping her hands in his hair. "Please."

"Please what?" His smirk easily returned to his face. "Use your words, sweetheart."

"I need your mouth on my nipples, Cole," she pleaded. "I need to feel you between my legs. I don't care how it happens, I just need to come. Please, Cole!"

"God," he hissed at her filthy words. "You're such a dirty little witch." He bit at the underside of her breast, and she practically came unglued, legs scissoring underneath him. Pulling his head back, he looked down at her; she was flushed with desire, gasping for breath while she tried to push his head back to where she wanted it. "I can't wait to hear you scream my name again." He tilted down, inches away from taking her pebbled nipple into his mouth, when a loud rattling sound filled the air. *What the fuck is that?* Lifting his head slightly, Cole narrowed his eyes in confusion.

The noise sounded again, and he finally placed it. His phone was vibrating on the nightstand. Blindly reaching a hand over, he rejected the call and went back to the molten witch lying in his bed. He kissed her desperately, rubbing his thumb over her taut nipple as he took her lips again. She breathed his name, the sound vanishing into his mouth when he slipped his tongue through her lips, teasing at her. Tasting her. *Fuck, she's delicious.* All traces of the ill-timed call vanished from his head as her hands ran down his naked back.

That was, they vanished until his phone started vibrating again. He glared at where it was dancing on the nightstand, damning whoever was calling him, his service provider, and the cell phone manufacturer itself into the depths of Tartarus. *Fuck no.* It was only 9:00 am, and he owned the goddamn firm. He practically lived at the office. He had competent staff for when he couldn't be there. They could deal with whatever problems came up this one fucking time.

He rejected the call again, but this time he didn't even get back to Evie before it started buzzing again. A blue haze descended over his eyes as he summoned his magic, torching the phone in an unearthly fire. He chucked it into the corner with a snarl before cold panic raced through him at Evie's gasp. Because his source was death, it was dangerous to touch him while he was using his magic. As a teen, he had once accidentally put a girl in the hospital because he lost control of his power while she was going down on him. Terrified, he pulled back suddenly. *What if last night was a fluke?* What if he had just endangered the only woman he had ever really wanted?

Beneath him, though, Evie was thriving, her cheeks flushed, goosebumps raising along her skin as she met his eyes.

His jaw dropped, and overwhelming possession burned through him. He knew it. He fucking knew Evie was it for him. She was the only person in the world that could touch him without repercussions when he was channeling death. *Fucking mine.* He needed to get closer to her. Now.

"I can feel your magic," she whispered. Almost like she was afraid she would break the spell if she spoke too loudly. He ran his hand down her side, blue flames still flickering between his fingers, reveling in the fact that he could touch her while channeling death. If the guttural moan she let out as the fire flitted over her skin, illuminating but not burning, was any indication, she was enjoying every second of his ghostly touch. "It feels so good!"

Cole lifted himself out of bed, almost cackling at her insane whimper. Her stormy eyes, flickering with her own magic, followed him as he dropped to his knees at the foot of the bed. Reaching forward, he gripped her hips and hauled her ass to the edge. "Fuck, I need to taste you," he said, lifting her legs over his shoulders before he lowered his head. "You're gonna taste so fucking good, aren't you, Angel?" He was inches away from paradise—he could see her pussy, all but had his tongue on her—when a shrill ringing filled the room.

Evie jumped, searching the room for the threat. Cole shook his head, trying to clear the fog of Evie and sex and magic so he could figure out what that goddamn sound was.

It wasn't the fire alarm. It wasn't the security system. It wasn't... awareness filtered in suddenly. Was that a fucking *landline*? He snarled and leapt from the bed, crossing the room quickly. Tucked into the corner sat an old-fashioned rotary phone that, if you had asked him minutes before, he would have bet good money didn't even work. The thing was a leftover from the previous owners, and he knew damn well he had never paid for a phone line. So how in the hell was it ringing?

Cole seized the handset and raised it to his ear. "This better be a fucking emergency," he barked.

The voice that answered him shook. "I'm sorry, Mr. Aidoneus, but you told me, that is to say, I'm sorry, sir... "

He cut off the stuttering voice with a harsh tone and zero sympathy. "Who is this, and what the fuck do you want?" Evie sat up, drawing the sheets to her chest. *I'm going to kill whoever's on the other end. Inches away from tasting my witch. Fucking inches.* He turned towards the wall; maybe if he wasn't looking directly at Evie, he would be able to think straight.

"I'm so sorry, Mr. Aidoneus, this is Nyx. I'm the law clerk at your office." He tried to visualize the woman but couldn't put a face to the name. "You—I'm so sorry, sir, for waking you up—but you have to be at court in 5 minutes."

"Why are you only just now contacting me?" He was aware he was acting like a brute, but he couldn't stop it. Apparently, his knee-jerk reaction to being inches from everything he had ever dreamed of and having it ripped away was to act like a depraved maniac. “We have protocols in place to ensure this doesn’t happen.”

“Yes, sir,” she responded. “I know, sir, but you didn’t answer any of my calls or texts this morning. I started calling you at 8 but couldn’t get through.”

Cole glanced at his phone, currently a charred brick in the corner of the room. Couldn’t verify whether that was true or not, although he was inclined to think it might be. A small seed of guilt threatened to bud. “Ah.” A hand touched his arm, and he looked down to see Evie, her heart-shaped face tilted towards him, her tangled hair curling around her naked shoulders. *She touched me first.* His lungs all but stopped working at the feel of her skin against his, knowing that she had sought him out.

“Cole, what’s wrong?”

Without thinking, he wrapped an arm around her lower back, pulling her into his chest just in time to hear the law clerk go, “Mr. Aidoneus? Sir?” like she had been waiting for his response for a while.

“I’ll be there, Nina.” He moved to drop the phone, only just hearing her say in an aggravated tone, “It’s Nyx, you asshole” right before he set the phone in its cradle. If she had said that to his face or held off until after he hung up, he might have been impressed. As it was, it showed poor decision-making and even worse timing. Guess they would be looking for a new law clerk soon. Since he didn't remember hiring the old one, that wasn't a problem.

“Cole?” Evie’s voice carried up to him from where she was nestled against him. “Is everything alright?”

Cole winced, preparing for an unexpected end to his time with Evie. He knew how this usually went when he got pulled away from any woman for work. It typically went badly. Extremely badly. He could only imagine that it would be ten times worse with one he actually cared about. “I'm sorry, Evie, I forgot about a hearing, and I have to leave, like... 30 minutes ago.” With a sharp pang of regret, he set her away and walked into his closet to get ready for an apparently necessary day of work. She trailed behind him into the massive room.

“A hearing?” Her brow crinkled as she worked her way through the context. “Like a courtroom hearing?”

His eyebrows jumped into his hairline. "Yeah, like a courtroom hearing. I'm sorry, I keep forgetting that you may not know the finer points of society and legal careers since you lived in the bayou." At her scowl and pointed glare, he laughed, trying to swallow the sound before it could sneak out and irritate her more. "Although I promise I have been made extremely aware of the superior education you witches receive in the forest."

She nodded, seeming to accept his apology as her eyes tracked around his closet. "I've never seen so many clothes in my life. Why... when... how could you ever need this many clothes?"

As he shrugged into a white dress shirt, he examined the room carefully, trying to look at the room from her perspective. Many older New Orleans houses didn't have walk-in closets because they were considered another room under city ordinances at the time; to get around those ridiculous regulations, New Orleanians invested in armoires. So the fact that he had a walk-in closet at all, much less a dressing room like the one attached to his bedroom, was already fairly unique in the city. Its size and storage capacity were what made it truly enviable, though, in the city's cutthroat real estate market. Two walls bore custom cabinetry that spanned the length and height of the entire wall. Many of the deep drawers were empty, but his shirts, slacks, suits, blazers, and ties took up much of the hanging space available.

The room's ceiling was vaulted with regal arches that met over a wrought iron chandelier with dozens of intertwined arms that cast eerie shadows over the central island housing his watches, shoes, and other accessories. In a corner of the room sat a pink velvet fainting couch, courtesy of an ex-hookup who had tried to slowly move shit in... as if Cole wouldn't notice that he hadn't asked her to sleep over, much less actually move in. When he pointed those things out to her, she called him a pig, slapped him, and left the couch. What was her name again? Catriona? Catalina? Caroline? He was fairly certain it had started with a C.

He shook his head. The former forgettable hookup with the undetermined C name didn't have any place in his home while his witchling stood naked in the doorway in front of him. "When you reach a certain level of success, society seems to think you need to have an abundance of everything. Clothes, house, cars, whatever."

"That seems... wasteful." She stepped into the room. He strapped a watch to his wrist, barely noticing which one it was or whether it complemented the outfit he had also given exactly zero attention to selecting. "I never really saw clothes as necessary, but I wore them when I was away from the coven, exploring." Her eyes grew angry. "Creatures who come in to the forest tend to think they can take things that don't belong to them when a woman is nude."

His chest tightened with a completely irrational need to hunt down everyone who may have harmed the woman in front of him and offer her their head on a stake in the front yard. He was about to start demanding names or descriptions to accomplish that task when the house phone started shrieking again. Evie jumped a mile. For fuck's sake. Prior to this morning, he hadn't even known he had a fucking landline. Now the thing wouldn't shut up.

He strode past Evie, swinging her into his arms in a bridal carry on his way to the phone. Bracing her against his chest, he freed an arm to snatch up the phone just long enough to snarl, "I'm on my way," before flinging the phone back into the cradle.

Evie raised an eyebrow at him. "Do you usually shout at people just trying to help you? Or is that a special treat for this morning?"

He had been about to apologize for interrupting their morning, but his brain completely ground to a halt at her sassiness. The apology on the tip of his tongue was forgotten. "Oh, baby, we're gonna have to find a much better use for that bratty mouth of yours." The mouth in question dropped open in shock, and he leaned in to her, stopping just inches away. With a chuckle, he nibbled her lower lip. "Yeah, you got the idea, but you're gonna have to open your mouth a lot wider than that."

Her eyes glazed at the blatantly sexual comment, and, almost like she didn't know she was doing it, she slid her hand under his shirt collar as he carried her down the stairs. They had to get out of the bedroom or he was going to lose his mind, blow off work, risk a contempt charge for missing the hearing without notice, and spend the next twelve hours making her come so hard that she wouldn't even remember what a forest was, much less that she once lived in one.

Her nimble fingers played across the floral snake tattoo that serpentined from underneath his collar to his upper arm—the one that somehow paralleled her own, a truly mind-boggling thought of its own—and he nearly turned right the fuck around and went back up the stairs. *Nope,* he scolded himself, continuing the trek down the gracefully curved staircase with his arms full of Evie. *Have to get out of this house before she gets me to agree to anything and everything.*

The scent of coffee wafted out to him before he even entered the kitchen. Thankfully, the machine was already automatically brewing his morning roast. As he walked them into his favorite room of the house, he heaved a happy sigh that at least one part of this morning was going as planned.

The kitchen had been the deciding factor for him when he purchased this place. It blended the antique aspects of the 1800s Greek Revival style with practical, modern elements like the stainless steel equipment. The floor was a reddish stained wood that was original to the house. The cabinets were a rich deep blue, which contrasted with the white quartzite countertops and copper backsplash. All of that was stunning on its own, but it was the full wall of windows and glass doors overlooking the backyard that really made the space. They let in an abundance of natural light and allowed anyone in the kitchen to look out over the elegant terrace surrounded by stately, centuries old live oaks, gorgeous crepe myrtles, and colorful flowers.

Cole set Evie on the countertop gently, turning slightly to see if the coffee was ready. Although he wasn't looking directly at her, he could still pinpoint the exact moment the garden caught her attention and, more importantly, her attention caught the garden. Out of the corner of his eye, he saw one of the crepe myrtles extend a branch toward the windows, waving gently at her. Even his trees loved her. The little voice in his mind chimed in: *you don't stand a fucking chance, buddy. You need to accept this and tell her everything.*

"I didn't expect to see such vibrant trees in a city," she said suddenly. "And you've taken good care of them. They feel like they're in incredible health."

"I wish I could take credit for that," he responded, pulling a mug out of the cupboard and pouring a cup of freshly brewed coffee. With a questioning look, he offered it to her; she accepted it, taking a small sip before shaking her head, wrinkling her nose, and setting the cup down on the counter. A smile broke over his face as he retrieved it, sipping the strong black coffee that would keep him going until his second cup after court. He barely noticed that he took the time to seal his lips right over where she had taken her drink, hoping to get just a small taste of her. *Fuck*. He was so gone for her. "I have a gardener that comes in every week to make sure that all of the greenery gets taken care of. Good to get confirmation that he's doing his job, though. I don't know shit about plants, so I just assume that if they're alive, they're healthy." Technically, he knew more about plant life than that, but the childish part of him wanted to rile her up just a little bit.

His wish was granted when Evie scoffed and gave him a distressed look before pushing her hands against the quartz, looking like she was about to pop off the counter to run to the backyard.

He stopped her with a big hand that spanned the width of one of her legs, keeping her locked in place. His thumb traced lazily against the outside of her thigh.

She shivered at his touch, leaning slightly into him, her eyes still locked on the gently waving crepe myrtle. "Can I go out there?" she asked. "I'm not used to being indoors."

"Of course you can explore." His answer was quick. "You're not a prisoner, *ma petite sorcière*. I want you to be happy here." *Because there's no way I can let you go*. "But I do have to go to work, so I can't show you around." He checked his watch, letting out an irritated groan when he realized just how late he already was. Her movement dragged his attention back upwards where he saw her shrugging in response to his words. He took a quick gulp of burning coffee in an attempt to hide his displeasure that she didn't want him to stay. He could barely force himself to leave her here alone, and she was all but shoving him out the door? Just made him want to throw her in his car and bring her to court. "I wish I could take you with me."

At that, she laughed. Christ, her smile did things to him. He would do anything to make sure he kept seeing that stunning smile, no matter if she was mocking him. "What would I even do at your office? I don't know anything about the... law?" He nodded, confirming her educated guess about his career and choosing not to interrupt her with his lecherous opinions about the options available to her at his office. "Plus your co-workers may have questions about the naked woman that you're escorting in."

Oh, they would have questions all right. They would, in fact, remind him that he had lost his damn mind. Especially if they caught wind of the midnight construction abduction. They would never let him live that one down. That was the problem with going into business with your best friends; they had an obnoxious way of keeping you humble. "Be that as it may," he interrupted, setting down his empty coffee mug and cupping her face in his hands. She swayed towards him, resting one delicate hand on his chest while her big eyes stared up at him. Jesus Christ. He had waited most of his life for this woman to look at him exactly like that. Nobody and nothing else that came before her mattered, and there would be nobody after her. He had to convince her to stay with him. "I don't like leaving you home alone. Just don't go anywhere. Please."

Her brow furrowed, a small frown creasing her features. "You're holding me hostage." Not a question if her flat tone was any indication. "I thought you said I wasn't a prisoner."

That was definitely displeasure in her voice. Fuck, he hated that note of disappointment. "Not a hostage. And definitely not a long-term solution. Just for the short-term until we can figure out a way to keep you safe. Please, Evie," he requested, hoping that using her name would get her to listen to him better. "Don't go anywhere. Please. I need you to agree or I'm going to have to ward you too. I need to be able to trust you to stay, Angel. Please. Just for the next few days. I can't lose you." Cole hoped she wouldn't push back against his desperate need for her. He wasn't sure how to explain it to himself, much less her, how he knew, deep in his gut, that he couldn't let her go now that he had found her.

She sniffed in irritation, but it looked like she was considering his plea at least. Eventually, she nodded.

His heart lightened, and he pressed his lips to her forehead. "I swear to you, we'll find a better way. I'm going to ward the outside of the house and the grounds to protect against unauthorized entry and exit. You'll be able to go out into the garden and wherever you want within the house." He dropped his hands from her face, collected his car keys, and began his disappointed trek to his car. He wanted to stay, not go pontificate about gambling and bordello law to an officious, corrupt-as-fuck judge.

"If you do go out in the garden, please just... put on one of my shirts." He smirked at the naked witch still sitting in his kitchen drinking in her perfect curves so that he could get through the never-ending workday before he could see her again. "I would hate to have to threaten to kill my next-door neighbor. Again."

"Sure, I can—wait, did you just say again?" Evie hopped off the counter. "You've threatened your neighbor more than once?"

He crossed the kitchen rapidly, undoing all of his forward progress, and backed her into the fridge door, pinning her in place with a knee between her thighs. Ducking his head to her neck, he breathed her in, feeling the entire world settle into rightness with her scent. She smelled like oranges and cinnamon with a hint of fire. "He interrupted me while I was finger fucking you in the car, *mon ange*. He heard those little gasps you make when you're on the edge and saw just how beautiful you are when you're riding my fingers. He knows what my fucking witch looks like when she comes apart for me. He's lucky that all I did was threaten to cast his soul into the abyss." His thumb fixed at her chin, tilting her head back so he could crush his lips to hers, slide his tongue into her mouth in a desperate imitation of all the other things he wanted to do to her body. He finally pulled back, breathless, knowing that he was now unforgivably late and not giving a shit about it. "I'm the only one who gets to see you like that for the rest of our immortal fucking lives because you're mine, Angel, and I will happily destroy anyone who thinks otherwise."

Reluctantly, he managed to push himself away from her lush body, pushing a stray strand of hair behind her ear. Her eyes were glazed, and she was panting softly, her hands still resting where they had fallen to his waist when he pressed her against the fridge. Evie was all but melted into him, and, if his cell phone weren't currently a scorched pile of plastic and glass upstairs, he would have called the court that minute, told the judge to go fuck himself, and taken them both back upstairs.

Willpower, man. Have some fucking willpower. With a groan, Cole leaned in and gave her a bruising kiss. "I'll see you tonight," he told her. "Explore the house a little. Spend some time in the garden. Get some sleep. Take a bath. Whatever you want to do."

"Okay." Her fingers loosened on his hips. "It's fine, Cole. I'll figure out what to do with myself."

Upstairs, he heard the landline ringing again. Probably the mysterious, soon-to-be-fired Natalie the law clerk. With a low growl, he kissed Evie lightly one last time before he left the house, placing protective wards as he went.

Chapter 16

Evie

Garden District, New Orleans, Louisiana

The instant Cole left the house, it felt like Evie could think clearly for the first time since he had taken her. Without doing anything in particular besides existing, he somehow managed to absorb all the air in the room, make her feel like she couldn't breathe. Gorgeous, overwhelming man.

Also. What did he mean by "the rest of our immortal fucking lives?" Evie chewed on her thumbnail as she wandered around the kitchen, opening and closing cupboard doors absently while she considered everything Cole had said since they met. Witches weren't necessarily mortal, but they weren't immortal by any stretch of the imagination. And she didn't know the average lifespan of the "reincarnated god Hades," either, an idea that still made her snort. She briefly wondered whether he might be a lunatic human before shrugging it off. She had felt his magic, could feel it even now without him in the house. So, while the idea of Cole being a god was absurd, he was still a magical being who she would hazard a guess, based on his laugh lines, aged at a fairly human rate too. *So what was he talking about with that oblique reference to immortality*?

Evie pursed her lips. She hated not knowing things, and, in the last day, it seemed like that was all she was doing. Nothing made sense, and, with every minute she spent in this house, she became more confused than ever. Nodding sternly to herself, she turned away from the garden towards one of the two entrances to the kitchen. Time to snoop so she could try and get some answers. Which meant she was here for longer, a choice she was surprisingly okay with. For all her anger about him abducting her, she didn't actually want to leave. Setting aside that she wasn't wholly certain how to get back home, she liked Cole. He was funny and sexy and sweet. In the hours she had spent with him, she'd felt more than she had in her entire relationship with Marie. More passion, more amusement, more frustration, just more... everything. Not to mention her lifelong knowledge of him, which made that bond seem more real. It would be difficult to throw that away over a little thing like an abduction. And if he was serious about her not being a prisoner here? She found it difficult to imagine that she would want to leave.

She rolled her eyes at herself as she swept out of the kitchen into the room bordering it. There was forgiving and then there was delusional and, while she couldn't be sure, she would guess that ignoring an abduction fell more towards the delusional side of the spectrum. Ah, well. She hadn't really ever done things the normal way. Why should a seemingly fated connection be any different?

The kitchen opened into a room with a large, elegant black wooded table centered under an ornate chandelier. The dining room, she assumed. Although the coven didn't ascribe to human housing structures, their education extended to everything under the sun, which included, among many other subjects, anatomy, formal eating techniques, advanced mathematics, chemistry, and astronomy as well as lessons about their history—what little they could recall or was recorded of it following the witch purges in the 1940s—training them on understand their source of power, and how to use and control their magic. The absence of a true working day, which she understood to be standard in the human world, meant that much of their day was open for them to learn and explore.

Evie skirted the corner of the dining room and walked out through the open doorway, which led her into the entryway where she found the stairs Cole had carried her down that morning. Although the rooms she'd seen on the first floor were beautifully designed, she hadn't noticed anything that looked like his personal papers or books, if he even kept such things. She knew that the humans had... digitized, she thought may be the correct term, and used electronics instead of paper nowadays. That morning, Cole had even received a call on such a device before he set it on fire.

Her face flushed at the memory, and she almost tripped up the stairs. He had stripped her of all her boundaries—and her clothing—this morning. In addition to feeling exposed after sharing a lifetime of her experiences with his voice and eyes before they ever met in person, she was completely overwhelmed by how sensual his magic felt against her skin, how open he was about her taste and what he wanted to do to her, how incredible his long fingers and demanding lips were as they dominated her body. She fanned herself as she came to the second-floor landing. In no world could she have imagined a person quite like Cole, much less one who seemed so well suited to her sexually.

There was a bedroom directly across from the stairs. To her right was the room where she and Cole had spent most of the morning. Decided, she took a left down the hallway where she found another bedroom on the right. But, through the partially open door of the room to her left, she saw a desk. That may mean information.

She slipped through the open door into an elegantly decorated room. Her feet carried her across the wood floor and onto a thick rug in shades of purple ranging from a lavender so light it was almost white to a violet so deep it was practically black. The walls surrounding her were painted a striking stormy grey with violet overtones. Around the room were captivating paintings of a faceless, curvy woman with tangled curls. Evie tilted her head as she considered the portraits. The woman's shape and hair style mimicked her own fairly closely, but it was probably arrogant to assume it was her. Just because Cole admitted he had dreamed about her for years didn't mean that he would decorate his home office with figures that looked like her. At least that was her thinking until her gaze found the final painting sitting directly across from the desk. In all of the others, the subject was depicted in black and white with either the woman's face obscured or the composition of the painting placing her face out of frame.

However, the painting across from Cole's desk was brilliantly colored with the woman fully in frame. Unlike the others, which looked like her but could conceivably be anyone with a similar shape, this portrait was clearly Evie. She was nude, surrounded by trees sunk in shadows. A breeze appeared to sweep her auburn curls behind her, but a delicate tiara circling her forehead kept them from growing too wild. Her body bore more tattoos than Evie's currently held, and her eyes blazed a blue so vibrant that it dulled even the other colors in the painting. Standing behind her, a suited man with Cole's coloring watched her closely, one hand wrapped possessively around her waist.

Holy Hecate. This was... unexpected. It was one thing to hear that he had dreamed of her his whole life. It was completely different to see the evidence of that right in front of her, prominently displayed in his home office where he would see it any time he sat at his desk. On the one hand, it seemed like they were destined to meet. On the other, it was intimidating to know that he cared so deeply for her before he ever met her that he had commissioned a painting he could look at any time he was in this room. Unsure of her feelings and unwilling to unpack them, she crossed to his desk.

It was a massive L-shaped wooden behemoth with more drawers than she could fathom anyone needing. The top was clear of any paperwork, although she was pretty sure the slim rectangular glass box was a monitor of some sort. She touched it reverently, sliding her fingers down the long sides and across the sharp edges, awed by the craftsmanship, before she lowered her sights to the rest of the desk. Even before she touched it, she could feel Cole's carefully drawn wards sealing them tight against unauthorized intruders.

Evie channeled a burst of power at the wards to light them up so she could figure out how to break them. If she manipulated them the wrong way, it would probably alert Cole. Glancing at the symbols revealed by her magic, she slowly traced her fingers across the drawer front, drawing the counter rune that would naturally break Cole's defense. Careful spell work like this was often difficult during the day for her because the moon—her source—was below the horizon. Today, though, her power came readily, pouring easily from her with a radiant blue hue that matched the color of Cole's magic. Odd that it wasn't the usual gold color she associated with her own magic.

She shrugged dismissively as his wards disappeared, giving her access to the room's secrets. Carefully, she began the process of investigating, starting with his desk. While the top of it was neat, the drawers were decidedly not. The very first one she opened was stuffed full of envelopes addressed to Cole—some opened but most not—and a truly alarming amount of mints in all shapes and colors. The next two revealed no less than eight notebooks, tiny notepads with sticky backs in an array of bright colors, and a plethora of clamps and clips ranging in shape and size. One drawer was filled with financial information, which revealed that Cole was more than well off, and a will leaving all of his assets to someone named Charles Aidoneus. Bizarrely, she felt inexplicably relieved that he left everything to a person she assumed was a relative rather than a spouse or significant other. She slammed the drawer shut a bit harder than necessary in an attempt to ignore what that sense of relief meant about her feelings for Cole. The last drawer was just sealed snacks, including pretzels and chips and a bag of something called Jolly Ranchers. Evie scowled as she closed it. This was all interesting information about the man himself but nothing that gave her any insight into his immortal life comment.

She blew a strand of hair out of her face and rocked back on to her heels. This may have been a waste of time. She considered that possibility, chewing on her lip and drumming her fingertips against the top of her thighs. Maybe it was just a saying? Maybe it didn't actually *mean* anything. Always possible. With a shrug, Evie pressed her palms against her legs, starting to shift her weight to stand up—maybe she would go spend time with the plants outside, including the oldest tree, the branch for which was enthusiastically tapping on the window of Cole's office in a bid for her attention—when she noticed the edge of an envelope sticking out from a small-lipped drawer in the desk above his chair seat. She didn't remember opening that one; it would have been all too easy to miss given how narrow it was.

Evie wiggled at the drawer, popping it out easily. The envelope, larger than she had expected, sat unevenly atop the drawer's debris. A small laugh escaped her at this one last example of how messy Cole actually was as she pulled out the envelope. It was large and beige with Cole's name scrawled in almost illegible script across the front. Evie flipped the envelope over, sliding her finger under the flap to open it before removing the folder tucked inside. Even if this wasn't anything informative, it was still enjoyable to open all the different layers.

Standing, she rested her hip against desk, opening the folder as she did so. Inside sat a thick stack of papers, topped by a sheet that read "Evangeline Dyeus" with a picture of a toddler and biographical information. She flipped to the next page in confusion. News clippings about the trial of a Desmond Dyeus, charged with the murder of his wife. Behind those documents was a news article about Desmond and his deceased wife's missing toddler. A report describing the circumstances of the missing daughter. Amidst the ramblings, one phrase popped out at her: "child last seen with the mother, Luanne Dyeus, outside the Jean Lafitte National Historical Park and Preserve, specifically by a stretch of road near the Barataria Preserve Visitor Center."

Evie froze, blinking in surprise, before her fingers started moving, flipping quickly to the first page detailing Evangeline Dyeus' biographic information. Scanning quickly, she filtered past full name, sex, birth location before lighting on birthdate. February 01, 1989. The coven didn't observe birthdays, and Evie herself typically tracked time by the moon and seasons, but she knew that she was older than many of her sisters. She scanned the rest of the information on the page, much of which didn't provide anything interesting, before coming to identifying features. Eye color: grey. Hair color: red. Distinct marks: a birthmark shaped like a skull on the inside of her upper left thigh.

A high-pitched keening filled the room. It took Evie several seconds to realize that it was her. All of the other coincidences like eye color and hair—even the last known location—could be explained away. That birthmark, though... she looked down at her nude thigh where the small, skull-shaped birthmark sat. She threw the folder away from her in panic. It landed on the desk, the papers inside ruffled but still contained.

That meant she was... she had to be this missing little girl. Her mother was dead. Her father imprisoned. Her breath raced from her lips, uneven and unsteady, and she wobbled, only just catching herself on the corner of Cole's desk before she fell to the floor. Assuming all of this was true, it meant her whole life was a lie. That her sisters... her family... that they had taken her from her parents, one of whom was prepared to abandon her and the other one capable of committing murder. Evie's heart was racing, and black dots were sparkling across her vision. Why would the elders lie to her? Had they stolen her? A horrifying realization occurred to her: what if the coven was responsible for her mother's murder?

Evie's back straightened as rage pulsed through her veins. She deserved the truth, the whole damn story, directly from their mouths, and they would share it with her whether they wanted to or not. Out of the corner of her eye, she saw blue fire. Her gaze shifted down to where her hands clenched the edge of the desk. Vibrant blue magic sparked around her fingers. Was this just another thing that the elders had hidden from her? A separate magic source? A scowl spread across her face. She had to get back to the forest. Now. The coven elders owed her an explanation.

Spinning on her heel, Evie sprinted out of Cole's office to the bedroom where they had slept. She stormed past the bed, the sheets still tangled from that morning, and into Cole's closet where she snatched one of his shirts from a hanger and threw it on as she tore down the stairs. As she came to the front door, she slowed, remembering the wards he drew before he left the house just as the electric pulse of them hummed against her skin. She probed at them and cursed. These were significantly more advanced than the ones he placed on his desk.

Closing her eyes, she pushed her power outward, doing another sweep of the magic binding the house. A sigh slipped past her lips. He had specifically sealed his wards against all sources of magic, but... she paused, feeling a slight weakness. She probed at it, pressing against the fault in the protections, feeling for what was missing. Like lightning, it finally came to her. Cole hadn't sealed against death magic. Without a defense against it, death magic could unravel his protective measures.

Evie glanced down at her hand. Minutes ago, it had been licked with blue fire. And upstairs, her spell work had radiated the same blue as Cole's. Maybe she could get through these wards using that same anomaly? Wincing nervously, she sent a small pulse of magic at the wards surrounding the front door. Her hands glowed that brilliant blue, and she saw through the world like it was shrouded in cobalt cloth. All the same color as the magic sealing the house. Channeling her magic carefully into what looked like a standard lock-and-key mechanism, she slowly unsealed the house, hearing her pulse beat in her ears with every second that went by.

After what felt like an eternity, the door went dark. No wards illuminated it, just sunlight glinting in through the glass windows lining the front of the house. Evie grasped the doorknob and felt no magic. For a second, she considered waiting for Cole to get home so he could go with her but dismissed the thought just as quickly as it arose. This was her discovery, her confrontation. If her entire life was going to be laid bare in front of her, she needed to find that out on her own. She had apparently waited over 30 years to have this discussion if the biographical sheet was to be believed.

More importantly, though, Evie had no idea why Cole had that folder of information about her. Had he been stalking her? What was he to her? *Who* was he to her? No. She shook her head. It was too dangerous to wait for a man whose role in her life she didn't understand, who had started their physical relationship by abducting her from her home.

She slipped out the door silently, closing it tightly behind her. When they arrived at Cole's house in the early morning, the street had been pitch black, barely illuminated by the street lamps lining the street like iron guards. She had felt death all around them but didn't know where it came from. Now, in the midday sunlight, she saw the quiet street and houses surrounding her but also the sprawling cemetery directly across from the road.

There was no way to stop her feet from carrying her across the road to the cemetery. It almost felt like a compulsion, something Evie couldn't explain drawing her to this vast city for the dead. She reached out a hand to tug at the lock on the gate, but it just tapped against the metal barrier, a discordant note in the quiet. Since she wasn't getting past the locked gates easily, she simply looked in through the bars, taking in the uneven rows of deteriorating slate headstones, tilting drunkenly, surrounded by limestone monoliths and marble mausoleums.

Just being this close to the cemetery, she could feel the dead. Could feel magic coursing through her at the abundance of death just feet away from her; it felt like her body was on fire. There was so much magic. Besides when she had reconstituted an entire section of the forest with no knowledge that she was doing so, she had never felt this much magic flowing through her veins.

As much as she wanted to explore the cemetery and the magic pouring from her body, first, she needed to get home... no. To the coven. She needed to confront them about her life, her very existence. Evie pushed away from the cemetery gates, her heart aching as she backed away from the death that surrounded her like a warm blanket, her body almost cold as she turned towards the street.

Across the road, in the massive white stone house that sat next to Cole's, curtains twitched behind the doors leading to the second-floor balcony, and, for a split second, the sun illuminated a tall person standing behind the curtain. Evie squinted, trying to get a better look, but before she could see more, the shadow disappeared as quickly as it had appeared. Shaking her head, she dropped her gaze back to street level, trying to figure out which direction she should go.

Loud noises sounded just up the road from her, so she began walking towards the sounds, one eye still on the house next to Cole's in case the person watching her came out of the house. Her bare feet padded along the cool concrete of the sidewalk, the jagged concrete and stone rubbing along the callused edges of her feet. Although she was used to the feeling of running barefoot through the forest, it was almost painful to walk through the city without shoes. A car rumbled past her, loud music shaking its windows, as she dodged broken shards of glass and other trash. After another twenty feet, she finally came upon the street that she and Cole drove down that morning. Cars raced past her, sending up plumes of dirt and smoke. People bustled around her, but she paid them no mind.

Cole had driven them to his home. While she had been too disoriented from the night's events to track their journey, she still knew that a substantial amount of time had passed between when they left the preserve and when they arrived at his house. She sighed. Walking was an option, but she was barefoot and only wearing a man's shirt. Albeit a man's shirt that came down to her knees, but, given the looks she was seeing the people around her—mostly men but some women too—level at her chest, it seemed like it may be a problem. She sighed.

"Excuse me?" A voice called from her left. "Excuse me, miss?"

She turned to see a tall, elderly man wearing a black shirt with a white collar ringing the neckline staring at her. "Yes?" she asked.

"*Cher*, if you don't mind me sayin', you look a bit lost." He leaned down towards her. "Can I help you with somethin'?"

She looked up at him. She didn't know him, but... maybe he could help. Would it be foolish to ask this man for assistance? She had read stories of men taking women, hurting lost souls. But she needed assistance and, while it could be dangerous to ask for help, it was probably more dangerous to stand here in a man's shirt and nothing else. "I need to get home, and I don't have a car or a—" What did humans call those damn devices they used to call one another? Mobiles? Telemobiles? Phones? "—I don't have a way to call anyone." There. That was a nice, neat way to say that without acknowledging that she had no idea what the device used to call someone was.

"Well," the man said, guiding her across the street to a large white building with a large wooden cross gracing the front. *A church*, her mind supplied. "That's an easy one. I can call you an Uber that will take you where you need to go." At her surprised blink, he continued, "I'll call one right now, and we can just wait here for it to pick you up. Where do you need to go?"

Evie stared at him in disbelief until he nudged her elbow with his hand, a small device that looked like the one Cole had incinerated held in his hand. "Where are you going, *cher*?"

"The Barataria Preserve, please," she replied. It couldn't really be that easy for her to get back home, could it?

The man typed quickly on his device and gestured for her to sit down on the bench in front of the church. "John should be here in five minutes," he chuckled, displaying his device to her. There was a map and the name John.

"That's good," she commented slowly. Should she know who John was? "Is he a friend of yours?"

The man raised his attention from the phone screen. "No, he's just an Uber driver." Piercing golden-brown eyes settled on her face. "Where did you say you were from again, darlin'?" His voice sounded deeper than it had before.

Evie's skin prickled, a sense of wrongness settling over her. "I, uh, I didn't." She shifted slightly away from him, pulling Cole's shirt tighter around herself. The movement loosed some of that smoky mint scent unique to Cole, the smell comforting her even as the man stared at her with that unsettling gaze.

"What was—" His words were cut off as a sleek blue car pulled to the curb, and the driver shouted out the open window, "You my fare to the preserve?"

Evie popped up from the bench and practically threw herself into the back of the car, barely considering the danger of getting into a vehicle with someone she didn't know. All she knew was that she wanted away from the man, who had followed her to the car, his gaze still narrowed on her.

"You be safe now, darlin'," the man commented dryly, closing the door behind her once she was fully seated. "Can't have a magical thing like you in danger, can we?"

Pursing her lips, she nodded uneasily. "Of course," she responded through the open window. "Thank you for your help." Her voice faltered as the car whisked her away to confront her coven, those golden-brown eyes not leaving hers until the car turned a corner, and the old man was lost.

Chapter 17

Cole

Central Business District, New Orleans, Louisiana

Cole checked his watch again, barely suppressing his frustrated scowl when he saw that less than thirty seconds had passed since his last check. He had made it through court, only just stopping himself from turning the judge into a pile of ash, before being guilted back into the office by his best friend and business partner, Hayden Sopor. Upon his arrival, he realized it was actually a business ambush only after Hayden corralled him into a conference room with the firm's accounting team to review the quarter's financials, a topic that he couldn't give less of a shit about on a good day, much less a day when he had somewhere else to be. Apparently—or so his CFO told him—the meeting was on his calendar. *Who the fuck cares?* He would happily torch his calendar, the computer housing it, and, if he was being honest, the whole damn building down around their heads if it meant he could get back to Evie now.

From his seat across the conference room table, Hayden cleared his throat. "Hey, man."

Cole glanced up at him then frowned in confusion. Not five minutes before, eight accountants were fanned around the table, all fidgeting uncomfortably as he reviewed their work. Now, however, it was just him and Hayden separated by six hefty binders and a mostly empty carafe of coffee. "The fuck did everybody go? You dragged me back here just for this. I'm here. Where's everyone else?"

"Well," Hayden drawled, tapping a finger carelessly on the bound stack of papers in front of him. "Around your twentieth watch check and your ninth muttered 'this is a fucking waste of time,' I figured it might be best to excuse the accountants before either you fired them or they collectively quit. We need the money guys, buddy; they tell us whether we can afford to do anything around here, including keeping the lights on and paying our staff. They're all already scared of you. Seems like a good idea we don't make it worse." He closed the binder in front of him before fixing Cole with a pointed stare. "Now, *I'm* used to how much of an asshole you are, but this is extreme even for you. What's going on, man?"

At Cole's head shake, Hayden sighed. "You're going to play it like that? Really? The court clerk called over and mentioned that you called the judge a pompous ass. And not in your head or to me like you usually do but *to his face*. As if that weren't bad enough, Nyx, y'know, the highly qualified law clerk we spent months finding and weeks vetting, called me this morning in tears wanting to quit because you're a, and this is a quote, mind you, 'sanctimonious jackass who has the personality of cocaine bear and needs to learn how to not be a dick.' You set one of our computers on fire in front of your executive assistant, and we'll talk about you using magic in front of the humans later. Not to mention you look like you got dressed in the dark—I'm pretty sure you're wearing two different shoes."

Cole looked down and groaned internally; he was definitely wearing two different shoes, one of which was light brown, the other black.

"So I'm going to ask you again. What the fuck is going on with you today?"

Sighing, Cole met his friend's glacial blue eyes. With his sins of the last several hours laid bare, he really couldn't argue with any of it. Time to come at least a little clean. Of the many people in Cole's life, only a few knew of his prophesied role as Hades reincarnate and future god of the underworld. Hayden, better known as Hypnos, the immortal god of sleep and dreams, had stayed close to the Aidoneus family since the original Hades' untimely death. Unlike Hades, Hypnos had attained his immortality during the initial devastation and, at the Moirai's urging, remained with Aidoneus and Kore's child to ensure that, when his' memories and powers returned to a then-future descendant, the male had a knowledgeable guide. Of his friends and relatives, none would better understand the implications of Cole finding his fated wife then Hayden, who had been with Aidoneus when he first found his Kore all those generations before. Cole drew in a breath. Released it before tilting his head against the chair back. "I found her."

Hayden looked blank for a second before his expression lit with recognition. "Her? You mean... her her? You found the reincarnate?" Cole nodded, and Hayden practically beamed.

"Evie," Cole corrected absently. "Her name is Evie now."

"When did you find her?" Hayden rose to lock the door. "Where was she? Who is she?"

"I'm almost positive that she's Evangeline Dyeus."

"Dyeus," Hayden repeated, blinking at him. "Dyeus as in the Dyeus case from the '90's?"

Cole inclined his head. "The very same."

"Luanne was the wife. Wasn't Evangeline the—"

"The daughter?" Cole interrupted him. "Yeah, Evangeline was the daughter who got dumped in the preserve and nobody ever saw again."

Hayden's mouth dropped open in disbelief. "Everyone was positive she was a critter's dinner. You sure it's the Dyeus girl, man?"

"Pretty damn." Cole shoved his hand through his hair, his foot tapping a quick beat on the conference room floor. "Charlie brought me a file on her yesterday and said that the Moirai thought it was the Dyeus girl but couldn't read her lifelines. I told him I would check the preserve and see if there was any sign that anybody, including the daughter, was there. When I got there this morning, there was a woman there." His heart almost stopped in his chest as he remembered the vision she had made in that barely there white dress. "This fucking goddess just standing in a construction site in the middle of the night."

"Why was she at a construction site that late?" Hayden chuckled. "What, is she a serial killer?"

Cole stayed quiet.

"Is she a serial killer?" Hayden asked, his voice no longer teasing. "Not that that's a dealbreaker or anything, but it's probably something you should know before you tie your lives together."

"No, she's not a serial killer, you jackass," Cole snapped.

"Then what's the problem?" Hayden demanded. "What, is she ugly? Well, I'm sure you'll be able to have consorts—"

A low snarl poured out of Cole's mouth at even the hint that he would cheat on the auburn-haired beauty hopefully in his bed right now. When his words emerged, they were guttural and threatening. "I would never screw around with someone else. She's fucking perfect."

Hayden's eyebrows rose. "So she's got you turned upside down then, huh?" Cole dipped his head, and Hayden paused before asking, "Then what's the problem, man, if you find her attractive and you don't want anybody else?"

No escaping the Spanish inquisition. "Well, she's a witch."

Hayden flinched like he had been slapped. "I'm sorry. I must have misheard you. Did you just say that the reincarnation of Persephone—queen of the underworld, wife of Hades, and goddess of spring—is a witch?"

"Yup." Cole popped the 'p' on his response. "You heard it here first, folks."

"Fuck, man." Hayden's playful smile slipped, and he leaned forward, resting his elbows on the table. "You know the witches have their own prophecy that I'm pretty sure doesn't play well with the Moirai's."

Cole snorted. "Yeah, I know, I just can't remember the differences between the two. I was going to look them up, but Evie and I... well, we got distracted before I could find the old texts. I figured I would talk to Charlie, see if he could tell me."

"Oh, I bet you got distracted." A lecherous smirk slid across Hayden's face, and Cole chucked the water bottle sitting by his elbow at his best friend, who ducked. The mostly full bottle struck the door and fell to the floor, rolling under the table. "The good news for you is that I was around when the Pythia originally issued the witches' prophecy at Delphi. The bad news is that, if I remember correctly, it isn't great for you and your girl. The witches might be the harbingers of the apocalypse when the old gods return. Although the whole thing was in verse and about as clear as oracle predictions usually got. Which means it wasn't clear, y'know, at all. But a lot of the witches I've met over the years believe that they're supposed to roll out the red carpet for the end of humanity. So your girl may not want to stop the apocalypse caused by an unsettled Underworld and a shade-devastated earth. And if she's actually the reincarnate, she'll be in a crazy unique position to bring about the downfall of humanity." He paused, sighing. "Are you sure it's her?"

Cole's mind raced. Was he sure it was her? Given that he had dreamed about her all his life, felt like his skin was electrified when he was around her, and was prepared to murder anybody and everybody in this building just to get back to her? Yeah. Pretty damn sure. "Without a fucking doubt. And I need to get back to her. Like, now. Are we done?" He pushed his chair back from the table, starting to stand, but Hayden stopped him.

"What the fuck do you mean, 'get back to her now?'" His best friend asked, squinting at him suspiciously. "You're going back to the preserve?" For a split second, Cole froze, but he recovered quickly. Unfortunately, it wasn't fast enough for Hayden to overlook the misstep. "Where is your Evie?"

Cole cleared his throat, his fingers drumming against his thigh as he tried to figure out a way around admitting what had actually happened. "Uh. She's at the, um, she's at the house." He was stammering badly enough that he sounded like a bad Jeff Goldblum impersonator. Jesus, he didn't even convince himself that everything was above board with that stumbling response.

"Your house?" At Cole's nod, Hayden stood, walking to block the only door out of the room. "Cole, man, what did you do?"

Cole scowled as he realized there was no way out of the conference room without going through Hayden. "I brought her home with me," he responded coolly. There. No way Hayden could find fault with that perfectly chill response.

"And she came home with you, a man she didn't know, willingly?" Hayden huffed out a disbelieving grunt as he stared at Cole, whose only reaction to the question was to narrow his eyes at the other man. "Holy shit, you kidnapped her, didn't you? You found your girl at a construction site, she wouldn't come with you, and you kidnapped her, didn't you?" He was chewing on his lips, the corners of his mouth tilting up, right before laughter burst from him, his body shaking at its intensity. "Holy shit, you pulled an Aidoneus!" Cole glared at his best friend, now fully bent at the waist, slapping his knee like this was the funniest thing he had ever heard. "That's fucking hysterical, man. I never would have thought the legendary bachelor of New Orleans had it in him."

Cole glowered. "Fuck off, man." Hayden was laughing so hard he was officially wheezing. "It was about her safety."

"No, it wasn't, man." Hayden's laughter was slowing, but a big shit-eating grin still sat on his face. "You wanted your girl, so you took her. Bold move. Pretty classic Aidoneus move if we're being honest. I didn't think you had it in you." He stepped aside, gesturing at the door. "I'm assuming she hated that, didn't she?"

Cole rolled his eyes, making sure the expression was overexaggerated enough that Hayden maybe wouldn't second guess that he hadn't answered the question as he strolled towards the other man.

Hayden's gaze was knowing as Cole passed by him. "You have her locked in your house, don't you?"

"I won't dignify that with a response." Cole unlocked the door and walked out of the room, but Hayden's raised voice followed him down the hall as he walked to the elevators.

"Don't do anything you can't fix, man!" Hayden called. "You'll never forgive yourself if you do."

Shaking his head, Cole jabbed at the down button for the elevator, tapping his foot impatiently and checking his watch. Assuming traffic was fine, which was a huge assumption, really, he could get home in about fifteen minutes. He had just stepped into the elevator, pushing the button for the garage when an alarming realization hit him. Pretty much the only food he had in his house was coffee and bourbon. Possibly some very stale cereal. He winced. They would definitely need to pick up groceries; he was horrible about eating regularly, and he certainly didn't want to accidentally starve both of them. But that could definitely wait until after he got home tonight—being away from Evie this long had already been hard enough. He wouldn't stay away longer to go to the store when he could easily pick up dinner on the way home and have groceries delivered in the morning.

With a smile on his face, he walked off the elevator, crossing the garage to where he had angrily parked his car only—he checked his watch—fuck, six hours ago. He slid in to the driver's seat, slamming the car door a bit harder than necessary in his irritation, but the minute he was ensconced in the small space, the residual scent of Evie found its way into his lungs. His irritation vanished as quickly as it arrived, and it was with excitement flooding his veins that he started the car and drove off towards Evie. As he drove home, his mind wandered back to the first time he dreamed of the little redheaded girl with the stormy eyes . . .

He sat among trees that were as wide around as his little twelve year old body. The light filtered in through the leaves and branches above him, the dust in the air sparkling in the sunbeams that made their way to the ground. It was quiet but peaceful, soothing in a way that the pervasive silence of the palatial house he shared with his uncle wasn't.

He was alone, not that that was too different from his normal life. He was good at being alone after both of his parents died. At least in the forest nobody was around to pity him for being a little orphan boy.

At least he thought nobody was there until he heard tuneless singing coming from just beyond the trees in front of him.

"Hello?" he called out. "Is somebody there?"

The singing stopped suddenly.

"Who are you?" His voice trembled with nerves. "I know karate."

"Do you really?" A pale face with a button nose and massive grey eyes popped out from behind the massive felled log lying beside him.

He shrieked and tumbled backward, crawling away from the stranger.

"No, no, no, it's okay!" The owner of the face stood up, and he stopped moving. It was only a girl, maybe about his age, her delicate skin and stormy grey eyes surrounded by curly red hair. She squirmed over the top of the log towards him, her gaze never leaving his. "I'm so sorry! I didn't mean to scare you."

"I wasn't scared," he denied, even though his heart was still racing. Although that may also be because she was the prettiest girl he had ever seen. Cindie, the girl he had a crush on at school, had nothing on this girl.

The girl sent him a teasing grin. "You were," she corrected. "But it's fine. Everyone gets scared. I won't tell if you don't."

Although he felt like he should argue the point, he was too curious about her to care she thought he was scared or not. "Where did you come from?" he demanded.

She giggled. "I live here. This is my home." Her hands waved around her, gesturing around them.

"You can't live in the forest," he argued. "You're just a kid!"

"So are you," she snapped, her eyes flashing at him. "And I live here with my sisters."

"Don't lie to me. I know that kids have to live with an adult." He couldn't look away from her, this cute girl whose nose was scrunched, her hands balled at her sides. "What are you really doing here?"

Her eyes flashed molten gold, a sparkling gold hue forming around her hands. The trees behind her seemed to lean towards her, the limbs drawing closer to surround her. "I already told you. I live here. And if you're going to be rude, then I'm leaving." A scowl on her pretty face, she twisted around, stomping away from him.

She was almost twenty feet away from him when he called out, "No! You don't have to go. Please. Please don't leave. I'll be nicer."

She paused but didn't come back.

"I'm sorry. I didn't mean to be rude," he said. He wanted her to stay. She was weird and probably a little bit crazy, but that was okay. He was too. They could be weird together. "Please stay. I want you to stay."

She turned with a brilliant smile on her face that sent his heart stumbling in his chest. He would do anything to keep her smiling at him like that...

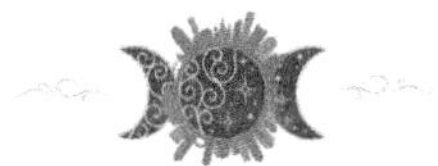

That had been the first of many dreams about the girl he now knew to be Evie. With each night, he learned more about her, became a little bit more obsessed with her. By the time they aged into their late teens, she was a knockout, all mouthwatering curves and luminescent skin that made him want to lick her from head to toe and back again.

Cole pulled into the parking lot of *Lagniappe*, a small dive bar that made some of the best burgers in the area, and went in, ordering enough to feed a small army, including a vegetarian meal just in case Evie didn't eat meat. Dauphine—the old Cajun owner who had known him since he was born—came out fifteen minutes later, her arms laden with two bulging paper bags filled with food.

"*Chèr*!" she cried, dropping the bags on the bar before darting around it, her wrinkled face crinkled in happiness as she threw her arms around his neck in a bruising hug. "It's been too long since you came to see me."

"Sorry, Dauphine," he responded, returning her embrace. His mother had loved Dauphine and her cooking, so much so that she made a point to bring the entire family for dinner at *Lagniappe* at least once a week. He had tried to keep up the tradition, but, as his work days grew longer and traveling became a more regular part of his professional life, the time between each visit grew longer. "I've been meaning to swing by."

"I know, baby, you're a very important man." She drew away, pinching his cheek. "And yet you still manage to make time for little ol' me."

"I could never forget you, Dauphine." He smiled widely at her. "You're etched in my memory, *belle*."

"Oh, you charmer you," she chuckled, walking back towards the bar and the grease-stained bags containing dinner. "That's a lot of food for just you... " Her voice trailed off, and she raised and lowered her eyebrows suggestively.

Cole shook his head at the old woman's digging. "You got a question, ask it, Dauphine."

"Well, I don't want to pry."

"I believe that about as much as I believe that 'A' inspection score on your window," he retorted, eyeballing a dead cockroach on the bar. "What, did you bribe the inspector?"

"Still a cheeky little thing, aren't you?" Dauphine responded, pinching his cheek again before swiping the bug off the bar top casually. "Fine. Does our little Cole have a special friend that he's taking dinner to?"

"A gentleman doesn't dine and tell," he taunted.

"Oh, baby, I see the gossip pages. You're no gentleman." Her voice was gentle but chiding.

Ouch. He knew he had a well-earned reputation around town—and everywhere else if he was being honest—but he hadn't thought it was so bad that even Dauphine knew about it. Under her scrutiny, though, he found himself telling the truth. Maybe the truth would make him seem a little less tarnished—not so much a man-whore—in his mother's friend's eyes. "*Ouais*," he responded, confirming the existence of his special friend in French. "I've known her for a while, but we finally connected. She's, uh—" He rubbed his palm along the back of his neck. *How the hell do people talk about their feelings? This is excruciating.* "She's someone really special to me."

"Oh!" Dauphine bounced a bit on her toes. "Oh, that's wonderful. All your parents ever wanted was for you to be happy. She must be a very special lady to be worthy of you." Seizing his arms, Dauphine dragged him back into a smothering embrace before releasing him and pressing a finger into his chest.. "You'll bring her here to meet me." It wasn't a question.

"I don't really have a choice, do I?" He knew how the old lady operated. "It's either bring her here or you show up at my house. I know how this works." His hands closed around the bags of food. "Now I need to get home to her. I got held up at work so I'm already running late."

"I'm honored that you took the time to chat up little old me when you have someone waiting on you, but you best get out of here, *chèr*, before you make your *petite amie* angry." She wrapped a strong hand around his arm before he left. "I hope she's the right woman for you."

Cole dipped his head, kissing her on the cheek. "She is." With a passing wave at the bartender—a long-haired stoner he had gone to high school with—he strode out the door, food in hand.

Chapter 18

Cole

Garden District, New Orleans, Louisiana

Cole pulled into the driveway. Traffic had been light, and the stop for food only took about twenty minutes, so, all told, he had gotten home to Evie earlier than expected. As he leaned over to retrieve the bags from the passenger seat, the hairs on the back of his neck rose. Something was very wrong. His head snapped around, his gaze darting from the backyard terrace then, past that, to the glass door that opened into the kitchen. Although he couldn't see anything wrong, something felt off.

With a frown at the back door, Cole summoned just enough magic to see if he could sense anything. Nothing. Which was odd in itself. Ordinarily, the wards he set around the house buzzed against his skin like small jolts of lightning, but now... Nothing. He sent a subtle pulse into the house to see if there was anyone in there who shouldn't be or foreign magic; he broke into a cold sweat when no magical trace came back to him at all. At a minimum, he should be able to sense his own wards and Evie, but he couldn't sense either.

Cole's fist tightened around the food bags, and he flung himself out of the car, throwing open the gate to the backyard and racing to the door. He jammed the key into the lock, blood pressure skyrocketing as it unlatched without him having to invert the wards. The door yawned open slowly, his keys still hanging from the lock. "Angel?" he shouted. Silence. "Evie?" No answer. He walked into the kitchen, dumping the bags on the counter as he paced around the island and into the dining room.

Wards down. Evie gone. What the *fuck* was going on? Nobody could get into this house except someone else whose source of power was death. Even human sacrifices to fuel magic weren't enough to unlock his wards. They could only be undone by someone who drew upon death itself to channel their magic. And people with that kind of ability were rare, bordering on nonexistent. He honestly thought he was the only one left... or he had until he walked into his house, its defenses easily dismantled.

But, most importantly, his witch was *gone*. His logic didn't matter when she was *fucking gone*. Cole couldn't breathe around the panic clawing its way up his chest. The house felt too silent around him, even with his own pulse thundering in his ears. A quick glance around the first floor revealed nothing. No Evie. He raced to the staircase, bounding up to the second floor, mumbling incantations to detect intruders as he went.

Each spell he cast came back with nothing, which, unfortunately, only told him that there were no human intruders or unskilled practitioners since there were absolutely magical beings that left zero trace of their presence. Shades, for example. A low grunt of concern rolled out of him. Cole knew better than most the damage those beings could do. His hand rose to where his throat was tingling at Aidoneus' memory of being stabbed through the neck by a vengeful shade who had been able to sneak upon him because they gave off no magical signature. Cole may only have the former Lord of the Underworld's memories, but it didn't negate their intensity.

His chest tightened in fear and rage. If somebody took her, if somebody so much as touched a single hair on her head, he would destroy their whole fucking world and then give his witch the match so she could torch the remnants.

The door to his bedroom was flung open, the sheets still rumpled from when they woke up that morning. He pressed his palm over his heart, the ache of seeing where they had slept together just hours ago almost palpable. A quick glance around confirmed that she wasn't anywhere in the master suite, so he went down the hallway, checking each room quickly from the doorway to see if there were any signs of a struggle. Each one looked exactly the way he had left it that morning. His panic ratcheted up with every step he took. It was only when he came upon his study door—wide open although he knew it was shut earlier—that he entered a room. Crossing the threshold, he cast a wary eye around the area.

Nothing destroyed. No obvious struggles evident. Nothing out of place. As he turned to walk out of the room, though, something on his desk caught his eye. He pivoted, noticing the file splayed open on his desk, the papers it held jumbled but still contained within it. His brow furrowed. He could count on one hand the number of physical files he still had. Much like every other profession, the legal field changed significantly—if a bit more slowly—as the world transitioned to digital. The legacy files he was required by the state bar to maintain were preserved in a climate-controlled storage unit in keeping with the law until the firm could find an intern to begin the arduous process of scanning them in. The few non-legacy physical files the firm had were all at the office; he never brought physical files home with him, preferring to do any work from home digitally.

Cole strode to the desk, picked up the file, and groaned, sinking into his chair. That particular folder held the background information Charles had given him just days ago on Evangeline Dyeus. The papers were disheveled as if someone had rifled through them, and it wasn't hard to guess who might have done that. To the right of the folder, far enough away that he knew Evie had to have picked it up and dropped it suddenly, was the page detailing Evangeline Dyeus' biographical information.

They hadn't actually talked about her life outside of the coven besides when he called her Evangeline that first time he saw her. She corrected him then, though, didn't she? Told him her name was Evie. He thought it was simply because she preferred to be called Evie, but what if it was bigger than that? He shoved a hand through his hair. Hell, they hadn't even resolved that she actually was Evangeline Dyeus, much less whether she knew who she might be.

But honestly? It didn't matter to him whether she was just Evie or the allegedly deceased Evangeline Dyeus. He only knew that he felt a connection with her that went deeper than anything he had ever felt before with anyone else. He knew her all his life through his dreams. When he was with her, the world felt stable and real and happy in a way it never had before. He had to find her. Now. He didn't give a shit who she had been, only that she was his now.

Dropping the file back on the desk, he pinched the bridge of his nose, thinking through the options. He had a theory about where she had gone. It seemed unlikely that she would just go on walkabout around New Orleans. *Much more probable that she returned to the forest.* In a haze, he stood up and walked out of the room and back down the stairs, eerily calm as he collected his wallet and keys and went to the car.

Todd stood on the other side of the fence, his attention turning from an unknown something in his backyard to Cole when the gate slammed behind him. "Hey, Cole," he said, his voice shaking a bit. Ah, the wonderful effects of a threat to drag one's soul into Tartarus. Cole gave the man a terse nod, already halfway into his seat when Todd gathered his wits about him just enough to say, "Hey, uh, I saw your girl from last night leaving the house this morning."

Cole paused, one leg planted in the driver's side footwell, an arm extended over the top of the car. "Which way did she go, Todd?" On a good day, he barely had time for Todd's particular brand of bullshit. Today? He couldn't even manage the niceties.

Todd's voice lost its uncertain waver at the direct question. "Towards St. Charles, I think, after she stared at the cemetery for a little bit." Seeming more comfortable now that they'd had an interaction without threats of violence, Todd added, "Pretty little thing. She looked like she would be a fun time."

"Excuse me?" Cole pressed himself away from the car and rounded the bumper, not bothering to close the driver's side door in his fury. All the fear, the rage, the absolute helplessness and madness he had barely kept a handle on since he got home to find his Evie gone now simmered to the forefront and found a target: Todd. His imbecile of a neighbor who appeared to have a death wish. "What. The. Fuck. Did you just say about her?"

To his idiot neighbor's credit, he worked out his error quickly and began sputtering apologies immediately. To his idiot neighbor's detriment, Cole couldn't care less about the lame attempt at reconciliation and was already stalking towards Todd, stopping only inches from the other man.

"I thought I made myself abundantly fucking clear when you saw her last night that you weren't to say a goddamned word about her or even look at her ever again, you inconsequential asshole." The world became soaked in blue as his magic surged. He could easily rip this shithead's soul from his chest with the magic flooding his body and—if the Underworld were actually open—chuck it into the depths of Tartarus alongside the Titans, who would surely have a blast with the puny human. With his magically enhanced vision, he could already see Todd's soul, ready to be stripped from his body, although—Cole frowned—it had an unusual, pitch black tar look to it unlike the incandescent glow most humans put off.

Without an open Underworld, though, Todd's separated soul would simply stay in the human realm, wreaking more havoc. Cole needed Evie to access the Underworld and, as much as he might like to destroy Todd right now, he couldn't send yet another shade out among the humans. There were too many of them already. So, for the moment, unhinged threats would have to do. "Let me explain something to you, Todd," he sneered down into his shorter neighbor's face. "You would do well to never speak about her ever fucking again. In fact, I would recommend that you forget about her existence altogether. I would hate to have to find out how great it would be to have a new neighbor because you just disappeared."

"Are you threatening me, Cole?" Todd's jaw tightened, his brown eyes narrowing on Cole.

Cole chuckled grimly. "Todd, you're not smart—you calling my woman a 'pretty little thing' proved it, just in case there was any doubt—but I would think you're at least intelligent enough to get that, yes, I am in fact threatening you. But, just in case you're unclear, let me clarify a bit. If you go anywhere near her, I will destroy you. I will remove your limbs from your body and dump them in the bayou for the 'gators to feast on right before I rip your worthless soul from your body and torture it in ways that even I can't fathom. You saw something you were never supposed to see and then you made the mistake of commenting on it when you should have kept it to your fucking self. And do you want to know something?" Todd blanched as Cole continued, but his icy gaze never wavered from Cole's. "Nobody will ever know that you went missing because no one cares about you. And, if by some miracle, somebody wonders where you are, nobody will think to look at the *lawyer*, the partner of an internationally recognized firm and local philanthropist, who lives next door." Todd's face was the color of curdled milk when Cole returned to his car and started the engine. "Anyways. Have a great day, Todd."

Cole pulled into the street, heading towards St. Charles. Todd hadn't specified when Evie had left, but Cole had been at work for—he snuck a quick look at the clock in the upper corner of the car's entertainment center and calculated quickly—a good seven hours before he left the office to come home. Add the thirty or so minute drive home and the panicked search of his home, and it was closing in on 5:00. She had a significant lead on him, assuming she figured out a way to get to the forest that was faster than walking.

His blood froze in his veins at the thought of her strolling along the side of the freeway. So help him, if she fucking walked to the preserve, he would put her over his knee, spank her ass red, then lock her in his fucking bedroom until she learned not to put her damn self in danger.

He kept his eyes peeled as he drove, but he didn't catch any sigh of a red-haired witch along St. Charles, the Westbank Expressway, or Barataria Boulevard. Her absence along the roadway just raised the question of how she actually managed to leave the city. Did she climb into another person's car? The hair rose on the back of his neck. Getting into stranger's cars was dangerous at the best of times. It took on an extra element of recklessness when you were a barefoot woman wearing what he assumed—what he hoped—was only one of his shirts since her dress was getting dry cleaned, courtesy of a lunchtime detour before the accounting meeting from hell.

And, fuck, what if he was completely wrong, and she didn't even go to the forest at all? Cole's imagination spiraled, providing him with a variety of horrific things that could happen to a small woman in New Orleans. It wasn't an unsafe city, but any city could be dangerous to someone unfamiliar with it. And Evie… well, she was as unfamiliar with the city as anyone could possibly be.

He took a few stabilizing breaths, forcing himself to be rational. He was known for being coldly logical everywhere; he needed to channel that, so he didn't lose his mind to the panic trying to overtake him. Evie was a powerful damn witch. She had reconstituted an entire section of the forest from a devastated construction site within minutes. She managed to undo his wards with death magic—a fact that still shocked him—without destroying his house, something few could manage; those wards were damn powerful, and improper manipulation would result in an explosion the likes of which the Garden District had never seen, not to mention a magical warning to him. If she left and somebody had taken her, he should probably be more concerned for the abductor than for her.

At least that's what he told himself. In reality, his heart was beating inhumanly fast as he pulled off to the side of the road by the reforested construction site. He threw open the car door and stepped out, drawing to his full height, gaze fixed across on the trees across the way as the humid winter breeze blew around him, tousling his hair and carrying the rich scent of the bayou to him. He slammed the car door shut and crossed the small shoulder between him and the preserve quickly, thankful for the complete lack of vehicle or foot traffic in the area. While the locals may not remember a random person walking towards the forest, they would probably remember a tall stranger in a suit who abandoned his car on the side of the road.

Four men stood shouting next to a digger hoisted high in the air and speared through its center by a tree trunk at least five feet in diameter. Fortunately, they were too wrapped up in themselves and the complete nullification of their work to notice anything around them. Without a sound, Cole passed them quickly, entering the forest unseen by the group.

Chapter 19

Cole

Barataria Preserve, Marrero, Louisiana

When Cole entered the preserve, sunlight dappled the forest floor and birds chirped around him. As his foot crossed over the threshold into the shadows cast by the trees, however, a cloud covered the sun, plunging the forest into darkness and, bizarrely enough, silence. The birds, the wind, the ever-present hum of the bugs, all of it had gone quiet. He frowned. Although he didn't spend much time in nature, he would have expected more noise if he actually thought about it. Instead, it was oddly still, almost as if the forest was... thinking?

Shaking off the oddness of it all, he summoned his magic. It flowed easily, just the way he expected it to given his setting. Nature was full of the dichotomy of life and death with no moral valuation of either; it was so very different, refreshingly so, from the human world where death was seen as the ultimate evil, despite, most of the time, lacking the intent necessary to be truly wicked.

He pushed his senses to their limit, searching for Evie's magical signature. The trees around him spiked, flowing gold vein running the lengths of their trunks, and he sighed in annoyance. He should have thought of that. Of course they would reflect her magic; she seeded and grew the damn things less than a day ago. Shedding his suit jacket, he dropped it on the ground carelessly—he had more just like it at home so no great loss—and eyeballed the trees ahead of him. Each one as far as he could see was lit with the gold strands of Evie's power.

The original construction site had been massive. At the very least, he would have to get past the edges of the newly replanted trees, plants, and other flora to get a somewhat accurate read of whether Evie was here. As he powered past trunks the size of small convertibles and tangled vines, he noticed that the trees around him were lit not just in the shades of gold associated with the moon but also a smidge of radiant cobalt blue, a color unique to death magic. *Interesting.* Had Evie been drawing on his own magic as she touched him?

Finally, he reached the end of the trees lit with that golden and blue hue, signaling that he was past where Evie's magic had detonated the night before. He put a bit more distance between himself and the trees at his back, so they wouldn't interfere with the signature blast he was about to put out. Breathing in deeply, he pushed his senses out to full intensity once more.

At almost 26,000 acres of wetlands, bayous, and forest, the feedback he received was immense, so much so he felt his vision blur at the enormity. Cole could sense signatures of pretty much anything associated with the grave, including dead and dying flora and fauna, long deceased animals, and anyone who used death magic. All around him, he felt small deaths: squirrels, birds, a tree decaying from oak wilt. Just northeast of him, he could detect a decaying human corpse. Scratch that: a *lot* of human corpses. Somebody was using the preserve as a dumping ground for their murderous activities. Not that it mattered right now.

He closed his eyes against the intensity of the feedback, inhaling sharply to brace himself for what was next. It would be all too easy for him to get overwhelmed, but he needed to stay focused. He needed to find his witch. Inhaling again, he recalled the taste and scent and feel of her magic rubbing against his own, using the memory to guide his search. There was the section of trees at his back. Little pockets of her magic lingered around the preserve, too small to actually be her. Further in, towards the lakes, her signature lingered a bit more, but it still wasn't enough. Further north, though... further north, near one of the bayous, the preserve practically exploded with magical activity, too vibrant to be anything but his witch herself. *There she is.* A ferocious grin spread across his face, his body tightening in excitement. She could never hide from him. All he had to do was get to her.

If he went directly through the preserve, it would be shorter in distance but so much longer in time. He would be going directly through critter-infested bayous with the trees, vines, and nature in general doing their damnedest to slow him down, not to mention every predator in the area trying to make him their dinner. And that was the best-case scenario. The worst case was Evie finding out that he was here, not wanting him to find her, and actively siccing the forest on him. No thank you. He would take the slightly longer route that was more likely to ensure his arrival at his witch's doorstep.

Turning on his heel, he walked back the way he came, grabbing his suit jacket from where he had dropped it to the ground. He strode past the tree line, passing the group of men, which had expanded from four people to seven, all yelling. Their voices went quiet behind him, but he didn't pay any attention to them as he dropped into the driver's seat of his car and powered it on, pulling out onto the street and following Evie's magical signature.

Fifteen minutes and six wrong turns later, Cole finally turned into the parking lot for a local tavern, the closest point to where he felt Evie that wasn't in a residential neighborhood. The wrong turns he attributed to driving through a magical haze. While it wasn't necessarily dangerous to use magic and drive, he had only been loosely paying attention to his driving, more concerned with finding Evie than driving.

It certainly surprised him that he hadn't been pulled over by a Jefferson Parish deputy. For all that they weren't far from New Orleans, the local law enforcement took great pleasure in ticketing and arresting city folk. Among the raised trucks and older sedans on the road in the more rural area, his EV stuck out like a sore city thumb that said, "please arrest me on charges of suspected reckless driving" on a normal day. Given that he had been driving erratically at best, the likelihood of getting stopped by the police skyrocketed. Had they pulled him over, the magical blue light dancing in his irises would have been more than enough for any good deputy to kick the charges up to suspected possession of some form of narcotics.

Fortunately, he hadn't seen a single deputy, a fact for which he was extremely grateful. Talking himself out of a ticket—at best—or criminal charges—at worst—would have eaten up time he didn't want to waste on anything other than retrieving Evie. He turned off the car and climbed out. It was almost dinner time, but the bar was closed, the parking lot empty. He paid these things little attention as he crossed the empty street, past a muffler shop and across an open field, into the trees. Let them tow his car when the bar opened; he didn't give a shit.

Like before, the minute he passed into the preserve, the world went dark and silent. Thankfully, his attention wasn't split by the reforested site anymore; all of his focus remained on the witch whose presence he could feel like a physical ache. He trekked through the soundless forest, course correcting towards Evie's signature each time he wandered in the wrong direction. In the brush around him, scurrying sounds rustled intermittently, and he kept catching glints of deep red eyes that vanished as quickly as they appeared. He didn't stop to figure out what it was or where it went, just kept moving forward. Anything that wasn't Evie didn't matter unless it was actively attacking him.

Every few minutes, Cole felt a flare of Evie's magic light up the forest in front of him. Further reassurance that she was not only here but alive too. After what felt like a never-ending walk but was probably only about ten minutes, the forest opened into a massive clearing in front of him, and he felt Evie like a punch to the gut.

One problem, though. He couldn't see her. The area appeared empty.

But magic flooded the area, sending shivers through his body. It was thick in the air, so much so that it almost made it feel like he was swimming through too-thick air with every movement he made. As he passed a hand in front of him, magic whispered and flowed over his flesh; a whiff of smoke tinged the air. All of it underlining the scent of his witch: that spicy, fruity smell of her.

There was something here. Something he couldn't see. He brushed a hand over the air in front of him again. It wasn't a ward, or he would have felt the vibrations against his skin. Instead, it almost felt like an oily residue. A protection spell, maybe? He scowled; he had the powers of a god. A coven that didn't even have fucking electricity shouldn't be able to keep him from his witchling.

Summoning more magic, he gathered it in his palms, bright cobalt smoke collecting around his hands, tangling through his fingers. There was nothing for it but for him to punch his way through whatever magic protected the clearing. The world washed away in a haze of blue. All logic abandoned him as the intensity of his magic overpowered his human side; the possessiveness that had been dancing over his skin since he met Evie at that construction site finally taking over at the idea that she was *here,* but he couldn't get to her. His last thought before releasing the cataclysmic amount of magic needed to break through the spell was that Evie wouldn't thank him for this.

Chapter 20

Evie

Barataria Preserve, Marrero, Louisiana

After an uneventful journey in the car the strange man called for her, which dropped her at the foot of the preserve by the visitor center, she had lit through the trees rapidly, driven by an overwhelming need to confront her coven. Was she Evangeline Dyeus? Had the elders taken her from a loving family? The trees and vines she was running past, sensing her inner turmoil, bent towards her, extending themselves in her direction, gently stroking any part of her they could reach in an effort to soothe her.

Once she arrived at the clearing, she drew the inverted symbols needed to lift the protection spell and walked into absolute chaos. Her jaw dropped as she glanced around, taking in the devastation around her. Trees were toppled across the clearing. Conical piles of sand filled with boiling water were scattered around the area, and cracks fissured from where she stood, extending beyond where she could see.

"Evie!" A slight figure raced towards her, slamming into her with so much force that Evie stumbled to the side, barely catching herself before she fell. "Where have you been?" The question trailed off as Sandrine burst into tears.

Evie wrapped her arms around Sandrine. "Please don't cry, little sparrow, I'm here now." Her eyes tracked the clearing, catching sight of the small group of witches gathered around the fire.

One woman popped her head up from the group gathered around the fire, squinting at where Sandrine and Evie stood. "Evie?" she called, rushing towards them. "Evie, darling?"

"Hi, Chloe," Evie greeted the witch who had raised her in a soft voice.

"We were so worried about you!" Chloe gave Evie a quick hug, pressing a motherly kiss to her forehead. "Where were you?"

Evie paused, her mouth not quite able to form the words to describe everything that had happened in the last day. All she could think was that there was a strong likelihood that Chloe—the hedge witch who had raised her, the elder who had trained her in lunar magic as best she could, the maternal figure who cared for her when she was ill—had lied to her. And not just a small lie. A massive one that spanned her entire life if the file on Cole's desk was to be believed. "I was just exploring," was what Evie chose to say instead. "What happened here?"

Sandrine pulled her head from Evie's chest, giving her older coven sister a confused gaze, at the same time Chloe shot her a strange look. "The earthquakes, Evie."

Evie shook her head. "Earthquakes? As in plural, more than one?"

Hesteia and Thea walked up to them. "The three earthquakes over the last day, love," Thea responded, rubbing her hand over Sandrine's back soothingly. "You didn't feel them?"

Evie thought back to the moment she saw Cole, that first kiss where she had felt like one or both of them was shaking. Assuming that was an earthquake, that accounted for one. *When were the other two?* "No, I didn't know. When did they happen?"

Hesteia's mouth was pursed, her eyes calculating as they locked on Evie. "Two were before sunup, not too far apart. The third happened a few hours after the sun rose."

Evie froze in shock. If the first earthquake happened when she and Cole kissed that first time and the second occurred not long after that... Not long after that had been the driveway. She flushed, the memory of Cole's low voice growling in her ear and his fingers rubbing over her, plunging inside her, sending a spark of arousal through her body. And a few hours after sun up, she had been in Cole's bed, wrapped in his arms. No earthquakes since they had parted ways. What if... no, that was too absurd to even think about. She was forcing connections where there weren't any to be made. "I'm sorry I wasn't here," she said, dropping a light kiss on top of Sandrine's hair and giving her sister one last hard squeeze before dropping her arms. "How can I help now that I am, though?"

"We've cleaned up much of the damage already." Hesteia waved a hand at the felled trees. "And unless you feel up to reseeding the damaged trees, I don't think we have anything for you to do." With a single authoritative gesture, she herded the small group that had gathered around them towards the eating area where the rest of the coven was slowly gathering at the long tables. "But we do have dinner ready for all of you so if you're hungry, now's the time."

Evie trailed behind Hesteia and the others, staring blindly across the clearing. Not a day ago, she had raised a completely devastated section of the forest, bringing hundreds of dead plants and long dormant flora back to glorious life. At the time, though, she had so much magic coursing through her veins that it felt like her skin couldn't contain all of it. How much of that could she attribute to Cole's presence?

A gentle hand touched her elbow, and she jumped, glancing wildly where the touch came from. Chloe stood next to her, tears running down her narrow face. "I was so worried about you, Evie. I thought something might have happened."

Something did happen. It just wasn't death or physical injury. It was emotional damage. Mental. Evie took the bowl of warm stew that Thea brought her, nodding her thanks at the witch, before turning her attention back to Chloe.

"I'm fine. I didn't even notice the earthquakes." She shuffled her feet awkwardly. "Chloe, would you mind if we went back to the house? I have something I need to talk to you about."

"Of course, Evie." Chloe nodded, accepting her own bowl from Thea with a smile. "You're always welcome at home."

Evie followed Chloe to her small home nestled in between two dwarf palmettos, where the walls—such as they were—were composed of small saplings and vines. It was a prime location because the moon shone down perfectly and directly onto the house. It was also where Evie had grown up. She glanced at the small room she had lived in for much of her life; it looked exactly the same as it had before she moved to her own house in the forest canopy. Chloe hadn't changed a thing since she left, claiming that she wanted Evie to always feel welcome.

"Sit down, Evie darling." Chloe dropped into one of the two chairs in the main area, resting her bowl on her lap. "It has been too long since you've been home."

Evie lowered herself into the other chair, perched at the edge of the seat. Her mind raced as she tried to figure out the right time to demands answers as to whether her whole life had been a lie. It didn't feel like dinner conversation.

"How was your explor—" Chloe began.

Screw polite dinner conversation. "Tell me again how you found me," Evie interrupted her.

Chloe shifted backwards in a movement that almost looked like a flinch. Her skin paled just a bit, but then she straightened. "What do you mean?"

"That night you found me when I was little." Evie placed her elbows on her knees and leaned forward, her bowl sitting forgotten on the ground beside her. "Tell me again what happened."

"Beyond the fact that we found you, it was just like any other night." Chloe's smile was beatific, but Evie noticed that it was frayed around the edges, not actually reaching her eyes. "Why do you ask?"

Chewing on the inside of her cheek, Evie observed the woman who was like a mother to her. "So there was nothing out of the ordinary then?"

Chloe blanched, but she held on to her smile. Barely. “No. Just a beautiful little witch who became part of the heart and soul of our coven.”

“So… there was nobody else with me?” Evie pressed. “No man shouting for his daughter, no woman carrying a toddler into the preserve? Nothing like that?” Based on the news clippings from the folder, she was guessing that was what had happened. Now was the time for Chloe to correct her. Offer an explanation.

Instead, Chloe’s face fell, and she looked at her adoptive daughter with a distinct look of guilt and fear and burst into tears.

That was all the answer Evie needed. “You… lied to me?” Her voice wavered. “You took me from my family?”

“No!” Chloe cried, emotion thick in her voice now that the truth was coming out. “We would never do that! We found you at the edge of the forest. Just like we did all of your sisters!”

“Are you saying I was… abandoned?” Evie shook her head. “That doesn’t make sense. I’ve seen the news clippings. I had parents! My father was looking for me that night.”

Chloe’s face darkened. “You weren’t alone.”

“What does that even mean? If I wasn’t abandoned but I wasn’t alone, how did you not take me? Those are mutually exclusive things.” The world was creeping in around Evie, her thoughts muddy. She needed to breathe, but her heart was beating too quickly, her lungs struggling to work, enough so that she couldn’t get in the air she needed.

Chloe was opening her mouth to respond when the world blew apart. Around them, Chloe’s tree-sheltered home shook; screams echoed through the forest. For the first time in the Barataria Coven’s recorded history, the lights that lit their forest home went dark, going from the pale color they usually held to a deep blood-red scarlet. The color symbolized an attack. War. That was almost scarier than the explosion. Almost.

Shoving herself out of her chair, Chloe raced out of the house into the clearing, calling behind her, “Evie, come on!”

Feeling like she was struggling through molasses, Evie followed, barely able to reconcile the little Chloe had shared about her history with what she had thought. to be true. In a matter of minutes, the entire foundation of her life was destroyed. And now, it appeared that the coven's home itself may be destroyed as well. Her fingers trembled at the idea that every constant in her life was about to be stripped away, but, as she walked into the clearing, Evie felt his magic. Felt him. The most constant part of her life standing right in front of her.

The minute she saw Cole, her chest pulsed with familiarity. He was hers: the man who had haunted her throughout her life, the only one who knew her.

His eyes, lit radiant blue, traced the clearing, catching sight of her almost as soon as she walked out into the open air. A dark, fiery crown graced his head and magic poured from him, sending shivers down her spine. Behind him, she could see the tattered edges of the protective barrier behind him; he had punched through it like it was nothing. As she neared him, she felt more than heard the low-pitched growl rolling from his chest.

"Come here, little witch," Cole rumbled, his voice distorted.

Evie took three steps towards him before her body checked in with her brain that going to him was actually a good idea. Once she starting thinking again, she came to a screeching halt, but it was too late. She was already in arm's reach of the dark god before her, and he didn't seem willing to be separated from her for any longer.

Cole snatched her into his arms, pulling her feet fully off the ground. A satisfied huff emerged from his mouth as he nuzzled into her neck. "Don't run from me again, Angel," he breathed into her ear. "I'll always fucking find you, no matter what. You'll never be free of me." His arms suddenly tensed around her, and he started snarling again.

"Back off," Evie snapped. "It's probably a bad idea to try and come any closer." Cole's snarl intensified, and she threw up a shield, biting back a laugh when she heard a yelp as somebody came into contact with the invisible wall blocking them from the coven. Although she could hear whispers around them, she turned her attention back to the man holding her, who was still glaring over her shoulder. "Cole."

Cole drew back, his gaze fixing on her face. The intensity of his magic was slowly fading the longer he held her and, with it, the overwhelming dark energy that she could feel between her thighs. Now he just sounded tired, concern replacing the dangerous expression he was wearing when he first entered. "You left. You put yourself in danger. Why the fuck would you do that?"

"I had to—" Her voice caught as she remembered the conversation his untimely and destructive entrance had interrupted. "Oh gods, I had to talk to my mother." A surge of pain and no small amount of anger struck her heart. "The woman who raised me. Chloe. I don't know what the fuck to call her, but I found something in your desk, and I needed to talk to her about it."

His brow furrowed. "Why didn't you wait for me? I would have brought you back to talk to her. Evie, I need to be with you. I need to stay with you."

"Why didn't I wait for you," she repeated his question back to him as a statement, her irritation with him flaring suddenly back to life. "For starters, you abducted me. You were the one who actually had the information that made me come back. You warded your house against me leaving!" As she listed his various missteps, her voice increased in volume until she finally shouted, "Should I go on? Why the fuck should I have trusted you, Cole?"

To his credit, he did actually look ashamed, his shoulders slumping forward, his head tilting down until his forehead rested against hers. "I'm sorry, Evie. For all of it. I never meant to take away your free will. Or your freedom."

Well. It was hard to stay angry at him when he apologized. Harder still when he was clutching her to his chest like he would die before letting her go. "Fine. That's... well, thank you. For the apology. But why did you have any of that stuff about that girl—me, I guess—in your study?"

A wince crossed his handsome face. "I think we need to talk about that somewhere else. You know. When your family isn't staring at us?" They both glanced up and around, finally taking in her coven.

The members had taken defensive positions around the barrier spell Evie had cast. At their attention, Hesteia stepped forward, fire ringing her arms, the flames licking up to her shoulders. "Who are you?" she demanded.

Evie maintained the barrier on the off-chance that Cole lost his temper again.

Cole inhaled then breathed out slowly, the air of his exhale whispering against her cheek. "My name is Cole Aidoneus," he responded authoritatively, and Evie couldn't help but imagine that this was what he sounded like in a courtroom. A small streak of desire—never far when Cole was around—throbbed through her veins, and she pressed closer to him.

Hesteia scowled, her face illuminated by the fire surrounding her, looking every inch the powerful red witch she was. "What do you want, Cole Aidoneus? Why are you here? The witches have done no wrong to you, and you've threatened our home and one of our sisters in a short time."

Cole's arms tightened around her. A signal. Even before Evie saw his eyes narrow in rage, she knew that was the wrong thing for the coven elder to say. His voice was ice cold fury when he spoke. "Correct on one of three counts, *putain*. I threatened your home because your protective spells were hiding *my* witch from me, which I consider to be a wrong done to me by the witches. But I would never hurt Evie. She's mine to defend. Mine to protect. And I will never let anything happen to her." He tilted his head down to Evie, lowering his voice so only she could hear his next words. "You know that, right?"

"In theory, yes. But you said we need to talk about why you had that folder, and I think we need to do that before I can fully believe that you want to protect and defend me." She pushed at his chest. "But before we do that, I need to talk to Chloe and the coven elders. I need to understand where I came from before I can go anywhere else with you." And, with a wave of her hands, she lowered the barrier blocking the other witches from coming near them.

Chapter 21

Evie

Barataria Preserve, Marrero, Louisiana

Cole didn't let go of her hand once while she helped clean up the area and reset the barrier spells to correct the damage caused by his entry. Even when the coven elders were giving him pointed glares and scared younger witches were crying when they saw him, he held her hand through it all. He seemed determined to see everything in their home, his eyes excited as they took in the uniquely styled living quarters, the orbs overhead—which had calmed from the blood-red scarlet hue to an orange glow that reminded her of the sunset—the roaring fire. No matter how much he looked at everything around them, though, his eyes always came back to her, his gaze almost a physical touch each time it landed on her. He kept up a low-level of commentary the entire time: seeing the youngest of the red witches playing with fire magic elicited an alarmed "holy contributing to the delinquency of minors Batman," whereas the sight of her home high in the canopy above them drew a worshipful, "goddamn" from him as he crowded into her, his semi-hard length pressed against her stomach while he swept a strand of hair behind her ear, his thumb lingering against her cheek.

Eventually, everything was set more or less back to rights. Sandrine easily got over her initial fear of Cole after she heard him humming tunelessly and was now following them closely. "So who are you?" she demanded from her place by Evie's elbow.

Evie heard something that sounded suspiciously like a chuckle come from the man at her side, but, when she looked over, Cole's face was serious.

"I'm Cole." He reached out the hand not holding hers to her little coven sister. "And who might you be?"

"I'm Sandrine. Evie's favorite sister." Sandrine placed her hands on her hips, pointedly not shaking his hand, and drew herself to her full height of a little under five feet, a stern expression on her face. "I'm her protector."

Cole nodded, dropping his extended hand without a word or any sign of awkwardness. "I'm sure you're very good at it." At Sandrine's sharp look at where Evie's fingers were tangled with his, he added, "I'm not going to hurt her, Sandrine. I would rather destroy myself than do that." He squeezed Evie's hand, almost as if he were trying to reassure her of the truth of what he was saying.

It seemed that Evie wasn't the only one who melted in the face of the man beside her because Sandrine's look became a little less harsh under Cole's sincerity. "Please promise me you'll take care of her," her coven sister whispered. "She's all I have."

"Sandrine," Evie scolded lightly. "You have the rest of the coven too."

"Yeah, but everyone else treats me like I'm annoying or silly," her beloved sister responded, eyes glassy with unshed tears. "You're the only one who doesn't."

Evie swallowed against the lump in her throat, tugging Sandrine into her side and resting her cheek against the girl's braids. Tears were blurring her vision at the damage—however unintentional it may have been—that the coven did to people they viewed as other, but she could still see Cole step out from beside her and kneel down in front of Sandrine. Even kneeling, he was barely shorter than Sandrine.

"Sandrine, I promise you," Cole said, voice grave and eyes unwavering on her sister's. "That I won't let any harm come to Evie, and I won't hurt her. She will always be safe with me."

Sandrine nodded, dashing away the tears running down her face, before lunging at Cole, wrapping her thin arms around his neck in a hug.

"Sandrine!" Hesteia shouted, and Sandrine jumped away from Cole like she had been slapped. "Get away from him!"

Her coven sister walked meekly to the coven elder, who shooed her away to the safety of the red witches' living quarters.

Evie glanced around, noticing that, sometime in the last several minutes, the clearing had emptied of everyone but her, Cole, the coven elders, and Cassandra, the coven's seer. Everyone's eyes were locked on her and Cole, their expressions ranging from intrigued to murderous.

Cole tugged her to him, one hand wrapped possessively around her waist.

Hesteia's lip curled at the gesture, but otherwise she didn't respond. "Shall we sit?" she asked politely, gesturing to the benches surrounding the fire.

They gathered around the fire, the coven elders and Cassandra on one side, Cole and Evie facing them. Before Evie could sit, though, Cole gathered her in his arms, settling her into his lap.

This time it seemed Hesteia couldn't help herself. "You know she's capable of sitting on her own rear, don't you?" Beside her, Thea tutted at her wife in displeasure. "No, Thea, Evie was fine without this man, but now he thinks he has a right to her."

Evie glared at the red witch. "How dare you presume to know what's best for me?" she hissed, her words dripping with venom. "When you've been lying to me all my life."

Hesteia's face fell. "I—I—I don't know what you mean," the usually composed witch stammered.

"Don't insult me by lying more," Evie snapped. "I know who I am. I've seen the records. I know that you took me from at least one loving parent who was looking for me." Her gaze narrowed on Chloe. "Chloe all but confirmed it earlier. I want to know why."

Chloe was curled in on herself, looking more frail than Evie had ever seen her, when she raised her eyes to Evie. "Darling, I know this must be... difficult."

Evie shook her head angrily. "I appreciate the attempt at sympathy, really I do, but let me just say that you have no idea how I'm feeling. In the last 24 hours, I've left the forest, found out I have a history you all never saw fit to share with me, discovered that the elders took me from a father who wanted me, and am capable of using magic on a level I never dreamed of." The air hung heavy around them as she came to the end of her list. "Before Cole arrived, you were going to tell me something, Chloe. What was it?"

"Speaking of Cole," Hesteia interrupted. "Could somebody please tell us who this man is to you and why he is here?"

Cole's head swung sharply towards the witch, but Evie responded before he could jump in with a profane rejoinder that would undoubtedly include some combination of the words "fuck" and "you." "No, I don't think we will, Hesteia. On the topics we need to discuss this evening, the man who came to find me and wants nothing more than to protect me isn't even at the top of the list. You know what is?" Although Evie's voice shook, it still rang clearly across the clearing. "My life. You've all hidden far too much from me for years. I want to know who I am. I want to know how you found me alone but somehow also didn't kidnap me. I want to know everything including why you all treated me with kid gloves, like I was a danger to the coven."

"My darling," Chloe whispered. "We never—we never wanted to treat you like you were any different than any of our sisters."

"Chloe, that doesn't tell me anything," Evie said coolly. Out of the corner of her eye, she saw a proud, fond smile tilt the corners of Cole's mouth. That one small expression gave her the push she needed to continue. "And while you may not have meant to treat me like I was different, you did, and you know it. I've known all my life that the coven treated me oddly, that it meant I wasn't like others in the coven, even disregarding everything else that you all have done." Beside her, she felt Cole turn slightly, squinting at her. "And whenever I confronted any of you about it, you all dismissed it. I need to know the truth. I deserve to know the truth."

Chloe lowered her head slowly, a tear rolling down her cheek. "You're right. But, Evie, it's not—it's not a happy tale, my dear. Your early years were... tragic. We found you when we were sourcing food... "

Chapter 22

Thirty-Two Years Earlier

Barataria Preserve, Marrero, Louisiana

Chloe slipped a hand underneath the plate-sized cap of the mushroom in front of her, a beautiful, plump Chanterelle that would feature marvelously in a dish. It was rare to find such a delicacy in this area of the forest; it was so close to a roadway, which, even though it wasn't regularly traveled, still meant very little chose to grow here. As an accomplished hedge witch who could commune with the plant life, drew her very magic from it, Chloe knew the car fumes and uneven sunlight coverage resulted in poor growing conditions for the little loves. She felt her way down the mushroom's root system, pushing it to extend further into the soil, encouraging its growth and propagation.

When she opened her eyes once more, the area was flush with mushrooms, waving happily in the breeze. She smiled down at them before removing the large Chanterelle she had first noticed. *What a wonderful evening*. She cheerfully tucked the mushroom into her bag, humming softly as she did so..

Behind her, a sharp cry pierced the quiet night.

Chloe spun, looking for Cassandra, the coven's seer who had come with her on the trip. The woman was shaking, the movement visible even from feet away. Running toward Cassandra, Chloe slipped her arms around her sister's shoulders in a tight embrace. "What's wrong, love?"

Cassandra's face was pale as she withdrew from Chloe's comforting hug and pointed towards the roadway silently. Chloe turned, unsure what to expect, but once she took in the sight before them, she recoiled violently.

A silent toddler, maybe a year or two old, sat on the ground beside the road. Her big stormy eyes observed the two sisters from a pale face beneath a shock of thick red curls. None of these were what had drawn Cassandra's attention, though—it wasn't odd for female children displaying magical abilities to be deposited at the forest's edge, even in this modern age.

No, the upsetting thing was that the little girl was splattered in blood, the crimson stains creating lace-like patterns along her pale skin. Next to the girl sat a black dog with three heads, each one bearing two ruby-colored eyes burning like embers as it stared distrustfully at Cassandra and Chloe.

On the other side of the toddler lay a dark-haired woman on her back, arms and legs sprawled inelegantly around her. A deep slash across her throat gaped like a second smile below her wider-than-fashionable plum-colored lips that would never rise in happiness again. Her life's blood pooled around her, soaking through her clothes and drenching her hair before it drained away into the forest floor beneath her.

"No," Chloe gasped, rushing toward the toddler and woman with Cassandra close behind.

The dog growled, a low-pitched warning. From several yards away, the witches heard a man's voice. Screaming. Scared. "Evangeline! Luanne? Where are you? Evangeline!" The voice held an edge of hysteria, fraying and scratchy as if he had been shouting for hours. "Please! Please don't leave me! Luanne, bring our little girl back!"

Chloe couldn't see him from where she and Cassandra knelt. As a prophet, Cassandra was inherently sensitive to murder victims—a more common occurrence in their forest than one might expect—so Chloe left Cassandra to retrieve the infant and figure out how to deal with the dog while she tended to the body. The woman's body hadn't even cooled; she must have only just died. She flinched back at the feel of unfamiliar power tangling around the woman's corpse. This magic felt odd. Old. Like nothing she had ever experienced. What in the realms could leave an imprint like that?

For the second time that night, Cassandra cried out. Chloe's head jerked up in response as her sister's face went slack, eyes unseeing, as she fell slowly to the ground. A prophecy. Garbled words, unintelligible to Chloe's ears, poured from Cassandra's mouth. Even the mutant dog seemed uncomfortable at the witch now lying prone in front of it if the way it let Chloe ease closer to her sister and the toddler without putting up a fuss was any indication.

Although she wanted to confirm her sister was alright, Chloe knew better than to touch Cassandra mid-prophecy. She knelt next to her sister, waiting for her writhing to stop while taking note of the one phrase that Cassandra kept repeating, sometimes in whispers, sometimes as an outright scream that Chloe was surprised didn't draw the attention of the man on the road: "The grave will find her; she is darkness. A lovely death. A deathly love." Fear trickled down Chloe's spine, but she maintained her vigil by Cassandra's side, one eye on the dog and infant.

Mere breaths later, Cassandra gasped, a rattling sound in the silent night, and sat upright. She jerked, hands outstretched, reaching desperately, blindly, around her. "Chloe!"

"I'm here, Cassie, my darling," Chloe replied, resting her hand on her sister's cheek. The dog remained at the toddler's side, silent but watching. Around them, the night had grown silent once more, the man's cries vanished into the stillness of the bayou. "Are you alright?" At Cassandra's shaky nod, she asked, "What did you see?"

"I—I—I—" At Chloe's urging, she paused. After a deep breath in, she tried again. "I don't remember much. I just... there was blood. So much blood. And fear and magic and something so... old that it didn't even have a name." Tears trailed down her cheeks. "The child. The girl."

"What about her, Cassie?"

"I don't know who or what she is, but she did this." At Chloe's questioning gaze, Cassandra clarified, pointing a shaking hand at the corpse lying just feet away from them. "That woman is dead by that little girl's hand."

Chapter 23

Evie

Barataria Preserve, Marrero, Louisiana

Evie's body was shaking, partially at the enormity of the coven's lie but mostly from disbelief. Shocked tears poured down her face. "I killed my mother?"

Cassandra shrugged a shoulder, the move shifting her long ponytail. "I don't know whether you killed her or not. I could never see that much of your history, although, trust me, I did try. So many times I tried. But all I could ever see—all I could ever sense—was blood and death and ancient magics. Nothing more."

"That's why you always treated me differently. Why you did all of those spells over the years." Evie sat up a bit straighter within the protective cage of Cole's arms. "What, were you worried I would turn on the coven?'

"No!" Chloe exclaimed, reaching out toward the girl—no, woman—she had raised. "No, we never thought of you as anything other than a sister! We loved you just the same."

Unease lay thick across the circle as the coven elders noticeably shifted. "No. You didn't." Evie stared at them in confusion. "Why would you lie to me now?

There's no benefit to lying anymore. Not after... not after everything that's happened tonight."

Above her head, Cole's voice rang out unexpectedly. "What happened to the dog?"

For the first time since her outburst, Hesteia spoke up. "You're the one who caused all of this, trespasser. We don't owe you any answers."

"No," Evie interjected frostily. "No, you don't get to pin any of this on him. Yes, I found out about all of this because of Cole. But this... you all were the ones who hid it from me for... " She trailed off as she tried to quickly calculate her age based on the barely remembered birthdate from the folder, but it was Cole who quietly supplied, "Almost 32 years." He folded her back into his chest when she began shivering again. "You hid this from me for so long. So you'll answer any question I have. Which includes any question that Cole may have since he's the only one here who hasn't lied to me my entire life. So answer. What happened to the dog?"

Chloe sighed deeply. "It just... vanished."

"What? How does a *three-headed dog* just vanish?"

The two women's shoulders shrugged in sequence, but Chloe answered for them both, holding Cassandra's hand while she did. "After Cassie woke up and told me what she saw—"

"What I could remember of it," Cassandra interjected.

"—What she could remember of what she saw," Chloe amended. "We were distracted. When we finally turned our attention back to you, the beast was just... gone. We were still reconciling that this innocent-looking child was responsible for a grisly murder, so, not only were we a bit shellshocked, but we were also more concerned with our safety than the missing dog."

As if Chloe's mention of the dead woman was a signal, Hesteia raised her eyebrows at Cole and commented mildly, "Mr. Aidoneus, you seem remarkably unfazed by the fact that our Evie may be a murderer. Why exactly is that?"

Chapter 24

Cole

Barataria Preserve, Marrero, Louisiana

As a well-respected attorney barred in three states and admitted to practice before several federal circuits, Cole was used to opposing counsels doing their level best to undermine him before the court. It was practically second nature for him to be constantly wary of unexpected attacks—physical or verbal—from any direction. So while the unexpected question from the witch in front of him didn't take him aback, the vitriol she spewed about his witchling, still curled in his arms and shaking, did. And the cruelty of her words triggered every protective instinct in his body. As Hayden often joke—usually to Cole's never-ending irritation— #lawyermodeactivated. "You forfeit the right to call anybody your anything when you casually call them a murderer over actions committed when they were a toddler who couldn't form the necessary criminal intent," he bit out coldly.

Chloe rebounded as if he had slapped her, and even Cassandra looked uncomfortable with his assessment.

Hesteia shook her head, though, glaring coolly at Cole. "Cassandra saw her association with that woman's death," she argued. "What does that make her if not a murderer?"

Evie shook harder in his arms, and he tucked her head into his chest, dropping his chin to nuzzle her hair. "It's okay, Angel," he murmured, rubbing his hand down her arm. The sleeve of the shirt she wore—his shirt, he thought viciously, possessively—was ripped from her earlier trek through the forest, and the torn fabric scratched harshly along his palm. "Don't pay them any mind." He pitched his voice low; his reassurance and gentle words were for her ears only. Not for these judgmental assholes. "You hear me?" His rage made his accent thicker than it had been in years. Her head nodded slightly, almost imperceptibly against his chest.

He pressed a kiss to her hair before lifting his head, the anger he felt flooding on to his face, quirking his lips into a rage-filled scowl. "If you love her as you claim to, you know that people grow and develop. You know that nobody is the same person they were in adolescence, and that's doubly true for when they were a fucking toddler." Ignoring Chloe as she sputtered denials he continued, "If you want to accuse me of something, go ahead and do it. But don't disguise it as an indictment of Evie for actions she doesn't remember and can't be held responsible for because, as we all acknowledge, she was a goddamn infant when they happened." Evie's fist clenched a bit on his shirt, but he didn't know whether it was in thanks for defending her or horror at what these women thought of her.

"Fine." Hesteia's voice rang out. "You want us to accuse you of something instead of attacking Evie? You want us to accuse you, a known invader of our peaceful home, of something? Very well." The flames wavered around her face, drawn by her impassioned outburst. "What interest do you have in Evie? Why are you not surprised by Cassandra's prophecy?" He blinked at her, and the witch's lips turned up in a victorious smile. "Are those questions clear enough for you?"

Cole's chest clenched. All excellent questions. But all had answers that Evie deserved to hear from him first. There was no way this conversation should be had for the first time in front of Evie's family, particularly when they had a vested interest in arguing against everything he had to say. He needed to get her out of here, so they could have that discussion together first. Alone. "I'm interested in Evie for a multitude of reasons, not the least of which is that our magic resonates in a way that none of you have seen before. Which also happens to answer your other question. My magical source is death. Evie is the only other person I've ever found who shares that source in any way." Disturbed murmurs rose from around the fire. From below, Evie's head tilted in an almost feline way that indicated just how closely she was listening to the conversation. "Any other interest that I have in her is between us. Strictly speaking, y'all have no right to unpack and pick at any part of our relationship." *Jesus Christ*. He was more upset than he thought if he was casually dropping "y'all"—a word he had been convinced he had purged from his vocabulary—in conversation.

"Death magic?" Thea asked, twining her fingers with Hesteia's as her eyes grew wide. "We thought that was a myth. Our lore doesn't speak of anyone but the old gods having death magic."

Fuck. Cole swallowed. They were starting to get far too close to the reality of it all, truths that were best shared privately with Evie first. "Well, Evie has it. It would explain how she was able to raise an attack against her mother when the woman was planning on abandoning her to the elements." It would also explain why a three-headed dog with burning red eyes, which he strongly suspected was Cerberus, had been protecting her at the forest's edge until he felt she was safe, but that was neither here nor there.

For the first time in several minutes, Evie spoke up. "Why did you take me in if you... " She lost the sentence to her trembling voice. "If you knew that I had murdered that woman. Why would you bring me home with you?" Silence reigned around the fire. "You could have endangered everyone. Why would you risk the coven that way?"

Chloe exchanged a loaded glance with Cassandra that Evie's tear-swollen eyes tracked. "What?" Evie demanded, sitting straighter in Cole's lap. "What aren't you telling me, Chloe?"

Chloe wasn't the one who responded, though.

"You were a little girl. We couldn't leave you to the bayou. You would have been eaten by animals or starved or died of sepsis, to name just a few ways you could have perished." Hesteia spread her hands, palms up. "So we lobbied the Witches' Council to allow us to take you in. After many tied votes, we finally received a unanimous vote by a narrow margin. They agreed to let us bring you in if we agreed to certain... requirements." For the first time during the evening, Hesteia's tone was tentative, her words carefully chosen. After all his years as a litigator, Cole recognized the tells when a person was trying to protect themselves or someone else: the hesitation, the stilted style of speech, the lack of assurance. He saw all of those signals in Hesteia, and he knew, in his gut, that she was dancing around even more unpleasant realities. "They wanted... to see what you remembered and ensure that the covens had someone to protect us. Someone who could... do what needed to be done if the need arose."

"Excuse me?" Evie sprang to her feet, nearly knocking Cole to the ground. "Are you saying that the Council agreed to allow me to stay so I could be your resident executioner? Am I hearing you correctly, Hesteia?"

At Hesteia's stern look, Cole rose quickly behind her. Whatever Evie had in mind, he was on board. If she wanted to leave, he would hold her hand as they walked away. If she wanted to dismantle her coven members with her death magic, he would pour his own into her and watch them scatter into ash on the wind. Whatever she wanted—whatever she needed—he would give it to her.

"We would never say that!" Chloe choked out. At Evie's mutinous snarl in her direction, she curled back into Cassandra's arms, crying softly.

"Is that why you've put me through memory reversions every year since I was pubescent?" Her voice was pitched low, vibrating in rage but controlled.

Even still, Cole went cold with fury. Memory reversions were a useful but deadly magical tool to bring forth a person's lost memories of their current and past lives. When used on a person whose memories of this and their previous lives were positive, it could reveal beautiful possibilities for their emotional and mental growth. But when used against a witch like Evie—a witch who was responsible for her own mother's death, who had at least one previous incarnation soaked in blood, death, and grief—it practically invited madness. It was a miracle Evie hadn't succumbed to a murderous rage in the absolute best case, a catatonic state in the worst. A growl echoed around the clearing. It took Cole several minutes to realize it was coming from him.

The witches clocked it long before he did, and he felt them begin drawing upon their magic to stall him.

Joke's on you, fuckers, the dark voice in his head whispered. *I can tear your world down around you and barely break a sweat.*

"As soon as I started seeing," she fluttered her hand in his direction, "Cole. As soon as I started hearing him. Having the nightmares. You forced me into reversions, no matter how much I begged and pleaded with you not to. Was it just so I could remember and become the Council's perfect little murder tool? Their failsafe in case something went wrong?" As her voice rose, the hanging vines started to sway as if called to her rage. "And you agreed to do the reversions every year just so you could bring me back to the coven with you, even though you knew how much pain those spells caused me each time we did them?"

At her pause, Cole jumped in. Evie hadn't mentioned the danger aspect of a memory reversion. Did she know just how much risk they had exposed her to with their continued use of dangerous magic? "Did you know?" he asked Hesteia.

"Know what?" Although her voice was level, Cole's ability to detect bullshit was finely tuned. And this lady was still hiding something.

"Did you know the dangers associated with memory reversions on someone with a bloody past?" He felt rather than saw Evie's back stiffen. Recognized the exact moment the words seeped into her consciousness. "Did you know you could have driven her to madness? Made her a shell of herself? Memory reversions are only intended for those whose lives have been peaceful. Were you aware of that?"

Silence followed his question. No one spoke until Chloe stammered, "N-n-no?"

"Are you asking me or telling me?" he demanded. This was the Cole Aidoneus that other attorneys hated to respect. This was the Cole Aidoneus he needed to be for his little witch right now. All of his life, his education, his experience, all of it was leading to this exact moment when he had to defend his goddess. This had nothing to do with who Kore had been to Aidoneus millennia before; it had fucking everything to do with the effervescent girl who had haunted his dreams, who had been his steadfast companion his entire life. He had been in love with her since he was twelve, craved his devastatingly beautiful dream woman since he was old enough to feel sexual desire, and, in the 24 hours since he met her in person at the construction site, had felt more... everything, every emotion under the sun, from lust to joy to rage to possession, then he had ever felt before her. And these witches in front of him could have destroyed her with their reckless magical experimentation, annihilated his opportunity to ever meet her outside of his dreams. "Did you know that you could have magically lobotomized Evie with your memory reversions?" To a one, the witches gaped at him, each of their jaws dropping. "Yes or fucking no. It's a simple question."

The sound of crickets chirping was the only sound in the clearing.

"So either you knew and did it anyways because the Council told you to," he continued. "Which is despicable and, I would argue, abusive. Or you had no idea and used magic that you didn't understand because the Council told you to, which makes you reckless, both with Evie's life and the coven's safety. So which is it?" At their downturned faces, he scowled. "You know, I don't really need an answer, but I'm fairly certain Evie deserves one."

Mere steps away from him, Evie was practically vibrating in fury. The blue hue of death magic tinged her eyes, but it seemed like she was maintaining a thin line of control. "Yes. Evie does deserve an answer," she said in a dark tone that simultaneously spiked a bolt of arousal through him and scared the shit out of him. Around them, the trees were practically quivering, their limbs and the moss dangling from them thrashing to get to her. The vines wrapped around their trunks slid to the ground, slithering snake-like to get as close to her as possible. "Tell me. Now."

The witches weren't stupid, but they were definitely alarmed. Hesteia eventually responded for all of them. "The Council... we knew. And we took... a calculated risk."

At her words, the world around them exploded.

Chapter 25

Evie

Barataria Preserve, Marrero, Louisiana

The world was obscured by blue fire. Evie could feel the decay, the utter death in the miles of bayou around her, running through her veins, the same way she felt the quicksilver tug of the moon. Around her, she heard howling, felt the wind whipping past her as the trees flailed their branches wildly and the vines cracked like whips around her. Deep in her core, she felt an intense wrenching as deadly flora and fauna she had only ever seen in books spontaneously bloomed from the forest floor around them. She could hear screaming too, now that she thought about it. But none of it could touch her. It all felt removed. Distant.

A hand cupped the back of her neck, the touch instantly calming the madness inside of her and causing her to fall back into herself. She turned, only to see Cole's eyes shimmering a mystical blue in his lean face. "Cole," she whispered.

"Yeah, Angel," he murmured as she wrapped herself around him once more, her arms locking behind his neck, his hands dropping to rest on her hips. The movement was so natural, so unbelievably familiar, that she found herself lulled into some sort of comfort, even though she was still wrecked inside. "What do you need?" She knew that voice, had heard it more days than not over the course of her life. Never in her wildest dreams did she imagine that not only was its owner real, but that he would be standing beside her looking at her like she was everything he had ever wanted.

She barely recognized her own voice, sultry as it was, when she responded. "I need you, Cole. I need you to get me out of here, away from here. Take me with you."

"Are you sure?" He rested his forehead against hers as if they had all the time in the world. As if they weren't surrounded by her coven, who had lied to her, blindly endangered her, for all of her life, who were readying for battle as the forest around them roared with Evie's rage. "There's no going back from this, baby. If you leave this forest with me, I'm not gonna be able to let you go. It's gonna be you and me together. And there are still things I need to tell you that could... change how you see me. Us."

Evie paused, considering everything he was saying and the subtext underlying it. "Have you lied to me?" He shook his head. "Are you going to kill me?" He shook his head again, violently this time, the blue magic in his eyes flaring with his response. "Once you've told me whatever you need to, are you going to hide anything else from me?" Another head shake. "Are you going to experiment on me without my knowledge and complete consent?" He hissed out the words, "absolutely fucking not," in response to the final option as if the thought was so abhorrent to him he couldn't bear not to respond verbally. "Then I am already safer and more cared for with you than I have ever been here."

"And you're sure?" He braced his thumb against her chin, tilting her face to his. "I need to hear you fucking say it."

"I'm sure." Her eyes slid shut in pleasure at his touch before opening again, taking in the growing excitement on his face. "Take me with you, Cole."

He crushed his mouth to hers in a quick, possessive kiss. "I promise I will be everything you ever need me to be. You won't regret this, *mon ange*." Wrapping his arms around her waist, he picked her up easily and, with no thought to the witches surrounding them, strode quickly out of the circle, past the protective spell the elders had cast to keep other coven members from overhearing and the small groups of witches peering curiously at them.

Sandrine gawked at Evie and Cole and sprinted towards them. "Evie, where are you going?" Her forward progress was halted by Hesteia, who had followed them out of the circle and grabbed one of the younger witch's thin arms to stall her run towards Evie. "Evie, no!" Sandrine cried pitifully, struggling against Hesteia's grasp, while Cole walked them towards the edge of the clearing. "Evie, please don't go!" Her final cry was punctuated by sobs and then a small gasp of pain as Hesteia dragged Sandrine backwards forcefully.

"No," Evie snapped, her temper close to redlining once more, summoning a massive tree branch to swing at Hesteia's head. The elder ducked just enough that the hit missed her, but her grip loosened enough that Sandrine was able to wriggle away and run towards Evie. "Don't you *touch* her!"

Cole hadn't stopped, looking down at her without slowing. "We'll come back for her. We'll come back for anybody, for everybody, that you want, but we need to get out of here. They're not going to be distracted by your arboreal foot soldiers for much longer, and they aren't going to want to let you leave now that you've shown a proclivity for the very magic and knowledge that the Council wanted out of you."

Evie glanced over at Sandrine, who had just caught up to them as Cole paused at the cusp of the clearing. "Little sparrow," she said, her lip trembling. "I have to go."

Sandrine stared at her, tears rolling down her face. "Then let me come with you. I'll be good, I promise."

"I know you would, but now's not the right time." She cupped her sister's cheek and pulled her close, kissing her forehead gently. Behind them, the trees raged, limbs lashing out and drawing the attention of the elders. But Cole was right; the distraction wouldn't hold them forever. "I'll—we'll—come back for you. For now, keep your head down and be safe. The coven will take care of you the way they always have until we can get you." Tears dripped down Sandrine's face, and Evie's heart ached at the sight. Her sister meant everything to her, and choosing to leave her home permanently, to leave her sister behind even temporarily for the man holding her and the foreign magic flooding her veins practically ripped her in two. "This isn't forever, little sparrow."

Sandrine's gaze snapped back to hers, familiarity flashing in her eyes. "It's just for now," she finished, a watery grin splitting her face at the saying they broke out whenever Evie went exploring without her.

"We'll come back for you," Evie repeated, kissing Sandrine's forehead again. "Go back to the elders for now, though. It's alright."

Sandrine stepped away, Evie's hand falling from her face, and backed towards the elders, her eyes never leaving Evie's. "I love you, Evie," the little girl whimpered.

"I love you too, Sandrine," she called just as her sister turned and walked back to the red witches' living quarters, passing the elders by like they were nothing.

Cole kissed the top of her head, dragging her attention away from Sandrine's retreating form. "We'll come back for her, Angel, and we'll take her with us if she wants to go. But now... " Cole jerked his chin at the protective circle ringing the clearing. "When I tried to get in, I got tased. You got any tips on getting us out of here?"

A hysterical giggle threatened to spill from her lips as she prepared to leave her life—her family—behind. "They don't care about who leaves, just about who's getting in. And they wouldn't have the time or power to extend the protections against us exiting, given all of—" she gestured around them at the forest that was still very much alive and raging to defend her. "—This."

Chapter 26

Cole

Barataria Preserve, Marrero, Louisiana

"Alright, then." Squaring his shoulders, Cole stepped a foot forward towards the barrier, bracing himself for the shock of pain. His toes went through like the protective measure didn't exist. No damage whatsoever. "Fuck, yeah!" he shouted gleefully, plunging them through the magic into a world where the forest was still except for a mysterious rushing sound above them. He tilted his head back, glancing towards the night sky, as he continued forwards. His eyes widened as he took in the cause of the noise.

The rushing sound was bats. Thousands upon thousands of bats flooded the air, practically blacking out the moon and stars. He nudged Evie, nodding upwards. "I've lived in Louisiana all my life, and I've never seen anything like that."

"Did you know that Western cultures consider bats to be evil omens and harbingers of death whereas many countries in Southeast Asia consider them to bring good fortune?" Her question was contemplative, her voice low—probably still back in that clearing with her beloved coven sister—but her eyes shone with happiness as she peered at the colony of bats flying away from the witches' clearing with singleminded focus.

"Which do you think it is?" he asked, sauntering towards where he had abandoned the car earlier that day, calmer now than he had been on his initial tear through the forest. They had spent the last day in varying states of arousal, irritation, and fear; if someone had asked him what meeting the woman from his dreams would look like, nothing that had happened since the construction site would have made the list of options at all. None of it mattered, though, now that Evie was in his arms, chattering about folklore of all things. Their situation was far from perfect, but listening to Evie made the world feel right. He wanted nothing more than to hear her opinions on superstitions. On everything.

She chewed her lip. "I don't know. I like to think it's a bit of both. That they're bearers of good fortune to those who intend only good but harbingers of death to those who would cause harm." A laugh bubbled from her, a welcome sound after the tearful exchange with Sandrine. "A bit vindictive, isn't it?"

Cole shook his head, long legs eating up the distance. "I don't think so. Seems more pragmatic than vindictive." It also sounded very much like the perception of death the goddess of the underworld would have, particularly one who balanced death and life-based magic sources the way she did. "Do no harm and all that Hippocratic bullshit."

"*Primun non nocere*," she murmured.

"You know Latin medical creeds?" He couldn't have been more shocked if she had invited him to participate in a blood orgy on the full moon.

With a small chuckle, she finally turned away from the bats still careening overhead, her eyes meeting his. "Which part of that is surprising to you? The Latin? The medical knowledge?"

"Honestly, a little bit of both."

"I like to read and learn." Gaze growing distant, she mumbled, "After each memory reversion attempt, I was always so sick. The elders never told anyone what specifically was wrong with me, mostly because we're generally forbidden from using magic like that against another witch. So my sisters were warned to stay away because an illness could potentially devastate the coven. We don't have the natural immunity that most humans do, so they were careful to keep their distance. Well, all of them did except Sandrine. She would sneak to the doorway of wherever I was laid out and sing to me. But the elders would shoo her away pretty quickly." She was quiet for so long he thought she had fallen asleep until she added, "I was so lonely and, well, books were pretty much my only consistent companion during those times. Besides you, of course." A fleeting smile touched her lips before vanishing.

His fingers tightened on her thigh in rage. All of his control was now dedicated to not destroying the sadistic fucks—her coven elders and the Witches' Council alike—who put his witchling through near-constant torture in an effort to, what, fulfill some ancient prophecy? Preserve and protect their way of life? Despicable.

Unfortunately, she misread his fury as exhaustion. "You don't have to carry me all the way," she said, unraveling her arms from around his neck and pushing against his chest.

Although he was still furious about her kind's reckless disregard for her life, his caveman brain—the part of him that thought it was an excellent idea to throw Evie against one of these trees and fuck her until she couldn't even remember all the pain those assholes had put her through—must have taken over his speech center because, before he even thought about how to respond, he was growling, "Angel, you're not going anywhere, so put your damn arms back around my fucking neck."

"But I know that I can't be light to carry." She waved her hand across her body. "Although all bodies are beautiful, even I know that I have more body than some of my sisters. Plus, you expended a huge amount of magic earlier, which must have made you tired. You can put me down; it's okay. I won't be offended."

It looked like growling was the only form of communication available to him anymore. "First off, your body isn't just beautiful. It's a goddamn work of art that I want to worship for the rest of fucking time. Second off, that 'more' you're talking about isn't heavy to carry. Third, and I'm not gonna say it again," he rumbled, staring into her piercing eyes, now back to their normal stormy color. "Put those arms back around my neck right now."

She looked shocked then pleased, a slow smile breaking across her face as she followed his order. "Are you always this bossy?" Even though she was being a tease, her arms were back around his neck and the happiness on her lips was finally reaching her eyes. After everything that had happened, that was all that mattered. Well, that was what mattered *now* at least. Later, he would punish her for her sassy mouth.

"Nah." He leaned in, nuzzling the delicate shell of her ear before nipping at her earlobe. She shivered against him, and his rationale for not finding a good tree stump to bend her over went pretty damn fuzzy. "Usually, I'm much worse." It would feel so amazing to sink into her beautiful little body, better still to feel her come all over him as he filled her up. He shook his head, trying to bring his thought back into focus.

A list. That's what he needed. A list of all the reasons he couldn't get distracted. One: they were on the run from witches who had committed unspeakable acts against his Angel. Two: he didn't know whether the coven would follow them or if they even could follow, given the green army Evie had raised in her magnificent ire. Three, four, and five, respectively: she had just discovered a devastating secret about her past, left her beloved sister behind—even if it was only for the short term—and abandoned her entire life to come with him. It was not the right time for *anything* sexual. For now, he needed to be sensitive. He needed to remain focused. He needed to stop fucking staring at her breasts testing the fabric of the shirt she had borrowed from him.

Cole gulped, forcing his eyes away from her perfect tits, and kept his pace consistent as they reached the field he had raced through only hours ago. Even though his life had changed irrevocably in that time, the world around them didn't seem to have gotten the memo since it still looked exactly the same. After checking both ways, he crossed the untraveled street, more careful now that Evie was in his arms, and passed into the tavern parking lot.

When he had parked, his car was the only one there. Now, though, the lot was crammed full of trucks, reliable old beaters, a few motorcycles, and even a local patrol car. The tavern was hopping, music and the scent of good food and cheap beer pouring through the open doors.

"You hungry?" he asked as her stomach growled audibly. *Something something, the care and feeding of his woman was probably important.* The voice in his head mumbling this advice sounded annoyingly like Hayden. In his head, he rolled his eyes at the future lecture he would undoubtedly receive from his best friend about caring for his woman; Hayden's recommendations were better suited to scene aftercare than general caretaking. "We should probably put a bit more distance between us and the forest, but we can stop to eat if you need to."

"Do you have food at your house?" After constant movement over the last 24 hours, an unexpected abduction, and some truly overwhelming revelations, he could hear her voice wobbling with tiredness, practically feel the exhaustion emanating from her. His chest squeezed uncomfortably at the realization that, without him, today would have just been just another normal day for her.

"Yeah, baby," he chuckled. "I got food at home." Balancing her weight on his hip, he used his free hand to depress the car's handle before sliding her into the bucket seat. She relaxed into the deep seat, drawing her knees to her chest.

When he dropped into the driver's seat, she was already watching him sleepily, one hand extended towards him. Fuck, he loved that she reached out to him like she hated being separated from him for the amount of time it took him to walk around the car. In all his thoughts of what his reaction to his fated wife would be, this possessiveness, this complete loss of irrational thought about her, around her, never crossed his mind as a possibility. Evie was turning his world completely upside down, and he hadn't even fucked her yet. He still remembered the taste of her on his fingers after she came, though, the feel of her thighs resting over his shoulders... at the memory of her body garbed only in his black sheets, her legs wrapped around his waist, her eyes hazy with desire, arousal fired through him. He opened his mouth to say something—he wasn't exactly sure what—but his throat seized around the words when he got a good look at her.

His witch's eyes were closed, though, her hand resting against his arm. As much as he wanted her, as much as he imagined that she would love waking up to him inside of her in any way, there were far too many things they needed to discuss, including consent, safe words, and, oh, that little thing called their shared destiny, for him to dedicate himself to hearing her screams at this moment.

As he started the engine, he couldn't help but lean over to kiss her forehead lightly. As he backed out of the parking spot, he couldn't stop himself from brushing a rogue auburn curl behind her ear, his hand lingering against her cheek. And as, for the second night in a row, he drove back to New Orleans with Evie by his side, this time by her own choice—a fact that made him want to throw a whole ass party—he slid the delicate hand resting on his arm down to his own, so he could intertwine his fingers with hers for the short ride home.

Chapter 27

Evie

Garden District, New Orleans, Louisiana

Evie woke slowly, unsure where she was but more comfortable than she had ever been in her life. Not only did it feel like she was floating on a cloud, but she was warm, her body tilted on its side with a wall at her back. *Wait.* Her eyes fluttered open in confusion. *A wall at my back?* She tensed, suddenly noticing a firm band around her waist as well, and tilted her head slowly towards whatever was holding her.

A soft rumble rose from behind her, and she finally peeked over her shoulder, straining to see in the pre-morning light filtering through the curtains. As her eyes adjusted to the muted light, Cole's face came into view. Ah. So the wall was Cole, the firm band his bare arm wrapped tightly around her waist.

She should probably wriggle away, put a little distance between them. For the life of her, though, she couldn't bring herself to do that. Her eyes slid closed as he tightened his grip on her, tugging her further into his body and nuzzling her neck in his sleep. She would only sleep for... just... a... bit... longer...

When Evie woke again, the midday sun was streaming in through the windows. Although she recognized Cole's bedroom, the man himself was nowhere to be found. The sheets on the other side of the bed were rumpled and pulled back just enough that she could see where his body had rested behind her. She brushed her hand over the imprint of where he had slept, a small smile lifting her lips. She should probably go find him in the sprawling house, but his bed was too comfortable, and she was so relaxed. After two days of pure adrenaline and emotion, she needed to feel safe. And that's what she felt here, wrapped in these absurdly soft sheets, surrounded by proof of Cole's existence. Protected.

Even last night, she found herself reaching out to him in the car. She hadn't missed that little nugget; when she needed comfort, she wanted him. She just wanted to touch him, know that he was there and, for the moment, hers. Potentially a side effect of having shared a good portion of her life with his eyes and voice, but—and she couldn't quite kid herself after spending hours with him—it was the reality of him too.

Unsettled, she shook her head in an attempt to dislodge the thought. When it refused to leave, restlessness rose inside her that she could feel this strongly about a man she had only known in person for two days—no matter what experiences came before—and she sat up, unsure what she was doing but knowing that she needed to do something other than sit here alone with her thoughts. The silky sheets puddled to her waist as she did so.

From the door, a sharp inhale sounded. "Fuck me." Evie looked up to see a shirtless Cole resting against the doorframe, holding a cup in his left hand, an awestruck expression on his face as he ogled her bared chest. Holy gods, did he look perfect like that. "I'm regretting the hell out of getting up now."

Her smile, which had vanished when her thoughts started racing, teased at the corners of her mouth again. "Well, you can still get back in. Nothing's stopping you." With him standing feet away from her, all of the fear, the panic she had been feeling seconds before, slipped away like it never existed.

The smirk fell away from his mouth. His face grew serious, and he walked over to her. "Sorry, Angel. We got a few things to talk about before I can feel okay about not letting you out of that bed for the next several days." Because he couldn't seem to help himself though, he swooped down and kissed her firmly, nipping at her bottom lip before passing her a spare t-shirt. "I ordered groceries this morning, so the pantry's full again. I'm making us some breakfast. Come on down when you're ready."

Evie watched him walk away, turning over the emotions of the last few days. She had been abducted. Found out her mystery man was real. Discovered her life was a lie. Kind of run away from home. She winced. In theory, she was now homeless after everything that had happened with the coven, although she imagined Cole would argue that fact. She missed her coven sisters—Sandrine especially—so badly it was like a physical ache. Yet, in spite of all of that, she was still happy, fulfilled in a way she hadn't felt in years. It seemed likely that at least part of that was due to Cole's now very real presence in her life.

Shaking out the neatly folded shirt, she pulled it over her head and rose from the bed. Now that she wasn't distracted either by Cole's touch or overwhelmed by a need to run, little details in the bedroom stood out to her that she had missed the morning before. Unlike his study, there was very little to distinguish this room as being regularly used, save for the bed. No art on the walls or personal decorations, save two small framed photos leaned against the wall above the fireplace across the room.

She crossed to the fireplace to take a better look at the pictures. In one, Cole was next to a man with light brown hair, curious icy eyes, and a sleepy smile, his arm looped around the other man's shoulders in a friendly half hug as they stood in front of a tall building covered in glass. Tracing her fingers over Cole's face, Evie took in the differences between the Cole of today and the one in the photograph—he had fewer laugh lines, and his hair was cut differently, but otherwise there was very little distinguishing him from the man currently cooking her food downstairs.

Her gaze shifted to the other photo, this one a rudimentary charcoal drawing of two teenagers holding hands: one bore thick black hair and green eyes and, she was fairly certain, was supposed to be a young boy, the other was a young girl with curly hair to her waist and wide eyes locked on the boy next to her. She picked up the portrait, looking closely for an autograph. Not seeing one, she cradled the frame to her chest and left the room, carrying the portrait downstairs as she followed the delicious scents making into the kitchen. As she entered, fragrant spices perfumed the air, and the sizzle of whatever was cooking on the stovetop filled the room.

Standing in the middle of it all was Cole. Facing the counter in front of him, he had his back towards her, sweatpants slung low on his hips and the fitted white shirt he'd thrown on sometime between when he left her in bed and now showing every shift of his muscles as he went from pan to pan. Almost as if he could feel her, he glanced over his shoulder, grinning widely before his eyes shifted down to the frame in her hands, His smile dimmed slightly.

Evie slid the drawing onto the counter, the young couple in charcoal facing upwards, and lifted her gaze to him. She knew her question was splashed across her face.

Cole shrugged in response, his jaw tense as he responded. "I was a lonely kid. Didn't have many friends because I couldn't control my temper, and weird things happened around me that couldn't be explained. Even the kids who didn't outright hate me avoided me. I couldn't figure out why I was different from everybody else. But you. You were there with me in my dreams almost every night, no matter how weird or dangerous or angry I was. You... " he traced a long finger over the girl's likeness, his fingertip skimming lightly across the glass. "You were my fucking everything, Angel. In a lot of ways, you saved me long enough for me to actually meet you." Swiveling briefly towards the stove to check the pan's contents, he said in a thoughtful voice that didn't even sound like he knew he was speaking aloud, "But I never could have imagined the reality of you, *ma petite sorcière*." His drawl was thicker than it usually was, the Cajun dialect rolling off his tongue as he turned back to her.

Evie couldn't breathe. This man was overwhelming every single defense she had. His honesty tugged at her heart, and she knew she had to tell him her truth too. "You did the same for me," she whispered, her voice so low she wasn't sure he could hear her over the sound of cooking food. "A lot of the time, I couldn't remember much, and what I could was jumbled—" His eyes flashed that neon blue at the mention of her memory reversions, a sign that she now knew meant his magic, emotions, or both were close to the surface. She pushed past the reminder quickly. What she had to say to him now was far more important than the dangerous magic she had been exposed to for years. "But I never forgot you. All those times I couldn't leave my home because I was sick from the magic they'd poured into me, I saw you. I heard you. You were the only person who talked to me while I was isolated. So I may have been your everything, but you were my whole world, Cole." A tear traced down her cheek as she remembered the crushing loneliness and fear of lying in her bed, her body shaking as it purged the foreign magic and ancient lives inside of her; all while the jumbled violence and memories and screams that no one else could hear filled her head. "I was so scared that you weren't real. Nobody else knew you existed—they couldn't see or hear you. And I could already see things and people that nobody else could... What if you were just another vision?" Her voice trembled, and, through her tears, she saw Cole come into her space.

His arms snaked around her waist, and he pulled her into him. "I can't say a lot with absolute certainty, but this? This right here? Me, us? I'm real. This is real." He gripped her chin, tilting her head up to face him. "And, baby, I'm not going anywhere. I'm here for as long as you'll let me stay."

The intensity shining in his eyes practically flayed her alive. She couldn't keep staring at him, but she couldn't bring herself to look away either. Cole as a person, not just her visions of him but everything that made him the man in front of her, holding her, was so much more than she could have ever dared dream in her home high among the trees.

He kissed her cheek gently before setting her away from him. "Now go sit down and eat some food. And stop looking at me like you want to eat me alive, or I won't be held responsible for what happens." At her pursed lips, he shook his head at her. "Nope, you walking around the house in my clothes is dangerous enough. I'm not strong enough to withstand that look on your face too. Go sit." He nudged her towards a stool on the other side of the island.

Sashaying around the bar to one of the tall plush chairs nestled underneath the countertop, she made sure to add some extra sway to her hips as she did so. A low groan rolled through the room when the shirt slid up her thighs a bit from the movement; she smothered a smirk, pretending not to hear it. When she finally took a seat, he was shifting uncomfortably, his eyes still locked on where her ass had last been. "What?" she asked innocently.

"You know exactly what, you little tease," he snipped as he slid a plate loaded with food in front of her. "I had no idea what you forest dwellers ate, so I made a little bit of everything." Although there was a bit of a snicker in his tone as he said it, his face remained completely serious.

Evie tilted her head, observing the plate. There were a number of things she couldn't identify, something that looked like bread although it was thicker than a normal slice of bread with a custard-like exterior and... berries! Those she recognized. She confidently popped one in her mouth, nearly moaning at the first taste of food she'd had in almost two days. *Oops.* Looks like she hadn't suppressed it enough if the pained look on Cole's face was anything to go by. "Okay. So I've never seen some of these foods. What are they?"

His eyes gleamed in amusement while he shoveled food onto his own plate. "I knew you didn't have a standard diet! Let me guess. Vegetarian? No. Gotta be vegan."

She snorted at him. "You're enjoying this way too much. But I guess you could say we survive on an extremely raw diet. Lots of vegetables, fruits, mushrooms, whatever we can find in the forest." She picked up the thick piece of bread, wrinkling her nose at the thick feeling of whatever was covering it under her fingers, and took a bite. It was sweet and fluffy, the taste so decadent her mouth started watering. "This is delicious! What is it?"

"It's *pain perdu.*" Cole placed a glass filled with what she recognized as syrup in front of her. "Usually people put syrup on it."

As he finished loading his own plate before taking a seat next to her, Evie drizzled syrup over the *pain perdu*, taking care not to use too much. Syrup was an extremely rare delicacy for the coven, so she didn't want to waste any of it. Instead of using her hands, she cut a small neat bite of it with the fork and knife by her plate. She gasped as she slid the cut piece of syrup-soaked bread into her mouth, the maple flavor complementing the texture of the dough. "That's amazing. I've never tasted anything like it!"

"It's my *maman's* recipe," he said, picking up his fork. "Even though I don't remember much about her, I know she was an amazing cook. She used to cook for everybody in the neighborhood, just spending all day over her gumbo pot, stirring and cackling like the Cajun witch everybody jokingly accused her of being." She hummed in amusement at the description. "So when I got my own place, I started teaching myself how to cook so I could make her recipes."

Evie took another bite of her *pain perdu*. "How old were you when she died?"

"Four. My dad died not long after, and I went to live with my Uncle Charlie. My dad's brother." Cole shoveled something that looked like a potato with some sort of meat in it into his mouth. "He's a good guy. You'll like him."

Evie slid her hand across the island, grasping his. "Even if your uncle was amazing, it doesn't make losing your parents any less painful."

Cole smiled, a wry twist to his mouth, before he picked up their joined hands and pressed a kiss to the back of hers. "Thanks, Angel. It was a long time ago, though." Loading his fork up with his free hand, the fingers of his other one still entwined with hers, he lifted the food to his mouth then paused. "Do you eat meat?"

Head reeling from the sudden turn, Evie barely followed the conversational leap enough to respond. Once she caught up, she barely stifled a giggle. Sitting across from the man who had haunted her for most of her life, and he was asking about her eating habits. "Um, yeah, of course we do. But we're careful to only take the lives given to us."

"Um." His eyebrows shot into his hairline "'Given to us.' What in the sweet name of *Pet Sematary* does that even mean?"

She crinkled her nose at him in confusion at the reference but ignored it in favor of an answer. "Well, we have witches who can commune with animals and talk to them all the time. Animals that are older or dying will give us their bodies in exchange for a painless death."

"Who grants them a painless death?" He looked intrigued, but his eyes narrowed when she started fidgeting. The silence grew thicker, more potent, as she remained quiet. Cole's gaze grew more intense with each passing second that she didn't answer his question. The sharp clatter of his fork against the plate broke the palpable tension. "Angel, who in the coven was responsible for giving those animals the painless death they sought?" At her whispered, "me," his lips tilted down in a scowl, and he stood quickly, his chair legs scraping against the floor. "Come with me," he ordered, extending his hand to her.

Without a second thought, she took his offered hand and followed him out of the kitchen and up the stairs. Little had changed since her illicit snooping the day before, but having Cole in the house with her sucked all of the air out of a room, particularly since he was fuming, practically radiating fury, although at what or whom she couldn't guess.

Chapter 28

Cole

Garden District, New Orleans, Louisiana

They were halfway up the stairs when the landline rang. The thing had never rung before three days ago, but apparently everybody had the damn number now. Cole choked out a snarl and ignored it, walking towards his study with Evie tucked into his side, still fuming at the revelation that the coven had made her—and only her—responsible for taking the life of forest creatures. Thankfully, after three rings, the shrill chime stopped. He had just opened his office door when the phone rang again.

"Should you get that?" Evie asked, glancing up at him.

"Nope. It's probably just a telemarketer." He ushered her in. "They'll stop eventually." Blissful silence followed his words, and he smirked in victory.

"If you're sure—" Her skeptical response was cut off by the beginning of the third wail of the landline. She giggled at what he was sure was the fully mutinous expression on his face. "It sounds like they're not going to give up. Go. Answer the... telemobile?" Her lips pursed into a cute moue as she struggled for the right name for the phone. "Whatever. I think that's what it's called." Pushing herself to tiptoe, she kissed his cheek gently and then dropped back to standing. "I'll be here when you get back."

"Fine." He went still as the line went quiet for the third time. "Or—" ^*Nope.* There it went again. "Fuck, fine." He gave her a light kiss, which quickly turned into something dark and passionate, Evie pinned against the wall with one leg around his waist, before he tore himself away. "I'll be right back, Angel."

She nodded, her eyes glazed, her mouth slightly parted.

Fuck. It took everything he had to make himself walk away from the beautiful, aroused woman still leaning against the wall like it was the only thing holding her up. "Don't go anywhere." With one final look, he stalked out of study to the master bedroom where the phone was still jingling merrily like the antiquated cockblocking hunk of junk it was. He snatched the handset out of the cradle, brought it to his ear, and snapped, "What?"

A long pause followed his terse greeting. "Well, hello to you too, my boy." His uncle's voice finally came through the speaker, a low laugh underlining his words. "Did I interrupt something?"

Cole pinched the bridge of his nose and closed his eyes. "Hey, Charlie." This was going to take longer than expected. He hadn't briefed Charlie sufficiently on anything that had happened that night at the construction site. And he sure as shit hadn't told him about openly declaring war on the Barataria Coven, at minimum, and the whole witch population, at maximum. *Jesus Christ.* He dropped into the chair beside the end table where the phone sat. "No, you didn't interrupt anything. At least nothing that can't be picked back up after the call."

"Hmm." Charlie hummed into the phone. "I'm sure your lady friend for the day can wait."

"What?"

"Cole, my boy, you're not getting any younger." *Ah, there it is.* This was Charlie's old song and dance, so well-practiced that Cole could practically recite the speech back to his uncle verbatim. "I know that marriage isn't something you want, but you need to at least think about the greater good. If you and the reincarnate don't take your seats in the Underworld and put the shades littering the human world back where they need to be, the world and everyone in it are going to be destroyed. Including you and whatever woman you've chosen for the given night. It's time to grow up."

Cole's head snapped up in surprise. That was new. Usually, Charles was circumspect about Cole's social reputation. Formal, awkward, and slightly disapproving, yes, but never attacking. He opened his mouth, but his uncle wasn't done.

"You don't have to love her or even be loyal to her, but you do have to find her. You have to do what needs to be done. You and your fated wife are the only ones who can."

Even the idea that he would be unfaithful to Evie was disgusting to him. An angry knot formed in the pit of his stomach at the thought of touching any other woman or, worse, any other woman touching him. "Well, I got good news for you," he interrupted his uncle, who had moved on to his more practiced lecture materials on duty and honor.

"This is what you were born—" Charles stopped. "Wait. What did you just say?"

"I said I had good news."

"Oh?"

"Yeah, I, uh, I found her." Cole leaned forward, resting his elbows on his knees, the headset still pressed against his right ear. "That night I went to the preserve. She was there."

There was a brief second of silence from the other end. Then his stoic, formal uncle let out a wolf whistle so loud it echoed in the speaker and reminded Cole of every one of his soccer games that his uncle had ever attended when he was a kid. "That's wonderful!" Charles exclaimed. "Who is she? Where is she?"

"Her name is Evie," Cole replied.

"The Dyeus girl?"

"Yeah." Cole inclined his head in confirmation, even though his uncle couldn't see him. "We confirmed it last night." He rubbed the side of his head, trying to figure out how to broach the subject of what she was with Charles.

"How do you know she's the reincarnate?" His uncle's tone was curious.

Cole froze. How did he not prepare for that question? He had expected it, sure, but the surprise phone call meant that he couldn't explain it with any dignity.

"Cole?" Charles asked. "Did I lose you?"

"No. No, I'm here, Charlie." He pinched the bridge of his nose again, hoping the sharp pressure would force his brain to work more quickly than it was. But no dice. "I know it's her, because... you remember that girl I started dreaming about when I was a kid? The one I asked you about."

"Yes... " Charles trailed off thoughtfully. "The little red-haired girl you were convinced was real?"

"Yeah, her." Cole bit his cheek then let it rip. "She's real."

"What do you mean 'she's *real*?'" Charles sounded condescending even through the phone. "Cole, she was a dream."

"No," Cole retorted. "No, she wasn't. And I know because she's sitting in my study right now."

Charles' voice dropped. "Are you sure it's her?"

"More sure than I've ever been of anything in my life." Cole glanced at the open door. "I know her—the way she looks, the way she sounds, her laugh, everything about her—better than I know myself. It's her." The final word pitched up in excitement, a fact that his uncle caught on to almost immediately.

"You're happy," Charles observed. "You're happy it's her."

"Yes." His answer was succinct. "You know how I've always felt about that girl. How badly I wanted her to be real. And now she's in my house with me, and everything feels right. Death magic is one of her sources too."

For the third time that afternoon, his uncle surprised him. "Holy shit." The profanity was quiet but still audible.

Cole tugged the phone away from his face and stared at it in shock. He could count on one hand the number of times he had heard Charles swear.

"That's wonderful, my boy." Charles finally spoke again. "I'm so happy for you that you found your Evie." Clearing his throat of the emotional gravel, he continued. "You said she's with you now?"

"Well, she's in the study, but yeah, she's home with me now." His heart thumped in excitement at the idea of them making this *their* home rather than just his.

"Does she know who she is to you?"

"Not yet." Cole scraped a hand through his hair, his foot tapping unconsciously against the floor. "I was just about to tell her when you called." He dropped his voice. "But I need some advice."

"Oh?" The surprise from the other end of the line was palpable.

"Yeah, oh." Cole chuckled. "I don't remember some of the particulars of the prophecy—" Charles let out an exasperated groan that Cole couldn't help but snort at. "Like I don't remember how exactly we open the Underworld."

"Now don't you wish you listened all those times we talked to you about your fate?"

"Yeah, sure, Charlie. Whatever you say." Big eye roll to that one. "Can you help me or not? I want to tell her everything. I want her to choose me, and I want the choice to take the crown to be hers as well. And I can't do that without having all the information."

"You really care about this girl, don't you?" Charles pondered softly.

"She's everything to me," Cole replied bluntly. "I want her to have everything she's ever wanted. Which means that this, all of it, me, the crown, and all of the immortality and other royal deity bullshit that comes with it, has to be her choice. So... will you help me or not?"

"I'm proud of you. I'm so proud of you, Cole, and your father would be too." Charles cleared his throat once more. "The texts say that the reincarnates will open the Underworld through... " Here, he paused. Coughed. "Through—" Another louder cough.

"You need to go get some water, *nonc*?"

"No," Charles barked. "No, I'm fine." Another pause and then he finished in a rush, "The reincarnates open the Underworld through sexual congress."

"I'm sorry. What?" Cole blinked rapidly. Like that would help him process what he had heard. "We have to have sex to open the gates of the Underworld?"

"Yes." Charles sounded relieved that Cole hadn't asked him to repeat himself. "Yes, precisely." His voice dropped. "To completion."

"Fuck's sake, Charlie." Well, there was no way he was ever going to forget that horrifying combination of words said by the man who raised him. Had Charlie ever even had sex? He was inclined to guess no if he referenced coming as 'to completion.' Cole shuddered again but pushed forward. "What if we were to have sex before she made her decision? What would happen then?"

"Well, the prophecy isn't all that precise regarding motivations or decisions," Charles answered, back on solid ground now that he was talking about family lore rather than sex. "But I would imagine that any sexual congress—" His voice dropped low again as he said the words. "Would trigger the opening of the Underworld."

Cole's mouth dropped open, and he stared at the wall in alarm. He had all but been inside Evie at least three times in the last two days, and, each time they touched, it got more difficult to stop. If she wasn't ready to accept the responsibility of the Underworld, if she wasn't ready to let go of her home, her sisters, her *life* the way it was before they found each other... He groaned. *Fuck.*

Chapter 29

Cole

Garden District, New Orleans, Louisiana

After saying goodbye to Charles, Cole hung up the handset and stared unseeing at the bed in front of him. Evie's scent still lingered in the room, which made thinking even more difficult than it already was with the erection from hell. He wanted nothing more than to touch her, bury himself in her. But if Charles was correct—and it was almost a guarantee that he was—then they needed to slow things down. A lot.

He dropped his head into his hands and shoved his fingers through his hair. On a good day, he wasn't particularly patient; on a day when he had a warm, aroused Evie in his arms... impulsivity was the name of the game, and patience was nowhere to be found. It got more intense when he factored in his own years of sexual fantasies about her and the ones he would bet his house and firm that she had about him too.

With a loud groan, he started working through what about his plans had to change for the day. He still needed to tell her about the Moirai's prophecy about the two of them, which could easily make or break her choice. It was a big decision for a normal person to tie themself to another in a standard human marriage that only lasted for one life. Factoring in the immortal life span they would both have if they accepted the throne made her choice all that much more difficult and impactful.

He leaned back, drumming his fingers on his thighs distractedly. There was no doubt in his mind that he had already made his own decision. Although most of his thirty-five years were spent pushing back against a destiny he had no choice in and navigating magic and memories he never asked for, his professional life was unbelievably fulfilling, and he had no complaints about his personal life up until recently.

Now, though, with Evie sitting down the hallway, he felt complete in ways he never had before. His experiences with happiness before her weren't even close to what he was feeling now; he was completely mystified that he had ever mistaken his previous emotions for fulfillment. So he was all in with her, no question. Now it was just a matter of getting the witch in his study to agree. The way to do that was to spend time with her and make her realize just how much better her life could be with him in it forever.

Cole's eyes popped open on an idea. Time for him to actually use this landline himself. He picked the handset back up and dialed the number for his personal assistant, Daeira, a truly terrifying woman in her mid-forties whose striking features and olive skin kept luring in husbands, who kept succumbing to mysterious deaths. Husband number four was still alive and kicking for now, but who knew how long that would last.

"Mr. Aidoneus' office." Her three-packs-a-day voice answered the phone after the first ring.

"Hey, Dae, it's me," he replied.

"Where the hell are you, Cole? There's a pool going on in the office that you're dead since you've never missed a day of work in your life."

"Don't be dramatic," he scolded lightly. You would think co-founding and -owning the firm would get him at least one day off in a decade, but, based on his employee's responses, they expected him to work 24/7. "I've missed days befo—" he trailed off, realizing he couldn't remember the last time he had called off work.

"That's right. You can't even finish the thought." Daeira was annoyingly smug through the phone. "So since you're clearly not dead, what do you want? Do you need me to overnight your passport to Mexico again?"

The one time he got drunk and accidentally crossed the border while sleeping off a bender in a random woman's backseat, and he never heard the end of it. Didn't matter that it happened almost a decade ago or that Hayden had been right there with him; everybody only focused on Cole's role in the whole thing. He glared at the phone. "No. I don't need you to send my passport to Mexico. Also, just remember that I sign your paychecks, Dae, so let's maybe feign respect?" He ignored her snort of ridicule and shook his head at the complete lack of control he had over his assistant's behavior. "I'm safely at home, but I need you to do me a favor. *Non*," he interrupted when she started to speak. "Don't try to guess what it is. I'm full up on being insulted for the day."

"Hmm." Daeira hummed disapprovingly into the phone. "Well, then. What can I do for you, Mr. Aidoneus?"

He rolled his eyes. The only time she acted professionally was when Hayden was around, and they were trying to prank him. "First off, say hi to Hayden for me." An audible male snicker sounded from the other side of the phone. "Second, take me off speaker." He waited a beat. "Am I off speaker?"

"Yes, spoilsport, you're off speaker. You ruin all the fun."

"I'm so sorry for making your job a little less fun. Whatever will you do now," he drawled. "But I do actually need you to do something for me."

"Fine. What?"

God, if she weren't so efficient and good at her job, he would have fired her ages ago. "I need you to have some women's clothing messengered over here."

The other end of the line went dead silent. A pin could have dropped in the firm's office, and he would have heard it through the speaker. "I'm sorry. You need what?"

"You heard me," he said.

"Is this some sort of code?" Daeira asked. "Are you being held hostage again? Do I need to call the police? Tap against the handset twice if you're in danger."

"Don't be absurd. I wasn't being held hostage the last time. It was just a one-night stand gone wrong. She only had a starter pistol, and the whole thing got blown way out of proportion."

"Fine," she sighed. "Do you have her size?"

He had gotten an eyeful of Evie over the last few days, so he was fairly certain he could spitball measurements. "I'm guessing a 36-inch chest, 29-inch waist, and 38-inch hips, but get clothes up and down one size from those measurements, just in case I'm wrong. Whatever doesn't fit, we'll send back. And shoes."

"Is there any type of clothing in particular you need for this woman?" She paused delicately. "Lingerie, perhaps?"

"Jesus Christ, Dae." Cole scraped a hand down his face. "Just basic clothes for the next few day: jeans, shirts, dresses, underwear, shoes, whatever."

"And when do you need this clothing for your mystery woman delivered?" His assistant's words dripped with suspicion.

"An hour from now. Two at the latest." A slight inhale from the other side relayed Daeira's displeasure. "We represent corporate customers across the damn city, including two major clothing retailers that I can think of off the top of my head, and the ones that we don't, we have relationships with through our fundraising efforts. This shouldn't be a big ask."

"Well, if I'm to supply your lady friend with a multi-day wardrobe from an as-yet unknown retailer in less than two hours, I need to get off of the phone with you, Mr. Aidoneus." Daeira's voice was frosty; he made a mental note to send her something in appreciation. "I'll send an intern with whatever I can find."

"Thank you, Dae," he responded gratefully, dragging out the last vowel on her name. "I owe you."

"By last count, you owe me several hundred times over, Cole," she sighed, her tone thawing a little. "I'll get this taken care of, and then I'm taking the rest of the day off, and you have no problem with that."

"I have no problem with that," he parroted back without hesitation. "Thanks again."

"Umhm," was all his assistant said before hanging up the phone, leaving the dial tone ringing in his ears.

Now that that was taken care of...

"Cole?"

At the sound of Evie's voice, he glanced up, only just realizing that he had probably been sitting here for upwards of half an hour. She was standing in front of him, still swimming in his t-shirt, her head cocked in confusion. That primal part of him that wanted her no matter what her choice may be was encouraging him to embrace the legacy of abduction associated with his family. His rational side was demanding that he lay out every ounce of the prophecy and history, so she could make an informed decision. The result of this internal battle? He froze in place, brain grinding to a halt, his mouth open but no words coming out.

Evie blinked at him and came a bit closer. "Is everything alright?" When he didn't respond, she came closer, resting her hand on his shoulder. "Cole?"

Her touch jerked him out of his self-inflicted freeze. "*Ouais*, Angel." He nodded, standing and tucking her into him once more in a smooth movement. "Yeah, I'm good."

She melted into him, tilting her head back to glance up at him. "Who was it?"

"Just my Uncle Charlie and then a quick work call to sort out some stuff so I can spend the day with you."

She ducked her face down into his chest but not before he saw the smile take over her face, the happy blush spreading across her cheeks.

An answering grin spread across his own face. It took everything in him not to jump up and down in glee that spending time with him was an exciting prospect for her. Instead of letting out an undignified screech of premature victory, he simply went, "Let's go back to the study. We got some things to talk about." She darted a quick concerned look at him, but he smiled down at her as he escorted her down the hall. "Nothing to worry about, *mon ange*. Just unveiling the last secrets I ever intend to keep from you."

Her smile came back, brighter than before and so beautiful he almost tripped over his feet. Shit, he didn't deserve a single second with her, but that wasn't going to stop him from trying to get her to commit to him. He was ruthless in every other aspect of his life. It took on diabolical intensity when it meant keeping his witch by his side.

He kept his arm around her as they walked into his study, and he rifled through the built-in bookshelves bordering the couch facing his desk until he found the tome he was looking for. It was one he had only pulled off the shelves—by choice, at least—a handful of time. Usually, his uncle or one of the Moirai had to bully him into reading it. The time had finally come to open it willingly since he needed it desperately to explain to the woman he wanted more than anything that, not only should she choose to stay with him, but she should give up her entire life as she knew it to do so.

Cole tugged Evie towards the couch and sank into it, pulling her into his lap, resting the book across her legs. Her eyes flicked down to the text that had changed his entire life and was about to change hers. From the outside, it looked like nothing special. The cover was worn leather, cracked in places, burnt in others; the pages were mismatched with different colors, textures, and widths, resulting in tattering and ripping to the wider page edges while the slimmer ones were tidy. It bore no title or author.

Inside, though, was a whole 'nother story. The book held the comprehensive history of the Aidoneus family, every solitary scrap of information about the prophecy that drove his entire life.

"Should I be concerned?" Evie finally broke the silence. "I'm pretty sure there's blood on the spine of that book. I'm wondering whether you've waited all this time to tell me that you're going to make me a ritual sacrifice?"

Cole snorted out a surprised laugh. "You caught me," he joked, and she smirked at him, eyes alight with mischief. It would be all too easy to get distracted by her, so he pulled away from his urge to talk to her, flirt with her, and nodded back down at the book. "Last night, your coven asshole asked me what you were to me." He ran a hand down her back. "And it was a good question.

A great question, actually. But it wasn't her story to get before I shared it with you."

"What exactly is the story, Cole?"

"I, um... " He trailed off. "I don't know if I'm gonna tell it right. I've never had to be the one to explain any of this to anyone. And definitely not to someone as important as you."

Her forehead furrowed, and she cast him a confused look. "Just tell it the best way you can, I guess. I'm not picky, and I'm not going anywhere."

"So." Cole exhaled. Tangled his hand in the ends of her long hair as he set the book to the side. If he read straight from the book, it would be wooden. Hollow. He needed to tell her this in his own words. "Sometime tens of thousands of years ago, the Titans, immortal gods with elemental powers, dominated the human world. Of them, Cronus was the most powerful, so much so that he ruled over both the other Titans and the humans with an iron fist. He left blood and destruction in his wake. Even weaker Titans weren't wholly safe from Cronus' rule. It was perfectly normal for them to go missing and never be heard from again. After millennia of bloodshed, though, Cronus found Rhea, the Mother of the Earth, and forced her to marry him. Years of rape later, she bore him four immortal children: three female, one male. But there was a prophecy that one of his children would overthrow him, and Cronus became convinced the only way to stop it from coming true was to eat all of them."

Evie lightly touched his arm. "If this is the story of the Titanomachy, I've read it."

"It is, but you haven't heard it this way." He shook his head, still running his fingers through her hair thoughtlessly. "What really happened. The myths got it wrong, Angel. Yes, Cronus ate the four children Rhea gave him, but, for some reason, he was so disgusted that she only gave him one male son, Hades, to eat that he whored her out to his generals. She bore two sons, one to Atlas and one to Hyperion. Cronus was so paranoid that he ate Poseidon, Atlas' son, but Rhea, now wise in the ways of her husband, secreted Hyperion's son, Zeus, away to Crete and gave Cronus a stone swaddled in cloth to eat instead. Once he was of age, Zeus became obsessed with seizing the power the Titans held, raising an army of their surviving children to do so. He ingratiated himself to Cronus, eventually becoming his most trusted advisor. Zeus worked for him for years. Eventually, one night, Zeus slipped Cronus an emetic that caused him to vomit up every child he had ingested. They never stopped aging after Cronus ate them, though, so they were all adults, and they were pissed. Partially 'cause, y'know, they were eaten, but mostly because they were stripped of their immortality by Cronus' stomach juices." Cole chuckled grimly. "Apparently being digested by the god of fucking time isn't conducive to maintaining immortality, who knew."

"Although they were mortal, they had the powers that they were born with and were powerful allies for Zeus, who was still immortal because he had never been eaten. Cronus' biological children, Hades, Hestia, Demeter, and Hera, and Poseidon, Atlas and Rhea's child, all joined forces with Zeus and his army to overthrow the Titans. After ten years of war, just absolute destruction, Rhea's children were successful in their mutiny. But they needed somewhere to keep the Titans who were still alive. And that's where the Underworld came in."

"As the only ones with power over earthly and celestial creation, Zeus, Poseidon, and Hades joined forces to create the Underworld and, in it, Tartarus, a hellish cage for the worst of the worst. They banished the surviving Titans there so that they could never escape and wreak havoc upon the world. Then, the three of them sent the millions of deceased souls occupying the human realm to the Underworld. The only problem is that there was no organization to the resting places in the Underworld, so the good were expected to live right alongside the evil. None of the Olympians could come up with an effective way to share the duties and no one wanted Underworld oversight, so, not only did it remain unguarded, but the souls inside weren't kept in places that aligned with how they conducted themselves on Earth."

"Within months, the situation in the Underworld reached a fever pitch. The souls lost their absolute shit being that close to Tartarus and the Titans; even the good go bad after so much exposure to the worst, most depraved souls. With nobody guarding the Underworld, they escaped into the human world, unleashing absolute rage across creation. The world was dying as the escaped souls, what we call shades, devastated everything in their path. Crops, the environment, even humans themselves."

Cole breathed in. This next part was make or break. "In the intervening time, Hades had taken on his mortal name Aidoneus. He met a powerful witch named Kore, the daughter of his sister, Demeter. Kore held unbelievable power over flora and fauna, and he was smitten with her the moment they met. The two fell in love, but Demeter wouldn't support their marriage, so, one night, they ran away together. Demeter, of course, claimed that it was a kidnapping, but Kore chose Aidoneus from the beginning. After the shades escaped, the Olympians decided that somebody should probably be overseeing the Underworld. Aidoneus' strength lay in death magic so, when Zeus, Poseidon, and Aidoneus decided which regions each of them would rule, it was only natural that Aidoneus take ownership of the Underworld. That meant capturing the roving shades, returning them to the Underworld, and establishing a living system within the realm to ensure the good received their rewarding existence and the bad... well, the bad were taken care of in the way most fitting to them."

Evie was listening closely, her back ramrod straight. Her gaze was unflinching on his, and he knew the gears were turning in her mind as she puzzled through the story he was telling her.

In spite of the nerves destroying his stomach, Cole continued. "Aidoneus told Kore she could leave, but she chose to stay. Chose a life of chaos with him rather than any straightforward existence they could have apart. When they assumed the role as the royals of the Underworld, they took on the proper titles—Hades and Persephone. Kind of asinine, but it was a branding thing more than anything else. Together, they began to slowly force the shades back into the Underworld after ensuring there were safeguards in place so they couldn't escape again, including Charon, the gatekeeper, and Cerberus, their trusted three-headed hound." A slight gasp emerged from the witch in front of him, but he was reaching the end now, so he powered through. "They did this for years, aging as the mortals did, only able to achieve immortality once all shades were returned to the Underworld. During one of their scouting missions, they were attacked. Not unusual, but the shade had insane powers they'd never seen one use before. It slaughtered Aidoneus as he held Kore and then brutally murdered Kore as she wept over her love's corpse. Before she died, though, she cast a curse using Aidoneus' blood and her own power, ensuring the return of their memories and powers to a couple in the future so they could reunite in some lifetime and finish what they started."

Deep breath in. Deep breath out. *Time to share the biggest piece of information.* "When I was young and I started dreaming about death and war, my family suspected that I was Aidoneus' reincarnate. When they realized that my magical source was death, it became almost certain. You showed up in my dreams around two years after that. My family and our supporters spent years trying to find Kore's reincarnate, but she wasn't prophetically tied to a family like I was." He bit his lip. "The same day we met that night at the construction site, my uncle brought me the file on you. You met all the prophesied markers, he thought, and, given the proximity of your mother's death to the forest and your father's allegations of magic, you may have survived and been taken in by the witches. I had to meet you, though, because the only way to truly know whether you were the reincarnate was to see if you shared an affinity for death magic."

"When I got to that forest... well, you felt what happened that night." He took it as a good sign she was still in his lap. *But who the fuck knows?* It wasn't like there was a manual for telling the woman you planned to spend the rest of your life with that she was the reincarnation of a murdered goddess. "You were the woman from my dreams. I never hoped that you could actually exist, although I wanted you to be real more desperately than I ever wanted anything. That was a huge coincidence on its own, but then you had an affinity for death magic. And you've seen me almost all your life."

"Cole... " Her voice was breathy. Uncertain. Absent from her tone, though, were fear or anger.

He looked deep into her stormy eyes. "It's you, Angel. You're Kore's reincarnate. You're my fated half in every way that could ever matter. You're the one who's meant to rule beside me in the Underworld for the rest of our days. That's the choice you have to make. Whether you want to accept that fate or not. But I need you to know something first." Cole took another deep breath.

"I've spent more than half of my life with Aidoneus' memories, more time than that with his powers, but I'm not actually him. I'm just... me. I don't have his emotions or his feelings for Kore." Her lips were parted as she stared back at him, whole worlds in her deep, silver eyes. "So when I tell you that I want you next to me because you are my goddamn everything, Angel, I'm not telling you that as Aidoneus to Kore. Or as the future king of the underworld. I, Cole Aidoneus, am telling you, Evie, that I want you in every fucking part of my life. And whether we take our rightful seat ruling the underworld together or not, I don't give a fuck. I just need you with me. That's the story, baby." Dropping his hands to the couch, he nodded. "Whatever you choose to do next is up to you."

Chapter 30

Evie

Garden District, New Orleans, Louisiana

Cole stopped touching me. In the wake of more life-changing news, that was the only thing Evie could think about. She should definitely have an opinion on the story Cole had shared. She should have some extremely important thoughts of her own to discuss. But, even though intellectually she knew these things, her brain kept cycling through only one thought: *Cole stopped touching me*. And what was worse? She knew exactly why he had stopped touching her. He wanted her to make a choice without his touch influencing her. Not that that was going to work. He was going to have to forcibly remove her from his lap if he wanted to avoid touching her.

She tried to shake herself into rational thought, but that one repetitive phrase remained.

"Angel?" Cole's voice brought her back. He still sat motionless under her. "You got thoughts on... any of that?"

"So when you told me you were a reincarnated god." Her voice trailed off. "That was... real? You weren't just being self-important?"

Cole snickered at her question but pulled himself together quickly. "First off, if I could have gotten out of this prophecy years ago, I would have. It's a huge burden for a kid to have around their neck. I never wanted to be royalty. Second off, I don't need to try that hard to be important."

"So all of it's real?" Evie asked softly. After everything in the clearing, all of their time together, there was no way that he was crazy or it was coincidence. Which meant that the gods of legend were real.

"Yeah, it's real. I wish it weren't. That we could be normal together, no pressures besides me being an idiot with the romantic intuition of a goat."

"Why did you tell me everything?" Seriously, that's what she was asking? Why he was being honest with her?

Based on his slightly raised eyebrows, he was also confused. "Why did I—wait, are you asking why I told you the truth?"

She wrinkled her nose but nodded even still. "It sounds like you need me for you, but that there's this whole other component. Why would you tell me any of this if you could just keep me here with you and surprise me with the rest?"

He gave her a deep scowl. "Because when you stay with me—and you *will* stay with me, Angel—I want it to be because of me. And if, beyond that, we choose to rule—I want it to be because you chose to do that too. I don't want to trick you into *anything*." With a sigh, he continued. "And there are going to be a lot of people who know the magical lore surrounding us. I never want you to feel like you were ever a person I was 'stuck with.' You're here with me because I can't fucking stand the idea of you *not* being here with me, not because of some damn prophecy."

"But Kore's curse. She did that to reunite their memories and powers, but you said it was also to finish what they started." She was going to stay with him, of that she had no doubt. Yes, she loved her sisters and her life in the forest, but she had a feeling that anything she felt for this man would make the change bearable. But she wanted to know everything first. No lies, no half-truths. "What does that mean for us?"

Cole scrubbed his hand over his face. "We would have to do a lot. We would have to access the Underworld, which has been sitting for millennia. No one can access it, either entering or exiting. Hell is empty, and all the devils are here." He heaved a small almost laugh at the Shakespeare quote. One of her favorites, if she was being honest; of course her mystery man would use it in conversation. "We would be the king and queen of the Underworld, tasked with setting up a court and a living system down there. And we would have to retrieve all of the shades. We could enlist help to do that, but we would have to bring back every single shade that escaped way back when plus every soul that has died and stayed on this earth for millennia. It's a massive undertaking."

"What does accessing the Underworld mean?"

"Without a deity leading it, the Underworld is, for all intents and purposes, closed for business. So, right now, nobody, including the souls of the recently deceased, can enter or exit the Underworld. It's just there. The king and queen must take their rightful place, vow their lives to the throne." Cole saw the question cross her face before it left her mouth.

"How do they do that?"

Evie saw him struggling with the answer, almost caved and let him get away without telling her, but didn't. Eventually, Cole spoke once more, but it was a mumble. "What? I couldn't hear you." Raising his voice slightly, he tried again but still... only an incomprehensible mashup of words. "Try again. This time clearly, Cole."

Clenching his teeth, he gritted out his response. "They consummate the relationship."

"They consummate the relation—" Her mouth dropped open as she realized what he was saying. "You're saying that the key to opening the Underworld is to have sex." A nod. "And if we have sex, then the Underworld just . . . magically opens up?"

A shrug was her response. "I think we're already seeing the effects of us being close," he commented. "The earthquakes are too weirdly timed to be anything else."

"They've only ever happened when we've been together." She turned over the idea in her mind, squinting as she puzzled it out. "Is that the Underworld, what, welcoming us home?"

"I honestly don't know," he responded. "We're the first since Aidoneus and Kore that it would recognize as its rightful rulers. There's basically no rulebook except the old texts and, no offense to my ancestors, but they're pretty fucking useless. It's a lot of guessing, most of the time. Although Charlie is usually good at interpreting these things, especially whether my ancestors sanitized stuff while on their puritanical bullshit or not. Like, one of my ancestors said that marriage was a requirement to take over the throne, but it didn't line up with anything else, so we threw that one away as nonsense. Sex, though. That's always a requirement."

Evie tangled her fingers together. She would feel so much better if Cole was actually freaking touching her for this discussion. "So in every scenario, us having sex will open the Underworld? That's why the earthquakes are happening when they do?" She paused. "They're happening because we're one step closer to taking on the roles?"

He shrugged. "That's my best guess. I confirmed with Charlie that sex for any reason will do the trick, which, by the way, was a hysterically uncomfortable conversation to have with the man who raised me." She giggled. "But I don't actually know about all the lead-up stuff since I've been, y'know, chasing you through forests and shit." A smirk tugged at the corners of his mouth, and his voice lilted up playfully. "You know I got a job, right, witchling, that isn't stalking your pretty little ass through the forest?"

"Well," Evie responded, trailing off. She knew what she wanted to say. She knew she wanted Cole's hands on her, especially if they were having a conversation about their future. "If you're going to talk about my pretty little ass, you should probably have your hands on it, right?"

Cole's eyes lit up, but he groaned, almost like he was in pain. "I can't believe I'm going to say this, but my hands need to stay off that perfect body of yours until you decide." At her slight snort of disbelief, he grimaced. "I'm trying to do this right. I don't want to distract you. This decision is huge, and I want you to feel like you have a choice in all of it. I really do." He grew serious once more, his face stark in its intensity. "But let's be clear: your choice is whether we take our seats as rulers of the underworld. You made your decision to stay with me when we left that clearing together."

In a second, Evie's mirth vanished. "So, in the forest, when you said me leaving with you was it? That there was no coming back from it. You meant it?"

"Every fucking word, Angel.

"So why did you stop touching me, Cole?" she asked. "If I made my choice—and I did because I left my coven with you after you told me what that would mean—why would you stop touching me when you gave me a choice?"

"I didn't want to distract you or sway you or anything."

Leaning forward, Evie nuzzled his face, whispering a kiss across his cheek. "Cole, you are unbelievably distracting, but your presence is not prohibitively debilitating. I—"

Her voice cut off in a yelp as he slid a hand under her ass and gripped a cheek tightly. "If you can think straight while I'm touching you, I must not be doing this right." He traced his thumb across her lips, tugging down her lower lip slightly with the tip of his finger before pulling his hand away with an angry sound. "You need to think about this one, Angel, and think about it hard. We can decide not to rule. We can pass off the reins to somebody else. But it's a long and hard process, and it means the Underworld would be exposed while we try to find somebody to take the throne. Beyond the difficulty of finding somebody who wants to do the job, it would be kind of like the mafia don leaving their post. If they give up their position of power, their replacement will always think they're going to try and take it back. Same thing goes if we abdicated. The myths are pretty clear that the gods are a paranoid bunch."

"Cole." He was offering her everything she had ever wanted. To be someone's first choice. To be with someone who wanted her, would choose her over everyone else. "I want to be with you. Whatever that looks like. However that looks."

"*Ma petite sorcière*, I want that too." He bit at his lower lip, his head tilting back against the couch. "More badly than you know. But I don't want you to feel pressured into anything."

"I don't," she said immediately, but he wasn't done.

"I want you to take at least the day to think about it." He lifted his head, his gaze intense but steady. "You've had a shitton of trauma in the last few days, and this is a huge fucking decision."

"Do you not want me?" Her mouth trembled at the idea.

Cole blinked once. Then again several times in rapid succession. "What?"

"You said that we would be together no matter what and the only question was whether we would be ruling the Underworld. If we're staying together, but we're not ruling, then... what, are we just not going to have sex? Ever?"

"Fucking hell." A low groan rolled out of his mouth. "Of course we're gonna have sex, baby."

"Then why are you so reluctant to touch me?"

"Because—" His expression turned ferocious, his arms locking around her waist as he leaned into her, his grip the only thing keeping her from falling to the ground. "I would crawl inside of you right now and stay there for the rest of our fucking lives, prophecy and duty and destiny be damned. Once I'm inside of you, though, I know I'm never going to want to pull out of that tight cunt of yours."

She gasped at his filthy words, already so turned on by what he was saying that she couldn't think straight.

One arm unlocked from her waist, and he gripped her hair, rocking his hips against her ass. His hard length settled in between her cheeks as he tugged her head back. His eyes flashed. "So don't get it wrong—the only reason I'm not fucking you right goddamn now is because I want you to make your decision regarding our rule without *any* pressure." He pulled her head back further. Nipped at her neck before licking the slight sting away.

She was panting, practically writhing in his lap, and his breaths were ragged against her throat.

"Trust me when I say that, as soon as you know what your choice is, regardless of what it is, I'll be ripping off whatever you're wearing and bending you over the closest piece of furniture."

A shrill ring echoed through the house. Not the same sound from before but a different higher pitched one.

"Now, though, Angel." His emerald gaze was still far too piercing—so much so Evie almost couldn't look him directly in the eyes—but Cole sat up enough to put some space in between their bodies. "I've got a surprise for you."

Chapter 31

Cole

Garden District, New Orleans, Louisiana

"Mr. Aidoneus?" A gangly early-twenty-something kid carrying a handful of branded bags stood on his doorstep, looking more concerned than he probably should at being face-to-face with his employer. "Daeira sent me with all of this."

"Yeah, kid, c'mon in and set it down." Cole winced when he realized that he should probably know the intern's name but definitely didn't. He only knew him as "that kid who fucked up the appellate brief's formatting, which the paralegals had to stay late to fix." Honestly, calling him "kid" seemed less rude than calling him an imbecile.

The intern walked in, his head swiveling around to take in what he could see of the house. "It's a nice hou—holy shit."

Cole's hackles raised at the worshipful tone he heard in the kid's voice, his head cranking around so quickly that his back cracked. In seconds, he saw what had caused the response: Evie bounding down the stairs, wearing nothing but his shirt. The kid's eyes were glued to her curves so lovingly framed by the worn fabric. Fury burned through his veins that this barely grown asshole was ogling *his witch. How fucking dare he*? A growl rolled out of his mouth, but the little prick wasn't paying attention to the fact that his employer was about to murder him.

Cole stalked past the kid to Evie, shoulder checking him hard enough that he staggered. With the intern's attention diverted, Cole wrapped himself around Evie, pushing her into the wall and pressing a forceful, claiming kiss to her lips, one that left them both breathless and Evie's eyes glazed when he finally pulled away.

The kid was still staring at Evie, eyes wide as dinner plates.

I'm going to scoop this fucker's eyes out with a melon baller. Magic was flooding through him rapidly. Every passing second, he lost track of a bit more of himself and the rationale for exactly why it would be a bad idea to murder some kid in his foyer. His vision was blurring when a small hand rested delicately on his chest, a soothing stroke of familiar yet foreign magic rubbing alongside his.

"Cole." All Evie said was his name. Just his name in a soft tone meant for his ears only. She might as well have shouted it for how much it caught his attention.

Cole's legendary temper was still redlined, but his magic faded enough that he wasn't seeing the world in vibrant shades of blue. When he finally spoke, his voice was distorted with rage. "Set the bags down, and get out. When you get back to the office, pack your shit up—you're fired."

"But—"

"I thought I was pretty clear, kid. Get the fuck out." He heard a tiny laugh from the region of his chest, but when he looked down, Evie's face didn't have a hint of a smile on it.

The kid—Cole was fairly certain his name was Dylan, now that he thought about it—dropped the bags and sprinted out of the house, barely remembering to close the door behind him.

"So that was your surprise, hmm?" Evie peered up at him, the smile she had been suppressing breaking through. "Scaring the absolute life out of a child because he ogled me?"

Cole growled at her, pressing her back into the wall. "And I would do it again."

She laughed, her face breaking into an open expression of pure joy to accompany her bright, happy sound currently lighting him up inside. "I'm yours, handsome. I know it. That kid knows it. Mother of witches, the corpses across the street know it." The hand still resting on his chest slid up to cup his cheek. "You have nothing to worry about."

He rolled his head to the side, kissing the inside of her palm. "I'm well aware that I have nothing to worry about from your end, Angel, but it doesn't make me want to rip their entrails out any less just because they won't get anywhere with you."

Evie licked her lips. "That level of Neanderthal shouldn't be attractive, but it is. Whatever. If you have to gut somebody for looking at me, just do it in a place that's easy to clean and where I can't see it, I guess?" She glanced around him at the stack of bags laying haphazardly on the floor, courtesy of the now long-gone intern. "So... what's in the bags?"

"That's actually part of the surprise," he said, taking her hand and walking her into the entryway. "They're clothes for you."

She tilted her head at him in inquiry.

"Just enough to get you through the next few days until I can take you shopping for real clothes that you like." He gathered the bags by the handles and picked them up in one hand, leading Evie back up the stairs to the master suite and setting everything down on the chaise lounge in the dressing room. "If anything doesn't fit, we'll take it back."

"Why do I need clothes?" Evie asked, eyebrows raised.

Dumbass. Should have led with that. "That's the other part of the surprise." Nerves threaded through him as he realized that he was about to ask the woman of his dreams out on a date. "I wanted to take you out. Like on a date. If you want to go." Where the hell was his legendary charm? He had been smoother in kindergarten when he asked Cecile Fontenot to be his girlfriend and presented her with a Ring Pop as offering. Come to think of it... would a Ring Pop have made this whole thing less awkward? *No, that's crazy.*

Evie's mouth curled in a stunning smile, her eyes warm on his. "I would love to go on a date with you, Cole."

"Really?" He almost winced as the eager, surprised word shot out of his mouth. *Have some self-respect, man.*

"Yes, really." Evie glanced over at her new clothes. "How should I dress for it?"

"Just pick whatever feels right to you as long as it's comfortable. Honestly, you could wear a burlap sack, and I would be happy with it." He gestured towards the lounge. "Fortunately, I'm sure we've got something a little bit better here for you."

Evie went on tiptoe. "Thank you for sending someone to shop for me, love."

His heart pounded at the endearment that slipped off her tongue so quickly he wasn't sure she knew she said it. When he spoke again, his voice was raspy. "*De rien, mon bel ange.*" He stepped back as she reached to pull off her shirt. "I better go before you get undressed. I won't be held responsible for my actions if I see you naked."

Her eyes glittered at that, her fingers toying with the hem of the fabric. "Well, then, you better move fast."

Cole grunted at her but turned and walked down the stairs as quickly as he could, each step a battle with himself. He wanted to turn right around and go back to her, carry her to the bed, and not leave it for days. Instead, he forced himself down the staircase and into the kitchen, leaning against the fridge door and looking to the ceiling for strength. He lost track of time just standing there in frustrated meditation.

A subtle cough drew his attention, and he looked over to see Evie standing a few feet away from him in a black sundress with bold graffiti-style sunflowers in yellows and burgundies splattered across it. It cut low across her chest and flared out at her hips, draping softly down her legs and ending just above her knees. Her feet were encased in slip-on flats in a burgundy that complemented the sunflowers on her dress.

Holy hell. He was the luckiest asshole in the world to have this goddess interested, much less wanting to go on a date with him. She deserved to have him fall to his knees at her feet and give her anything and everything she could ever want. What he did instead was walk over to her and give her a light kiss, fighting against the urge to deepen it and plaster himself against her. "You look stunning, Angel."

A blush stained her cheeks, and it was all he could do not to skip everything and just propose marriage to her on the spot. "Thank you." She raked her eyes over him. "Do you need to get changed too? I don't know...."

He glanced down and frowned. He hadn't realized he was still wearing his sweats and t-shirt. "Yeah, I should probably get dressed. I'll be back in five."

Evie nodded, her eyes trailing to the garden as he walked away, bounding up the stairs and into the master closet. He changed quickly into a pair of worn black jeans and a plain white t-shirt, throwing a well-loved green cable knit sweater over it all and tugging on a pair of black boots, quickly tying the laces before darting back downstairs.

When he strolled back into the kitchen, the back doors were thrown open, the brisk February winds carrying the sweet smell of coming rain and flowering trees into the house. Through the doors, he could see Evie, just feet away from the Crepe Myrtles in the backyard. They were bent towards her, their limbs drifting around her and gently stroking her face. Her murmurs carried to him across the paved way, loud enough for him to hear her melodic voice but quiet enough he couldn't make out what she was saying.

A long vine trailed across her waist, and, for a moment, Cole forgot it was a plant. All he could see was something touching his Evie, and the world narrowed to a blue-tinged scope.

"Hey, hey!" Evie's raised voice broke through his rage. "Stop growling at the trees! You're scaring them."

"Well, tell the trees to stop fondling my witch, and I'll stop growling at them." She gave him a long-suffering look. "No?"

"No," she scolded. "You know you can't threaten everything that looks at me for longer than two seconds, right?"

"I can, Angel, and I absolutely will. With zero guilt."

Evie rolled her eyes, and his hand itched to spank that perfect ass for her sass. All he had to do was bend her over the outside table and pull up her sundress... he could practically feel her warm flesh under the palm of his hand. It took an inhuman amount of effort for him to rein himself in, pull himself back from the idea of punishing the brattiness out of her. He closed his eyes. Breathed in deeply. When he opened his eyes, she was staring at him, her brow furrowed in confusion.

With a smile, he extended his hand to her. She placed hers lightly in his grasp, and they walked back into the house, Cole closing, locking, and warding the back doors behind them. Then he walked her through the sitting room and out the front door, repeating his protective measures on this side of the house.

"So where are we going?" she asked as they strolled towards St. Charles.

He glanced down at his curious little witch, her hand wrapped in his, even as she reached towards the trees around them, her touch trailing gently over the trunks of every one. A small smile sat on her face as each one greeted her in their own way. His heart squeezed at the sight of her just walking next to him. Being next to him. He had dreamed versions of this moment almost all his life, never believing it would ever happen. To have her here with him was a dream come fucking true. He braced himself—this was the biggest deal of his life, one he had to close. There was zero room for error here. "I thought you might like to see one of the green spaces in New Orleans."

Evie's eyes went wide as her head snapped towards him, the trees around them all but forgotten. "There are green spaces? Here? In the city?" she demanded excitedly.

"*Ouais*," he responded, barely noticing the French slang rolling off his tongue. Before Evie, he almost never used the tongue that his mother taught him unless he was pissed off. Around Evie, though, he found himself lapsing into it more and more, realizing the happiness of speaking his mother's elegant language to the woman he hoped to make his forever. "Nothing quite so grand as where your coven lived but still beautiful and historically significant. Does that sound good to you, Angel?"

She was practically vibrating with excitement next to him. "Yes," she squealed. "I would love to see it!"

That one thrilled sound did it. Nothing in his life—not graduating in the top 10% of his class at Tulane, not passing the state bar, none of his professional accomplishments, not even his charitable ones—could make him feel quite so victorious as making Evie this happy.

"How are we going to get there?"

The light changed, and they strolled across the busy street to the neutral ground splitting St. Charles. "You seemed interested in the streetcar when we were driving in, so I figured that you might have fun riding it rather than driving. We will have to walk a little bit once we get off."

"We're going to ride the trolley?"

"Sweetheart, please don't ever call the streetcar a trolley again. I'm pretty sure there's still a city ordinance on the books making it a criminal offense to call them anything other than streetcars."

"Okay, fine, the streetcar," she drawled at him in a passing mimicry of his own accent. "We can ride it?"

"We can." A low horn blew, and he looked over, seeing the faded green streetcar making its way towards them. "There it is." Fortunately, the stop closest to the house wasn't a crowded one so they were able to get on, pay in cash because he still hadn't replaced his melted cell phone, and take a seat on one of the wooden benches next to a grimy, partially open window. Cole saw all of the imperfections of the transportation, after having lived in New Orleans all his life and being subject to countless streetcar-related traffic issues. With Evie sitting next to him, though, her eyes darting around excitedly, taking in every single inch of the historic conveyance, he couldn't remember a single negative thing about them.

The streetcar jerked to a start, the entire body of the vehicle shaking with every move. Evie was bouncing next to him. He suspected it was only partially due to the uneven, jostling ride, given that her eyes were taking everything in, and she was maintaining an almost stream-of-consciousness-style conversation about their surroundings, which seemed to require no input from him.

His lips quirked upward in satisfaction. *She's happy.*

With each stop, the seats around them filled, but that didn't stop his little witch, who was still pointing out everything she saw through the window to him. They were closing in on Canal Street when she turned to him and said quietly, "I've never seen this many people all at once before."

"Is it too much?" he asked, tightening his grip around her shoulders.

"No, not at all!" she exclaimed. "It's wonderful. I just... I never knew the world could look like this. I mean, I've seen photographs, but it doesn't really give you the full idea of what it's like. It must have been incredible to grow up in this place."

"Yes and no." He thought back to his childhood. "Don't get me wrong, New Orleans is an amazing city, and I can't imagine living anywhere else. But there's a fine line between wealth and poverty here and really no one living in between the two extremes. I grew up in vastly different circumstances than I live in now. My parents weren't poor, but they were definitely working class. I grew up a little over a mile from where we're going in one of the most culturally diverse areas of the city. Even though we were all different, we were still family and shared our food, our stories, our lives with each other in a way that I've never experienced where I live now." Chuckling, he grimaced. "Or maybe that's just the nostalgia of a little kid who missed his parents and his home when they weren't there anymore."

Evie leaned into him, petting his chest comfortingly. "Why can't it be both?"

He tilted his head at her. "Why can't what be both?"

"Why can't it be both nostalgic and true?" Her stormy grey eyes were thoughtful. "You can crave the familiarity of your childhood while still knowing it's true that you were close to everyone in your neighborhood, even if you weren't actual family to most of them. Just because something's nostalgic doesn't mean it can't also be real."

Cole blinked at her rapidly. He was doing that a lot around Evie, but she kept surprising him at every turn. And the insight that she just gave him about how her mind worked? Fuck, that was hot. Hot enough that he was now sitting in the middle of a crowded trolley, his dick half-hard, and needing nothing more than to kiss the sense right out of her. He was leaning down to do just that when the streetcar screeched to a halt at the end of the line.

"Last stop," the operator called. "Time to get off, folks."

People streamed past them off the bus, tourists garbed in tacky t-shirts and beads—even though Mardi Gras was still weeks away—mixed in among the professionals wearing headphones in a last-ditch effort to block out the noise. Once everyone was off, Cole stood, pulling Evie up with him, and ushering her down the aisle ahead of him.

Evie stuttered to a stop as soon as they stepped off the streetcar, and he couldn't blame her. There was nothing quite like Canal, even late in the afternoon on a random Wednesday. Colorful townhomes and ultra-modern skyscrapers lined the street, fighting for dominance. Neon blazed everywhere from the bar signs to the traffic lights, and cars filled the road as far as the eye could see. The noise was a dull roar, a symphony of horns, streetcars, people, and music, both from street performers surrounding them and the piped-in bar tunes.

Cole wrapped his arm around Evie's waist, moving her down the sidewalk so that the people trying to get on the streetcar going back towards the Garden District didn't decide it was a good idea to fight her. Out of the corner of his eyes, he noticed her hand dart up, quickly wiping something from her face. Leaning down, he asked, "You good? We need to head home?"

She whirled in his arms, palms flying up to rest on his chest. Her eyes were glistening. "Don't you dare, Cole Aidoneus. This is stunning." A tear slid down her face. He traced his thumb over her cheek, worry coursing through him. "They're happy tears, I promise. I never thought I would ever see anything like this in my life, and I got overwhelmed by how wonderful it all is. Please don't take me home yet," she pleaded.

What she didn't know was that he would take her anywhere she wanted, no questions asked. And when she requested something in that pleading tone like she wasn't used to getting what she wanted or was scared to ask for it? He was powerless to do anything but agree. "Not going home," he confirmed, his heart pulsing as her face lit up. "We've got a bit of a walk ahead of us, though."

She looked almost amused at his words. "I regularly run through a forest," she reminded him gently. "Is it likely to be more distance than that?"

He snorted. "It most definitely is not. Alright then, witchling, you ready?"

She nodded enthusiastically, and he guided her down Canal, taking a right onto Rampart Street. Her head swiveled with each step they took, taking in everything around them as they passed historic buildings now housing local businesses, more realtors than he could count, dive bar after dive bar, and the tall green lampposts lining the center of the street.

Finally, they reached Arch Armstrong, the tall white archway designating the public entry to Louis Armstrong Park. Through it, the brass sculpture celebrating the tradition of the second line was visible. Surrounding it all were massive trees, live oaks and bald cypresses all holding court over Congo Square.

Evie walked in through the archway, running her fingers along the steel structure, before turning her attention to the brass statue of the jazz musicians in front of them then on to the trees surrounding them. Before she could make her way to them, she hissed and turned suddenly. "Cole." Her eyes found his, and he was shocked to see them drowning in radiant blue. "There's so much death here."

"Yeah, this land has a lot of history associated with it." That was a nice way of putting it. "I didn't think it would hit you this hard, though." He could feel the magic rising in her, his own power and body responding immediately to her. *Fuck. This is bad*. King of the relaxed date, that was definitely him.

Without any sort of instruction from his brain, he found himself plastered against her, his hand tangled in her hair, tugging her head back so he could ravage her mouth. His tongue stroked along hers as her hands dragged down his chest and around his waist. *Jesus Christ.*

"Cole." Her voice was needy against his lips, her hips rocking against him. "Please."

He pulled back, breath ragged. As he cupped her face in his hands, an almost painful electric shock tingled through his fingers. "Angel, I'm not going to fuck you in a public park. Not for the first time at least." The idea of his mouth planted over hers, tasting her cries while he plunged in and out of her tight little body in one of the dark unused rooms in the park theatre was almost more than he could bear. *The theatre, though.* That was an idea. They could work off this overwhelming desire then go back to their sexless afternoon together.

Nope, that's not going to work, dumbass, he thought even as he dipped his head back down to kiss Evie. It was practically guaranteed that, if he took her to a dark room to relieve their ache by finger fucking her and jerking himself off, he would end up balls deep inside of her before he could even get a hand on his own dick. And, as much as he would maim, torture, and kill somebody to make that happen, it had to wait. She was going to choose this. Not be magically roofied into it.

With a groan, Cole tugged himself away, their lips separating slowly.

Evie whimpered lustily, nibbling at her kiss-swollen bottom lip.

"Not like this, *mon ange*."

She closed her eyes for a second but nodded in agreement. "I know."

"Jesus Christ, you two, get a room," somebody yelled, the unexpected shout breaking the tension.

Evie clapped a hand over her mouth to smother her giggle, but the sound poured through her fingers anyways.

"You still want to see the park?" Cole asked, shaking his head in a half-hearted attempt to clear his vision of blue and his brain of the desire fogging it.

"Yes," Evie responded immediately. "But can you tell me about it while we stand here for a few minutes?" At his confused look, she added, "My legs are a little wobbly right now."

"Fuck, baby, you can't say things like that right now. I'm barely holding my shit together here. That just makes me want to drag you to the first private place I can find." Evie's lips twisted in a wry grin, letting him know that she was perfectly okay with him doing exactly that. "No." He pointed a finger at her. "Absolutely not."

"Okay," she muttered. "Even though I know exactly what I want, and I don't need to wait to make any decision." At his pointed glare, she raised her hands in surrender. "Fine. Fine. Yes, sir, I'll behave."

His dick twitched behind his zipper, and he wondered if his witchy temptress knew just how fucking hot the idea of her calling him sir actually was to him. "Good girl," he said. Her eyes flashed at him, that rosy blush settling back over her cheekbones. "Now, c'mon, Angel. Let me show you the park."

Chapter 32

Evie

Tremé, New Orleans, Louisiana

For a man who claimed not to know how to date, Cole made their day unbelievably enjoyable and special. Not like she had much to compare it to, but she imagined that this was what a dream date would be like. After their magic-fueled make out, he took her hand and walked her into a large open area laid with light stone and filled with people. Massive trees surrounded the area; it took them no time at all to sense her and curve towards her.

A small smile on his face, Cole explained the historical significance of Congo Square as the *Place Publique*, a social and religious gathering point and market place for slaves in the 1800s, then its importance to Tremé, the neighborhood he had grown up in. All the while, across from the bench where they sat, an older Black man picked out a tune on his saxophone. The music echoed across the area to them, each note clear and poignant. And although Evie was sure Cole was ready to leave, she wasn't ready to go anywhere with all the history and magic and music around them.

Through the trees, a block filled with older looking buildings was just visible. A perfect mix of city and forest, just removed enough that it felt like it wasn't steps away from the hustle and bustle while still allowing for those fleeting visions of New Orleans. Not for the first time, Evie sighed in contentment, snuggling further into Cole's side, even as a sharp, unexpected pang of longing for her sisters bolted through her. Sandrine would love this place.

They sat there, listening to the music until the sun was about to go down and the street lamps came on, their glow luminous in the foggy evening.

"You ready to go, Angel?" Cole nuzzled into her neck, the chilly tip of his nose against the delicate skin under her ear sending a shiver down her spine. "I'm pretty sure I need to feed you."

As if in answer, her stomach grumbled, loudly enough she could hear it over the music.

Cole burst into unexpected laughter beside her, the rich, warm sound wrapping around her like a blanket.

Evie's mouth dropped open in surprise. If she was overwhelmed by him when he was serious or aroused, Cole laughing was something else completely, something she was completely unprepared to deal with. He was sweet and funny and smart and so beautiful it almost hurt to look at him… and she wanted to keep him. Needed to stay with him.

"That's my cue." Cole stood and pulled her to her feet. She went with him easily, tucking herself into the warmth of his body without even waiting for him to move. A low sound in his chest rumbled against her ear as he wrapped an arm around her. They strolled back through the park and out through the walkway, Cole's arm and body keeping away the worst of the chill.

After a short walk, Cole led her to a sprawling brick building on the corner of a block. Massive windows gave her a good view into what looked like a restaurant on the first floor and, overhead, a simple iron railing rounded the balcony on the second story of the building. "Give me a sec. I'm gonna go grab us a cab 'cause it's getting too cold for you to be walking outside in what you're wearing." He squeezed her hip before striding away towards the front desk.

Evie watched him saunter across the room, her eyes tracking each movement. She knew that if he looked back at her, he would see every feeling she had for him emblazoned on her face. Forcing her gaze away from him, she glanced around the space, taking in the marble flooring, the decorative flowers, and, best of all, the ornate chandeliers blazing overhead. The light bulbs illuminated what must be thousands of crystals, reflecting kaleidoscopic prisms all around her.

Her gaze was still locked on the chandelier when an arm snared around her waist. Before she could be alarmed, the smoky mint scent of Cole surrounded her. "Our ride's here."

She nodded and, with one last lingering look at the opulent light fixtures, followed him out to the car waiting for them at the curb. Sliding in through the door Cole opened for her, she relaxed into the cracked leather seats as he dropped in beside her.

With a grunt of greeting, the driver took off for their next destination, weaving wildly in and out of traffic like his drive was going to be timed. Although the sun had set, the city was somehow brighter than before: the street lamps releasing a flickering yellow glow, the traffic lights painting the inside of the car in reds and greens, and the neon signs illuminating the world around them in every shade under the rainbow. Their drive took them from the liveliness of the area they had been in into a quiet neighborhood filled with small, well-lit houses in vibrant colors.

"Where are we now?"

"This is Tremé," he replied, eyes on the scenery passing around them. "Where my parents and I lived." His accent was thicker than she had heard it before, a slight note of sadness seeping through his words. She rested her hand on his knee, smiling when she felt his fingers wrap around hers, squeezing tightly. The car pulled to a stop at a red light, and Cole nudged her, gesturing with his chin out the window next to her. "If you look down that street... you see the second house down the street, the light blue one?" She followed his instructions, nodded when she caught a glimpse of it just before the driver stomped on the gas, the car shaking as it hurtled forward. "That's where my parents and I lived before we moved to the cottage in Gentilly just before they died. Even though we left the area, though, they always made sure to bring me back to see our close friends. So I would never forget where I came from."

Evie turned in her seat to face Cole. Taking in the grief on his face, she tightened her fingers around his knee. His expression made it clear just how much showing her this meant to him. "Thank you for sharing it with me," she said quietly, kissing his cheek.

The harsh edges of mourning on his features softened. His free hand stroked over her arm. "I got to see where you grew up. I wanted you to see where I came from too, I guess."

Blood pounded in her ears as she stared into his oh-so-familiar eyes, barely noticing when the car jerked to a stop at another traffic light. With each confession, he was crawling his way further into her heart, into that place only he—as the friend visible only to her—had ever occupied. She wasn't sure she could get him out if she tried. Honestly, she wasn't sure she ever *wanted* to get him out.

The car came to a stop in front of a bright blue house with cheery yellow accents. A weathered sign reading Gabrielle Restaurant ranged over the porch roof that sloped slightly over the sidewalk, protecting the two small turquoise tables sitting underneath it from the elements.

"Fare's already been settled," the driver said. "You gonna need a ride home, too?"

"Yeah, man, that would be great." Cole glanced at Evie. "Can you be back at 8:30?"

"I can do that." He shook Cole's hand. "Enjoy your dinner, you two."

Evie shot the driver a quick smile before sliding out of the car behind Cole, taking the hand he had dropped down to help her to a stand.

He shut the door firmly behind her; the car pulled out immediately, almost getting sideswiped by an oncoming car. "Six in one hand, half dozen in the other whether he shows back up," she heard him mutter beside her. "Jesus, I gotta replace my phone soon."

As they walked in to the small blue house, the warmth of the room and the delicious aromas of carefully prepared food surrounded her.

Cole held up two fingers after a quick conversation with the hostess, an older woman who greeted him by name like he was her long-lost son before turning a smothering hug on Evie. In no time, they were being escorted past the long, low bar bordering the side of the room to a two-person table tucked into a corner. "This was one of my *maman's* favorite restaurants in the city. Probably didn't hurt that it was so close to home and pretty affordable in addition to just being amazing food."

Dinner was a blur of, as promised, incredible food and conversation that flowed more naturally than any she'd ever had. By the end of it all, Evie was full and so comfortable she could easily fall asleep at the table.

"It's 8:30," he said, signing the receipt in front of him with a flourish and standing. "Let's see if our friendly neighborhood cab driver actually came back for us."

She followed him out of the restaurant, the hostess waving a cheerful goodbye at them.

Against all odds, the car was sitting at the curb. The driver leaned against its side, smoking. "Where to, boss?" he asked, dropping his cigarette to the ground and stomping it into oblivion before he climbed back into the driver's seat as Cole and Evie slid into the back.

Evie heard Cole's response but didn't take it in. Her eyes slid shut briefly, but she shook her head, forcing them back open.

A low chuckle sounded next to her. "Angel, go ahead and fall asleep. We'll be home soon."

She shook her head. "No, no, I'm okay."

"That would be a lot more convincing if your eyes weren't closed when you said it." Cole's voice was rich with suppressed laughter. "It's okay, *ma sorcière*. Go to sleep." One large hand cupped the nape of her neck and tugged her head to rest on his chest.

Evie was about to doze off when a question she had wanted to ask earlier came back to her. Although she didn't open her eyes, she did ask what she wanted to know. "What happened to the home you lived in with your parents after they died? Who lives there now?"

She felt Cole's head tilt down towards her. "They leased our Gentilly house, but they owned the house in Tremé outright. For some reason, they didn't sell it when we moved. It was held in trust until I came of age." He stroked a hand over her hair and down her back before it finally came to rest at the bottom of her spine. "After I received the deed when I was 21, I connected with some of the local realtors to purchase the houses surrounding it."

"Why?" she yawned. He didn't answer. After a few minutes of silence, she lifted her head, pushing her eyes open enough to look at him. "Cole?"

"I wanted to give back to the area so I, uh, I worked with a local charity to make the houses available at no cost to women and children escaping domestic abuse situations with nowhere to go. They can stay as long as they need. The charitable arm of my firm takes care of any and all bills associated with the housing, and the charity I work with ensures they have whatever else they need."

Evie's eyes flared fully open. "That's amazing."

He shrugged. "Anybody would do the same."

"I'm not sure that's accurate," she corrected gently, resting her head back on his chest, her eyelids sliding closed once more. "You're incredible, Cole Aidoneus."

She didn't hear it when he whispered, "Not half as incredible as you."

Chapter 33

Her hands wrapped around the bulbous flower heads, their petals silky against her skin. She was careful not to squeeze too hard, knowing that, although they were strong enough to withstand a significant amount of pressure, too much of it would destroy the beautiful flowers. Not too different from herself, she thought bitterly, her eyes unfocused as she gazed across the field of roses.

It appeared to be another beautiful day in paradise, but that too was deceptive. Her home—an idyllic jewel box of a garden—was a stunning cage, one in which she was trapped as much as the flowers that surrounded her. She had no visitors, no friends, except for the goddess of the harvest's acolytes. Though they weren't friends so much as rats who gleefully reported her every move back to their deity, hoping that disclosing her actions would earn them favor with the stern goddess. Not just a stern goddess, though. Her mother. A strict disciplinarian who locked Kore away from the world, held her captive with spellwork so complex that Kore herself couldn't undo the boundaries.

All she wanted was somebody to spend time with. A person who wanted to be with her because of her, not because of who she was to her mother. It was painful to be this lonely. No. Not just lonely. Utterly alone.

From behind her, she heard footsteps. Her mother's acolytes were silent, always trying to catch her in some sort of mischief, so it was probably her nursemaid,

Kalligeneia. More a mother than Demeter herself, Kalligeneia practically raised Kore, and it had been too long since her last visit. A smile bloomed on Kore's face, and she whirled around in excitement, the nymph's name on her lips.

But the person behind her was not Kalligeneia.

Behind her stood a tall, dark-haired man with vibrant green eyes settled like jewels into an angular face that was too stark for beauty but somehow still captivating. His head was canted to the side, an amused smirk tilting up the corners of his lips. "Hello, little flower," he said in a deep voice.

"Hello." She couldn't look away from him. She had never seen a man before outside of the Galli, the castrated priests who served her mother; none of them looked like the man in front of her. Her stomach clenched as she took in his form. None of them made her feel like this man, either. "Who are you?"

The man took a step forward, his long legs closing the distance between them. "I'm Aidoneus." The name was exotic on his thin lips when said in his remarkable voice. "And you are?"

"I'm… " she trailed off, realizing that she might be about to reveal too much to a stranger. Even though the stranger was overwhelmingly beautiful. "I'm not sure I should tell you who I am. I don't know you."

Those lips, too thin for beauty, almost a cruel slash in his face, curled into a true smile, and Kore lost her breath as surely as if she had been punched in the stomach. This Aidoneus smiling was stunning.

"No," he murmured. "No, you don't, but I would very much like to know you."

Unfamiliar warmth settled in her chest. Something that made her feel at peace and at ease. Was this what happiness felt like? She had never experienced that particular feeling, despite reading tales of it often.

"What if I were to guess it?" Aidoneus raised a hand, curling a strand of her hair around his finger gently.

"Guess what?" she asked dumbly, too distracted by his touch—a touch she couldn't even feel, no less—to follow. Later, after Aidoneus had gone and she was alone like she always was, she would probably be ashamed at her dim-wittedness. Now, though, she was too stunned by his mere presence to care.

"Your name, little flower. If I were to guess it, would you tell me?"

A giggle bubbled out of her throat, and her fingers reached to her throat, astonished at the sound. She had never made that happy, lilting noise before.

His eyes were on her, too intense and far too observant. "Is that a yes, petal?"

"Yes." She nodded emphatically. "But shall we put some rules around this game? We wouldn't want to make it too easy for you."

"Of course." Aidoneus tilted his head back and laughed, a rich sound that reminded her of the noise the wind made as it whipped through her trees. "I want it to be a fair contest. I can never have my future wife accuse me of cheating to gain her affections."

Kore's head jerked up, alarm coursing through her. She had heard too many stories from the acolytes about men taking whatever they wanted from the women surrounding them, including a horrific tale about Poseidon forcing himself upon a virginal priestess of Athena, who was then punished for the god's crimes.

"Don't you worry, flower," Aidoneus said, unfurling his finger from her hair then tracing it along her cheek. Sparks followed the small touch, and her skin tingled under his fingertip.. "That's a discussion for another day. Now—" His eyes burned with excitement. "Shall we play a game?"

Evie

Garden District, New Orleans, Louisiana

Evie jerked awake, her heart pounding. Her eyes darted blindly in the darkness for whatever had woken her from Kore's memory, but the room was still and quiet, save for Cole's deep breathing beside her.

She didn't really remember getting home or getting into bed, after all but passing out from exhaustion in the car. Raising the comforter, she glanced down at herself, finding that she was draped in a shirt—one of Cole's if the size was any indication. Guess he meant what he said about not touching her until she had made a decision. A small groan emerged from her lips, and she sat up, Cole's arm falling away from her waist as she did so.

The room was still lit by the moon, the sky outside dark even through the curtains. It was either extremely late or far too early, but these moments, when the moon was high in the sky, were her time. She slipped out from under the covers, careful not to wake Cole, whose response to her absence was a strange snuffle of disappointment. With quiet steps, she crossed the room and stole out into the hallway, closing the door behind her gently.

As she slipped down the staircase, she took in the stillness around her. The house felt different at night, large pieces of furniture casting long shadows in the moon's dim light. The gas lamps outside the front door lent little illumination to the front entryway, their small and yellow flames barely breaking the darkness. The overall effect would be eerie if Evie hadn't spent so much of her life frolicking under the moon in the forest, surrounded by more ominous shadows than this.

The wards around the front door pulsed as she walked past them, but, unlike before, they didn't glow and repel her. She traced a finger through a door, sending a small pulse of magic at the spells so that she could read what they protected against. As they came into view, her face broke into a smile. Cole had built in an exception for her lunar magic in addition to the one already existing for death. She could come and go as she please. It seemed he meant it when he said he wanted her to choose him, even going so far as to make sure that the house was no longer a prison for her.

She padded away from the front door and crossed the sitting room into the kitchen, passing the island and strolling out through the glass doors into the backyard. The minute she stepped foot outside, her body flooded with power in response to the full moon above her, raising goosebumps along her skin and sending the glimmers of sorcery across her skin. In addition to the usual cool gold of her lunar magic, though, she noticed a vibrant cobalt too. She had assumed that her ability to source power from death was temporary, but it had been days, and she could still feel the grave around her: the corpses across the street, some odd sense of death that she didn't understand emanating from the house next door, both of them almost as potent a pull as the moon above her.

Her feet carried her past the crepe myrtles to one of the live oaks at the back of the yard. Its limbs reached out to her, the leaves passing over her face in greeting. "Hi, beautiful," she cooed, running her fingertips along the branches. Through the rough bark, she could feel the tree's health like a heartbeat in her head, vibrant and pulsing against her skin. "Cole's taken good care of you, hasn't he?" The branches shimmied happily against her fingertips in answer.

"Would you mind giving me a lift?" she requested.

The live oak was only too happy to oblige, a limb lowering delicately in front of her feet in seconds. She stepped onto it and was suddenly rising high into the air, finding herself among the canopy of the same copse of trees in the backyard. Once there, she arranged herself until she was seated comfortably, her legs crossed in front of her. At this height, she had a direct view into Cole's study where the book he had pulled off the shelf yesterday still sat on the couch.

Evie tilted her head back, eyes on the night sky above her. Cole had begged her—all but ordered her, actually—to think her way through this choice. And he was right to do so. It had been a traumatic few days.

Leaving him was never an option. She knew that deep in her heart. While she wasn't willing to call it love—yet—he held a piece of her heart she knew instinctively that she would never get back. She was his in a way that felt bigger than anything she had ever experienced, and he was hers. There was no going back to the way it was before.

If she was being really honest with herself, she didn't *want* to go back to the way it was before. Even before she knew his name, before she was ever aware of his very real existence, Cole had crawled under her skin and made a home there. His eyes a constant companion, his voice the consistent refrain of her life. He was as much a part of her as her magic. She refused to let him go. That was all there was to say on that matter. She wasn't going anywhere. *Not that he would let me.* She snickered at the thought, knowing that wherever she went, Cole would follow.

Which brought her to the second decision. The bigger one with life-changing implications. She chewed on the inside of her cheek, considering. Did she legitimately believe that they were reincarnated gods? As the chill wind passed through her hair, the heavy strands lifting in the breeze, she could finally admit that she did. If their complementary magic wasn't enough, if the dreams and visions they had both had of each other since childhood weren't sufficient, Kore's memories slowly coming to her through dreams were.

With each choice she had made since that night at the construction site, she felt herself drawing further and further away from the life she knew. She loved her coven, no matter how betrayed she felt by the elder's lies. She loved Sandrine more than life itself. Her home—her sisters—were an essential part of her. Was she ready to leave that behind?

Yes, she was ready to start something new. Start a life with Cole. And when they left, he made it clear that she wasn't leaving behind her sisters if she didn't want to. All she had to let go of was the life she knew in the forest, one she had felt increasingly trapped by. With Cole, though, she didn't feel caged, except for that first day. She felt free. Supported. All things that had been missing during her life with her coven, who loved her, certainly, but didn't understand her. So was she willing to give up her home in the forest? Yes. Could she accept a life in the Underworld? Unknown.

A sneaky voice in the back of her head whispered: *Are you ready to make Cole give up his prophesied destiny, though*? That was the truth of it, wasn't it, if she wasn't willing to accept an immortal life tied to the Underworld. There was so much depending upon Cole—them, technically—fulfilling their shared destiny. The implications of not accepting their role as the formally titled Hades and Persephone, Lord and Lady of the Underworld, and putting the shades back into the Underworld were apocalyptic. Could she live with herself if the entirety of humanity was devastated by escaped souls?

No. No, she couldn't.

The sky was lightening around her, murky yellows, oranges, and blues fighting for dominance in the sky. And as she caught a glimpse of the sun emerging over the horizon, her choice became clear.

She wouldn't ignore the prophecy that bound her life to Cole's as rulers of an Underworld.

With a whisper to the tree, the branches lowered her back to the ground. Steps purposeful, she strode into the house and back up the stairs, down the hallway to Cole's study. He had told her the story, not read it to her. It was still early, and Cole would probably sleep for a while longer. It was time for her to learn his past and understand their future.

This was her choice.

Chapter 34

Cole

Garden District, New Orleans, Louisiana

When Cole woke, it was to midday sun pouring into the room and a bed empty of his witch. He barely took a second to consider that he never slept this late before bolting upright in bed and shouting, "Angel!" His blood was pounding in his ears, panic racing through his veins that she might have left. He was about to leap of out bed when, barely audible over the sounds of his body trying to kill him with fear, he heard her voice outside the room.

He was racing to the door before he even recognized that he had moved. "Angel?" he called again.

"I'm down here, Cole. In your study." Her voice was exasperated but clear.

His feet took him down the hallway quickly until he was standing in the door to his study. Evie was curled on the couch, the oversized tome of his family's history sitting open in her lap. "You weren't in bed." It sounded accusatory even to his ears.

"I couldn't sleep." She shrugged. "So I had a lot of time to think. And read." Her finger traced a path down the page in front of her, and she finally looked up him. Her lips twitched as she took in his disheveled state.

He was wearing a pair of pajama pants that had a pattern of Scooby Doo and the rest of Mystery Inc. racing across them and no shirt. They were the only pajamas he owned— courtesy of a terrible gift exchange at the firm—and about two inches too short. Usually, he slept naked, but he had broken these out so there was no—well, less—temptation until she made her decision about everything.

"Hey." Her eyes softened. "I'm still here. I didn't go anywhere."

Cole strode across the room, dropping onto the couch and tugging her to straddle his lap, burying his face in her neck. Her fingers skated through his hair as he took in greedy gulps of her scent, that cinnamon and orange smell so unique to her. "I was scared you left," he muttered into her throat.

"I know." Her response was simple. "But I didn't." She tugged at his hair, and his head lifted until her big grey eyes were all he could see. "I'm not leaving you, love."

At the endearment sliding off her tongue, Cole's pulse ratcheted up, and he realized exactly how badly he had fucked up with this seating arrangement. They hadn't resolved anything; she hadn't told him she had made any decision. But his Angel was straddling him, draped in his shirt and only his shirt, and her lips were just inches away from his own. He could feel her magic seething under her skin; his uncle had always told him that when there was someone whose magic complemented his own, it would have an almost aphrodisiac quality. He'd scoffed—freaking laughed—right in his uncle's face. Now, he got it though. He had never been this hard in his life, and he was barely touching her.

Before he fell asleep last night, he had intended to start the day with the best of intentions. Make Evie breakfast, show her television, take her exploring a city she clearly loved. All of that went out the window when he woke up to an empty bed. He was operating on pure adrenaline now, and, as evidenced by that first night in the forest, that usually led him to impulsive actions. His hands tightened on her waist, and he tried to lift her off, but her thighs clamped around his. "Angel," he groaned as she rolled her hips over him.

"Hmm?" Her breath brushed across his cheek.

"Little witch, I think you need to stop moving those fucking hips of yours right now."

One of her eyebrows raised slightly. "Oh? And why is that?"

He cupped the back of her neck and tugged her forward. A small gasp escaped her, and he nearly ripped off his own pants at the sound "Because we will absolutely open the Underworld if we have sex, and I promised you I wouldn't pressure you into a decision." His thumb pressed into the flesh under her ear, a small stroke there sending a small shiver through her body. "And I care about keeping my promises to you. With you rocking your hips over me like that, though, all I can think about is how it would feel to be inside of you. What you would look like coming apart underneath me. The sound of you screaming my name. So I need you to stop fucking moving, Angel."

"Cole." She pushed back against his hand.

"Yeah?" He let her move her head back until she could make eye contact but couldn't bring himself to let go of her neck.

"I made my decision."

She made her—"Wait, what?" Time screeched to a halt, leaving him scrambling to catch up. He needed to think with the brain that made him one of the best attorneys in the city, the man who had co-founded an international firm, rather than with his dick, which was currently screaming at him to get inside of his witch. "You made your decision."

"Yep." A smile split her face as he stared at her. "I'm staying with you."

That was good to know, but that wasn't the most important of the choices he gave to her. "And the other decision." It wasn't a question. It was a demand. "Do you want to rule the Underworld and its inhabitants with me for the rest of our immortal lives?"

Evie raised her body, canting forward in his lap until she was only inches from his lips. "I want *you*, Cole. I'll take the crown if I have to so that we can be together."

Time stood still after her answer. "This isn't just because we've made the absolutely fucking horrible choice to have this conversation while you're in my lap, right?"

"I made this decision while I was sitting outside under the moon this morning, and you weren't anywhere near me." Her tone was straightforward, her gaze steady on his. "Yes, I want to have sex with you. But I'm not making my choice based on that, even though I don't think us waiting for years to make this decision makes it any easier or, frankly, us able to think more rationally about it." She pursed her lips. "I'm choosing this, you, because it's the right thing to do. I want you in my life. And I won't be responsible for an apocalypse because I'm afraid of change. With you by my side, it's not quite so scary. It's something we'll accomplish together."

Cole knew he should probably have questions. They should probably talk things through a bit more, figure out a game plan. Should probably call the Moirai to fact check the prophecy. But all of that paled in the face of Evie in his lap telling him she wanted him and a life together. His little witch. *My fucking fated wife*.

He pulled her in further, one hand wrapped around the base of her skull, tangled in her hair. "I'm assuming that you've never been with a man." Her breaths were emerging in pants, her eyes already dilated with lust. "Have you, Angel?" She finally shook her head, and a bolt of victory struck him. "But you've had sex before?" She nodded. "Baby, it's okay that I'm not your first, but I'll be your fucking last."

Rational thought faded as he picked her up and stalked over to his desk with her in his arms. Setting her down on the empty desktop, he scraped his hand over her cheek gently before stepping back. "Strip."

With an inscrutable smile, Evie gripped the sides of his shirt and slowly lifted it over her head. Dropped it to the floor behind her. And Cole forgot how to fucking breathe at the sight of her naked in front of him. She was absolutely stunning with plump breasts and curvy hips, seemingly made with him in mind. On her left arm was that delicate winding tattoo that ran to the middle of her forearm, even more nuanced than he initially thought and the perfect inverse complement to his own snake tattoo. Just another sign that she was made for him, even if he didn't completely understand any of it. She was an absolute vision, and she was *all fucking his.*

That single thought nearly took him to his knees. He had a lifetime to discover everything about her, all the things that made her scream, moan, gasp, whimper, and every other sound in between, but right now, he desperately needed to taste her.

He stepped into her, crashing his mouth down over hers. A tiny moan slipped from her as he ran his tongue over the seam of her full lips, parting them, his tongue sliding into her silken mouth. She tasted exactly the way she smelled: oranges and cinnamon, just like a fucking dessert. *Her beautiful mouth, her delicious taste and scent, they belong to me now.* He dominated her, marked her as his.

Her arms were wrapped around his neck, her curvy body pressed against his. She was just as lost for him as he was for her, practically vibrating with need against him. He bit her lower lip, felt her sharp intake of air at the sudden sting, before he dropped to his knees in front of her. His head was right at the height of her breasts, her nipples tightening before his eyes. He nipped the taut buds, laved them with his tongue, and then bit down hard on one nipple while pinching the other. "Holy gods, Cole!" she cried.

"Angel," he growled. "You call my name like that again, and I'm going to forget all the ways I'm going to make you come before I fuck you like the dirty little witch you are." He palmed her breast again, his big hand making her look small as he rolled his thumb over her nipple. "But feel free to scream for me, *ma belle sorcière.*"

Varying the intensity of each bite, he bit across her chest and down her stomach, leaving imprints of his teeth across her skin. She was *his*; his marks only reflected that on the outside. She moaned and gasped at each touch; the chorus of her pleasure was driving him insane. "I bet you're fucking soaked for me, Angel."

Evie's eyes met his, her stormy grey irises nearly completely overtaken by dilated black pupils and tinged with lunar gold and neon blue. "Why don't you find out?"

Mouthy little witch, so desperately in need of punishment. Right now, though, he needed to feel her, craved his head between her thighs, desperate to have her come on his tongue. There was time for correction later. He slid his hand between her thighs, running his thumb along her slit. Completely drenched. Just for him. *Just like I knew she would be.* A low rumble left him, and he tossed his head back. She was going to be the death of him. He wouldn't survive long enough for them to claim their throne because his witch was going to kill him before he ever got the chance to fuck her. *But what a way to go.*

Cole slid a long finger inside her, slowly thrusting before adding a second finger. Evie was trembling above him, moaning as she rode his hand, rocking her hips for the friction she needed. "Jesus Christ, I need to fucking taste you." She whispered out a "please" in response. He was practically shaking himself when he slid his fingers out of her and ordered, "Spread your legs, Angel. Let me see your pussy."

Without a word, just a glorious whimper, she spread her legs, exposing herself to him. "God, you're perfect," he murmured as he made himself comfortable between her thighs. After draping her legs over his shoulders and taking a glance up at her stunning face, he leaned in and ran his tongue the length of her. "And fucking hell, you're delicious too, witchling." With that, he gripped her hips and dragged her to his face, licking her as if he could never get enough of her, refusing to even come up for air. He would drown in her before he would willingly stop.

Above him, Evie dropped to her elbows as she rode his face. Her breath was emerging in little gasps, raspy moans that carried down to where he knelt in between her legs.

With a small smirk, Cole finally sucked hard on her rigid clit. She let loose a keening moan, almost a scream, her legs clamping around his face as he slid two fingers back inside her, curling them at the perfect angle to make Evie lose her mind, and pumping, all while keeping up his tongue's relentless assault.

"Holy Gaia, Cole, please don't stop," she begged.

He wasn't going anywhere until he saw what she looked like when she came on his tongue. *Hellhounds couldn't drag me away*, he thought as her inner walls started fluttering around his fingers, her clit beginning to pulse against his tongue.

"Cole!" she screamed, body seizing and falling to the desk, hands shoving through his hair as she writhed against his mouth and sobbed out her orgasm loudly enough that it probably alerted the whole neighborhood. Good. Let them hear who she belonged to, the only fucking person who would ever give this to her.

Cole kept pumping his fingers into her, forcing her through her orgasm until the hands in his hair started pushing him away, and she giggled at the overwhelming sensation. Rocking back on to his feet, he stared unabashedly at his little witch, soft and satiated above him. That wasn't enough though. He needed every part of her.

He nipped her thigh before standing between her legs. Evie lay prone before him with a dreamy smile. She was too extraordinary for words. Too good for him. His heart stuttered, and, despite the overwhelming need crawling through his blood, he checked in with her. Gave her one last chance to stop this. "You can still say no, baby. We don't have to go any further than this right now."

Her tangled hair fell away from her face when she sat straight up, a fiery look in her eyes. "Don't you dare stop, Cole." His entire body was on fire as she ran her hand across his chest before looking down at where his dick was tenting his pajama pants. "I want you, and I will take everything that comes with you." She pulled on his waistband. "Now get inside of me or, I swear to the gods, I'm going to go take a shower once I can figure out how to turn it on and make myself come again—"

A growl rolled from his chest. "Like hell you will." He wound a hand in her hair, grasping enough of her auburn mane to allow him to establish a solid grip and crank her head back, exposing the long column of her neck. "You, *bel petit ange,* are going to have to get used to the fact that this cunt, your whole perfect body, belongs to me." He leaned into her, whispering savagely, "And you only get to come when I fucking say you do."

Her gaze intent on him, she reached for his pants, but he dropped his grip on her hair and wrapped his hand around her wrists, binding them behind her back. "Not yet, baby. You don't get to touch until I give you permission."

She made a low, grumpy sound in the back of her throat, followed by a muttered but indecipherable comment.

He raised his eyebrows. "We need to talk about that bratty mouth of yours, *vilaine fille*, because you can't keep thinking you can get away with that shit." Her mouth quirked into what was probably going to be a smirk, maybe a sarcastic response, but he shook his head at her. Swiped his thumb across her lips. "How about you control that urge to be a brat, so I let you come again rather than spanking that pretty ass red?"

She opened her mouth, closed it, then smiled angelically at him.

"That's a good girl," he purred. "Now I'm going to give you one of your hands back so you can take off my pants because I need to be inside you. Right. Fucking. Now."

Evie's face lit up as she pushed his pajama pants down with her free hand, the other still bound by his grasp behind her back. He stepped out of the loungewear and stood still, allowing her to take him in. Cole knew he was larger than the average man, which didn't really matter, but he also knew that she may want a look at him before he was inside her, especially since… "Are all men pierced?" she asked, sliding her fingers over his piercing.

He groaned at the feeling of her fingers rolling over the cool steel. "Not all."

"Why would you do it then?" She shifted her hand down his shaft, away from the piercing, lightly grazing her fingers along his length.

"Mostly because I got drunk and lost a bet." That little experience showed him why he shouldn't party with tattoo artists, especially relatives. Prohibitions against tattooing and piercing drunk assholes didn't really have the same weight when the artist was your distant cousin. He lightly removed her hand from him, tugging it behind her once more. "Angel, if you keep touching me like that, this is going to be over a lot sooner than I want. Now, if I let your hands go, will you be a good girl for me and keep them by your sides until I tell you you're allowed to move?" She nodded enthusiastically, and he released his grip on her wrists. "Hands by your hips until I say otherwise."

Her eyes were glazed with lust when he finally kissed her again, sinking into her lush mouth, trailing the backs of his fingers down her body. "Please, Cole," she begged. "I need you so badly." Her hands clenched on his desk, her knuckles white from the tightness of her grip, but she kept them firmly planted.

"I know, Angel," he murmured gently, running his cock over her clit before sliding to her entrance. Her back arched, pulling her eyes away from him. *That won't do at all.* He needed her stormy gaze on his this first time. Fisting her hair in his left hand, he tugged back her head until all she could do was look straight into his eyes. With an "Eyes on me," he gripped her curvy hip in his right hand and slid partially into her on a swift thrust. She gasped, a lone sound in the silence of his office. "Fuck," he swore softly into her neck.

He had to make this good for her—she had spent her life in the woods, and although he knew it had been a rich and full life with her coven sisters, this was still her first time having sex with a man. If he wasn't careful, he could hurt her, it could be painful for her... any number of thing could happen that would make it a less than enjoyable experience. He needed to make sure she enjoyed every bliss-soaked second because he intended to do this with her for the rest of their immortal lives. If nothing else, he needed to take it slowly. But she was so tight around him, her walls already clenching around his pierced cock, and he wasn't even halfway in yet. He wasn't sure his self-control was that good. "Goddammit, Angel, I never would have dreamed you'd be like this."

She smiled up at him, practically glowing in the harsh afternoon light filtering in, and laughed throatily. "Well, it seems like you were definitely able to dream of me like this." When he looked down at her in shock, her smile morphed into a mischievous smirk. "What, are we not joking yet that you've been fantasizing about me since you were a teenager?"

Cole pushed her sweat-soaked curls back from her forehead. Figures that she would be an absolute brat when he was too lost in her to even think of punishing her. "Maybe after I've made you come so hard you can't walk or see straight, maybe then it will be time for jokes."

She wrinkled her nose at him, rolled her eyes mockingly. And with those two small movements, the mood in the office shifted once more as he found himself needing to put his bratty little witch in her place. "Did you just fucking roll your eyes at me, Angel?" he growled at her, nipping at her nipple.

She squeaked and jumped a bit as that small bit of pain filtered through her. "So what if I did?" she asked, clutching his shoulders. "What are you going to do about it?"

Cole could have sworn that his heart stopped in his chest just a little bit, right before he shifted his hips back, slipping almost fully out of her. Evie's eyes grew large, her mouth falling open to start begging right before he slammed back into her. She rasped his name, almost shouted it, as he plunged in between her legs; her nails dug into his shoulders with each thrust.

He bit her lower lip and snarled, "mine" before kissing her roughly. *This is what obsession feels like.* The thought was dim in his mind, all his attention on the fluid shape of her as she arched her back, wrapping her legs tightly around his waist, her peaked nipples rubbing against his chest.

The hair on the back of his neck stood on end as magic flooded the room with each forceful thrust. Evie writhed under him, growing wetter and more wild as she took him deeper with every stroke. "Cole, love, please," she begged.

"Please what, Angel?" he growled into her ear. "'Use your words, *belle fille*, even though your sweet little cunt is telling me exactly what you fucking want." He could feel her bearing down on and soaking his cock, small flutters trembling around him as he plunged into her.

"Please, Cole, please let me come," she cried.

Items fell haphazardly to the floor as their magic intertwined, and the world shook around them, but the sounds were muffled. Indistinct. He couldn't say with certainty what was shaking the world: an earthquake, a cataclysmic combination of their magic, or an actual medical emergency. All he knew was he couldn't stop.

He dropped two fingers between her legs, strumming her sensitive clit. She let out a sharp shriek against his lips, bucking against him, clenching around him, as he rubbed with a bit more pressure on each stroke. The muscles in her thighs seized around his waist, and her moans were nearly constant as he kept up his grueling pace. "Scream for me, Angel. Let everybody in this fucking neighborhood know exactly who you belong to."

One last quick stroke of his fingers over her clit, and she fell over the edge, screaming as she came apart around him. "That's right, baby." His words were so guttural that he barely recognized his own voice. Couldn't even figure out what exactly he was demanding of her as she strangled his cock. "Jesus Christ, I can feel you coming all over me, Angel." She was chanting his name, soaking him with every thrust, her nails digging bloody pinpricks into his arms, when he came. "Fuck, yes, take my cum, baby!" he roared, shuddering violently as he pumped out everything he had into his Angel. His dream woman.

Chapter 35

Evie

Garden District, New Orleans, Louisiana

Lucidity returned to Evie in phases. The smell of smoke and mint surrounding her. The ache where Cole's body remained inside hers. The pressure of their combined magic chilling her skin.

She had, of course, had sex before with previous partners, but it had been enjoyable at best, perfunctory at worst. Never in her life had she experienced anything like what she and Cole had just shared on his desk. Her throat was sore from screaming, and she had come so hard she was almost positive she lost consciousness at one point. They had just finished, and, although she should be satiated, she could easily go again with the man currently sprawled across her.

Not to mention, her magic had *never* responded like that during sex. It had almost been an active participant, flooding the room, intertwining with Cole's own. Cole had said that their magic complemented each other's. It had felt that way in little doses each time they had been intimate before this, but, when he was inside her... it was cataclysmic.

Her thoughts were interrupted when Cole started moving, pushing his upper body off hers. His face was relaxed, but his eyes were intense as he stared down at her. He cupped her face in his hands, kissing her gently before asking, "You okay, Angel?"

She nodded, her heart melting at his concerned look. "I'm wonderful, love." Her voice was raspy, even to her own ears, cracking on her words.

"No regrets?"

"None."

"I didn't hurt you, did I?"

"Not at all. I'm perfect."

"Yeah, you are." Cole's face broke into a broad smile, and he nuzzled her hair, which had gathered into an uncontrolled halo around her head from their activities. "Why don't we go get cleaned up then pick up some clothes you actually choose? As much as I would love to keep you naked for the foreseeable future, I want to make sure you're comfortable first. Plus I'm pretty sure we have some things to take care of now." He slid out of her, both of them moaning in unison at the movement.

Her eyes had involuntarily slid closed at the feeling when she heard Cole go, "What the fuck," softly but emphatically. She sat up quickly, concerned, until she noticed what he was staring at.

Before, his study had been utilitarian, the only pop of color the vibrant painting of his dream of her on the wall behind the couch. Now, though, the room was crowded with flowers and greenery growing from everywhere. Wisteria wound down from the ceiling; bushes had bloomed along the walls, dinner plate-sized rose blooms exploding from their branches in a dizzying array of colors. Lilacs weaved along the exposed beams in the ceiling, and ranunculus had burst into life seemingly through his desk. As if all of that weren't enough, the window beside his desk was shattered around the oak tree branch that had extended its limbs into the room and up toward the ceiling.

"This, um. This happen to you a lot?" Cole's lips were twitching as he glanced around, taking in everything.

"Besides that night in the forest?" Cole was starting to let loose small puffs of air through a growing smirk. "Other than that, this is new to me." A mild sense of guilt churned her gut at the glass shards sparkling on the floor from the broken window. "I'm sorry about the window, though. Kind of. I enjoyed myself too much to really be sorry, though, so... I'm mostly sorry?"

Cole finally lost the battle with his amusement, bowing his head down as he howled in laughter. "It's never gonna be boring with you, is it?" he said, picking her up by her thighs and carrying her down the hall—now lined with arching rose vines that definitely weren't there earlier—to the bathroom. "Time to get cleaned up, Angel, so we can go get you some clothes and see what happens next."

Evie wrapped herself around him, biting his shoulder lightly. He smelled so good there—even though he was slick with a fine layer of sweat—and he tasted better. A deep sound rumbled from his throat as she nibbled her way along his collarbone. "You're not gonna distract me."

"Not trying to distract you," she murmured, shifting her weight forward so she could keep biting her way along his chest. "Just want to taste you."

He turned on the shower. "Angel," he groaned down at the top of her head. "You gotta stop."

"What?" She glanced up at him through her eyelashes and, unraveling her legs from around his waist, allowed herself to drop to her feet in front of him. Turning slowly, she sauntered towards the walk-in shower. A small smirk crossed her face when she heard Cole's feet moving swiftly behind her right before he snatched her into his arms.

With her back to his chest, she could feel his growl before she heard it against her ear. "One of these days I'm going to bend your bratty ass over the bed and spank you until you learn a lesson, but right now, I don't have the patience for it." He walked them into the shower, letting her slide down the front of his body in an achingly slow movement while they approached the far wall of the walk-in. "Now... bend over and place your forearms against the wall."

Hinging at the waist, she braced herself against the side of the shower, exposing herself to the predatory man prowling behind her. He dragged a possessive hand down her back, palmed her ass roughly. "If this gets to be too much for you or you want to stop for any reason at all, say the word 'marshmallow,' okay?" Her head bobbed up and down in confirmation, but Cole's hands paused on her behind. "I need to hear you say it, Evie."

"Yes," she murmured. "Yes, I'll say the word 'marshmallow' if it gets to be too much."

"That's good. Now I know you might be sore, Angel, but remember that you brought this on yourself." Her whimper filled the room at the same time he brought a heavy strike down on her ass cheek.

She cried out, her back arching at the sudden pain.

"Fuck," he bit out. "God, you're so beautiful." He struck her ass a second time, this time on the other cheek, slowly sliding two fingers of his other hand inside her as he did so.

She rose to her toes, letting out his name on a keening cry. His fingers alone felt incredible inside her, but she needed more, especially as the pain from his spanks slowly morphed into something brutally pleasurable, her clit throbbing with each hit. Tossing her head back, she sobbed out his name, grinding against his hand, tightening around the fingers he was fucking her with.

With each slap of her ass, each pump of his fingers, he kept up a constant stream of filth in a low, distorted voice. "Look at you, so goddamn needy for my dick. You're such a dirty little witch, so wet and already filled with my cum but needing me to fill you up again."

Evie was not above begging. "Cole, please for the love of all the gods, please let me come," she whined, slanting a look at him over her shoulder.

"How can I say no when you ask so nicely," Cole teased, lining himself up with her entrance and slamming into her in a single thrust. She cried out, the sound mingling with Cole's shouted, "Fuck, baby!"

Although he had fucked her slowly with his fingers, his pace now that he was inside her was ravenous, his thrusts intense and quick. He had one arm resting on the shower wall above her, the other wrapped around her waist as he drove his hips relentlessly.

She was screaming now—had no idea when her voice had ratcheted in volume that quickly—the concert of her ecstasy mixing with his feral demands to echo through the bathroom. "Angel, drop your fingers to that sensitive pussy of yours," he ordered, maintaining his brutal pace. She obeyed him immediately, strumming her clit desperately, already feeling her inner walls clench around him. "You're gonna come for me, and, when I fill you up, you're gonna take every fucking drop of me, aren't you?"

"Oh gods," she cried, her muscles tensing as she neared her orgasm.

"There's no other god here, just me. Now beg your god to let you come, baby."

"Please let me come, sir," she pleaded, the honorific rolling off her tongue without thought.

His thrusts paused, and she was almost sobbing for relief when he picked back up his pace, an overwhelming growl pouring from his throat. "That's right, Angel, come all over your sir's cock. Make a fucking mess of me," he ordered.

Her muscles seized around him, and the world vanished into stars as she screamed out his name, clamping down around him, her body writhing in pleasure. Behind her, she dimly heard him bellow, and then he was pouring himself into her, fucking her through her first orgasm and tumbling her into a second.

Cole's head slumped to her shoulder, his uneven breaths coming hot against her shoulder. "Seriously, I think you might actually kill me," he breathed. "I'm not sure I'm young enough for marathon sex anymore."

Evie snapped her head around, glaring at him. Although the coven shared all its worldly goods and convened to share powers for larger spells, there was no way in this realm or any other that she would share *her* Cole. When she spoke, her voice was frosty. "Maybe let's not talk about your previous sexual conquests while you're still inside of me."

Cole's eyebrows rose, and he chuckled as he slid out of her. "You jealous, witchling?"

"No, not at all," she lied, slowly standing before turning to face him. "But just in case, give me their names—"

The chuckle bloomed into a full-throated laugh. "Angel, you're not gonna curse them."

How was she the only reasonable one here? Cole was hers, and anybody else who had ever experienced him needed to go. "It wouldn't be a real curse. Just, like, a little tiny one."

Cole gripped the back of her neck, his thumb stroking along her pounding pulse. "Look at me," he commanded. Her eyes flew to his at the stern tone that had replaced his laughter. "I'm only going to say this once, because it's laughable that you think that any of the other women in my past could hold a fucking candle to you. Are you listening to me?"

She nodded.

"You're it for me, Angel. There will never be another fucking woman in my life that makes me feel the way that you do. None of the women I've fucked before—" she harrumphed but shut her mouth at the dark look he gave her. "None of them matter now, and honestly, I don't even remember any of them. You want to know why?" He paused, tightening his grip around her neck just slightly, enough to show he meant what he was saying. "Do you want to know why?" She finally inclined her head in a nod. "Because they weren't you. You're the only person I want—have ever wanted—in this damn world, even before I knew your name. Even before I knew you were *real*. I fantasized about you while I was inside them, wished with every minute that it was you begging me to make you come. So don't bother thinking about any of them because you are all I have ever wanted. The only woman I'm ever thinking about. I only want you." Green eyes met hers. "So believe me when I say, you have nothing to be jealous of."

Chewing on her lower lip in thought, she finally conceded the point by stepping back under the water and drawing him with her.

Interlude

Chugach Coven

Chugach National Forest, Seward, Alaska, United States

Three girls hid behind the trees at the edge of the forest where they lived, peeking out at the small village near their wooded home. Lights danced in faraway windows, and behind the glass, shadows of people flickered, offering a small glimpse into the home life of villagers the girls would never know.

It was a quiet, cold area at what seemed like the edge of the world to most, but to Natalya, Amaruq, and Stephanie, it was home. Well, the only home that they had ever known. The coven elders made sure they knew the stories of how they each came to be there, though. Stephanie had been born in summer and sent down the barely-thawed rivers to the forest days later, swaddled in a thick blanket. An Inuit elder had escorted four-year old Amaruq into the forest and sat with her until the forest bade the elder to retreat. Natalya was dumped at the edge of the forest, too young to defend herself and half-freezing.

Now in their late teens, they knew who and what they were. They knew why they had been abandoned, and their adopted mothers—the High Priestess and the other elders—taught them the craft, alongside their sisters. They stayed in the forest for their own protection, knowing that humankind embraced the fantasy of witchcraft, not the reality.

On uneventful nights, Natalya, Stephanie, and Amaruq loved to sit, carefully hidden, at the edge of the trees, observing the daily lives of the local villagers and, illuminating the sky like the glow of faeries, the far-away lights of Anchorage, all of it surrounded by millions of stars. They told stories about what it might be like to see it up close.

But these weren't uneventful times. The night before, an unexpected fire had ravaged their still-frozen forest—sparking spontaneously before disappearing just as quickly—and devastated the area surrounding the witches' home. After that, they needed an escape. A way to experience some normality and dream of what it may be like to be somewhere new.

"Do you think we could do it?" Natalya whispered to her sisters. "Do you think we could go to the village? Akna would never know we were gone. And it would only be for just a little while."

Stephanie snapped her head back, eyebrows raising high, almost disappearing into her black hair. "Oh yeah, great idea. Do you think they burn witches here or just send them naked into the snow to die? Plus Akna not knowing something? Are you crazy? She knew when you stole food from the larder while she was away."

Natalya glared. "That's because you told her, you little snitch." Over Stephanie's snickering, she asked Amaruq, "What do you think? Should we do it?" At Amaruq's silence, she wheedled, "Come on, it would be fun!"

"I guess. But Akna would know. And I don't think she would like it. At all." Natalya's face fell so Amaruq hurried to add, "But you know the prophecy says that someday the witches may be seen by the outside world. After last night, who knows. That may be closer than we think."

Natalya snorted. "Amaruq, that is not nearly as reassuring as I think you meant it to be. We were almost burned out of our home yesterday. If this is the start of the prophecy, it's not going to be sunshine and rainbows. We would be leaving to render apocalyptic judgments under the old gods' authority and raining fire and bringing death to all around us. Purging the world of all humanity. I don't know about you, but that's definitely not the way I saw myself going into the village."

Giggling, Stephanie poked her sister. "You know it sounds really bad when you say things like that? 'Purging the world.' It sounds like genocide."

"Well, you know it kind of is genocide. But it's an inspecific sort of genocide, which I guess makes it better?" The three girls fell quiet, as silent as the village they could see but never enter.

"Girls!" A booming voice rang out behind them, unexpected and echoing in the clear, snowy night. "What in the holy name of Rihannon are you doing?"

The three girls swiveled as one, each bearing an identical look of guilt. "Nothing, Akna," they chimed, staring at their feet as their High Priestess loomed over them.

Sighing, Akna wrapped the three girls in her arms and escorted them back into the forest. "What is our most important rule, my daughters? Especially after last night." The trees rushed around them as she shooed them deeper into the frozen tundra.

"We don't set fire to our sister's homes. Even if it's by accident." Natalya's charcoal-colored eyes danced with mischief.

Akna exhaled once more, pinching her most impish daughter on the upper arm. "No, my darling, that is *your* most important rule. What is the coven's most important rule?"

The three girls fell silent for a brief second before chorusing, "Don't be seen by the outside world."

"And why is that?" Akna prompted as they entered the small copse that marked the beginning of the witch's territory. Before her, faerie lights became evident, revealing trees twisted into the walls of houses. "Have you forgotten the stories? Have you forgotten what happened to our sister covens around the world? The systematic extermination of Europe witches during World War II? The Rwandan genocides? The slaughter of Vietnamese witches mistaken for combatants during the War? To mention but a few."

Once again, the girls were silent. They all knew the stories—they were the first ones they had heard as children, after all, warnings against leaving the forest, lest they be hunted. Even after the witch trials, the 1900s had not been kind to their kind, resulting in mass extinction across Europe, Africa, and Asia, and the overall depletion of power as witches died around the globe. Thousands of years of records were destroyed, including those chronicling their most important prophecy as apocalyptic harbingers. That information now lived exclusively in the heads of the small population of witches that had survived the exterminations.

"But that could never happen here, Akna." Stephanie glanced pleadingly at their High Priestess. "This is a peaceful area. They would never hurt us, even if they found us."

Akna placed her hand on Natalya's head as the girl began to shake, her eyes haunted. "It depends on what you mean by hurt. They don't need to physically assault us to injure us. Sometimes cruelty or selfishness are sufficient to hurt. They can destroy our natural resources. They can imprison us. Mankind has no limit on innovation when it comes to the destruction of its fellow beings."

Amaruq burst out, "But that would be an act of aggression against us. We could protect ourselves if they attacked us like that!"

"An ye harm none, do what ye will." Akna intoned the witches' creed. "Even if they are aggressors, we may not harm them. As witches, it is our duty to maintain the balance. Only when the balance is irredeemably upset, as prophesized, may we act."

"But that's stupid," Amaruq argued. "How are we supposed to comply with the prophecy if we're not around to do just that? If we're murdered by *them*—" She flapped her hand in the direction of the village. "—or they destroy the resources allowing us to survive or some other horrible thing, why can we not protect ourselves with violence if necessary? The early witches who wrote the creed were peaceful, not stupid!" Gesturing to indicate their ice-ridden home, blanketed by snow, now surrounded by fire-charred trees, she glared at their High Priestess.

"Go home, girls." Akna pushed them towards their respective caretakers. "I know it does not make sense now, but this is our sworn duty. We have been tasked by our gods with the purity of the world. We may only become involved when men have destroyed the Earth and turn on one another. Now, however... " She gestured them once more towards their adopted mothers. "You must go to bed. We have tasks to complete come morning."

As the three girls trudged to their homes, Akna's gaze flitted across the women and girls that she thought of as her children. They were all precious, and she loved them all. She turned as her wife, Malina, approached her, appearing to shine from within.

"How did your travels go, my love?" Malina asked, resting her cheek against Akna's shoulder. She felt Akna shrug before responding.

"The fish are dying, and the glaciers are melting. People are attacking those of different skin colors than themselves and just yesterday, I watched a group stone a man who loved other men." Akna rubbed her temples before wrapping her arms around Malina, hoping to shed the feeling of hopelessness seeping into her bones. "The hatred and vitriol that spew from men's televisions... it is horrifying. And with the fires of late? They nearly destroyed our home! At what point do you think we call the Council together? The news anchors seem to indicate that this problem is global. If so, then the prophecy's day may have come." She sighed. "Regardless of whether we agree with our ancestors' interpretation of it or not."

"It's possible that you may have to wear your bone tiara once more. The prophecy implies that we will know for certain, though, no doubt whatsoever. I do wish we hadn't lost the records of it during the extermination. An apocalypse is so final, and pursuing violence against the world... " Malina bit her lip, shaking her head. With a huff, she turned to a different topic. "We did receive news from the Barataria Coven in Louisiana while you were gone, though."

"Oh?" Akna escorted Malina back to their home, wanting nothing more than a good night's rest.

"Two messages, technically. The first inquired about an earthquake that hit New Orleans and did a significant amount of damage to their forest. The second... " Malina trailed off.

Akna sat at the foot of their bed, untangling her hair, glancing up when her wife remained silent. "The second?"

"The second let us know that they've been attacked."

Hands flying to her face to cover her gasp, Akna leapt to her feet. "They were attacked? What happened?"

"Do you remember the toddler they found all those years ago? The one with the dead woman?"

Akna nodded. It was almost completely unheard of for there to be anyone with a child when they were left to the witches. When the toddler was found not just with another person but with a corpse? That raised concerns in covens the world over. It grew worse when Barataria shared that their seeress identified the toddler as the murderer and shared the cryptic phrases she kept repeating during her prophecy. Some of the older witches and more traditional covens had argued for the young girl's ejection from the forest. The truly traditional among them had demanded that she be put to death. Fortunately, neither of those demands were met, although other extreme safeguards had been put in place as a compromise; even still, that decision had resulted in schisms between the covens for years.

"She went missing then returned with knowledge she shouldn't have about who she is. A man named Cole Aidoneus followed her, broke their protective boundaries with death magic, and disclosed that the girl herself has death magic. The girl *left* with him after turning the forest against the coven."

"Why did she turn the forest against them?" Akna asked absently, her brain turning over the name Aidoneus. It sounded so familiar. Aidoneus. *Where have I heard that name before?* Even as Malina responded to her question, she was barely paying attention, walking over to the books lining the walls of their home. As if they might have an answer. *Aidoneus, Aidoneus, Aidoneus, Aidoneus*, she recited in her head as she ran her finger along the spines of their library.

"Why do you keeping saying 'Aidoneus,' my love?" Malina sounded slightly exasperated, leading Akna to think that this might not have been the first time she posed the question.

Scratch that, apparently I was reciting the name out loud.

"I know that name. It sounds... I recognize it. From somewhere?" Her voice lilted up in a question as her finger ran across a book on world mythology.

Aidoneus. Startled, she tugged out the thick tome, flipping to the index where her eyes raced down the page until she found *Hades - 1, 47, 56 - 60, 63.* Her fingers flipped quickly through the pages until she lit on a page entitled **Hades**. Siblings, spouse, children, history, powers... and there, buried at the end of the pages detailing the god, was a small section labeled **Other Names**. Aidoneus was the first among them. Akna froze.

From where she stood looking over Akna's shoulder at the open book, Malina gasped. "You don't think—"

"That the old gods may have returned in the form of Cole Aidoneus and this witch?" Akna's heart beat fast. "I'm scared it may be a very real possibility, darling. We'll need to call the Council together. Quickly."

Chapter 36

Cole

Garden District, New Orleans, Louisiana

After their shower, Evie more or less passed out, despite the sun barely having set. With his witch curled in his bed, her hand and head resting on his chest, Cole felt more at peace than he ever had in his life. That peace, unfortunately, hadn't followed him into sleep as he fell into dreams that were filled with darkness and angry shadows and screaming.

Now, at 5:00 in the morning, Cole was wide awake with no chance of falling back asleep in sight. After tossing and turning enough that he was concerned he might wake Evie, he left the bed long enough to take a detour through the flower-saturated halls, which now had floral archways spanning the doorways after their shower, into his newly-greenhoused study to retrieve his laptop and his glasses since it was way too early for contacts. As he walked back to the bedroom, he considered the upkeep it would take for their menagerie of exotic flowers to thrive. The moment he crossed the bedroom's threshold, though, all thoughts of floral care and maintenance drained from his head at the sight of

Evie nestled in the black silken sheets. Exactly where she was always meant to be.

He crossed the room and crawled in next to his Angel. Still deep in sleep, she nestled back into him, extending an arm across his waist before sighing softly. A small smile tilted his own lips at the feeling of her wrapped around him. Settling back against the headboard, he rested his laptop on his thighs, turning it on and settling his glasses on his face as it booted up. He had taken off work for the last two days—and was more or less fully off grid generally since he still hadn't replaced his melted phone and apparently only a few people had that cursed landline number—so his inbox was sure to be a thing of nightmares.

Once he logged in, he dimmed the brightness and muted the damn thing. He wouldn't risk waking Evie up for something as trivial as work. Groaning softly, he finally loaded his email and the firm's messaging app. Sure enough, 514 emails sat glaring at him from his inbox. The messaging app finally started up and—oh grand—only 72 messages there. Time to triage the damage, organizing the communications into the things that needed to be immediately addressed, those that could hold forty-eight hours, and those that could go into his trash bin without any action. He pulled up the messaging screen, only to see fifteen DMs from Hayden, whose own circle showed him as available.

we have the depo at 2:00. did you want to be there?

you good, man?

seriously, where the fuck are you?

are you dead?

guess no depo for you then.

The messages tapered off once the deposition started at 2:00, but at 2:30, Hayden's messages got more urgent.

dude, everything's fucked over here. massive earth-quake just took down the building next door, a few of our windows shattered. nyx got hit by some of the glass when the windows went out and we're getting her to the hospital asap. everybody else seems to be fine, but something big's going down.

Cole squinted at his computer. What the fuck? And who the hell was Nyx? He knew that probably wasn't a relevant question, but he hadn't expected to get hit by this news either.

power's out. check in, cole. this shit is bad. you good?

cole, you have answered messages while you were getting blown. where the FUCK are you, man.

The messages only grew more intense and insulting from there until, in an intense burst of profanity and caps lock, Hayden threatened to come over to the house to see whether Cole was "a-fucking-live." That threat came at—Cole checked the message—3:30 am. The final message at 4:58 am made ominous noises about dreamwalking to ensure Cole was alive. Cole's eyebrows shot up at that one. That was definitely a bold move from Hayden, flexing his power to enter dreams as the god of sleep, especially against his best friend who was also his king.

Cole checked the message receipt times again. Although he hadn't been keeping a particularly close eye on the time, he felt pretty good guessing that the 2:30 earthquake took place right around when he was sinking into Evie for the first time. His brain and body took very different approaches to that memory; rationally, he knew that an earthquake taking down buildings at the same time he and Evie were having sex for the first time was both a very big deal and not at all a coincidence. Physically, however, he wanted to slide the covers back and wake Evie with his tongue between her legs.

He was still battling the diametrically opposed impulses when his screen lit with an incoming call. Hayden. After kissing Evie's forehead, he unwrapped himself from her arms and quickstepped into the hallway to answer the call.

On the other end, Hayden looked harried, an unusual expression for the usually collected man. "Where the *fuck* have you been, Cole? Nobody can get ahold of you, the building is crumbling around our goddamn ears, we've got an employee in the hospital because she got hit by glass shrapnel—"

"Man, I get the gravity of the situation, but lower your fucking voice," Cole snapped, taking a look at the closed bedroom door as he made his way to the study. Evie had had a big few days; if Hayden woke her up, Cole would rain hell down on him, best friend or not.

"Lower my—where are you?" Somehow, Hayden's face grew more disgruntled, which Cole would have bet wasn't possible. Fortunately, Cole made it to the study and had the door closed before Hayden started yelling. "Are you serious? You went missing for *two entire goddamn days because you were fucking the Kore reincarnate*!!!"

In the moment, Cole's eyesight went vibrant blue as his magic built in rage. Mostly, though, he saw himself crushing his best friend's head in his hands. His words were clipped when he actually found himself able to speak once more. "Don't. You. Ever. Fucking. Talk. About. Her. Like. That."

At his furious, clipped response, Hayden's icy gaze narrowed on Cole, the astute asshole recognizing that his shouted question still hadn't been answered. "Cole, man, you didn't actually say why you vanished during an earthquake that all but took down the building and injured our employees. Did you fuck the Kore reincarnate?" At Cole's irate glance at the laptop's camera, he rolled his eyes. "Fine, made love, had sex, did the boom boom, what the fuck ever."

"Yes," Cole gritted out. "And before you ask, you nosy motherfucker, yeah, I'm pretty sure the first time we had sex was around when the earthquake hit."

"Does she know what that means for the two of you?" Hayden demanded, just as the door to his study creaked open.

Cole looked over to see a very naked Evie, still half asleep by the looks of it, standing in the doorway. "Hey, Angel," he greeted her, interrupting Hayden's stream of consciousness speaking. "Did I wake you up?"

She shook her head slowly. "No." Her hair was disheveled, her voice hoarse from sleep, her eyes barely open. He had never seen anything look so good in his life. "I woke up, and you weren't there. When I heard yelling, I came to see what was wrong." She moved towards the desk, but he stood before she came into view of the webcam, wrapping her in the blazer he kept on the back of his chair for Zoom hearings. It hung past her knees, completely dwarfing her petite, curvy frame, but at least it covered all the essentials.

"Is that Evie?" Hayden shouted, clearly shifting into his role as obnoxious best friend meeting the significant other. "Let me see her!"

Cole gathered Evie in his arms, drawing her into his lap as he sank back into his office chair. She stared owlishly at the webcam, auburn hair tousled from sleep.

"You Evie?" Hayden asked.

"Last I checked," Evie snipped at him. "Who are you?"

"I'm Hayden, Cole's best friend, business partner, and life coach." Cole and Evie snorted simultaneously at the clear bullshit emerging from Hayden. "Hey, that's not fair," Hayden—an immortal god whose good looks appeared to be of a man in his late 30s—pouted childishly in response to their mockery. "You two aren't supposed to gang up on me. When you finally got a girl, Cole, she and I were supposed to gang up on you. It's the rules of friendship."

Cole shrugged, smothering a smirk as Evie nestled further into his arms. "I don't think Evie's gonna agree to that. Think she's showing a strong preference for me."

She yawned but nodded. "Definitely going with Cole. No question."

Cole looked down at Evie, commented quietly, "Angel, we're gonna get you back to bed soon. Think you still need some sleep after yesterday." A blush rose along her cheekbones, the color intensifying as he nuzzled her ear and whispered, "We've got a lot of missed time to make up for." Her eyes went lusty; she leaned into him, running her hand along his chest. Before he could get distracted by her, Cole turned back to Hayden. "Ask me again what you asked before Evie got here."

"Whether you two have had sex? I'm pretty sure by the way you're pawing at each other that I already know the answer to that one."

"No. Whether she knows."

Hayden's face went serious once more. "Evie, did Cole tell you what being intimate meant for you? For the two of you?"

"Are you talking about the fact that we're reincarnates? That we're meant to rule the Underworld together? That we're fated in some kind of way?" At Hayden's nod, Evie's spine stiffened. Although her tone was pleasant when she spoke again, her face belied her anger. "Or are you actually asking whether your best friend hid information from me to have sex and trap me in a long-term relationship?" She was now turned fully towards the camera, ass resting on Cole's cock, which was rapidly hardening as she came to his defense.

"Let me make myself perfectly fucking clear, Hayden." She spat out his name like a curse. "I chose Cole. I've chosen Cole every night since I was a child falling asleep with his voice in my ears and his eyes in my sight. And when I met him in person, I chose him then too. He told me everything before we ever had sex. He made sure I knew I had a choice before we had sex and wouldn't touch me until I had made my own decision about what I wanted to do. It was infuriating." Hayden's snicker echoed through the speakers, but Evie's voice drowned it out. "And I chose to have sex with him too because Cole is my whole godsdamned world and always has been, and I would be proud to rule by his side as his queen. And I really don't appreciate you thinking that he would hide something like that from me." She settled back into Cole's lap with a huff of irritation.

Her frustration only lasted a moment when she recognized just how hard he was. She gave a soft wriggle against him that almost had him ripping open the blazer she wore to feast on her, camera be damned. "Now, Cole and I are going back to bed. Whatever is going wrong with the office or the world or whatever we have to do can wait until we wake up, and then we'll meet you—" She looked at Cole.

"We'll meet you at the office, man. I'm gonna take my girl back to bed." Cole shut the laptop lid on Hayden's murmured, "This is a good match, Cole Aidoneus."

Without checking whether the call had dropped, Cole tilted a giggling Evie into a searing kiss before carrying her back to bed where he stripped his suit jacket from her and proceeded to remind her who she belonged to.

Chapter 37

Cole

Garden District, New Orleans, Louisiana

Cole woke to the morning sun streaming in through the curtains and Evie curled next to him, her hair spread across the pillow and body relaxed in sleep. One of her legs was splayed across his own.

Sifting his fingers through her silky hair, he watched the light catch it, drawing out all of the colors that made up her unique auburn; vibrant rich reds, deep mahogany, and even hints of gold glinted in its depths. He let the strands slip through his fingers before lifting his head to scan the room for his phone so he could check the time. It took him about thirty seconds of wild searching before he remembered that it was currently a melted blob of plastic somewhere in—he glanced to the right of the bed—yep, right over there. Sitting on the floor, useless and ruined. They needed to go shopping today before heading over to the office to check in on Hayden and make sure that everything hadn't been destroyed in the earthquake. He frowned. Was the damage isolated to New Orleans? If not, they needed to check in on their other offices and staff too. After doing that, though, they needed to go to his uncle's house to catch him up on everything and introduce him to Evie.

Charles had been a confirmed bachelor for much of his life, save a small blip in his thirties that he never talked about except when he was half a bottle of bourbon in. Although his uncle said he never regretted his lack of a romantic life, Cole knew that Charlie had always wanted more kids than just the angry, magical orphan that he got by accident. Specifically, he knew Charles wanted a little girl to spoil. Hopefully, a daughter-in-law would meet that wish.

He caught a glimpse of the digital clock sitting in the bathroom. 8:30 am. Most shops in the area didn't open until 9:00, Hayden didn't get out of bed before 10:00 and was never at the office before 11:00—noon if Cole was being honest rather than charitable—so there was really very little point to getting out of bed right now. That gave him a little bit of time to wake up his Angel the way she deserved. Cole's lips lifted in a predatory grin.

A small whimper rose from next to him, and Evie rolled to her back. Her legs scissored back and forth; his name emerged from her mouth on a whisper. After they returned from their early morning phone call with Hayden, Cole had bent Evie's pretty little body over the side of the bed and railed her through three orgasms, the final of which had her squirting all over him and the sheets, which prompted the hardest nut of his fucking life as she drenched him. Screamed for him. God, he would never get tired of her sounds.

Time to make her give him some more of those magnificent cries. With a gentle tug, he freed his arm from under her neck and slid down the bed, settling her legs over his shoulders. One long finger swept down her slit, and he nearly came out of his skin at how wet she already was for him. He kissed the inside of her thigh before dropping his mouth to her pussy, giving a decadent lick that ran from her ass to her clit before settling in to devour her. He growled into her. Gods, her taste was ambrosial, coating his lips and tongue.

She whimpered again, not yet awake, as he slid two fingers deep in her tight little channel, crooking them as he pumped slowly. The hair on the back of his neck stood up as his magic rose in response to her own awakening. She was still asleep, but her legs were already subtly trembling against his shoulders.

With absolute disregard for easing Evie awake, Cole wrapped his lips around her sensitive clit and sucked.

Chapter 38

Evie

Garden District, New Orleans, Louisiana

This dream was more salacious than any she had ever had before. After Cole took her in ways she wasn't aware existed before last night, she had fallen into a deep, dreamless sleep. But now... now, she was dreaming Cole was between her legs, licking her as if he were starving for her taste. Gods, she didn't know a dream could make her come, but she was already so close to the edge. She moaned, the noise sounding unexpectedly real to her ears;and her eyebrows creased in confusion. Suddenly, other small details started to come into focus too. She was a little sore. Her left ankle tickled. Her legs were elevated on muscular shoulders. Magic prickled along her flesh, skimmed across her throbbing nipples. Her eyes fluttered open. Yeah. She was definitely awake.

The most important detail of them all was Cole lying in between her legs, alternatively sucking and licking ravenously at her clit while his fingers surged in and out of her, crooked just enough to hit her g-spot. His eyes glinted up at her mischievously as she writhed under his tongue and fingers.

"Cole," she moaned, dropping her hands to his hair. "Cole, please."

He shook his head, resting his chin on her pelvis and staring at her. "You're to call me 'sir' if you want me to let you come, Angel. You think you can manage that?"

Evie raised herself to her elbows. At one point, she had read a book on sexual dynamics, and it felt like this fell into one of those categories. Tilting her head, she gazed down at Cole, whose own facial expression was stern. Intense. Passionate. His eyes were swirling with the colors of his magic, but they bore a feral look of possession that she knew was just for her.

"Can you manage that?" he repeated.

In response, she lowered herself back to the bed and said, "Yes, sir."

The groan that Cole let out was sudden and sharp but not nearly as abrupt as his next movement. Without any warning, he surged up the bed to the pillows, laying on his back and fixing his gaze on her. "Come sit on my face."

"What?"

"Crawl up here and sit on my face, Angel." He gestured to where he wanted her. She hesitantly followed his orders, hovering over his head uncertainly. "Now, put your hands on the headboard and ride my face while I tongue fuck your sweet little cunt."

Evie moaned at his filthy words, settling her hands on the headboard before gingerly lowering herself over his head.

Cole slapped her ass and snarled into her core, "I said sit on my face, *belle*. So sit on my fucking face." With her center of gravity off balance from his spank, her full weight dropped, her pussy coming to rest right over his mouth. Before she could move, his hands wrapped around her thighs, holding her down. "God, I love the way you taste," emerged from between her legs right before he wrapped his lips around her clit and sucked.

"Sir! Fuck, sir," she cried out. Suddenly, she was rocking her hips over his face, all decorum and concerns gone. He devoured her like he would die if he couldn't taste her; it was absolutely destroying her. Her back arched as she moaned above him.

"Please don't stop," she begged, barely conscious of what she was asking as he laved her clit with his tongue, lightly teasing it with quick flicks before sucking it back into his mouth. The orgasm he had stirred up while she was sleeping sat just out of reach. "Sir, please!"

One of his hands moved from her thigh, dropping out of sight. Twisting her head, she saw his hand wrapped around his dick, pre-cum welling at the tip as his muscles flexed while he stroked himself. The sight of him so overwhelmed by her that he had to fuck himself was more than she could bear, and her rhythm faltered against his talented tongue. His mouth curled into a smile that she could feel against her core just before his free hand spread her wide with his fingers, curling two of them deep inside her and pumping intensely, rubbing along her sensitive inner wall. "Sir," she gasped. With one final stroke of his finger, one last firm lick of her clit, her body seized, magic pouring from her as she toppled into an intense and overwhelming orgasm, fueled by the sound of Cole's shout against her as he came.

Evie was still floating when Cole lifted her off his face to rest beside him in bed while he carelessly wiped his cum off his chest with his shirt, discarded on the floor next to the bed after one of their many act breaks the night before. After chucking it in the general direction of the bathroom and missing wildly if the sound of clothing hitting carpet was any indication, he pulled her into his body, nuzzling into her hair, kissing her forehead. "Morning, Angel." Neither of them paid much attention to the weeping willow that had bloomed in the far side of the bedroom, thanks to her seemingly limitless ability to magically cause spontaneous plant growth whenever Cole made her come.

She shivered at the feel of his fingers running down her side. "Definitely a good wake up." Her voice was hoarse, a fact that her far-too-astute lover more than caught onto. Under her cheek, a quiet laugh rumbled.

"I would say. I'm pretty sure we woke up about half of our neighbors. The other ones only slept through it 'cause they're dead." His lips settled against her forehead once more. "You've got a helluva set of lungs on you, Angel. It's sexy as fuck."

Propping her chin on his chest, she looked into his oh-so-familiar eyes. "Why do you call me Angel?" she asked. "Don't get me wrong: I love it. I just don't understand why that pet name."

Cole sighed and paused long enough that she wasn't sure she was going to get an answer. "When I first started seeing you in dreams, I thought you were my guardian angel." At her quizzical look, he clarified. "I was a kid and dumb, but you were this absolutely radiant, pretty girl who talked to me, no matter how stupid and angry I was. I figured the only way you would want to talk to me is if you were, I dunno, assigned to protect me." Her throat clenched at the idea of Cole as a small boy, alone and scared, just looking forward to spending time with someone who was happy to see him. "As we got older, you just got more beautiful, and you became the ideal that every other woman had to live up to. You had to be an angel because it was impossible for someone to be that fucking stunning. When I saw you that night at the construction site, god, it was like I'd gotten struck by lightning. And when we confirmed that you were actually Evangeline Dyeus, this pet name I've had for you in my head most of my life became a nickname because—"

"Angel is in my birth name," she interrupted.

"So you're my Angel because you're too beautiful to be of this earth—which, as it so happens, is actually true since we'll be ruling the Underworld soon—and because it's your name." He heaved a breath. "And speaking of ruling the Underworld, we have to get out of bed."

"Why?" Evie hated the whine in her voice, but she was lazy, satisfied, and almost positive that if they got out of bed now, their day could only go downhill from this perfect morning.

"Well, for starters, I need a new phone. If I have to hear that landline one more time, I swear to god, I will not be held responsible for my actions. Then we gotta get you some clothes that you choose rather than my forty-five-year-old assistant. She may have great taste, but it's not yours. You need to have clothes that make you happy. Plus, we have things to do in the outside world, and—" A murderous look took over his face unexpectedly, and his eyes flashed that intense blue. "I will put anybody who sees you half-dressed in the fucking ground."

Smothering a smile, knowing that she would be the exact same way if any person were to so much as dare to try and catch a glimpse of Cole like this, much less actually try to touch him, Evie rubbed his cheek reassuringly. "Purely hypothetical. Nobody is ever going to get to see me like this but you. I'm yours, love. Just yours."

His gaze softened, the fury draining from his face as quickly as it appeared. "So after we go shopping for new clothes for you and a new phone for me—" Her eyes dropped to the melted brick on the floor, her snicker at the memory of him burning it slipping past her clenched lips. "Then we need to go check in at my office because, apparently, a massive earthquake yesterday tore up the building real bad."

Evie gasped. "Because of us?"

Cole stayed silent, but she could see the truth of it in the tenseness of his jaw and the depths of his emerald eyes.

"Cole." Her voice was stern. "Don't try and hide things from me."

"I would never. Even if I wanted to, I doubt I could get away with it. You have a way of seeing through my bullshit that no one else does." His mouth kicked up in a gentle smile before he pressed a soft kiss to her lips. "But, in answer to your question, yeah, I think it was because of us. The earthquake happened right around the first time we had sex, and it was bigger than anything New Orleans has ever seen before. Makes sense that we would be the cause."

Her lips parted, a puff of air sliding through them. The witches' creed demanded that a witch harm no other living being, but something she had done—technically, they had done—had probably hurt people.

"Hey, hey," Cole said, no doubt seeing the panic in her eyes. "This is something that was going to happen, no matter what, now that we've found each other. And the alternative to us opening the Underworld is far worse. The shades will destroy this world if they stay here longer, and humans... well, humanity doesn't need any help from the shades to be awful."

"I know." She nodded sadly. "I mean, yeah, I know all of that. And I know that this was my choice, and there's no way we could do this without any violence. I just didn't expect it to happen so soon."

Cole tucked a stray curl behind her ear, his hand cupping her cheek. "I get it. You don't have to bear this burden alone, though, *ma petite sorcière*. I'm here with you to share in the weight of anything and everything we do."

Evie's heart clenched at the man in front of her promising her that she would never be alone or unsupported. They were a team of two. Pushing herself upwards by pressing her palms to his chest, she stretched herself over his body and kissed him hard, passionately enough that they were both breathless when they pulled apart.

"Fucking hell, though, Angel, you do make a compelling case for staying in bed." Disheveled and aroused Cole was dangerous to her.

"What?" she drawled the word at him sarcastically. "I thought we had 'errands' to run." Her fingers made scare quotes around "errands."

"You're bratty but right." Cole clicked his tongue and grimaced. "I also need to take you to meet my Uncle Charlie. Would you be okay doing that today or tomorrow?"

Her eyes widened. How had she not realized that she would be meeting his family? "Umm, sure?" It sounded like a question even to her ears.

"You sure?" Cole asked, one eyebrow raised. "We don't have to yet if you're not ready. I can put him off for however long you need."

"No, not at all." She hurried to explain. "I didn't think about meeting your family. What if they don't like me?"

Cole smiled widely. "Oh please, they're going to love you. In fact, I would be surprised if Charlie didn't prefer you." She snorted indelicately at the absurdity of that. "But, and this is never going to happen, if they don't like you, then fuck them. I lo—" His eyes went wide, and his mouth slammed shut. When he spoke again, his voice was hesitant. "I like you, and that's all that matters."

Evie's heart raced in her chest. He had been about to tell her he loved her, and she hated that he had corrected himself. Because she already knew how she felt about him.

"Alright." Cole groaned, sliding out from under her. An undignified squeal left her mouth when he scooped her into his arms, holding her tightly as he walked them into the closet. "Time to get out of here, *mon ange*." He set her down on the chaise lounge and turned to pick out his own clothing while she picked through her options from the bags on the floor, wondering if it was normal to be terrified to meet a lover's family.

Chapter 39

Cole

Garden District, New Orleans, Louisiana

Two hours later, after replacing his cell and getting a phone set up for Evie—which she had already managed to leave in the store, lose twice, and almost break once—they finally made it to the Garden District Free People. Cole figured the bohemian-style clothing the shop specialized in wouldn't grate on Evie's nerves too badly, especially since she seemed drawn to looser fit clothing.

The two staff members currently overseeing the store stared at them intently, which could be because they were the only people in the store. Or it could be that his witch was standing in their shop in her now-cleaned dress from their first night together, which Daeira had sent over with the intern. Beyond being practically transparent, it barely covered anything. He glowered at the clerks from behind her. *Why in the hell did I let her out of the house in that dress when there was probably a perfectly good alternative sitting in the bags Dae sent over?*

"Can we, um, can we help you?" The braver of the two finally greeted, his eyes on Evie's bare legs. "We've got some stuff that would, uh, that would definitely look good on you."

Cole's response was sharp, drawing the boy's attention away from *his witch's legs*. "We'll take care of things from here," *you little fucker*, he finished in his head. His tone left little room for argument as he swept Evie deeper into the store towards the jeans. He lowered his head and voice so that only Evie could hear him. "Angel, we have to cover up those legs of yours if you're going out in public."

The little tease tossed her hair back, shooting him a brazen smile that nearly had him escorting her into one of the dressing rooms for some privacy. "I would have thought you wanted as much of me on display as possible."

"I want you displayed for me. The rest of these assholes don't get to see what's mine." He nipped her ear. "Now behave and pick out some clothing."

Evie hummed a bit while she toured the store, running her fingers and the backs of her hands across clothing. It only took him a few minutes to figure out what each of her little noises and movements meant. Softer fabrics got a "hmm" of approval; rougher fabrics had her snatching her hand back like she had been burned and walking away with a disgusted look on her face, almost like the clothing had insulted her. Note to self: she was tactile as hell. Throughout it all, Cole just followed behind her faithfully, enchanted by the witch darting around in front of him. Anything that got her happy hmm, he nodded to the older salesclerk—the one who wasn't staring at Evie's legs—to figure out sizing and pull into the dressing room.

Every time he gestured for the saleswoman to add something to the stack in the dressing room, she squinted at him as if to confirm that he was aware of the cost. He just shrugged and gestured to her to place it in the dressing room or take it to the register if it was loungewear or anything that didn't require attention to size. He and Hayden had spent years building their firm into a top-tier, extremely successful international boutique. In addition, Charles had established a trust for him that paid out when Cole completed law school. After years of saving and investing and having almost zero expenses since the house was paid outright, he had more money than he could spend in several lifetimes. So why have a fortune if not to spoil the fuck out of his witch?

By the time their merry crew of three had looked at everything in the store, there was a massive pile of clothing, including jeans, shirts, dresses, jumpsuits, and a few pairs of shoes, neatly placed in one of the larger dressing rooms. The saleswoman ushered Evie towards it, dropping her hand quickly from Evie's shoulder when she caught Cole's frigid look. "Miss, your dressing room is this way."

"My... wait, my what?" Evie stopped in her tracks and turned to Cole. He dismissed the saleswoman and crowded Evie into the dressing room where she finally saw the mountain of clothing. The room was plenty large enough for the both of them with a chair for him to watch her from.

"Sir," the saleswoman called. "Sir, we require the men to sit outside of the dressing room."

Cole leveled a steely glare at her. "I think we're fine here," he snapped, drawing the curtain shut against her disapproving gaze. When he took a seat in the chair, he glanced back at Evie. Her eyebrows were raised practically to her hairline. "What?" He gave her an innocent look.

"Be. Nice." She closed in on him and dug her fingers into his hair. "Just because you're going to stay here whether they're going to let you or not doesn't mean you have to be rude about it. So be nice."

"Let me tell you something." Cole tugged her toward him. Ran his hand up the back of her leg and relished how she shivered at his light touch. "That asshole at the front was staring at you so hard he might as well have put his hands on you. He's lucky I didn't burn the store down with him in it." A small moan slid out of her when his hand slid under her dress to palm her ass. He felt himself hardening at the sound, wanting nothing more than to run his fingers between her legs. So he did because he couldn't help himself, and he didn't want to stop.

Passing one long finger over her core, he swore quietly, which barely covered the sound of her whimper. "Fuck, sweetheart. You're always so wet for me. Gods, I bet you want me to just drop you down and fuck you right here in this chair, make sure everybody in this store knows you're mine." Her lips parted on a small gasp, and he couldn't help but take them in a bruising kiss, fisting his hand in her hair to hold her steady so he could devour her mouth. It was sloppy and sexy and intense as hell. When he finally drew back, they were both panting, and she was straddling his lap, grinding against him desperately.

"Angel, as much as I want to drop you onto my cock right now and give you exactly what those beautiful eyes of yours are begging me for, we've got errands to run." And what fun errands they would be, starting with a field trip to his office so he could assess exactly how bad the damage was.

He had only had a phone again for a short time, but a quick search online proved that Hayden hadn't exaggerated the intensity of the earthquake that damaged their building. At a magnitude of 8.1, it was the most significant tremor to ever hit New Orleans and had devastated large pockets of the city, including, apparently, the foundation of the levees that protected the city from flood waters. New Orleans wasn't the only unexpected environmental anomaly to occur in the last day; according to the web, a tsunami had annihilated large swaths of seaside Japan. A deadly category five hurricane had overwhelmed Puerto Rico, leaving much of the island without power or potable water. At least three Caribbean islands had vanished after a five-hundred-mile-wide hurricane appeared out of nowhere. A flash fire had burned quick and dirty through hundreds of miles of California forest while a similar fire had raged in the frozen Alaskan wilderness. And that was just what he had seen in five minutes on Google News and the BBC.

On the way to the office, he needed to call Charles. Evie had agreed to meet his uncle on the drive to pick up their phones, and, although he could tell she was still nervous, she sounded surer about the idea than she had this morning. It was the only reason he would agree to subjecting her to his uncle and whatever other immortals Charles saw fit to invite to the clown car gathering.

Cole grazed his thumb along Evie's cheek. She tilted her face into his hand, pressed a kiss to his palm. "Pick your favorite clothes to wear out of here. We'll take the rest home and return whatever doesn't fit."

Evie pulled back, eyes wide as she took in the piles of clothing surrounding them. "Cole, there's no way I'll will ever need this many clothes. Plus, I have no way to pay for them."

"First of all: I've been waiting all my life to spoil you, Angel. Please let me do this." He rose to his feet, her legs wrapping around his waist as he lifted her from his lap. Barely stifling a groan at the feel of her, he continued. "Second of all: you will never have to worry about money ever again. What I have is yours—" She opened her mouth to argue, but he simply talked over her sputtering. "And I have more than enough to take care of us for all of our lifetimes together. Now. Let me buy you the damn clothes, Evangeline."

Stunned at the use of her full name—possibly because she had never actually heard it used in reference to her before—she dropped her legs from their place around his waist and slithered down his body until she was standing in front of him. While he tried to get himself under control from her sinuous movement, she dressed quickly in a pair of black lace panties, soft flare jeans, a black velvet bralette layered under a long, black sweater with big, hot pink hearts splashed across it, and a pair of lavender high-top Converses. Fully dressed, she turned to him, a smile on her face as she fingered the soft material of her top.

Even cozily dressed with no makeup, she was easily the most stunning woman he had ever seen. His heart pounded in pride not only that he was the one with her now, but that she wanted him with her. She chose *him*. Stepping forward, he ripped the tags off the clothes she wore to have them scanned, took her hand, and threw open the curtain.

There was a new sales associate at the register, this one a young woman with blonde hair cut a chic haircut. She caught sight of them from across the room and beelined for him. "Can I help you, sir?" She preened, pressing into Cole's space.

He frowned, but before he could tell the sales associate to back off, Evie was plastered against his side, arms around him. "No," she bit out, even though the sales associate was still openly ogling Cole. Her harsh tone drew the clerk's attention; the woman scanned Evie with a barely-concealed sneer. His frown grew into a scowl at the woman's blatant disrespect, and he opened his mouth to say something, but his little witch needed no help from him. Her shoulders were back, her elegant chin tilted at an angle he could only call regal, and her grey gaze was so haughty on the salesclerk that it was almost painful to see.

The clerk, who had started the conversation so confidently, started twitching under Evie's cold stare. Evie hadn't said a word.

Cole smothered a grin—she was going to make an incredible queen. Waving over his shoulder to indicate the clothes in the dressing room, he said mildly, "We'll take everything in there and all of the stuff at the register as well." Wrapping his arm around Evie's shoulder, he walked her to the checkout counter, murmuring in her ear as he did so, "Silly woman risking your wrath by flirting with your man."

Evie turned her face up to his, her intense gaze piercing his soul. "I'll put her in the ground if she does it again." Venom dripped from her words.

His heart pounded in his chest with an emotion that he knew, without question or doubt, was a life-changing love. Less poetically, his cock, only slightly calmed after their time in the dressing room, hardened at her vicious, jealous response. "That's sexy as hell, Angel, but let's call that tomorrow's agenda."

With the help of the little fucker who was still staring at Evie's now-covered legs, the flirty sales clerk brought all of the clothing to the front and passed it off to the older saleswoman to check them out. Scornful glare still on the blonde, who in turn was still eye fucking him, Evie didn't notice the massive amount of clothing going into the bags or hear the total amount.

When the clerk finally read him out the total, he passed over his card without a fuss. Honestly, he barely heard the damage, amused as he was by the scene playing out in front of him. Evie's eyes were now sparking blues and gold, her magic rising in response to her fury. The potted orchids sitting around the cash register were growing and reaching towards the blonde, who was only seeming to recognize the very real danger a jealous Evie posed. No matter that she didn't fully grasp the magical gravity of the situation; Evie's irate expression more than conveyed her willingness to murder the flirty woman.

Before Evie could strangle the woman with potted plants or discover how to wield her death magic for its true purpose, Cole lifted the four bags loaded with clothing in one hand and grasped Evie's waist with the other, using the grip to tug her out the door and to the car.

He knew with absolute certainty that this witchy woman with the brilliant brain and bratty mouth, who was prepared to tear down a building because one woman had looked too intensely at him, who was as hungry for him as he was for her, was his whole damn future. Regardless of whatever bullshit Hayden may pull or his family's response to any of this, she was his, and he was hers.

Chapter 40

Evie

Central Business District, New Orleans, Louisiana

Evie was still fuming when Cole parked on the street closest to his building. She didn't remember much about the trip over besides a phone call between Cole and... somebody. Honestly, she couldn't recall who the person on the other end of the call was or any detail about their voice, much less any of the conversation's content.

And she hadn't paid a lick of attention to what was going on outside the car, either. Although she had been staring out the window the whole time, she hadn't taken in any of the sights around her. She was taking faith that they were still in New Orleans.

And the entire reason for her fury? That damn girl from the store. How *dare* she get into Cole's space like that? How dare she try to *touch* Cole, *flirt* with him? He was off-limits. The girl was lucky Cole had pulled Evie out of there when he did because she had been well on her way to strangling the girl with the sad, half-dead orchid sitting on the sales counter. *She would have deserved it.* Evie scowled, cracking her fingers as she glared at the skyscraper beside them.

"Hey, Angel." Cole's voice interrupted her homicidal musings.

She turned toward him, only to see a smile on his face. "What are you grinning about?" she snapped.

"Here I was thinking I was the only one who was insanely possessive," he chuckled. "But I'm thrilled to see that's not the case. It would have killed me if you weren't at least a little jealous."

"Jealous?" Evie spat. "I'm not jealous, I'm furious. She tried to touch you. How *dare* she?" Her voice kept rising, but she couldn't control it. "You're mine, and that was so obvious, but she tried to get close to you and put her hands on you." The more she thought about it, the more her blood boiled. "Take me back, Cole."

"Take you back where, *ma petite sorcière jalouse*?" An eyebrow raised in question.

"Back to the store. I have to take care of something."

Cole shook his head at her. "I'm not taking you back. You'll have to murder the salesclerk on your own time." He leaned over the center console. "But fuck, it's hot when you get jealous."

She growled at him. "I'm not jealous, Cole. I'm pissed."

"Why are you pissed, Angel?"

"Are you serious?" Evie's back straightened at his question. "She was all over you! And she kept staring at you."

"So you're angry because she was eye fucking someone that belongs to you?" His voice lilted up at the end like he knew the answer already.

Evie frowned at him. There were only two possible answers to that question: yes or no. Given the smug expression on his handsome face, it looked like that may have been intentional. "This is an interrogation tactic, isn't it?" Evie demanded.

Cole snorted. "Yeah, it's called cross-examination. I was banking on you not recognizing it since I can't imagine there's a lot of courtroom drama in the coven. Almost forgot that your brain is as sexy as the rest of you." His eyes narrowed in on her mouth, his tongue swiping out across his lips. "Fuck, Angel, you know there's no one else for me." He reached out, gripping her chin between his thumb and index finger to bring her closer. "I don't want anyone but you."

"I know you don't," she bit out. "Doesn't make me want to claw their eyes out any less."

"And that's because you're—?"

"Fine." She rolled her eyes. "It's because I'm jealous. Are you happy now?"

"Unbelievably. It's sexy as hell that you're this possessive." His voice was harsh when he dragged her that final inch to his lips, giving her a bruising kiss that curled her toes and had her all but crawling across the console into his lap. His hands were in her hair, angling her head so he could take her mouth the way he wanted, plunging his tongue in between her open lips, when a quick double tap on the window interrupted them.

Cole drew back, his head turning so slowly even she could see the threat in the movement.

Evie tilted her head to the side so she could see around Cole's tense frame. The man on the other side of the glass waved aggressively at her, a friendly smile splitting his face. He was handsome with close cut light brown hair and stunning eyes, his irises an uncanny blue so light it was almost white. "Is that Hayden?" she asked quietly, recognizing him from the early morning phone call.

"My soon to be ex-best friend," Cole snarled.

"So... Hayden?"

"The very one."

"Should we get out?"

"Probably." Cole sighed. "He won't stop so unless you're willing to be subject to the whims of an immortal woodpecker masquerading as the god of sleep... " He trailed off, shrugging slightly.

Hayden was still tapping on the window when Evie shoved open her door, standing quickly and fixing him with a stern expression.

As Evie walked around the car, Hayden scanned her petite frame just long enough for Cole to notice and stiffen before saying, "Nice to officially meet you, Evie. I'm Hayden." He held up his hands when her mouth opened, her eyes firing. "I come in peace. As for before, I wasn't trying to imply that Cole would lie to you. All of this is a lot to tell someone." His eyes flicked over their now-joined hands. "And with you naked in his study, I was... concerned that his decades-long obsession with you had beat out his common sense. I was wrong."

Evie listened to him in silence. "Yes. You were. I appreciate you looking out for me, but don't ever make the mistake of thinking Cole didn't tell me something again. You're what? Thousands of years old? Be smarter, god of sleep."

"Touché," Hayden commented. "I think you and I are going to be good friends, Evangeline Dyeus."

"It's Evie," she corrected.

Hayden gave her a quizzical look.

"I may have been born with that name, but I don't know it. Not really." She lifted her shoulders. "The first time I ever saw my birth name was in that folder in Cole's study. My coven only ever called me Evie."

"So you are a witch then?" Hayden's tone was neutral, but his eyes were mesmerizing. Hypnotizing, almost like he was trying to see into her thoughts.

"I am."

"Interesting." Hayden rubbed his fingers over his chin. "Unexpected." She was about to demand he explain the cryptic comments when he clapped his hands loudly and strolled away. "Shall we go see the damage then?"

"Seems like a weird thing to get this excited about, man," Cole drawled, sauntering after his best friend, Evie by his side. "Maybe take it down a couple notches until we figure out how bad everything is and see who all is hurt."

"Fifteen total injured, four hospitalized. Three of those were blood loss from glass shrapnel, one got flattened by the hutch in conference room three." Hayden tugged open the doors into the building.

Once they were in the lobby, Evie gasped at the sight in front of them. Glass shards covered the richly appointed room. The wintry breeze outside blew through the empty frames where windows had once sat. To their right, the front desk was crushed under the heavy weight of one of the light fixtures, which appeared to have ripped out of and fallen from the ceiling above it. And that was all from her first glance.

"Holy fuck." Cole's hand tightened around hers. "Are we even able to get onto our floor?"

"Nope." Hayden popped the 'p' at the end of the word. "The earthquake may have fucked the foundation, so the building's owners are having an engineer come over to check it out."

"Hayden." Over her head, Cole leveled a probing look at his friend. "We're the building's owners."

"Yep, and you're welcome for taking care of that while the two of you were having some much-needed adult playtime."

"Where's our staff?" Evie heard Cole ask as she released his hand and wandered into the center of the room, her lavender shoes crunching over the glass. She couldn't believe that they were responsible for all of this. Not that she regretted choosing Cole. She would do it again in a heartbeat. All of this devastation was overwhelming, though. Inhaling deeply, she reminded herself that the temporary damage of them opening the Underworld was far better than the shade-caused apocalyptic extinction that was otherwise on the table.

An unsettling creak sounded above her. Glancing up, she noticed cracks extending through the vaulted lobby ceiling and lights dangling haphazardly from their fixtures. None of these things looked safe, and, with each glance around her, she grew less comfortable with the idea of them remaining here. Maybe them actually being in the building at all was a bad idea?

She was turning to ask whether they should move out of the potentially unstable skyscraper when a feminine voice cried, "Cole! Baby!" Accompanying this shout was a slender blond woman in heels clambering through the shattered window.

Chapter 41

Cole

Central Business District, New Orleans, Louisiana

"Where's our staff?" Cole asked, one eye on Evie, who was crunching over the glass towards the center of the room. Every ounce of his being was demanding that he go bring her back, but she wouldn't appreciate him restricting her freedom. Had, in fact, demonstrated aggressively and memorably how much she wasn't willing to accept boundaries on her ability to roam free by breaking his wards and returning to the forest by Uber—a fact that still shocked him—at the first opportunity after he took her from the construction site. So instead he kept a careful watch over her, ready to intervene if he needed to.

"You sap." Hayden punched his shoulder lighty. "She's got you wrapped around her little finger."

Cole shrugged. No reason to fight an obviously true statement, not that he wanted to. "Yeah." Evie tilted her head back to stare at the ceiling, her curls falling back from her face, and he was reminded viscerally of her in bed that morning, head canted back just like it was now, mouth opened on a moan. He shifted, widening his stance as desire coursed through him. *Why the fuck are we here again?* The crunch of glass under one of their shoes brought him back. *Right. The earthquake. Employees. Focus, man.* "Where are our employees?"

"After the earthquake, I sent everyone home to telework until we had a better plan. Honestly, some of them acted like it was the best news they'd gotten all year. I got more victory cheers over that than I did when we announced the company-wide pay raise."

"I bet they did," Cole muttered. Given the type of work they did, they couldn't let their staff go fully remote, a point of contention for many of their employees, which they tried to make Cole and Hayden's problem. Suffice it to say, it was a sore spot for both of them. "So everybody's working from home then?"

"Yeah, except—" Hayden's voice was cut off by a woman shouting. He winced. "Except Mina. She posted up at a coffee shop across the street."

The voice grew louder until Mina, their receptionist, tottered in through one of the broken windows. "Cole!" she cried. "Baby!"

Goddamn Mina. Cole glared at his best friend before turning to the blonde bombshell now approaching. He hadn't slept with her, not that she hadn't tried. And tried. And tried again. With each rejection, she got more aggressive and her behavior escalated. The most recent incident was the memorable holiday party where she got drunk, dumped egg nog all over his crotch, then dropped to her knees in front of him to try and lick it off. It had gotten disruptive enough that he and Hayden reorganized the reporting structure so that Cole didn't have to be the one to deal with or fire her. Under Hayden, she had gotten nominally better, but she was still committed to being way too familiar whenever she saw him.

Like now, when she had managed to cross the broken glass with remarkable speed and was swiping her hands all over his chest, cooing, "Where have you been? I was *so* worried about you."

From the corner of his eye, he saw Evie turning at the slow speed of a horror movie slasher, her hair rippling in a nonexistent wind. He couldn't see her face, but he had a feeling that Mina should be afraid.

Grasping Mina's wrists in one hand, he pulled her off of him, lightly pushing her a few feet back before releasing his grip. "Mina, we discussed this. You're not to touch me."

"But I'm just trying to make sure you're alright, silly." Her glossy lower lip jutted out in a pout.

Cole's mouth tightened in irritation. Before Evie, Mina was frustrating as hell. Yeah, he played hard, but when he was at work, he was at fucking work. The women he employed weren't up for grabs. After Evie, though? Well, after Evie, Mina was infuriating because no one in this or any other world, much less the woman who was practically stalking him, could compare to his Angel.

Around them, the glass started jingling against the floor, the shards bouncing in ways that defied gravity. Cole's gaze slid to Evie, whose eyes were the neon blue of death, not a hint of gold lunar magic to be found. Holy shit, she was *livid*, which was somehow both concerning and a turn on. *Who knew?*

He shook his head at her lightly, willing her to get that Mina wasn't an ex, just a deeply sad and lonely person who believed that sexual harassment was socially acceptable. Unfortunately, that was a lot to pack into a single look, and, based on the look of fury on his witch's face, she wasn't in the headspace for nuance.

Hayden all but leapt in front of Mina when she stepped toward Cole again, but she wouldn't be stopped. The leggy blonde shoved past Hayden to Cole. "I tried to call and make sure you were alright, but your phone just kept ringing to voicemail."

Shit, he had changed his number after she got ahold of it on Valentine's Day. How had she gotten the new one? He was working his way through that puzzle when he felt a delicate palm slide across his arm and down to his hand. A slow smile took over his face—this was who he wanted touching him. Glancing down, he almost swallowed his tongue at the ethereal being standing next to him.

Evie was practically crackling with energy, her eyes radiant with magic, her hair drifting around her, her feet raised from the floor until only her toes were touching it. All around her, the shattered glass was pulled off the ground by invisible hands, floating in the air like tiny, brittle pieces of shrapnel.

Mina's eyes lasered in on Evie's hand entangled in his, completely ignoring every other unexplainable thing happening in the lobby. "Who are you?" she demanded.

"I'm Evie," she responded. "Cole's witch. And who do you think you are?"

Beside them, Hayden snorted.

"I'm Mina." Her eyes were steel on Evie's. "Cole's girlfriend."

Cole's softly uttered "What the fuck?" was drowned out by Evie's, "I don't fucking think so." Had Mina gone full on Fatal Attraction? He didn't have a pet, but, for some reason, he was suddenly concerned for all of the animals in his vicinity.

"Well, I am!" Mina cried. "He promised me that we would see each other."

"At work, you idiot. As in I would see you at the office. I was being polite," Cole snapped. This was way past enough. "An office you no longer work at. Mina, you're fired."

Mina's eyes flashed. "What?"

"You're fired. Get the fuck out. Now. This is long overdue."

"H—h—how could you?" Mina stammered. "After all I did for you? All I ever wanted was to be with you!"

Rolling his eyes, Cole sighed. He should probably be more accommodating, but he was long past caring about the receptionist they should have fired months ago and far more concerned about his ticking time bomb of a witch. "Get lost." He squeezed Evie's hand and bent down to her ear. "Angel, there's nothing between Mina and me, never has been," he whispered. "She's just got no sense of boundaries."

"And a hard-on for Cole," Hayden muttered.

Without looking at him, Cole snapped, "Not helpful, man."

"Wasn't trying to be helpful, just trying to be accurate," his best friend quipped. "If your girl's going to turn our former receptionist to dust, I think she should know what's going down."

Mina had drawn herself to her full height. Her gaze was locked on Evie, a dangerous smile cracking her mouth. "You're going to pass on all of this," she demanded in a voice entirely unlike the airy one she usually used as she gestured to her body. "For some little witch bitch? Oh, Aidoneus, I thought you were smarter than that."

What the actual fuck? Cole opened his mouth, but no words came out.

Hayden's head whipped around, his face furrowing in a scowl. "I know that voice."

"Oh, god of sleep," Mina cackled. "Getting high on your own supply of magical sand hasn't done your mental powers any favors."

Hayden squinted at her for a few seconds, and then his eyes grew wide. "*Minthe?* No, it can't be. You died. I saw Kore kill you."

"No." Mina rolled her eyes. "You thought you saw me die, but my father protected me all these years, brought me back to health."

"Minthe?" Cole repeated. "Why does that sound familiar?"

"Jesus Christ, man, read your damn family history. Just once for me," Hayden pleaded. "Minthe was... "

"The naiad consort to Aidoneus before he found Kore," Evie spoke from beside him, her angry tone at odds with her words. "According to your family's archives, Kore drowned her because she kept pursuing Aidoneus." At his astonished look, Evie raised a shoulder lazily. "I read the book before you woke up yesterday.'

"You're incredible," he breathed, brushing a kiss across her cheek. She shivered at his touch, and, for the first time since Mina showed up, the intensity of the magic around her lessened a tiny bit, the sound of thousands of shards of glass falling to the floor ringing around them. "That's right, *ma petite sorcière*, let down your magic. It's okay. She's no threat to you."

"Oh, for the love of Zeus," Mina snapped. "This forest trash doesn't deserve you. Aidoneus, come with me." She reached for Cole's hand one last time. That one attempted touch was all it took, though

"You're right, love." Evie's head tilted eerily to the side, an unsettling smirk spreading across her face. "She's no threat. But I am." Mina's fingers had just touched Cole when Evie reached out, magic flaring around her, and laid her hand on Mina's shoulder.

There was a scream, a sharp, blinding burst of blue followed by a horrifying shattering that sounded like bones being crushed. Then nothing.

"Where'd she go?" Cole looked around for Mina, but she wasn't anywhere in the lobby. "I'm gonna getting a restraining order this time, I swear to god."

"Um, Cole?" Hayden said, his focus trained on the ground. On a small... plant? That hadn't been there before. Had it?

"Was that here before?" Cole joined Hayden in staring at it.

"Nope." Evie's voice chimed in. She sounded almost normal again, nothing like the dark goddess that had stood beside him seconds ago.

"Is that... "

"Yep," she singsonged, hinging at the waist to reach down and pick up the mint plant now sitting on the lobby floor. "That's your ancestor's former consort who wanted to become your whore. Doesn't she look so much better this way?"

Cole could only stared at his dream woman, who bore a small vindictive smile on her beautiful mouth while she held the mint plant that was his firm's former receptionist.

Chapter 42

Cole

Lake Pontchartrain Causeway, New Orleans, Louisiana

Cole glanced over at Evie, looking serene in the passenger seat on the drive to his uncle's Mandeville house. Like she hadn't just turned a woman, apparently an immortal concubine of his ancestor's, into a mint plant. Hayden, as a member of the Aidoneus family in all but name and a powerful member of their future court, followed behind them, Mina—no, Minthe—buckled in his backseat.

"Are you going to keep staring at me?" Evie finally asked.

"Well, *mon ange*, you did turn someone into a plant." You would think that would alarm him. He had never been one for relationships or the jealousy and drama they brought, but it seemed those concerns didn't really apply to Evie. In fact, her possessiveness was a huge turn on for him.

"Do you want me to apologize or something?" She frowned, her shoulders going back until she looked every inch the warrior queen she was. "Because that's not happening. She's lucky all I did was turn her into an herb. At least she's useful in this form."

He bit back a grin. This little beauty. Completely unrepentant. "Not looking for apologies, just curious."

"About what?"

"You ever turned someone into a plant before, Angel?" No good way to ask that question so might as well rip off the band-aid off.

Evie rubbed a hand along her cheek, her haughty expression falling. Suddenly, she looked exhausted, and, when she spoke, nervousness threaded through her words. "I don't really... know. I have a terrible memory." Her foot tapped against the floorboards so hard that her leg was bouncing.

"Yeah, that's probably all of the reversions they put you through." Cole placed his hand on her thigh, caressing the outside of her jean-covered leg with his thumb. "But you don't think you have?"

"I—no. No, I don't think I have." She bit her lower lip, turning her head to stare out the window.

Before she did, though, he caught a look of concern in her eyes. That wouldn't do. He gripped her leg a bit more tightly until she glanced back at him. "What's going through that complicated head of yours, witchling?"

"I just—" she began. Cut herself off. "Apparently, I killed my biological mother. And there're stories about me turning a coven sister into dust. Urban legends. At least that's what I think they are. It's the scary story they tell around the fire. Don't misbehave or Evie will get you. I don't know if they're true or not after the last few days... "

Fury lanced through him, hot and fast. *How fucking dare they?* His hand on the wheel clamped down hard, his teeth clenched, but he did his best to keep a neutral expression on his face.

"I don't think they meant anything by it," she rushed to clarify. "It was a joke. I think. But if I hurt someone, I violate the witches' creed and can be brought on charges before the Council and ejected from the coven."

He raised a curious eyebrow at her. The Witches Council he knew. They were the decision-making body of witches, overseen by a Judiciary of three deities who got involved when the coven elders couldn't reach a consensus of their own. Given who sat on the Council Judiciary, though, it was more than a little hypocritical of them to have any hard and fast opinions *against* violence. "So are you scared because you might be removed from the coven for violence?" That one felt like a knife in his chest. He knew the coven was her family, but the idea of her leaving him to go back to them? Yeah, no. That wasn't going to happen. She made her choice the night she left the forest with him

"No, I left the coven when I came with you. I made my choice when we left the clearing that night, and I have no regrets." He almost punched the air in victory at that one, but this wasn't about him. This was about the woman sitting next to him. Evie was quiet for long enough that he thought she was done talking. He was opening his mouth to say something when she spoke back up. "I'm scared because I don't care about the consequences of what I just did."

His head snapped back in surprise.

"I don't care at all that I turned her into a plant. I would happily do it again if she tried to put her hand or any other body part on you." Residual rage flared across her face, and her words dripped with scorn. "Reprehensible bottom-dweller that she is. She doesn't even care that you're not actually Aidoneus and don't have any history of your own with her."

Yeah, he had caught that, too, a weird little delusion from his apparently millennia-old stalker.

"And is it bad that I don't feel awful that I turned a woman into a plant and would have done so much worse if I knew more about how death magic worked?" Evie's voice dropped to an almost whisper. "That I just spat in the face of the witches' creed? Doesn't that make me more violent and dangerous than others?"

Fuck, those coven elders did a number on her. Cole had never been so glad that the Lake Pontchartrain Causeway finally had emergency shoulders because this conversation couldn't wait. Without looking in his side mirrors, he cranked across the outer lane. The driver of the Aston Martin he barely missed hitting laid on their horn and flipped him off as he pulled off onto the shoulder at speed, slamming on the brakes hard enough that Evie bounced against her seatbelt.

"Cole, what in the sweet name of Selene are you doing?" Evie demanded, rubbing her chest where the seatbelt had caught her. "I've never driven, but even I know that was dangerous."

He ignored her question and swiveled towards her, gripping the back of her head in his palm and turning her to face him. "Now, listen to me and listen good, Angel." He paused to make sure he had her attention. "That's all bullshit."

"What?" Her eyes darted up to his, confusion clouding them.

Smooth. Don't you talk for a living, dumbass? But he had so many emotions flowing through him right now—fury at her coven for every time they had made her feel dangerous, intentionally or otherwise, concern about that torn look on her face, a deep need to make sure that she knew that no matter what she did, she was perfect to him—that his words were failing him. "When your coven didn't understand things about you, the darkest part of your magic that draws from death, they made you feel like your abilities were something to be scared of, right?" A hesitant nod. "And let me guess, every time you did something that made them remember you had that darkness inside of you, they recited the witches' creed to you." Another nod, this time slightly less tentative. "*Ouais*, so there is absolutely nothing wrong with you besides that you were raised by people who didn't understand you. You turned Mina into a plant because she thought she was entitled to me, thanks to a relationship she had with my ancestor. You didn't attack her randomly; she tried to take me from you. Frankly, you behaved better than I would have if somebody tried to do the same to you." He rested his forehead against hers for a slight moment, her minty breath fanning across his face. "Yeah, you're dangerous. So fucking what? It's incredible, not to mention hot as fuck, that you can destroy those who fuck with you and yours."

"But—"

"No buts, Angel," he interrupted. "There's nothing wrong with you. You defended me. You laid your claim to me in front of someone who needed to be put her in place." His hand gentled in her hair, and he tugged her to him for a quick kiss. "You're fucking perfect, sweetheart. You hear me?"

She pursed her lips but didn't respond. Her narrowed, disbelieving gaze told another story though.

Bratty Angel. "I said, do you hear me, Evie?"

His use of her real name had her gaze snapping to his. "Yes. Yes, I hear you.'

"That's my good girl." He kissed her again, deeper this time, harder and more possessive. When they separated, Evie's lids were heavy, her breaths ragged. Tearing himself away from his lusty little witch was more difficult than it should have been. Jesus, he was already hard as rock from just one kiss, which was ridiculous given the sexual marathon they'd had over the last day. He breathed deeply, thinking of case law and old judges who pissed him off. There was no way he was walking into his uncle's house with the erection from hell. This time was all about Evie and making sure she was comfortable with his family.

Once he pulled his shit together, he steered the car carefully back into the traffic crossing the causeway that connected New Orleans to Mandeville, where his uncle lived. "Are you sure you're okay meeting my uncle? We can come back tomorrow or whenever you feel up to it if today has already been too much for you. It's just a quick call to reschedule."

"No," Evie said quietly before clearing her throat and repeating more firmly, "No, I want to meet your family."

He nodded, trusting his witch to know her own mind. "Okay, then now's as good a time as any to prep you for the madhouse that we're walking into."

Evie's eyebrows skyrocketed up, but she only commented, "Oh?"

"Yeah, oh." Cole toggled the left turn signal as they exited the causeway following the signs towards Madisonville, which would take them to the west side of Mandeville where Charles lived. "You've got Charlie, who's my uncle on my dad's side. After my parents died, Charlie took me in and raised me. He's my only living relative besides a distant cousin on my *maman*'s side who's around my age, but I haven't seen in almost a decade." They came to a stop at a red light. "Then you got Hayden, who you already met. And there's the Moirai: Essi, Cleo, and Addy. They're the immortal fates who read the past, present, and future using people's lifelines. Kind of creepy, if I'm being honest." They took a right onto the main road where the guard manning the gate waved Cole through into the exclusive neighborhood where Charles lived.

Evie perked up as soon as they passed through the main gate, her head swiveling every way, wide eyes taking in everything. Unlike other gated communities in the area, Beau Chêne took great care to balance the wildness and raw beauty of its location bordering the Tchefuncte River with the well-manicured flower beds and lawns expected of a ritzy neighborhood. The effect was stunning and unique, particularly to his little witch. He was having a blast watching her take it all in as they drove further into the neighborhood where his uncle lived on a desirable and remote cul-de-sac.

Cole pulled down the long, hidden driveway that led to the house, passing soaring live oaks and stubby cypress trees covered with moss. Almost as if they could tell Evie was in the passenger seat, the trees swayed towards the moving car, leaning in like they wanted nothing more than to be close to her. He chuckled; he could definitely empathize.

As they drove up to the house, Cole frowned at the line of cars parked around the driveway. There should only be three cars here, maybe four if Essi drove herself. He saw the usual suspects' cars: Hayden's low-slung opalescent Porsche, Essi's Fiat, which bore a crunched-in side panel since she was often distracted by lines of fate while driving, and the small black pickup truck Cleo and Addy shared. Cole knew Charles' own modest Hyundai was tucked away in the garage. That should have been everybody accounted for.

But no, there were five additional cars sitting in front of the house. He pinched the bridge of his nose. *Fuck.* He should have expected this, but he had assumed Charles would want to meet the closest thing he would ever have to a daughter in an intimate gathering. Rookie mistake. Charles was more gung-ho about the prophecy and Cole's destiny than anyone else, and it looked like he had invited the *entire Underworld pantheon that they had accrued over the years* to this conversation. "I'm sorry, Angel. I had no idea he would do this." Should have guessed but didn't actually know.

"Are they all here to meet me?" Evie's eyes were wide and slightly panicked. "Cole, I'm not actually that interesting!"

Even in his irritation with his uncle, he couldn't help but shoot her an amused look. "You are exactly that interesting to me. Probably also to these people too for a wholly different reason." Her knuckles were white on the edge of the seat. Reaching over to retrieve her hand, he threaded his fingers through hers and brushed a kiss across her soft skin. "It's going to be okay, though. We're calling the shots here, sweetheart, since these people are technically our... court, I guess you would call them?" Her back relaxed slightly at his words. "If we want to leave—and, with these people, there's about a 95% chance that we'll want to abandon ship in less than ten minutes—we will." A garbled laugh emerged from Evie, a subtle hint that she was terrified of meeting another family that she thought she might disappoint. "They're going to love you, though."

"Thank you, Cole." She leaned over the dash and kissed him gently. "You are, without a doubt, the best thing to ever happen to me."

Sitting in his car, staring at the most unexpected and wonderful surprise of his life, he knew he had to say the words before they went into that house full of crazy immortals and their sky-high expectations. As she tried to open the car door, he tugged her back by the hand he still held.

Her brows knitted together in confusion before she said, "I'm fine to sit here in the car instead, but I think they may notice. This place feels fancy, and I'm pretty sure that people don't sit in cars watching houses in this neighborhood. I mean, it had a gate to get in, I'm pretty sure that means they're always watchi—"

"I love you," he blurted, interrupting her tangent. She went silent as her mouth fell open. "I'm in love with you. I've adored you since I was twelve but knowing you, the real you, made it real. It made me realize that I love you more than anything else in this world. It has nothing to do with the fated reincarnate memory bullshit. I love *you*, Angel. All the things that make you you." Leaning towards her, he swept her hair behind her ear with his free hand. "You don't have to say it back. But I wanted you to know before we go into that house full of powerful lunatics." Her lower lip trembled. "Sweetheart, please don't cry—"

"I love you too." The grip she had on his hand was painful, but he didn't give a flying fuck about circulation when his Angel was telling him she loved him. She could rip the damn appendage off for all he cared, and he would probably thank her for it. "Gods, I'm so in love with you, Cole. You are everything to me, and I don't want to do this or any life without you. Nothing will ever change that. Not our ruling the Underworld, not my coven, and not even your family full of magical idiots."

Their lips met over the center console, sweet and gentle, almost tame when compared to the night before but no less powerful. This woman was his queen, and he would rule by her fucking side until the world went dark. They had plenty of time for all the unhinged filthy moments they could ever want.

Chapter 43

Cole

Beau Chêne, Mandeville, Louisiana

They were pulling apart when something tapped on the car. When they finally zeroed in on the noise, there was Hayden rapping on the driver's side window, grinning like a dumbass.

"You guys gonna come in or are we going to have to do this little reunion in your car?" he mocked through the glass.

Cole grunted. "You sure you don't want to leave? Deal with these morons another day or, y'know, never?"

"Too late to escape now, love. Unless you want to run over your best friend." A grumpy look took over her face. "Which, I'll be honest, I could be okay with. I'm still angry that he thought you would lie to get me into bed. Actually, come to think of it, let's run him over."

"You know he's immortal, right? He'll recover just fine."

"Oh, then that's handy."

His jaw dropped in amusement at his bloodthirsty witch, perfectly willing to maim his best friend simply because Hayden had the audacity to make sure

Cole wasn't a lying asshole. "You're sexy when you're protective." He reached over again and kissed her hard, quickly. "But let's get this over with."

Once he was out of the car, Cole scowled at Hayden, who was grinning widely at him. "You dick. Way to ruin a moment. You're lucky I didn't let Evie convince me to run you over." Hayden's eyebrows drew together over his nose, but Cole pretended not to notice. Lowering his voice, he added, "In all seriousness, though, I need you to help me manage these fuckers. Evie's nervous, and I will gut anyone who makes her feel even a little uncomfortable, family or not. So I need your help running interference."

"I got you." Hayden gave him a quick once over before Evie could round the car to them. "I never thought I would see you like this. Love is a good look for you, man."

Evie rounded the car, and Cole took her hand, bringing it to his lips. As a unit, the three of them turned toward the house where half of the family was surreptitiously watching them through the expansive windows lining the front of the house.

As they walked up the stairs leading to the house, the curtains were drawn shut with startling speed. The three of them snorted simultaneously. "So subtle," Evie commented wryly. "Wonder what they thought we were gonna do in the middle of the driveway?"

Hayden opened his mouth, a lascivious smile crossing his face, but Cole cut him off. "Man, don't you dare say a threesome or, I swear, the cops will never find all your body parts."

"On advice of counsel, I have no comment," Hayden said instead.

They reached the front door, which opened to reveal Charles. Barely 15 years older than Cole himself, Charles wore his 51-year-old silver fox status with pride. "Come in, you three." He ushered them in, clapping Cole on the shoulder before he looked down at Evie. "Welcome to my home, Evangeline," he said, shaking her hand, his eyes warm on her face.

"It's, um, it's actually just Evie," she corrected with an uncertain laugh. Cole, feeling her uncertainty, wrapped her into his chest, a gesture Charles noticed immediately. Neither of them cared, though, since Evie melted back into him, their joined hands sitting over her rapidly beating heart.

"Yes, of course." Charles turned his attention to the man standing behind them. "Good afternoon, Hayden." His eyes dipped to the mint plant in Hayden's hands, his eyebrows rising in confusion.

"Hey, Charlie," Hayden greeted their host, brandishing the mint plant in front of him. "I have something for you."

"Oh? And to what do I owe this... " Charles took the mint plant tentatively. "... pleasure?"

"It was my fault," Evie blurted before Hayden could respond. "I may have—well, I actually definitely did turn someone into a plant."

"Hmm." Charles turned the pot in his hands. "And did you have a reason for this drive-by planting?"

Hayden responded before Evie could. "It was Minthe."

Charles blinked. "I thought she was dead."

"Yeah, me too, but apparently not so much." Hayden shrugged. "She's been posing as our receptionist for the last few years and tried to get a little handsy with Cole today. And, thus, the plant."

"Ah, thus the plant," Charles repeated.

As Charles looked lost on what to do with the pot of mint he was holding, a woman in her mid-thirties swept into the room. "Cole, *cher*," she cried out, wrapping her arms around his waist. "You're home!"

"Hey, Magda," he greeted his uncle's housekeeper, a woman he had long suspected of holding a torch for Charles. "This is Evie."

"Of course you are, darlin'." Magda's smile grew wider as she drew Evie into a warm hug. "It's so nice to meet you." Beside them, Charles shifted and Magda's eyes darted over to him, gaze catching on the plant he held. "Umm, what's that?"

"The firm's former receptionist," Cole answered dryly.

"Oh, if that's all, then." Magda released Evie and seized the herb out of his uncle's hands. "I've been needing some mint, so I'll just take this into the kitchen with me." The plant leaves trembled, but she ignored the movement. "I have to head back in to start gettin' dinner ready anyways. Charles, why don't you take your family into the livin' room? You've kept them in the entryway for far too long," she tossed over her shoulder as she walked away.

At the admonishment, Charles jumped to attention and led them from the foyer past the sweeping staircase into the living room.

"Relax, Angel," Cole whispered into Evie's ear as they followed Charles. "The only time your heart should be beating this fast is when I'm inside you." Her strangled chuckle was music to his ears. He drew a thumb down her neck, sneakily checking her pulse, which was already calming as he held her. "It's okay, sweetheart. Remember. These are our people, and we can leave whenever we fucking want."

She nodded and squared her shoulders, walking into the room like the queen she was.

When they entered the spacious living room, Cole ground his teeth to see eleven people already seated on the plush furniture. The Aidoneus family had spent generations finding gods who had achieved immortality during the Shade Wars and whose powers were beneficial to or could be associated with the Underworld, all in preparation for the reincarnation of Hades and Persephone. Of course, these people weren't easy to find and not only because they didn't want to be found. Many of them had taken on mortal-sounding names to blend in with the humans. However, over millennia of intense searching with a lot of help from the Moirai and some luck, the Aidoneus clan had built an odd, jumbled extended family of extremely powerful deities. There were, of course, exceptions like Cole and, now, Evie, but the two of them would achieve their immortality once they stepped foot in the Underworld and took their place as its rulers. At least that was what the Moirai had said when a young Cole had asked why he could become immortal without collecting all of the missing shades like Aidoneus and Kore would have had to do. Since prophecies made very little sense to start with, he took their word at face value.

All in all, they gathered around twenty immortals over the years, all prepared to swear fealty to the Underworld's rulers once they reincarnated and take their role in the Pantheon. And it looked like Charles had invited the vast majority of that twenty. With each introduction of both the god's name and their power, Cole grew more irritated.

Hayden was, of course, the god of sleep (and dreaming, if they were being technical). There were the three Moirai, the goddesses of fate: Addy, the eldest sister responsible for the threads of life, Essi, the middle sister who apportioned designated lots of life, and Cleo, the youngest who cut life short. Charles himself was a powerful warlock. Seated among the members Cole saw most regularly, though, were others with whom he was far less familiar. Cate, the goddess of magic and witchcraft. Alex, Meg, and Isabel, the Furies. Ash, the god of pain, and his demon wife, Orphne. Phoebe, the goddess of nightmares. Aria, the goddess of curses. And a dark-haired young woman he didn't recognize that Charles introduced as Nyx.

Cole turned to Hayden. "Who the fuck is that?"

Hayden stage whispered back, "Y'know, Nyx, our law clerk that you made cry?"

Cole squinted in confusion. They had hired her? He didn't even recognize her. "Why is she here?"

Charles interrupted the less-than-subtle exchange with a pointed look. "Nyx is the goddess of night."

Cole glanced at Hayden with a look that said more clearly than words, *then why the fuck is she clerking for us?* Hayden simply shrugged in response while Charles continued speaking, ignoring them both, as he had since Cole was a child and first latched on to the much older Hayden as a much-needed best friend. "Cole is my nephew, the reincarnate of the great Hades himself. As I understand it, he has brought a guest with him. Cole? Would you do us the honor of introducing your friend?"

His flesh prickling in frustration at his uncle's formality, Cole stepped forward, bringing Evie with him. Charles already knew who Evie was. It was absurd to put her through this dog-and-pony show before she had the chance to get to know his close family.

Although Evie's eyes were wide as saucers, that was her only sign of nerves; her shoulders were drawn back, her chin set at a pointed angle. His Angel looked every inch the queen she was. *His* queen. "Everyone, this is Evie Dyeus." Murmurs filled the room as many of them recognized her last name. Like Hayden, most of them had closely followed her father's sensationalized murder trial. "She is the reincarnation of Persephone." He glared daggers at his uncle—this could have, should have, waited until she was more comfortable—as he announced, "And my beloved queen."

The room erupted. Some cheers, some surprised profanity, some shouted questions. Evie drew into his side, somehow making it look like a coordinated gesture of love rather than the seeking of comfort that it actually was. "Ignore them, Angel," he murmured into her ear. Her arms wrapped tightly around his waist. "They'll probably settle down soon."

"I know," she whispered back, face tilted up to his. "I'm okay, I promise. I just... I wasn't expecting quite so many people. This is your family, Cole. It kind of matters to me whether I make a good impression."

Even though the room was still chaotic, with everyone shouting over everyone, Cole leaned down and kissed the top of her head. "After my parents died, these people became my family, yeah. But you're my family now, Angel. And it matters more to me that they treat you well than that you make a good impression on them."

Her eyes went glassy just as Cate walked up to them. Looking over Evie's head, Cole greeted the goddess while Evie collected herself. "Hi, Cate."

"Good afternoon, Cole," she greeted him warmly then looked down at Evie, still wrapped in his arms. "Evie, it is lovely to meet one of my kin."

"One of your—" Evie wrinkled her nose, a clear sign she was shuffling through the overabundance of information Charles had shared. "The goddess of... "

"Witches, my dear," Cate finished. "Among other things. You might know me as Hecate."

"Hecate?" Evie yelped. "Holy mother of witches, it's you! I thought you were a myth."

"All myths have a basis in fact." Cate smiled. "You are a witch, yes?"

"Yes, I am." Evie stepped towards the woman, only for Cole to drag her back into his side. She could talk to whomever she wanted, but he needed to keep touching her. His possessive gesture didn't phase her. In fact, she seemed to barely notice it at this point. "How did you know I'm a witch?

Cate's answer was drowned out by Nyx, who had sidled closer to them and was now shouting, "You're a *witch*?"

Chapter 44

Evie

Beau Chêne, Mandeville, Louisiana

There were many different kinds of silence. The peace of the forest after a rainfall. The breathless quiet just after sex. The stillness of a cemetery. But Evie had never experienced a silence quite like the one that fell over the room after Nyx shouted, "You're a *witch*?" It felt almost... hostile.

"Umm, yes?" Evie answered, her voice lilting up on the confirmation. Why did that sound like a question? She knew what she was. Firming up her voice, she repeated, "Yes."

Cate wore a small smile on her face as one of the women, a person she was almost positive was a goddess of nightmares (or maybe it was curses?) spat at Cole, "And you knew this?"

Evie flinched, preparing for the worst possible response. Cole told her he loved her, but what if his family having an issue with who and what she was proved to be too much for him? Besides Sandrine, she had never had someone who wanted to protect and defend her. Even the rest of the coven had tried to hide away the bits of her they didn't like or couldn't understand. She tensed, starting to draw into herself, her brain dreaming up all sorts of horrifying comments that could be directed her way.

Instead of doing any of that, Cole rubbed a calming hand along her back and drew himself to his full height, glowering at the woman who asked the question. "Of course I knew."

And with that one answer, Evie knew he was it for her. Forever.

The Furies launched into a tirade that drowned out almost everyone else in the room, but Charles' voice carried only to the small group now clustered around Cole and Evie. "I think we should discuss this separately."

Cole glowered at his uncle, his eyes ferocious as he stared him down, his voice low but menacing. "Oh, now you listen, huh? Not when I called you to ask if I could bring Evie, who you knew was a witch, so she could get to know my immediate fucking *famille*? You just thought you would bombard my goddamn queen with everyone?" His arm was locked around her waist, his accent thicker than she had ever heard it. "*Piké twa, nonc.*"

Despite the fact that she was currently surrounded on all sides by Cole's immediate family with others shouting in the room and Cole himself rumbling in Cajun rage, she had never felt safer than she did right now with Cole's chest firmly against her cheek, his arm such a firm band around her waist that her feet were barely touching the ground. "Get them the fuck out of here or we're gone."

"Cole—" Charles began in a conciliatory tone.

"No, Uncle Charlie. You have five minutes to get everyone but you, Hayden, and the Moirai the fuck out of this house or Evie and I are leaving. You can bring everyone back tonight, tomorrow, two years from now, I don't care when, but we're not doing this with everybody here right now."

"Cole—" Charles tried again.

"No." Cole's voice was firm.

Evie reached up and touched his cheek. "Love, maybe we don't throw *everyone* out."

Cole glanced down at her, his scowl replaced almost immediately by an amused smile.

"We need these people... gods... whatever. We need them, right?" Under her hand, she felt his slight nod. "What if we just told them to come back tomorrow for breakfast so I can get to know your uncle—y'know, the man who raised you so not too far out of the realm of possibility—and best friend and—" She gestured to the three Moirai now standing to their left. "What are you three? The prophets?" She shrugged. "It makes sense that you would want me to meet your family. That's what couples do, right? Then we can avoid all of this—" Another gesture, this time to the inexplicable fistfight that had broken out between the three Fury sisters, rallied on by several onlookers. "Right now and reconvene with a united front later." She stopped, noticing everyone staring at her. "What?"

Cole jolted, almost as if waking from a stupor. "You're brilliant." She gave him a haughty smirk and a slightly condescending pat on the face. Although the loving expression on his face didn't change, his eyes darkened, his hand on her hip transforming from a protective rub to a claiming grip. She could practically see the words *brat* and *punishment* cross his mind and knew that she may not actually be able to cute her way out of his punishment this time. "Uncle Charlie, tell the troops the new game plan. We'll meet you five—and *only* you five—in the kitchen." He gave her a slight push toward what she assumed was the kitchen, his palm low on her back, almost resting on her ass, as he closed in behind her, leaving Charles to deal with the menagerie in the sitting room.

In front of them, Essi turned, her wizened face cracked into a grin. "Cole, I like this one."

"Me too," he responded, stepping aside, Evie safely enfolded in his arms, to let Essi and the others pass. She started to follow behind them, but Cole caught her braid in his hand, pulling her back against his chest so he could growl into her ear, "But don't think that just because I love you means you're not gonna get punished for that bratty mouth of yours."

Evie gasped, loudly enough that Cole placed his hand over her mouth, clucking softly at her. "Baby, you're gonna have to be quieter than that." Swatting her ass, he shoved her forward. "Now, go sit at the table like a good witch."

With an extra swish to her hips, Evie sauntered away. She shot a look over her shoulder just in time to see Cole adjusting himself as he stared at her ass.

By the time they made it to the kitchen, the Moirai and Hayden were already seated, and Charles had come up behind them. "I've managed to placate everyone. They'll return tomorrow to meet your queen." Charles gestured them to their seats before filling two glasses of water and placing them in front of Cole and Evie before taking his own seat. "You'll stay here tonight, of course."

"Awfully high-handed of you, Charlie," Cole responded. His hand was clenched around her thigh, so she rested hers over top of it. Almost instantly, his muscles loosened, his grip loosening as he relaxed.

Evie ducked her head, trying to hide her shock. She was so used to her touch being met with resistance, even among her own coven members. Although it made sense now after everything she had found out, it still didn't make the isolation hurt any less badly. To have someone who found comfort in her touch... she could become addicted to it.

Charles merely raised an eyebrow in his nephew's direction before turning a piercing look on Evie. "Now, Evie, it is truly wonderful to meet you. My nephew told me very briefly what happened during a phone call a few days back, but, as is his usual, he was fairly chary with the details. It seems that he is quite taken with you, so I and the rest of our little family would love to hear about you."

Evie nodded, nibbling on her lower lip before beginning the story, Cole providing color commentary as needed. It took almost an hour to walk his family through their childhood experiences of each other to the construction site and the powerful magic that drew them to one another and reconstituted the forest to the earthquakes that seemed to coincide with their intimacy to their decisions about ruling the Underworld. Seemingly, there was no topic that was out-of-bounds. Once they finished their story, Evie took a small sip of water.

"So am I correct in assuming that the two of you have consummated your relationship?" Charles asked, his distinguished face flushing lightly as he posed the question. "Hayden led me to believe that was the case."

Beside her, Cole's foot began tapping out a quick-paced rhythm of discomfort while Evie nearly choked on her water. There was definitely no shame in a consensual sexual relationship, but she hadn't quite expected Cole's stoic uncle to bring it up so... formally at the kitchen table. Eventually, Cole gave a sharp nod in response.

"And you discussed what would happen once you consummated your relationship?"

Evie shifted in irritation. Why did everybody think that Cole would trick her? "Yes. Cole was completely transparent with me, and I made the choice to be with him *before*—" she emphasized the word, glaring at Charles. "We had sex."

Throughout the entire conversation, Charles had maintained the utmost decorum, his face stern, his words regal. At her bald use of the word "sex," though, his cheeks turned bright red. She rolled her eyes at his prudishness. Gods, these people had such difficulties discussing healthy sexual expression. He tried his damndest to talk through his embarrassment, but his voice was strangled. "So am I to, uh, understand that the two of you had, uh, consumm—, hmm, uh, had sexual relations yesterday afternoon?"

Cole was barely concealing his amusement at his uncle's obvious discomfort. Knowing that he was more or less useless at the moment, she responded, "Yes. We had sex for the first time yesterday afternoon."

One of the Moirai sisters—Essi, she was pretty sure—leaned forward. "It would coincide with the unexpected environmental disasters that occurred yesterday." She ticked them off on her gnarled fingers as she listed them. "The tsunami in Japan. The hurricanes that wiped those Caribbean islands off the map and devastated Puerto Rico. The New Orleans earthquakes. The Alaskan fires. The volcanic eruption in Iceland." As Essi continued detailing disasters from around the globe that had taken place in the last day alone, Evie's heart sank. She and Cole had done...*this*?

Suddenly, she was moving. A small squeak of surprise snuck out of her lips as Cole dragged her into his lap, situating her so she was resting against his chest. "This isn't our fault, Angel," he murmured. "The Underworld has to be opened, or the shades will devastate this world far worse than we ever could. They're already doing that just by being here." He rested his palm on her cheek, turning her face towards him. "You get that?"

Evie nodded slowly. Maybe he was just trying to make her feel better, but the story he had told her about the Shade Wars made it fairly clear that the shades were the worse of two evils.

"Angel, tell me you understand." His eyes took on that dominating gleam, his voice that confident tone that never failed to make her want to strip down and ask him what he wanted her to do.

"I understand." The final word of the sentence was quiet, right next to his ear. "Sir."

Cole's body went taut against hers, a quiet growl emerging from his chest as he hardened under her. He adjusted her over him, her body blocking his erection from view. Her core clenched, and she felt herself grow wet. There were conversations going on around them, but she was having difficulties paying attention to them, a fact of which Cole seemed well aware if his whispered, "Baby, I need you to focus for a little bit longer," was any indication.

Evie dragged her attention back to the conversation just in time to hear Addy, the youngest of the Moirai sisters, say, "The lines of fate always foretold that the Underworld would open if the reincarnates ever established a relationship. We didn't know what that meant, but we assumed that it had some form of sexual connection required but no emotional one. Which, considering that Cole was always resistant to entering a real relationship with the fated reincarnate, was a good thing at the time." She raised her eyebrows at where Evie was curled in Cole's lap. "Although I'm assuming your stance on that matter has now changed."

"Consider that stance very changed," Cole answered. "Irrevocably changed."

A smile teased at the corners of Evie's mouth at the firmness of his tone.

Essi's face was serious. "We'll need to read the fate lines to see exactly where the portal to the Underworld opened. That should be a fairly simple task. But—" She leaned forward. "Now we need to discuss Evie's heritage. Was Cate correct in her assessment that you're a witch?"

"Yes." Evie nodded. "I was raised by the Barataria Coven based out of New Orleans."

"Are you aware of the witches' own prophecy?" Cleo finally spoke, her voice grave.

"Yes. Well, I know of it. Many of our records, including the one documenting the prophecy I think you're referencing, have been lost d the various genocides committed against us, so mostly they're oral history by this point. Interpretations are driven by those who remember, so it's highly dependent upon the individual covens. Barataria really isn't all that traditional." Evie cast her memory back over what she remembered of the prophecy being discussed by the elders. "But there are far more traditional covens that keep to the letter of the prophecies as they understand them, including the apocalyptic one, and hold true to them. In my coven, we always considered them morality tales."

"They are certainly far more than morality tales, Evie, as much as I hate to admit it," Essi replied. "And they do conflict with the prophecy in which you and Cole play a critical role. The witches themselves are meant to be harbingers of the apocalypse."

"What?" Evie's voice was loud in the kitchen. "So the prophecy is intended to be literal? As in the covens are literally intended to roll out the annihilation of humanity? But the witch covens are supposed to be peaceful."

"Well, the interpretation of the prophecy as literal versus not is, as you said, highly dependent upon the coven." Essi shook her head sadly. "But a witch herself can be peaceful. The covens themselves are not guaranteed as such. If I remember correctly—and I do—" For the first time since bringing up the subject, Essi chuckled lightly at her own joke, a bell-like sound that was far too whimsical to come from the wizened crone sitting next to Evie. "The witch's prophecy is that, when the old gods return, the witches will emerge from the forest and bring the world to its natural end, although there is some fairly significant language about a witch's choice in there. All told, it's a fairly silly prophecy, especially given that most of the so-called old gods have been here all along, but that's what you get when it's foretold by the Oracle at Delphi." Her voice dropped, and she muttered something under her breath that sounded like, "Fraudulent hack."

"Yeah, Hayden was hazy on those details when we talked about it." Cole sighed, shooting the other man a grimace. "So I'm assuming they think Evie and I are the old gods?"

"Well, now that you poked your head out in front of Evie's coven and *identified yourself as an Aidoneus* and took one of their witches, who they discovered uses death magic... yeah, I think it's quite plausible that they made some leaps and believe the two of you are old gods." Essi's eyebrows rose high on her forehead in mockery while Hayden cracked up beside her.

"You done fucked up, A-aron," Hayden cackled. "And all because you had to go retrieve your witch!"

Cole glowered at his best friend's amusement before shrugging, somehow imbuing the gesture with pride. "I have no regrets, and I would do it a-fucking-gain if I had to. She belongs with me."

Evie patted his cheek lovingly before turning to the Moirai sisters. "I don't wholly understand why the witches' prophecy would be in direct conflict with yours?"

"Our prophecy has always presumed that the Hades and Persephone reincarnates would stop all apocalyptic opportunities by opening the Underworld, collecting the shades, returning them to their rightful place, and establishing a judging system to determine where souls should live after death."

Cleo jumped in. "Whereas the witches' prophecy presumes that, at its core, humanity is not savable and, when a number of prophetic portents are met including the return of the old gods, the witches must ride and rain down the apocalypse. With the covens now suspecting that their old gods have returned, shades devastating the world at a catastrophic rate, the two of you causing all sorts of environmental disasters, and humanity being, y'know, awful, those portents keep looking like they're getting met. It would be easy for the witches who interpret the prophecy literally to connect the dots and assume it's the end."

"Fucking hell," Cole swore. "So it's two diametrically opposed positions. The world and humans in it deserve to be saved or that humans and shades have fundamentally damned the world?"

Six of the seven people at the table began talking over each other. Of them, only Evie was silent, doing her best to digest all of this information. That night in the tree, she had chosen to accept Cole and their rule. The witches' prophecy hadn't even factored into that decision. Now, with the Moirai saying the prophecy wasn't only real but potentially imminent as well, she had to figure out whether that changed her mind.

"And I—" Evie's voice cracked, but it still cut through the chaos. "And I'm the one who has to choose which prophecy to follow?"

Charles' gaze was heavy on her. "Yes. It's not fair to you, but yes, Evie. You have to be the one to decide. We could force the issue—force you to take the crown, force you to go through with the Moirai's prophecy—but—" A growl followed by a sharp, "Fuck that" emerged from Cole, bringing a fond grin to Charles' face. "I assume my nephew would object to that course of action."

"You're damn right I would," Cole gritted out. "Evie gets to choose whatever *the fuck* she wants to do. And if she wants to burn the world to the goddamn ground? Then I'll be right fucking beside her with the fucking match."

"Ah, love in the time of arson," Essi sighed. "So romantic."

Evie blinked at the crone and realized, for the first time in her life, she had somebody else to talk to about all of the darkest things. With that came clarity: she wanted to talk to Cole. Alone. Now. "Could you all give Cole and I a moment?" she blurted.

Chapter 45

Cole

Beau Chêne, Mandeville, Louisiana

Cole watched as his family filed out of the kitchen before turning his attention to the witch in his lap. "You know they're just going to eavesdrop from the hallway, right?" He loved them all, but they were nosey on a normal day. For a conversation like this with potentially world-ending implications, he just assumed that they would become even more overbearing. "I'm pretty sure I can see Charlie's shadow on the floor right there." The dark splotch on the floor moved subtly, proving his point.

"I kind of figured they would be a nuisance." From the hallway beyond the kitchen where he knew his family was gathered, there was an indignant snort (Cole was guessing Hayden) followed by a grunt of pain (undoubtedly one of the others trying to quiet Hayden). "Is there someplace else we can talk?"

"Yeah, let's go out on the deck." He gestured her through the French doors separating the kitchen from the porch, making sure to rest his hand on her back as he escorted her outside. If she was going to align with or not directly oppose the witches' prophecy, he wanted to touch her as much as he damn well could before the world imploded. He shut the door behind him with his free hand.

Evie stepped away from him, and he almost grabbed her back, only barely stopping himself. She opened her mouth to speak, but her focus was torn away by the deck's view, which looked directly down on the Tchefuncte River through ancient cypress trees. "This is where you grew up?"

Cole nodded, even though her back was to him, hiding a smile as he watched her reach a hand towards the bald cypress nearest the deck. The tree's thin limbs swayed towards her, oddly gentle as they stroked along her palm.

"Did you mean what you said?" The question came seemingly out of nowhere, breaking the comfortable silence surrounding them.

"About what?" She twisted her head, threw him a disbelieving stare over her shoulder. "I'm just asking, Angel. I've meant everything I've said to you, and I've never lied to you, so you're gonna have to narrow it down."

"Fine." She was finally facing him, stomping over to him with a look that, under any other circumstances, would have him bending her over the nearest piece of furniture or, in a pinch, his knee and seeing whether her ass was as spankable in true punishment as he imagined it was. "Did you mean what you said about me picking a prophecy? That it was my choice, and you would stop anyone who tried to force me into anything?"

The sharp winter wind blew the wispy tendrils escaping her braid around her face. In the late afternoon sun filtering through the trees surrounding the property, her eyes took on an almost violet hue, and he was certain she could see straight into his soul. He reached his hand out, cupping her cheek in his palm. "Angel." He paused just to drive his point home. "I meant every fucking word." She gasped, but he wasn't done. "The world's going to shit, and while of lot of that can be attributed to the shades, humans play a big role because they're, y'know terrible. Do I think they need to be apocalyptically purged? Not necessarily. Will I support you every step of the way if you decide they do? Fuckin' a."

She took another small step towards him, almost close enough to touch his chest.

"And I want to make this crystal clear to you in case you didn't believe me before. You're it for me, Angel. I don't want any part of this world, this life, or any lifetime that comes after if you're not in it with me. So we need to end this world tour on an apocalyptic bang because you want it? Yeah, baby, I'll do that for you." A tear slid down her cheek. God, that one tear fucking wrecked him. "Please, sweetheart, don't cry—"

His breath flew out as she took the final step into his arms and tugged his head down to hers. "I made my decision that night I sat in the trees while you slept. What the Moirai told us doesn't change a thing. I just found you, Cole." Gaze steady on his, her pulse raced under her skin, so pale that he could see the blood rushing through it, as her voice rose. "And I'm not giving you up for anyone, especially not some blood-soaked, apocalyptic prophecy passed down millennia ago that most witches think is fable anyway and violates every nonviolent belief we're expected to hold."

In her passion, she was every inch a queen. He would never deserve her, but he would do his best.

"I get to choose? Well, then I'm deciding to follow you into the Underworld, rule beside you, and keep this world from self-destructing. And it's purely for selfish reasons because I'm not going to let you go until *we* decide that we're ready to... turn into stars or become part of the universe or whatever it is deities do when their time is done."

"I love you, Angel," he murmured, dropping his head the final inch needed to bring his mouth to hers. Her lips fell open at the smallest swipe of his tongue, and he took full ownership of her lush little mouth. She was his. *Mine.* It was with that one thought in mind that he seized her waist, lifting her effortlessly. She wrapped her legs around him right before he turned and pushed her up against the expanse of windows lining the deck of his uncle's home, his hands quickly making their way under her fluffy sweater. *She chose me.*

Arms wrapped around his neck, she lined herself up against his rock hard dick, a muffled cry rolling into his mouth as she ground herself against him.

"Fucking hell, baby, you're already soaking for me," he murmured, feeling her wetness even through both of their pants. "God, I need to be inside of you—"

He had one hand on the button of her jeans when the French door beside them swung open and Hayden stepped out, looking everywhere but at the two of them. Cole dropped his head to Evie's neck with a groan of frustration. He just wanted one interruption-less day with his witch. Was that too much to ask?

Hayden's face was pained as he stared pointedly at the sky. "Charles said that it looks like you two have made up your minds so please come inside and don't fornicate on his porch where his neighbors can hear you."

"You are a 5,000-year-old immortal god," Cole snapped. "Get better timing or you won't make it to 6,000."

Hayden, prick that he was, snickered. "Cole, buddy, I know you can smoke me in a fight, but I'm more scared of Charles than I am of you."

"Guess you better work on that," Evie whispered into his ear. He cast her a fake betrayed look. "Can't have a ruler of the Underworld whose own court doesn't fear him." Her eyes were wide in mocking innocence.

"Don't think I'll forget that, naughty little witch." Cole dropped her to her feet and swatted her ass as she walked away. After adjusting himself for what felt like the thousandth time since they had arrived at Charles' house, he followed Evie and Hayden into the kitchen where the rest of the family made no secret that they had been watching.

Essi fanned her face lightly. "Damn, Cole, if I hadn't been around during your childhood and seen what a nasty little beastie you were then, *I* would be climbing you like a ladder."

Cole smirked at the idea of the old woman doing anything of the sort. "I'm sure you would, Essi." A hard pinch on his inner bicep brought his attention down to Evie, who was staring at the two of them mutinously. He loved this possessive, jealous side of her just as much as he did the sassy troublemaker. "Relax, Angel, there's no comparison."

"Oh, honey." Essi jumped in with heartfelt reassurance. "Don't you worry about a thing. I see the way this boy looks at you; you will never have anything to worry about with that one." Although her tone was jovial, her face fell. "I'm just a lonely—" She paused. "A lonely, old lady is all."

Evie moved towards Essi, her brow furrowed in concern at the Fates' flat tone, but Charles interrupted her march to check on the woman. "So am I to understand that the two of you have reached a decision?"

Evie glanced up at Cole, but he spread his hands, indicating the floor was hers. It had been her decision to make; it was hers to announce as well. He wouldn't take a single ounce of agency away from his witch.

"We'll be fulfilling the Moirai prophecy," Evie announced, her voice steady even though her hand shook in his. "Cole and I will be taking the throne and setting the Underworld and the human world to rights." She turned to Essi, Cleo, and Addy. "Please roll your bones or tie your strings or... however you divine so we can find the entrance to the Underworld."

"Very well." Charles bore a proud expression on his face as he watched the closest thing he would ever have to a daughter toss around orders. "For those who would like to stay, dinner will be served soon. Magda is just putting the finishing touches on a lovely meal now. Cole, can we chat?"

Cole nodded, following his uncle out of the kitchen and down the hallway to Charles' study. Once they reached it, though, Cole paused at the threshold, battling the childish impulse to talk to his uncle from the door. As a kid, he had been expressly forbidden from entering the room given his tendency to wreck everything he touched. As an adult nearing thirty-six years old, that inclination to never enter his uncle's inner sanctum lingered even still.

"Come in, Cole," Charles called from where he stood behind his desk, his back turned to Cole as he swung a painting off the wall to reveal an intimidating-looking safe. Intrigued, Cole stepped forward—he never knew Charles had that. "So. Evie, hmm?" Charles popped the combination on the safe, pulling open the door and rifling through the contents inside. "She's a firecracker."

"She is." Cole had no idea where his uncle was going with this. Might as well play along until he got the point, even though every instinct Cole possessed demanded that he return to Evie.

"And you seem quite taken with her." After shutting the safe, Charles turned and settled into his chair, gesturing Cole into the wingback lounger resting on the other side of the desk.

"If by 'taken with her,' you mean 'in love with her?' Then yes." He knew he was being short with his uncle but didn't particularly care.

Shark-like eyes narrowed on his nephew, Charles finally asked the question he had been dancing around since entering the study. "Is this you in love with Evie?" He steepled his hands together on the desk. "Or is this the reincarnate in you recognizing the reincarnate in her?"

Cole stilled. They had never really discussed his own experience being the reincarnate of Aidoneus, the heir to the Underworld. It was just assumed that he was the one after he began meeting the signs of the prophecy. "You never asked me what it was like to have that side of me."

"It was never relevant." Charles didn't waver. "It is now."

"Why does it matter now?"

"Because now you are bringing a significant other into the fold, a beautiful woman who has made the choice to follow you. To tie her life to yours." Tapping a finger on the desk in contemplation, Charles paused before finally finishing his thought. "She has given up her life as she knows it to be with you. So I'll ask again. Why do you love her—is it because she's the fated reincarnate? Or do you love your Evie for her?"

"The original Aidoneus' memories and powers are a part of me," Cole began. "But they don't control me. They never have. They're just there, same as you knowing the experiences of your own past." He leaned forward. "And in this? In Evie? This is me, my love as Cole for her as Evie. I've loved her since I was a kid when I first saw her in my dreams. You know that, even though you didn't believe she existed. She is brilliant and kind and funny and snarky and fucking gorgeous. She makes me feel alive for the first time in my life. She is everything that matters to me. Does that answer your question?"

Charles grinned widely, a look so out of place on his face that Cole almost found himself checking his uncle's temperature. "I thought that might be the case." With that, Charles dropped a hand to his pants pocket and drew out a jewelry box. Flipping it open, he displayed a vintage ring with black diamonds inset into a floral design cresting both sides to surround a large alexandrite stone.

"A ring, Uncle Charlie? It's a backwards state, but I think even Louisiana frowns on blood relatives marrying."

The levity dropped from Charles' face, and he stared across the desk, unamused. "This was your mother's engagement ring. Before your father died, he gave it to me to give to you if you ever found a woman that you loved and wanted to share your life with. He made me promise that I wouldn't give it to you for just anybody. She had to be someone that you would burn the world for, the same way your father would have for your mother." He slid the ring box across the desk. "I think you've found her. Whenever you're ready for that step, whether it be now or in three months or in 300 years, I wanted you to have this."

Cole wrapped his fingers around the small box, feeling the weight of his father and mother's love as he picked it up. They died too early for him to really see them together—his mother passing unexpectedly when he was four and his father following her a few short months after—but he knew that they had loved each other more than life itself. "Thank you, Uncle Charlie." He stood, rounding the desk to give his uncle a hug. "This means the world to me."

His uncle clutched him close, and Cole was struck, not for the first time, by the vicious realization that not only had he lost a father, but Charles had lost a brother too. "You're welcome." Charles' voice was thick with emotion. "You look so much like him that it's hard for me to remember that he's not here anymore. Regardless of how long he has been gone."

Cole patted his shoulder gently until his uncle stepped away, clearing his throat. "Now, let's get back to the kitchen and see what Magda has prepared for us tonight."

Chapter 46

Cole

Beau Chêne, Mandeville, Louisiana

With Evie's choice settled, dinner was a fairly chill affair with the family clustered around the table, catching up on minutiae and eating Magda's gumbo and honey-soaked cornbread. Even with the incredible homemade meal, his first made by somebody other than himself in months, he found himself jittery, planning ways to get out of the requisite after-dinner drinks so he could sweep his bratty witch to bed.

His uncle seemed to read his mind—or at least his impatience—and, instead of letting Cole and Evie escape after dinner, showed Evie to the bedroom they would share, told her where she could find the towels should she want to take a shower, and strong-armed Cole back downstairs.

Almost an hour of aimless conversation and half a glass of rum later, Cole was prepared to throw something heavy at his uncle's head. He couldn't quite work out whether he wanted to throw it by hand so his uncle would see it coming or telekinetically so it would be a surprise. Regardless, he was going to lose his shit if they kept him here any longer. Either that or he was going to walk the fuck out. *Hey. There's an idea.* He blinked, stunned that it had taken him so long to come up with the most straightforward solution.

Cole set his glass on his uncle's desk—feeling petty enough that he placed it so far away from the coaster that Charles winced—and stood. Then, without a word, he turned and walked out, slamming the door behind him for good measure.

Behind him, Hayden's loud laughter crackled through the house as Cole stormed down the hallway and up the stairs. It would be worth it for him to calm down so he didn't storm into their bedroom with the energy of a feral hyena, but knowing Evie was somewhere in there lit a fire in him that he couldn't control. His mother's ring sat in his pocket, not forgotten but also not relevant to what he was about to do.

Cole opened the bedroom door and stepped in quickly, shutting it behind him with a quiet click. As he turned, Evie stepped out of the steamy bathroom, toweling herself dry. Her hair was gathered on top of her head in a messy bun, but several delicate tendrils had escaped, highlighting her graceful neck. Water droplets glittered on her pale skin, making her look more like a faerie than a witch.

All rational thought abandoned him at the sight of her. He was already halfway across the room before she noticed him. Already in front of her when she opened her mouth to greet him. Already devouring her mouth as she started to speak. The words she had started to say filtered into his mouth on a small moan as he pushed her against the wall, ripping the towel from her hand and tossing it onto the floor.

He pulled back to gaze at his little witch. Her eyes were already glazed with lust, her breaths coming fast. Reaching out a hand, he cupped it around her breast, ran his thumb over her taut nipple. "Hey, Angel."

"Hi, love." Her voice was husky.

Slowly, he drew closer, letting one of his legs slide between hers, just enough to stimulate her, not high enough to actually let her grind against it. "Do you remember what I told you earlier?"

A dimple flashed in her cheek when she finally responded. "That you needed to be inside me?"

Cole tsked at her. "Oh, and here I was thinking that you wanted to come, sweetheart. But my *ange* just can't help herself, can she?" She shook her head ruefully, a cute whine emerging from her throat as he pulled away. "What I said—and I know you remember it because you were practically grinding on me in the kitchen when I said it—was that bratty witches get punished."

She stared at him hungrily as he sat on the settee resting at the foot of the bed. "Now crawl to me, little witch."

Her eyes went wide, but she still dropped to her knees and prowled naked across the floor to him.

Gods, that's the fucking sexiest thing I've ever seen. Once she settled in between his knees, he tugged her to his mouth, nipping at her full lower lip, before lowering her back to a kneeling position and placing her hands on his knees.

"Obviously, I can't trust you to be quiet, so I'm going to have to give that gorgeous mouth something to do." She whimpered as he gripped her thick hair in one hands. "Unzip my pants, sweetheart." Her eager hands made quick work of his zipper, but he tightened his grip on her hair before she could free his aching cock. "Put your hands back on my thighs." She tilted her head in confusion but obeyed him, shifting her small hands back to their original place on his legs. "You're gonna be taking me in that pretty mouth of yours, Angel. You may not be able to take me all the way down your throat right away, but we're gonna train you to." He ran a thumb over her throat, a long, extended column of pale silk, thanks to the hold he had on her hair. She let out a shaky breath, her eyes darting from his own to his cock straining the tensile strength of his boxers.

"You're gonna need to breathe through your nose when you take me. It may feel like you're choking, and you may gag or cry. It's gonna be hot as fuck, though, so I won't be able to stop myself from fuckin' that mouth of yours harder." Her tongue swiped out to wet her lips as her gaze took on a predatory sheen. "Baby—I need you to pay attention now—while your mouth is full of my cock, you're not going to be able to speak. So if you need me to slow down, squeeze my thigh. Like this." He wrapped his free hand around one of hers and clenched down on his thigh with it. "Now show me."

"Now?"

"Yes now, Angel." She tightened both hands around his thighs. He hummed his approval, murmuring, "Such a good girl." Her eyes shone at his praise. God, the Angel with a praise kink and a bratty mouth was going to be the death of him. "If we need to stop immediately, tap twice. Make sure you do it hard enough for me to feel because I'm going to be lost in that sexy mouth. I want to make sure I know if you need me to stop."

"Can't I just magic you against a wall or something if I want you to stop?" Her eyes glittered in mischief.

"You could if you want me to spank that ass of yours so red that you can't sit tomorrow." He leaned back again. "Now tap me like you would if you need me to stop." Her hands came down twice firmly on both legs. "Good little witch."

She whimpered again, leaning forward until his harsh grip on her hair stopped any forward movement. She had never gone down on a man, but she was already starving for him. An unstable breath rattled out of his mouth. "One last thing and then you can finally suck me down like your body is telling me you want to. It's okay to stop for any reason. I won't be mad. We've got a lifetime of this ahead of us, and we need to make sure you enjoy it. Understand?" She licked her lips again, nodded enthusiastically. "Fuck, baby, I know you're hungry for my cock, but I need you to use your words. Do. You. Understand?"

"Yes, sir." Her words were little more than a whisper.

Cole leaned back against the bed, lowering his boxers far enough to release his cock. As soon as he did, Evie tilted forward and, before he could even give her an order, licked the crown, running her tongue around his piercing and lapping up his precum. "Fuck, *mon ange*, that's right, baby."

Without any direction from him, she wrapped one of her hands around the base of his shaft and shifted further up on her knees to get closer. "Such a good fucking girl." She hummed in appreciation before lowering her mouth further down his length. "You're doing so good, Angel." With the hand fisted in her hair, he drove her down his cock, her moan vibrating along his shaft as she took him deeper. She choked, tears starting to roll down her face, as he used her hair to force her to take even more of him.

"Breathe through your nose, *mon amour*," he ordered as he rocked his hips up, sliding that last bit down her throat. "That's right, you're taking me so well." He was driving his hips hard, watching himself disappear between her pouty lips. "Fuck yes, you were born to suck my cock, baby." His stomach tightened, his release drawing closer. He was fucking her mouth now, that bratty, brilliant mouth that drove him crazy, all but silent now as she sucked almost every inch of him greedily down her throat.

Evie was his. Now. Forever. His balls drew up, and he knew he had only seconds before he came. "*Mon petit ange*, I'm gonna come. You're going to take me, beautiful girl, drink my cum down."

Her grey eyes met his, and she let out a sharp moan as he shouted out his release, coming violently down her throat and ordering her to swallow all of him.

She had only just pulled away, licking her lips hungrily, when he gripped her waist and tossed her onto the bed. His body was still shaking from the cataclysmic experience of coming down Evie's throat, but, more than anything in this entire world, he needed to see how wet going down on him had made her. He ran one finger along her exposed pussy and groaned. "Fucking god, you are goddamned drenched for me. Such a naughty little witch getting so wet while she sucks on her sir's cock."

Evie moaned. "Gods, please, sir."

"Please what, Angel?" Cole flicked a finger over her clit, and her body arched on a desperate moan. "You have to tell me what you want."

She stared at him with glassy eyes, her mouth swollen from sucking his cock. "Please, sir, make me come."

He growled, dropping between her legs. "You're so pretty when you beg, little witch. And you took your punishment so well that I don't want to tell you no." Tapping the inside of her thigh, he gave her a pointed look. "Now put these legs of yours around my shoulders, and I'll give you your reward."

This Evie, this lusty goddess who sucked his cum down like she would starve without it and followed his orders perfectly, made him just as hard as the Evie who bratted at him. Her legs settled around his head, he tilted forward, slipping one finger into her core. She whimpered at him, her hips rocking desperately against his hand. "Does my witch need something more?" Her head bobbled on a nod as she gasped, "yes" at him. In one swift move, he drove two fingers deep, pumping them hard as he alternated sucking on her clit and lazily passing his tongue over it.

Her moans were louder now, coming more consistently. She was soaking his face with each lick of his tongue and stroke of his fingers, slicking her own thighs with how much she wanted him. It had only been minutes since she made him come so hard he almost forgot his own name, but he was already ready for her, could easily slide into her pussy and release deep inside her again. "Make sure you scream loudly enough to bring the house down, sweet witch. They kept me from tasting you for far too long, and I want them to know it." Her thighs were tensing around his face, her gasps near constant now. On a downstroke, he slipped a third finger into her, crooking his fingers so they slid against her g-spot. "I'm gonna suck on this little clit of yours, and you're gonna come hard for me, baby. You get one shot—if you don't come now, I'm going to leave you this wet, horny mess until I wake you up tomorrow."

With his threat issued, he continued pumping his fingers before sealing his lips around her clit and sucking. Evie went batshit insane, screaming his name followed by a string of creative profanity. Suddenly, unexpectedly, as his fingertips rubbed over the bundle of nerves lining her interior wall, her cum gushed over his palm, soaking him and the bed as she squirted all over him.

"Fucking Christ, Angel," he swore. *I need to be inside her right fucking now.* One hand braced by her waist, he shoved himself up the bed, sliding his fingers out of her as he did but keeping one finger rubbing along her clit. He lined himself up with her entrance and thrust through her clenching walls.

"Cole," she screamed, her nails digging into his back as he pounded into her, blood rushing in his ears. "Godsdammit, sir." Her wail was piercing when she tumbled into a second climax, clenching around him so hard he almost blacked out.

"Holy shit. Fuck, baby!" The headboard clanking against the wall kept time with his barely controlled thrusts. "That's right, sweetheart, milk me dry. Good fucking girl!" He went lightheaded as he emptied himself inside her, grinding against her while he filled her body with every last drop of his cum.

Cole dropped his head to hers, gasping.

"Holy mother of witches, Cole," she breathed.

"I know, Angel." He was panting like he had run a marathon, was pretty sure he was blind in one eye from the intensity of what they had just shared. Sliding himself out of her with a pained wince at his sensitivity, he rolled them on the oversized mattress until Evie was sprawled across his chest, warm and pliant in his arms. "You okay?"

"Mmmhmm." Her head barely moved and, when he craned his head to see her face, her eyes were already sliding shut. "So amazing."

He chuckled at her dazed, sleepy expression. "Yeah, it was." Her leg hooked over his waist, dragging her further into his arms. "Go to sleep, Angel." He brushed his lips over her forehead before switching off the lamp on his side of the bed.

The light went out, plunging the room into almost complete darkness. The only light left were the moonbeams peeking through the plantation shutters, seeming to illuminate Evie alone. He had a brief moment of clarity—something about her being his light in the darkness—before sleep took him too.

As he dozed off, he could have sworn he heard somebody outside their door yell, "They're done fucking! We can finally go to sleep now!" but he was certain that had to be a dream.

Interlude

Council of Witches

Megiddo National Park, Jezreel Valley, Megiddo, Israel

Hesteia stared at the ruins that made up Megiddo National Park. The blazing Israeli sun shone high overhead while they stood baking beneath it in silence. They had spent the last fourteen hours traveling, using the chaos portals that naturally occurred within each coven's home—thanks to the high saturation of magic in those places—to travel. As they did so, other coven elders and high priestesses joined them in their travels until finally, almost 500 of them descended upon Megiddo. The birthplace of witches. The home of the Witches Council.

Sweet Selene, the whole thing was so pretentious it made her want to vomit. "It's not even the real birthplace of witches," she mumbled to Thea. "The witch of Endor was just a biblical fairytale."

With a patient smile, Thea nodded. "I know, my love." Having long been subject to this particular rant, she was well used to it.

"And they always make us go through those godsforsaken chaos portals that take forever when there's a perfectly good Council-sanctioned portal in the gathering chamber. But nooooo." She stomped her foot, well aware that she was acting like a child, then lightly pouted for good measure. "It can only be used to travel *from* the chambers, not *to* the chambers."

"Hesteia, you know why—" Thea started, but her wife cut her off.

"I *know* it's because of what happened the last time they let it be used as an entry," Hesteia grumbled. "But it still annoys me."

"Just a wild stab in the dark." Akna, the Chugach Coven's High Priestess, swept over. In the bright light, her golden-brown eyes sparkled with mirth at Hesteia's fit of temper. "Is it possible, dear sister, that you're annoyed not at the gathering location but because you've been traveling for so long?"

Hesteia gritted her teeth. "Extremely possible." She raised her voice. "What are we waiting for, sisters? It's time to descend—" Dropped her voice. "Into the hellmouth." Next to her, Thea choked in laughter, rubbing her lover's back in reassuring circles.

The collection of witches began their descent into the ruins. The oldest among them went down the roughly hewn stairs first with the youngest waiting behind them. Their group was diverse with witches from Oceania—who were extremely removed from society and unbelievably traditional—to a "cohort" from Los Angeles who lived in townhomes built in a greenspace and married non-witches. For all their differences, all of the elders gathered there believed in witchkind.

Even with their similarities, though, their allegiance to the long-held Council prophecies varied wildly. Many of the newer generations believed they were legends or metaphorical—the mythology of witches, really—while a small but vocal contingent of the powerful, older witches believed that they were prophetic and must be followed to the letter. All in all, it made for an interesting dynamic when a decent portion of their membership believed that it was time for the extermination of humankind while the others thought those members were overly literal, homicidal, and prepared to violate the witches' creed of nonviolence at a moment's notice. Given the purpose of the summons they had all received, there was no way this meeting of the minds was going to be anything other than deeply uncomfortable.

With all coven members finally in the ruins, Hesteia led them quickly to the staircase leading to the aqueduct tunnels before they could draw attention. Not only were there almost 500 of them, ranging in age from mid-thirties to wizened old crone, but some of their members were in unconventional clothing. Although the crop tops and high-waisted shorts of the Onzo-Borrego Coven were odd at a holy site, that wasn't even the most outlandish garb of the group. The wizened crones among them wore cloaks embroidered with metallic threads that glittered with magic. It was crucial that they not draw any more attention than necessary when getting to the Council chambers, but the sheer size of their group and the appearance of their members made it difficult to keep a low profile.

Hesteia escorted the first ten elders down, pretending that she was a tour guide so as not to draw attention. Once in the tunnels, she walked halfway down the broad path before turning to the wall and sketching a quick series of runes along the stone. The completed etchings flared briefly, bright flame in the dreary tunnels, before the wall seemingly fell away, revealing yet another tunnel. Unlike the one in which they currently stood, this one wasn't lit or paved, only packed dirt tracking into the darkness. One hand extended, Hesteia summoned a series of fiery orbs that lingered along the ceiling, lighting the way for the witches now traveling along the tunnel's length.

Dozens of trips later, Hesteia found herself alone in front of the tunnel entrance. She was tired, sweaty, and irritated and not just because of her disheveled appearance. Many of the elders were quite vocal about their thoughts on the witches' role as apocalyptic harbingers, and the more traditional their beliefs, the louder they got. Some of them were almost gleeful at the idea of wiping out humanity. She shook her head, her sweat-soaked braids clinging to her cheeks. Frustrated and concerned was certainly a *fantastic* way to approach not only the other Council elders but the Council Judiciary as well.

After adjusting her dress and realizing that there was no way to fix her hair, she inverted the wards, drawing the magical entry closed behind her. She walked slowly down the tunnel, an ominous feeling thrumming in her veins. Her heart was pounding. Gods, she felt bad about this. The summons that brought her here made her skin crawl. Now that she was standing on the precipice of this discussion, all she wanted to do was turn and run. Out of this tunnel. Out of this cursed set of ruins. But her love and several of her sisters were in the gathering chambers, and she couldn't—no, she *wouldn't*, she corrected herself—leave them behind to the jackals.

It was with this thought in mind that she took her final step into the Council gathering chambers. The room was massive, easily the size of a human football field, and carved deep underneath the historic site; whether it was made with magic or by witches' hands, she didn't know. Long, low wooden benches surrounded the outside edge of the cavern, leaving a wide space in the center for the elders to gather or, during discussions, present their case. At the front of the room was a long table of black wood with three large chairs behind it. Orbs similar to those that lined her coven's forest home hung overhead, shimmering bright, white light over the room and the women gathered in it.

Many of the elders hadn't yet taken seats on the benches, instead choosing to cluster in the room's open center. The hair along Hesteia's neck rose the instant she stepped into the chamber proper. The witches near the back turned to greet her, but she stepped past them quickly, looking desperately for Thea and her coven. That feeling of unease only grew as she wandered through the chamber, searching desperately for her love's tawny mane of hair. Finally, she caught sight of Thea and rushed towards her.

Startled by her wife's sudden appearance, Thea jumped. "What's wrong, love?" She rested her palm on Hesteia's cheek and drew her in, nestling into her wife. "Are you alright?" Her eyes darted around wildly, scanning the chambers for anything suspicious. "Is something amiss?"

"I feel... wrong. I'm jumping at shadows and sounds. I feel like something... like we're in danger here, Thea." Hesteia pressed her body against Thea's. "Something is very wrong."

Beside them, Chloe, Evie's adopted mother, spoke quietly, low enough that she wouldn't draw attention from the witches not associated with their coven. "I feel the same. Like something isn't right. Should we leave?" Her hazel eyes were wide with concern; when Hesteia glanced around at the other Barataria Coven elders, she saw the same look on every one of their faces.

"Do you all feel like this?" To a one, they all nodded. Hesteia winced. She had no idea how to respond as her wife and sisters stared at her like she would have the answer. Gods, she wished Cassandra was here; she would be able to determine whether this sinking feeling had any basis in the potential future. "I don't—" She never had the chance to finish that thought.

"Sisters!" A loud voice emanated from the front of the cavernous room. "Please take your seats so we can begin the Council meeting."

Thea grasped Hesteia's hand, drawing her after the other Barataria Coven elders to take a seat at one of the benches surrounding them. Chaos reigned as witches from all over the world jostled for a place to sit. Once everyone was seated, all eyes turned to the front of the room where the Witches Council Judiciary had filed in.

The Judiciary were the three powerful witches who oversaw the Council and acted as mediators when the Council couldn't reach a decision on the issues. Its members sat primly at the high table; in front of the woman seated at either end of the table sat a large copper basin. To the left was Circe, a beautiful enchantress garbed in an ocean blue tunic with hair the color of seafoam. Around her arms wove gold cuffs, engraved with scenes of the sun rising and setting over water. Best known for penalizing those who rejected her advances with death or transfiguration, Circe's thoughts on any given subject were anybody's guess. She was unpredictable and self-centered, which were a truly alarming combination.

In the throne seated at the table's right end, Medea held court, her hair golden in the lights flickering overhead. The golden fleece itself—stolen from her husband's corpse after she murdered him, his mistress, and their children—was draped over her shoulders like a cloak, parting over her cleavage to reveal a fitted but severe black dress. She was a force of nature and absolutely terrifying, her decisions often severe, brutal, and bloody.

And, centered in between them, sat Hecate. The goddess of witches herself whose existence was a closely held secret of the Witches Council and the coven elders who sat on it.

Hecate was a stunning woman, which wasn't surprising for a goddess, but her beauty tread that fine line between light and dark, a vast contradiction in every way. Her purple-tinged, raven black hair flowed elegantly over her shoulders, but it had small bone fragments and tiny bird skulls tied into it with twine. Her beautiful eyes were a violet hue so intense it was almost black, so dark it almost hurt to look at them, but madness roiled in their depths. Draped around her throat sat a delicate necklace of three keys, but they were carved from bone. As most gods did over their immortal lives, she had updated her wardrobe to something both elegant and edgy. Now, she wore an all-black outfit topped by a leather jacket with elbow-length sleeves, which revealed her forearm tattoo of two black dogs sitting on a dark road. Not many knew that these were her familiars, incorporated into a more modern medium where they would be safe but could be called to her side at a second's notice.

It was Hecate's voice that echoed around them, a mellifluous sound that somehow still managed to be discordant. "Blessed be, sisters."

"Blessed be, Goddess," chorused back to her.

"It has come to my attention that the covens believe there may be a return of the old gods, which would allegedly trigger our darkest and most important prophecy. At the request of the Chugach Coven—" She fluttered her hand in Akna's direction where she sat near Hesteia. "We are meeting today to discuss whether Evie of the Barataria Coven and Cole Aidoneus are the old gods prophesied about many millennia ago by the Oracle at Delphi. If we believe that they are, we must then identify the proper course of action to take. Many of you know Evie as the young witch abandoned in Louisiana in the United States who was found next to her mother's corpse and a three-headed dog; this Council was last convened to address the question of whether the girl may be raised with the witches, in spite of the fact that the Barataria Coven's seer saw that she was responsible for her mother's death. As you all know, certain members of the Council and this judiciary strongly opposed allowing the coven to take her in, some even going so far as to advocate killing her. In deference to those voices, the Council required that the girl undergo certain procedures to ensure that she would not be a danger to future generations. We also required her to undergo magical attempts to recover her memories, both of this and past lives. To the best of our knowledge, those attempts failed." Hecate paused, her dark eyes skimming the crowd. "I would now request the testimony of Hesteia of the Barataria Coven to relay the events that bring us here today."

Hesteia stood, Thea's hand falling away from her as she did, and strode to the center of the room. "Thank you, Mother of Witches." She drew a deep breath and then shared every moment of the last week. Evie's unexpected absence. The earthquakes. Their contacting other covens to see if anyone knew what was happening. Evie's return with unexpected knowledge of her past. The destruction of their clearing's protective barrier by Cole Aidoneus, who was searching for Evie, and his protectiveness of and closeness to her. His proclamation of Evie's own death magic. Evie's abandonment of the coven and subsequent summoning of the trees to allow her and Cole to escape. Everything. The Judiciary and other Coven elders stopped her often to ask questions, which she answered to the best of her ability. By the time she finished, hours later, her throat was raw, and she was barely able to stand anymore.

"Hesteia, you have done well," Hecate said, gesturing her to a bench. "Please be seated and have a drink."

Hesteia crossed back to Thea, who promptly passed her a jug of water. She drank deeply as Hecate continued.

"Now," Hecate said. "To save time, I will confirm that Aidoneus was the mortal name of the god Hades and is considered a family name of sorts. Are there any others who would like to provide testimony, or shall we move to discussion?"

An older witch from one of the Oceania covens stood, walking haughtily to the center of the room. "I am Maia of the Cook Islands Coven. Prior to this, we have never heard of any being whose magical source is death. On its own, having two practitioners with death magic is improbable. For those two beings to be seemingly connected to each other is all but impossible. When you consider this man's family name, it is all but certain that he is somehow the returned king of the Underworld." A loud cry of agreement rose from many of those sitting in the circle. "And this girl, this *Evie—*" she spat out Evie's name like it left a bad taste in her mouth. "—is clearly his queen. If we had only left her to the elements as many of us in this Council voted to do when you found her, we might never have had to deal with this question."

Hesteia leapt to her feet along with the other Barataria Coven elders. Chloe, who was all but snarling at the inference that her adopted child should have been left behind, was the first to speak, though. "She was a child!" she snapped at Maia. "It would have been certain death!"

Maia folded her arms across her chest. "And that cost would have been well worth potentially avoiding this danger."

"You're talking about an infant's life!" Hesteia shouted. "An ye who harm none, do what ye will. Or have you forgotten our creed of nonviolence?"

Eyes cold, Maia answered, "That creed of nonviolence doesn't apply to murderers."

Hesteia saw red. She was preparing to launch herself at Maia when she felt a forceful push to her chest that knocked her and her sisters back onto the bench.

In the center of the room, Maia was silent. Her hands clutched her throat, eyes bugging from her head. A small shuffle of noise filled the room as hundreds of witches turned to look towards the high table.

Standing at the high table, awe-inspiring and horrible, was Hecate. Shadows swirled around her, practically obscuring the floating light orbs behind her. Her eyes blazed with a furious light and, pacing in front of the high table, were two enormous black dogs, fur bristling with menace. When the goddess did speak, her voice was unexpectedly breathy, eerie in its fluidity, but it carried across the chambers with ease. "I understand that tempers are high regarding this matter, but I will not tolerate incivility. You would *all* do well to remember that. Maia, I recommend that you remember that you are speaking of one of our brethren and to not do so quite so callously. And, Barataria elders—" she turned to them, her gaze softening. "I understand that you are upset and have a personal interest in the witch in question, but this is not the appropriate forum for a shouting match. No matter how out of line other coven members may be."

Hesteia nodded her head slightly to indicate her understanding, fingers clenched around Thea's hand.

Maia's own fingers were now scratching at anything she could reach, including her own throat, deep welts appearing as she raked her fingernails down her neck in an effort to get air back into her lugs. She was gasping to no effect, and her face was turning red as she struggled for air. One of her own coven members screamed at Hecate, "Stop it, please, you're killing her!"

Hecate's eyes flashed at the witch. "I never wish for the death of one of my children, but if I must allow it to prove my point, I will. All witches are welcome in this space, both to speak and give counsel. But if you ever raise your voice to me again, young witch, I will burn you to the ground with your own magic and walk through the ashes. Do I make myself clear?"

Properly chastened, the young witch nodded her head deferentially.

"Now, now, child. You were so willing to speak up before. You must do so once more." The magic of their goddess, the Mother of Witches, roiling through the room was almost tangible. It was truly a fearsome thing, more so because Hecate did not exercise malice with regularity.

"I—I understand, Hecate." Her voice trembled but still made its way to Hecate. "I apologize for my outburst."

"I accept your apology, young witch." The shadows emanating from Hecate vanished almost like they had never been there. She looked over the room with a fond smile before her gaze fell upon Maia, whose face had gone from the red of immediate suffocation to the delicate shade of blue preceding death. Her hands were lax at her sides. The smile immediately fell from Hecate's mouth. "As for you, Maia, I will allow you to breathe once more if you agree to be civil."

Maia, too air deprived to do much else, flopped her head forward, her hair draping around her face. With a single blink, Hecate released her hold on Maia. The Cook Islands witch dropped to her knees, gasping.

The silence following the show of power spoke volumes. Hecate allowed it to sit for several minutes, witches twitching in discomfort the longer the uncomfortable quiet, broken only by the sounds of Maia's ragged breathing, went on. Finally, with a smug expression, the goddess broke the silence. "Now, we must determine whether these individuals are the old gods. If they are not, then our inquiry ends here."

Ignoring the near death that had nearly just occurred, Circe glanced up lazily from where she sat at the Judiciary table twirling strands of coral-colored magic between her fingers. "It appears that we might be able to reach a consensus regarding whether the Aidoneus man and the witch are the old gods." With a slight shrug, she carelessly advised, "If it does not offend, Hecate, I would recommend that we cast our lots on this issue."

Hecate pursed her lips. "Circe, I believe you may have a point. My daughters, at this time, you may cast your coven's vote as to whether the prophesied old gods have returned. You will have twenty-four hours to do so. Pease consider the issue carefully and weigh all potential evidence fairly and impartially. Only cast your vote once your coven elders have achieved a majority consensus on the matter. Covens, send a blue key to rest in the bowl on Circe's side of the table if you believe that these people are the old gods. Send a red key to rest in the bowl on Medea's side of the table if you believe that they are not. Please return to your resting places to reach a decision. If we do not have your vote by the end of the twenty-four hours, your coven's vote will not be considered. If we receive all votes before the end of the allotted time, we will summon you to the chambers at once." With a clap of her hands, she vanished in a cloud of shadows, leaving the other Judiciary members and Coven elders alone in the chambers.

Hesteia, Thea, Bernadette, Chloe, and Adelaide fell into lock step alongside the others, departing the chambers for the day. The covens had twenty-four hours to issue their votes. It took less than three before they received the summons bidding them to return.

Hesteia and the other Barataria Coven elders trailed into the chamber alongside the hundreds of other witches. After a long, emotional day, she wanted nothing more than to crawl into bed and sleep for a year. Instead, she was heading back into the cavern by cover of nightfall while the moon was high in the sky. At this point, she had been awake for almost two days, thanks to the inconsistency of chaos portals and the hours of discussion about the first decision of the prophecy

At the head of the room, Hecate, Medea, and Circe sat, their faces inscrutable as they waited for everyone to take their seats. Although before the mood had been tense, now it was unbearable, and it seemed like everyone felt the shift because their actions were abrupt and quiet. There was no low buzz of talking this time. Everyone was determined to begin and wanted no distractions.

"My daughters." Hecate spread her hands. "All covens have cast their votes. The result was unanimous, so there is no need for the Judiciary to cast its own ballets to break a tie."

A deathly hush smothered the room. It had been quiet before; now, no sound of any kind broke the silence.

"The Council has overwhelmingly voted that Evie of the Barataria Coven and Cole Aidoneus are the old gods returned." Hecate placed her hands on the table in front of her and leaned forward. "At this time, we will discuss what our next steps must be and then put that issue to a vote."

Chapter 47

Cole

Beau Chêne, Mandeville, Louisiana

The house was quiet when Evie woke him up, her lips wrapped around his dick, sucking him down like she would die if he didn't come in her mouth. He, of course, couldn't deny her anything and came so hard he was pretty sure he blacked out. When he was finally able to move again, he glanced down to where she lay with her chin resting on his stomach, a smug smile on her face, and immediately flipped her onto her back, dropping between her thighs, licking and sucking her until her legs shook, and she came all over his tongue and around his fingers.

Reluctantly, he looked at his phone. 10:03 am. The message notification caught his attention, and he pulled up the text application as Evie snuggled deeper into him. Charlie had messaged him at 7:56:

> Your court will be joining us for breakfast at 10:30 am.
> Please be down promptly.

Cole snorted. Even just those fifteen little words conveyed his uncle's absolute discomfort with the radio show they had given everyone last night. *Let him stew*, he thought uncharitably. They had kept him from his witch.

Evie glanced up at him. "What?"

"Nothing. Just Charlie being Charlie." He rubbed a hand down her side, loving the feel of her silky skin under his palm, the way her curves seemed perfectly fitted to his body. "But we do have to get up. Everyone's going to be here in about twenty minutes."

She bolted up. "All of my clothes are still in your car, though. And I shouldn't wear what I had on yesterday, right? That's not mannerly. Right?"

He smothered a laugh, watching in amusement as she waved her hands about her in panic. "Angel, don't worry about a thing. I'll go get your stuff from the car, you just get ready however you need." Slipping out of the bed, he slid on his jeans from the day before and pressed a kiss to her hair before grabbing his shirt and throwing it over his head as he strode across the room. Her voice stopped him before he opened the door.

"What if they won't follow you because of me?" She sounded small and scared, her eyes wide in her pale face. "I'm a witch. What if everything you've worked for gets messed up because of me?"

"Well first off, *ma petite sorcière*, it's us they'll be following, not just me." He walked back across the room, tilting her face up to his. "Second off, you're the only thing that matters to me. As long as you're by my side, I can do anything. And third. I haven't been working for anything to do with this prophecy." She made a disbelieving sound, but he shook his head at her. "No, really. Ask Charlie. It has been a constant source of frustration for him that I didn't give a shit about my role in the prophecy." Pushing a curl behind her ear, he cupped her cheek. "They'll follow us because they would be fools not to put their faith in you, Angel. Now go get ready, and I'll be back with your clothes in a few minutes."

She nodded, and he left the room, sneaking down the stairs, out to the car, and back to their room without anyone catching him. He set the vast collection of shopping bags on the bed then swapped out his shirt for a spare he kept in the glove compartment for emergencies. When Evie finally popped out of the bedroom, she looked calmer, no evidence of her earlier panic on her face.

That was until she got to the bed. Her eyes went wide as she glanced down to the bags then back up to him. "What do I wear to breakfast with a room full of immortals who are theoretically going to serve on our court?"

"Whatever you want so long as you don't go down there naked." His growled threat—mostly a joke—did the trick. She giggled and rolled her eyes at him before picking through the bags until she found a light dress with lacy overlay that she liked. She dressed quickly, and together, they walked down the stairs into the kitchen with minutes to spare.

Hayden and Charles sat at the kitchen table, clutching coffee cups with matching traumatized expressions pasted across their faces.

Charles glanced up when they walked in. There was no greeting, just a terse, "All of the furniture in that room, especially the mattress and bedding, is yours now," tossed at them.

Evie's cheeks turned bright red, her mouth parting as she sputtered adorably at the comment. Cole only smirked at his stoic, buttoned-down uncle.

He turned his attention to Hayden, sitting in the chair to the right of Charles. "You got something to say too?"

Hayden's response was simple: "I know we kept you away from her, but the punishment definitely didn't fit the crime."

"Oh, I think it did," Cole corrected, wrapping his arm around Evie's shoulder. "Not like anything would have changed if y'all let me go upstairs with her when I wanted, but we might have tried to keep it down at least a little bit.'

Charles pulled a face but otherwise didn't say anything.

"Where are the Moirai?" Cole glanced around for the three sisters, but they weren't anywhere in the kitchen or family room that he could see.

"They had to head home to take care of something," Hayden replied. "Said they were already part of your court so they didn't need to be here."

Magda bustled past Cole and Evie, a bright smile on her round face. "Good morning, lovebirds," she greeted them. "I heard the two of you had quite a night!" She gave a cheerful laugh, patting Evie's cheek delicately. "Don't you worry about a thing, *cherie*, if I had a handsome man like Cole around, I wouldn't be shy about it either."

Evie's mouth pursed. "Thank you?" It sounded more like a question than an answer. "I didn't expect to be discussing our sex life this much."

"Well, when you scream as hard as you—" Hayden shut his mouth around the end of the sentence at Cole's blistering look.

"I dare you to finish that thought, Hayden," he said lightly. "See how it goes if you do."

"I'm good, man." Leaning back in his chair, Hayden held his hands up in a gesture of truce. "Nothing to say here."

"That's what I thought." Cole glared at his best friend.

"Charles," Magda interrupted, lightly brushing her hand across Charles' shoulder. "Your guests are here. I've shown them to the dining room where breakfast is set up."

Charles leaned imperceptibly into his cook's touch but, when he noticed Cole's eyes on him, straightened his back so thoroughly it looked painful. "Thank you, Magda." His tone was clipped, but Magda's warm look, still trained on his uncle's silhouette, never faltered. "Shall we go introduce Evie to your court?" he asked, standing quickly, coffee cup in hand. "Properly, this time."

Cole looked down at Evie, who nodded slightly, her face gone pale with the enormity of what lay ahead of them. "We'll follow everyone in."

The motley crew in the kitchen filtered out to the dining room. Once they were gone, he turned to Evie, taking her in his arms. "You ready, Angel?"

"Yeah." She dropped her head to his chest before raising it again. When she did, her voice was steadier than it had been. "Yes. Let's do this."

With her assurance, he took her hand and led them into the dining room where almost everyone who had been at the house to greet them yesterday sat. Only Cate was missing. Nine pairs of eyes shifted to them as they entered; only Hayden ignored them in favor of wolfing down the simple but delicious omelette and sweet rolls that Magda had made. The expressions on the immortals sitting at the table ranged from wariness to outright distrust to excitement.

"Good morning, all," Cole greeted them, using the voice he reserved for small children, insufferable clients, and idiot judges. It commanded attention and established who was in charge out of the gate while still being civil enough that the person on the other side of the discussion felt like they had a say in the conversation. Out of the corner of his eye, he caught Evie's slight grin at the authoritative tone; he shot her a conspiratorial smirk in response before pulling out a chair for her on Charles' other side.

She sat gracefully, and he took a seat to her right, resting his hand gently on her knee.

"As you all discovered yesterday, this is my beloved queen, Evie. She is the reincarnate of Persephone and also a witch, which shouldn't be too much of a surprise to any of you since Kore herself was a powerful witch." He leveled a glare at the gods surrounding them. Many of them dropped their eyes. "You have all served my family loyally for generations with the expectation that you would join the Underworld's court once the reincarnates took their place as its rulers. I know many of you have questions about Evie and what will happen next. That's understandable. We will answer your questions to the best of our ability, recognizing that we have about the same amount of information as you do. What I will not tolerate is any sort of disrespect to my queen." His magic rumbled through him, blue tendrils of power rolling across the table. "Have I made myself clear?"

Indistinct murmurs rolled across the table to him. His irritation ratcheted upwards, and he repeated himself, the words clipped and demanding. "Have. I. Made. Myself. Clear?" This time, their answers were clear and distinct yeses.

Evie nudged his knee with hers, and he glanced down, nodding at her when she opened her mouth to speak. "Yesterday, it came as a surprise to all of you—well, almost all of you," she corrected with a conciliatory glance at Hayden and Charles. "That I'm a witch. I assume that most of your questions have to do with whether I plan to ally with the witches on their prophecy or follow the Moirai's." Her back straightened under their collective gazes. "I have left my coven for reasons that are my own and Cole's. While I still adore my sisters, there is no love lost between myself and the Witches Council. I will not be assisting them in fulfilling their apocalyptic prophecy if they choose to pursue it. I will be taking my seat in the Underworld besides Cole to do what needs to be done." Her voice tapered off. "Um, thank you, I guess?"

Cole squeezed her leg, heart overfilling with pride. She was incredible, more so than even he had dreamed and imagined. He leaned into her, pressing a chaste kiss to her cheek and whispering, "I love you so much, Angel," into her ear. She murmured it back to him, ducking her head into his neck.

On Evie's other side, Charles cleared his throat, a disgruntled sound distinctly at odds with the soft look of happiness he gave them both.

"Right." Cole straightened, remembering where they were, although he didn't release his hold on Evie's leg. "Are there any questions?"

As it turned out, there were so many questions. The next few hours were dedicated to answering every single one of them, ranging from an insulting invasion of their privacy with, "Will the two of you have children?" to the more relevant, "Do the two of you have a plan on how to retrieve the missing shades?"

By the end of the now-turned brunch—since it was nearing mid-afternoon—Evie's voice was all but gone. Cole himself was ready to throw her over his shoulder and sprint out of his childhood home.

"Is that everything?" he finally asked tiredly, ignoring Charles' stern look at his rudeness. He honestly didn't care. He was exhausted. Evie was simultaneously drained and overwhelmed, after having fielded most of the questions since almost all of them were about her.

"One last thing," Hayden piped up after having been quiet for most of the meal.

Cole shot a questioning glance at the other man.

Hayden stood, walked around the table, and bowed deeply to Cole and Evie. "I will be proud to serve under your leadership, my king and queen."

Besides him, Evie's mouth dropped open in shock, so Cole was left to respond. "We thank you for your fealty, god of sleep." *Thank fuck for George R.R. Martin's books, or I would have no idea how to accept a pledge of loyalty.*

"I'll see you fuckers later then." With a grin, a punch to Cole's shoulders, an abortive hug-turned-nod at Evie after Cole snarled when Hayden tried to embrace her, the god sauntered from the dining room and out through the front door.

Almost as if Hayden was the breaking point, each of the immortals at the table stood and approached them, pledging their loyalty in turn and departing until only Cole, Evie, Charles, and Magda were left

"I think that went well," Charles commented, taking a sip of his now-cold coffee.

"I do too," Cole responded. "And it's great and everything, but we're leaving. Right fucking now." He seized Evie's hand, drawing her to her feet with him as he stood.

Before they could go, Magda approached them, a bag of food clutched in her hands. "You did so well, my darlings." She passed the leftovers to them before giving Evie then Cole warm hugs. When he went towards the stairs to retrieve their things, she stopped him with a firm hand on his arm. "I've already packed your car with everything that was in your room. You need to go home before your uncle comes up with something else for you to do."

Cole snorted out a laugh and hugged Magda again. "Thanks, Mags."

"Get out of here, you charmer," the older woman laughed before embracing Evie once more and vanishing back into the kitchen.

Charles followed them out of the house, giving Cole a sanctimonious look after Evie dropped into the car. "When do you want the bedroom furniture dropped off?"

"Wait, you were serious about that?"

"Oh very much so," Charlie replied dryly. "I heard the two of you last night. There's no amount of cleaning that can put that room to rights."

"I honestly don't care. Hell, just work with the nonprofit to get it dropped off at the Tremé houses for one of the families. They need the furniture more than I do."

Charles smiled. "You're a good man, Cole," he said casually, leaving Cole to stare at his uncle and wonder about body snatchers as Charles walked around the car to the passenger side. "Good bye, Evie. You're a wonderful addition to our family. I'm so glad that you and Cole found each other."

Evie let out a sniff before leaping out of the car and hugging Charles hard. Before she let him go, she whispered something in his ear that made him laugh.

"You're a sweet girl, Evie." Charles patted her on the shoulder before she released him, his eyes suspiciously glassy as he closed the car door once she was in the seat. He nodded at Cole over the top of the car. "Make sure you do this right, Cole. You love that girl, and she loves you. Don't fuck it up."

"Helluva support system, that, Charlie." Although he appreciated how much support Evie was getting from his family. It hadn't been easy for her growing up in that coven, and he wanted her to be surrounded by people who would love and protect her. Starting with him. He would give his witch every ounce of love he had for her and protect her until he had no breath left in his body.

"Oh." Charles tapped on the hood of the car. "And I believe Magda has taken care of that minty problem of yours. Maybe we'll start an herb garden." He bent down by Evie's window. "Evie, next time perhaps some oregano?"

Evie giggled, shrugging. "Perhaps," she drawled back in a fair mimicry of Charles' voice.

Cole smiled. "I'll call you later, Charlie." With his mother's ring in his pocket and their Underworld court lined up, he slid into the driver's seat and drove them home.

Chapter 48

Cole

Garden District, New Orleans, Louisiana

They spent the two days following the brunch at Charles' house catching Evie up on every bit of lore surrounding the Underworld and their duties during the day. At night, they talked long into the wee hours of morning about everything, discussing plans for the Underworld, their childhoods, their hobbies, literature. It seemed like no topic was off limits.

Evie even taught him about different types of trees and flowers, a lesson that he almost immediately forgot to her amusement. For his part, he spent his time sharing his favorite music and movies with her. She loved Fleetwood Mac—go figure, a witch loving a band fronted by the white witch herself—and, unexpectedly, Korn best of all but hated classical music with a passion that was borderline feral. Her attention span for movies was atrocious, so he downgraded them to TV shows. The shorter format kept her hooked, and he loved curling himself around her while they watched old Criminal Minds and Bewitched episodes. He even caved to the millennial nostalgia and broke out the original Charmed, which she was obsessed with. Her adoration for the character Cole made him jealous of a fictional man who bore his own damn name. *Who would have guessed?*

In their spare time, they dedicated themselves to christening his house as theirs by fucking on or against every surface that they could. He discovered that Evie was absolutely insatiable, often reading ancient texts while she rode him. His solution to her obvious distraction was requiring her to read the documents out loud, which had the added benefit of letting him hear her voice, first husky as she read then dissolving into moans and screams as she came all over his cock or tongue or fingers. Basically, whichever appendage he had dedicated to the cause.

Cole himself hadn't had this much sex since law school. But even though his body was older, it didn't seem to understand that fact because he was hornier than ever. One sight, one scent, one touch of Evie was enough to get him hard and have him immediately bending her over the nearest piece of furniture. Or wrapping her curvy little legs around his waist and sinking into her against the nearest wall. Or ripping off whatever piece of clothing she was wearing and licking her pussy until she screamed his name loudly enough to alarm the neighbors. Cole groaned as he hardened at the memory of her throaty voice begging for him, her hands tangled in his hair, her legs bracketing his head while he drank her cum down. *Fuck.*

Evie's sheer vocal range—his new favorite sound—had already resulted in five noise complaints and one police visit. He didn't regret a fucking thing, except maybe growling at the officer when he saw a flushed, satisfied, and partially-dressed Evie from the door. Fortunately, the officer thought it was a poorly timed cough and ignored the magic rippling from Cole's person as he kept trying to catch another glimpse of Evie. The asshole was lucky he hadn't left the house in a body bag.

After two days of half-assed working, he finally decided to meander into his study. Evie followed him, crawling into his lap and promptly dozing off with his arms clasped around her. He had been irritated as hell as the six hundred messages waiting in his inbox, but after Evie curled in his arms, it somehow became so much more tolerable. He glanced down at her, nuzzling his cheek against her hair as he used one hand to scroll through the egregious amount of emails that had come in while he was out and balanced Evie with the other so she didn't accidentally slide out of his lap.

His computer lit up with an incoming call. Hayden. Cole hadn't seen him since Charles' house, opting instead to work remotely. Hayden had spent an obscene amount of time cackling via text at this decision because Cole called remote work, "the lazy person's commute." Words he was happily eating with a sleeping Evie in his lap. The shrill ring of his computer continued as he scrambled to connect his headphones, finally feeling the plug slip in the jack, silencing the loud noise.

Evie stirred against him, her head lifting slightly.

"It's fine, Angel." He rubbed her hip. "Go back to sleep."

With muffled sound of agreement, she snuggled back into his as he toggled the Accept Call button. Hayden's face burst into full technicolor on the screen.

"You two are precious," Hayden snarked. "Have you even left each other's sight in the last few days?"

"What do you want, man?" He was quiet in an effort not to wake Evie up. Ignoring Hayden was often the best way to get to the actual substance of the conversation, so you could get on to whatever else needed to be done.

"You may want to wake your lady love for this one." Hayden's smirk dropped from his face. "We've got the Moirai and Charles in the room."

"They found the entry?" Cole straightened in excitement.

"Yep, but you're not going to like the location. So you may want to get your better half on the line."

Cole turned off his audio and video without preamble and rubbed a hand along Evie's cheek. She murmured something nonsensical into his neck and burrowed in deeper. His dick, always at least somewhat erect when he was around her, hardened against her hip when she wriggled her ass in his lap sleepily. A predatory grin found its way on to his face. "Angel," he purred into her ear, nibbling on her earlobe. Her lips parted on a soft inhale. "That's right, sweet little witch, it's time to wake up." Sliding a hand along her thigh, he traced his fingernails along the sensitive skin just under her sleep shorts. Her muscles tightened, twitched, under his fingertips. A soft sigh drifted from her lips, just as he slid his fingers along her slit. He growled at the feel of her, working a single finger into her. "Always so wet for me."

"Cole," she moaned, her eyes heavy lidded. He started pumping his finger slowly in and out of her, her small gasps sparking fires in his blood.

"You finally awake, Angel?" At her fervent nod, he chuckled. "You want another finger, don't you."

Not a question, but she answered anyway. "No."

Cole raised his eyebrows. "No?"

Even as her walls were clenching on his single finger, lazily fucking her, Evie pursed her lips. *Ah. There's my brat.* "No, sir, I don't want your fingers. I want your dick, and you know it. I want you to throw me down on this desk and fuck me until I scream and milk your cum from you." Her eyes danced with mischief. "So why are you teasing me?"

Fuck. Cole tilted his head back. Groaning at the ceiling, he made some quick, reckless decisions followed by even more rapid action. "Stand up and take your shorts and panties off," he ordered, voice cracking as she followed his orders perfectly. He slid his sweatpants down to his knees, slowly stroked a palm along his hard length while she stared at him hungrily. "Now come sit on my dick, Angel. Facing the computer."

With a sassy smirk on her face, she angled over him, sliding her wetness around the head of his shaft but never fully dropping herself on to him.

Cole seized her hip in one hand, tangled her hair in the other, and growled into her ear, "Enough teasing, brat," right before he drove himself up into her. "Fuck, sweetheart, you feel so goddamn good." Absolutely astounding that, despite spending as much time inside of her as he had over the last few days, the feeling of her still shook him to his core.

Evie's head dropped forward, her hands gripping the desk so tightly her knuckles whitened as she ground herself against him.

"Hey, you guys still there?" Hayden's voice echoed through the headphones.

At the tinny sound, Evie's head popped up in search of the source of the noise. Finally, her eyes landed on the single bud in his ear, the other dangling from the wire around his neck. Leveling a glare at him, she tried to stand.

"Absolutely fucking not, *vilaine fille*," Cole snarled, snaking an arm around her waist to lock her in place. "You're going to sit on me during this call. We'll be on video while I play with your sensitive clit under the desk, millimeters from where everybody can see. You move one inch and they're gonna see you split open on my cock, drenched for me like the horny witch that you are." Her breaths were sawing in and out, her inner walls clamping around him. "You fucking love the sound of that, don't you, my dirty Angel? Fuck, baby." He pulled his headphones out of the audio jack, tugging the bud in his ear out and discarding them next to the computer. "One last thing? Audio will be live the whole call so you're gonna need to be quiet unless you want everyone to know that you're stuffed full of my dick and begging to come." The index finger of his free hand rested on the mouse. "Any last words before I turn on the camera and mic?"

His name emerged from her mouth on a plaintive cry. "Such a needy witch," he chuckled. "Now, straighten up, baby, unless you want them to see you gasping and panting for your sir." Not that he would ever actually let them see her like this, but gods, was it fun to threaten her with it.

With his help, Evie sat up, which had him biting back a moan at the sudden shift in angle. Before, she had been tight around him, but, resting against his chest, she was clenching around him even more acutely. Once he was under control and not about to throw Evie on the desk and pound into her like they had all the time in the world, he toggled the video and mic on. "Hey, everybody, we're here. Whatcha got for us?"

While Charles spoke, Cole dropped his fingers to Evie's clit, flicking slightly. Evie let out a squeak, clenching around his cock. He ran his fingers back and forth over the bundle of nerves, slowly enough to stimulate her, not enough to make her come. With each swipe of his thumb over her clit, she sank her teeth into her lip until he wanted to bite it with his, lay claim to her full mouth, branding her as his.

"Are you two paying attention?" Charles' voice cut through the fog, tense and unforgiving.

"Absolutely, Charlie." Cole dropped his hand to Evie's thigh, slowing the distraction enough so they could pay attention to the conference call. "But could you... say what you just said again. No particular reason. Just want to confirm what I heard."

Hayden barked out a laugh, and even Charles looked like he was considering smiling. "Cole, man," Hayden said. "Seriously, let your girl out of your sight every now and again, or you're gonna have a little Cole or Evie running around way sooner than I think either of you want."

Cole's chin was resting against Evie's shoulder, but something about Hayden's comments struck a chord through the cloud of arousal fogging his mind. It vanished just as quickly when Evie clenched tightly around him again.

While the two stooges yucked it up and Cole fought not to spill into Evie while they were on camera, Essi cut in seamlessly. "We said that we know where the entrance to the Underworld opened."

Evie's head snapped towards the screen. "Where is it?" she asked, the only external indication that Cole was currently balls deep in her a slight rasp to her voice and flush on her cheeks. He could feel her trembling around him, though, belying her seeming calm, her drenched cunt clamping down on him each time somebody looked at them by way of the screen. *Who would have guessed my little Angel has a bit of exhibitionist in her?*

"It's in Budapest," Hayden replied. "Sorry, Cole."

"Budapest," Cole repeated dryly. Although he didn't have a long list of cities he hated, Budapest was at the top of the list. Something about being arrested by the Hungarian Customs and Finance Guard within seconds of stepping foot in Budapest and investigated for falsified tax forms filed by a client before sitting in a Hungarian interrogation room for almost 12 hours had really soured him on the city. "Of course it's Budapest."

Evie's head tilted at his irritated tone and, despite being overwhelmed with pleasure, she still twisted around to kiss him on the cheek and rubbed the arm wrapped around her waist reassuringly. With those small touches, his irritation vanished. Who gave a fuck where the entry was when it was just a stepping stone to his queen being by his side for the rest of their immortal lives? "Okay, Budapest. That's, what, a 10 hour flight?"

"You taking the jet?" Hayden asked.

"Yeah, no way am I flying commercial for this." Cole snorted. At 6'5", commercial flying wasn't built for him. After he made his first $100 million and knew that he would have to fly internationally fairly regularly, he had invested in a private jet, so he didn't do long-term damage to his spinal cord in the cramped commercial seats. "When should we leave?"

Essi replied, "As soon as humanly possible. I'm seeing a great conflict in your future, although the participants are shadowy as of our last read. You must get to Budapest as quickly as you can before the potential for this danger becomes much more real."

Cole glanced at the clock on the computer. Going on 7:30 in the evening. No way they were getting out of here tonight. "I'll get everything arranged for the jet to take off first thing in the morning. First round will be just Evie and me, the rest of you can follow. Hayden, do you still have your place in Budapest?" At his nod, Cole instructed him, "Get the pilot your key so we have a place to crash if we don't find the entry easily." The group in the conference room were nodding in agreement. "Anything else?"

"The two of you have opened the Underworld. We assume it will recognize you as its rulers and tell you how to accept the throne and your immortality," Essi said mildly. "If that doesn't happen, please let us know and we'll reassess."

"Fine," Cole responded shortly. "Anyone else? If not, we have to go prep for an early morning plane ride."

After they said their goodbyes and hung up, Evie tried to stand. "Where do you think you're going?" he growled, gripping her waist as he stood and pressed her front down to the desk top. "I felt how much you loved me being inside you while everyone was watching, you dirty little witch." He pumped his hips shallowly. Her back arched as she pressed against him.

"But we have to go pack," she moaned.

"Yeah, baby, we do, but first I have to fuck you until we get another noise complaint." She tried to shove herself back on to him when he pulled out, but he held himself away from her. "Do you want me to make you come, Angel?" She nodded, hair splayed around her shoulders like liquid fire. A bolt of sudden clarity shot through him that this exact sight, this exact moment, would be branded on his heart for the rest of his life. "If you want to come, ask your sir sweetly to let you."

"Please, sir," she gasped, still pushing herself towards him.

"Please what, Angel?" His fingers bit into her curvy hips.

"Please, sir, let me come," she cried out.

"God, sweetheart, you're so pretty when you beg." He plunged into her, letting loose a shout at the feel of her around him. She cried out his name as he kept up his thrusts, making sure to keep his hips angled so his piercing ran along her inner wall.

Within minutes, she was squirming on his desk, keening his name. He dropped his palm between her legs once more, softly rubbing her rigid clit. Just enough to stimulate, not enough to get her off, and they both knew it.

"Fuck, sir, please." Her face was a stunning mask of need and lust. "Please, gods, please." By the final "please," her voice was practically a scream.

Cole's lower back was tightening, his balls drawing up. He was seconds away from coming in her tight pussy when he fingered her clit with the firmness he knew she needed. Evie's cries were constant when he leaned over her back and snarled, "Come for me, little witchling. Let me feel you."

As if his words were magic, she came apart around his cock so hard he saw stars. "Fuck, Angel, god-fucking-dammit, I can feel you milking my cock, *belle fille, ma putain d'épouse*." He could barely hear himself over the blood rushing in his ears but knew that he was claiming her, both with his words and his cum as he spent himself deep inside her, knowing that he would give her the world or destroy it for her if she asked him to.

The fog slowly cleared from his head as he breathed in that scent that was uniquely her, his body loose over hers. He had never been this happy before in his life. Despite that, though, he couldn't stop wiggling at an odd unsettling feeling. He kissed her spine gently, was enjoying the feeling of her flexing underneath him, when Hayden's comment about a "little Evie and Cole" finally sank in. His body went rigid against hers.

And, of course, his perceptive witch immediately felt the shift. "What's going on, Cole? You went-"

"We haven't been using protection." Cole dragged a hand over his face, sliding out of her and flipping her over on the desk to face him. "And I'm assuming you're not on birth control. Holy shit. How did I not think about this?"

"Hey, hey, breathe," she reassured him. "It's okay, love—"

"How did I forget to use protection? Holy fuck, I've never had sex without a condom." Cole was babbling, something about condoms being the first and only sexual requirement his uncle had taught him—he wasn't really sure—when Evie flicked him in the chest. Hard. His words caught in his throat as he stared down at her.

Evie glared at him, the mixed blue-gold of her magic sparking in her eyes. "I need you to calm down, Cole, and stop making inferences about you being with other women while I am freshly fucked on your desk."

He blinked. Nodded.

"How about you talk me through the whole mental departure you just had."

After a minute, he finally answered her non-question. "I never expected—or wanted—to be a dad. So I took precautions to make sure that it was a nonissue. But with you—" He shook his head. "I didn't even think about it. It was like I couldn't think about there being anything separating the two of us." His breathing was coming more easily, definitely less panicked, but he still wasn't calm.

"Cole, it's okay." Wrapping a leg around his waist, Evie drew him back into the cradle of her hips. "It's okay, my love. I'm not on birth control, but even still I can't have children anyways. I thought I told you that."

Cole reared back. "What? No, you never told me that. I don't understand. How can you not have children?"

Chapter 49

Evie

Garden District, New Orleans, Louisiana

Cole's gaze was steady, his body absolutely still against hers, but she could feel his magic whirling frenetically under his skin.

"I, it was—" Evie stopped. There was no way to tell Cole this without him losing his mind so might as well do it quickly. "I had to undergo a procedure when I was 18."

"A procedure." Cole was quiet for a second then his voice pitched into a soothing lilt. "And what type of procedure was that?"

"They, uh, it was meant to make me infertile."

When he cut her off, he was still using that detached, melodic voice. "You said you had to do it. Did you choose to do it?"

"No. But—"

"Were you forced to do it?" Cole appeared calm, but his eyes were lit neon blue in fury. In the back of her mind, she imagined that, if they took away the magic, this was his demeanor in a courtroom when he tore somebody apart on the witness stand.

The intensity of that stare, burning into her, was too much as she laid bare her biggest secret. Almost involuntarily, her eyelids slid shut. "Yes." Even closing her eyes didn't fully obscure the magical light of his own.

"Who forced you to do it?" A soft breeze of air passed her cheek just before he cupped her face. "Please open your eyes. Angel, I need you to look at me, or I'm going to lose my mind." When she raised her eyes back to him, he asked, this time in a normal voice, "Who forced you to do it? I need you to tell me everything."

"The coven elders. Well, the coven elders at the vote of the Council. They said that the only reason I was allowed to join the coven was on the condition that I undergo a surgical procedure that made me infertile. The Council knows of doctors who will practice medicine on witches in exchange for magical favors. They brought me somewhere, and, when I woke up, I had a new scar, and they told me I couldn't have children. I never asked why—" Her voice broke. "But now that I know how they found me... The Council was well within their right to mandate that."

A look of uncontrolled fury crossed Cole's face.

"Cole, I'm sorry—"

"Sweetheart, why the fuck are *you* sorry?" He kissed her deeply, brutally, before continuing. "You have nothing to apologize for. The Witches Council forced a teenager to go through a medically invasive, completely unnecessary procedure to sterilize her with fuck-only-knows what lunatic of a surgeon operating on her in a potentially unsanitary environment just so they could keep her from potentially birthing little murder babies to an unknown man in a coven full of women. All while forcing you to undergo annual memory regressions in case they ever needed to use you as their little enforcer. The coven elders that raised you *may* have done the best they could by you. But them. The Witches Council." The deep blue crown of fire— the one she had only seen twice before in moments of intense emotion—blazed to life around his head. His voice deepened, his eyes darkened. "Them, I will rip to shreds for laying a hand on my goddamn queen."

He lifted her into his arms, carrying her from the room, past the new flora and fauna lining the walls of Cole's office, thanks to her spontaneous sexual magical bursts, and back to their bed. Lowering her gently to the mattress, he pushed her hair back from her face. "Go to sleep, Angel. I'll pack a bag for you, and you can add whatever you need in the morning."

She nodded sleepily. "But don't you have to make arrangements for Budapest?" At his nod, she asked, "Do you need help?"

"Nah, witchling. I need you to get some sleep, so you're rested before we take off. I'll get everything taken care of." He crawled into bed beside her, resting his back against the headboard. "I'll be right here, though, assuming you can fall asleep while I talk on the phone."

Nodding again, she tucked herself up against his side, draping her arm across his waist and resting her head against his hip. His fingers sifted through her hair, a long, slow, loving slide, while his voice rumbled above her in a call.

Before long, she fell into sleep's warm embrace.

Interlude

Council of Witches

Megiddo National Park, Jezreel Valley, Megiddo, Israel

The Witches Council was deadlocked. It had been three days of women stuck in the cave shouting at one another over the prophecy. Three days of arguing over whether, with the Council recognizing Evie and Cole as the old gods returned, the prophecy's demand that the witches leave the forest and end the world was figurative or literal. Three days of rage and grief as the witches tried to work out whether they would annihilate everyone they loved. The traditional covens demanded that they comply strictly with the prophecy. The new generation's stance was that the prophecy was metaphorical more than anything else, not to mention millennia old and out of touch, while also making the witches judge, jury, and executioner in a way that was not only wholly unjust but violated their creed of nonviolence. The rest of the witches fell somewhere in the middle, more concerned about the apocalyptic end of their loved ones and their families than the hypothetical people out in the real world.

All of them were exhausted. Tempers were frayed. More than once, Hecate had to impose order through magical means. She even stripped one witch of her powers and memory, sending her into the world and away from her coven, after the woman had the audacity to accuse Hecate of being a fraud who didn't believe in the prophecy. Unfortunately, there seemed to be no end in sight.

"How are we supposed to put our faith in a prophecy that has been in existence since before anyone in this chamber, save the Mother of Witches, existed?" one of the Central Park Coven witches shouted. Like many of their American sisters, they believed in leniency for the world. "Especially when the records chronicling the prophecy are long destroyed!" A chorus of approving shouts rose around her while the traditionalists jeered and booed. One even threw something, although Hesteia couldn't tell what it was.

An older traditionalist from Nova Scotia spoke, spitting her words like a curse. "You new witches are cowards! You know nothing about which you speak. Your ignorance will destroy the covens!"

Hesteia rubbed her temples as a new generation witch from gods-only-knew where screamed from her wheelchair, "Whereas you traditionalists are demanding that we *actually* destroy the covens and the rest of the world because of a prophecy that's thousands of years old and has more than one interpretation, most of which wouldn't demand an apocalyptic end! Some of those interpretations could even command that the witches ally with the returned old gods to support what they're building."

The Nova Scotian sneered, but a new speaker jumped in over her derisive scoffs. "What is *wrong* with you traditionalists? You try to exclude witches from the covens arbitrarily based on magical ability or physical imperfections. Case in point: the little witch from the Barataria Coven years ago. You were prepared to let an infant die because the coven's seer prophesied that she was the cause of her mother's death. You are the narrowminded bigots here, not us. Your ignorance is tearing witchkind apart!"

After three days, the cavernous chamber was more or less a war zone with the two sides naturally selecting physical sides of the cavern as well. It was looking like a battlefield more and more each day.

A traditionalist witch across the way began shouting a curse, dark magic swirling around her as she summoned her power. Fortunately, she didn't get very far because Hecate heard her.

"*Enough!*" Hecate's raised voice echoed through the chamber. All conversation immediately ground to a halt. Despite the tumult of the last three days, Hecate had not raised her voice, not once spoken above her normal cadence. Now, however, she was standing, fury incarnate, with shadows in her eyes, her hair rippling with the force of her own magic. "*This is reprehensible behavior, and I am ashamed to call some of you my daughters.*" Her gaze locked on the traditionalist attempting to cast the curse. At first, it looked like she was only giving her a hard stare, but seconds later, two balls of light emerged from the witch, one from her chest and one from her head. They came to sit before Hecate, who banished them with a sweep of her hand. "*I will not accept any one of you trying to harm the others. Dire consequences will befall those who attempt to do so.*"

The witch's brow was furrowed as her eyes darted around the chambers. "Excuse me," she called. "Where am I?"

"You are nowhere, child," Hecate snapped. "You will be seen out." Once Hecate's legion of shadows removed the woman, who no longer bore any magical powers or memory, she turned back to the crowd. "I have been patient with all of you. I understand that this is a significant decision. But let me make myself extremely clear: if you attempt to curse or otherwise harm your sisters, I will remove your powers and memory and send you out into the world with no one to help you, care for you, love you, or support you. You will be completely alone, cast out from your coven." Her jaw tensed. "Consider this before you next speak."

She looked to Medea and Circe. "Given what just occurred, I think we have reached the time for the first vote." The two other judiciary members inclined their heads. "The question before the Council is whether, with the return of the old gods, the witches must ride to bring the apocalypse. As before, your coven will have twenty-four hours to cast your vote. Those who agree we must bring about the apocalypse cast a blue key to rest in the bowl on Circe's side of the tables. Send a red key to rest in the bowl on Medea's side of the table if you believe that the prophecy does not require the destruction of this world. Please return to your resting places to reach a decision. If we do not have your vote by the end of this time, your coven's vote will not be considered. If we receive all votes before the end of the twenty-four hours allotted, we will summon you to the chambers at that time. Come immediately back to the chambers at the end of the voting period if you are not summoned to return before."

Twenty-four hours later, the covens gathered once more in the chambers. Hecate, Circe, and Medea stood behind the high table; Circe and Medea faced off against their goddess, matching expressions of distaste on their faces. Unlike before, though, they were arguing, their words incomprehensible but their tone unmistakable to those slowly filtering in through the entrance. Medea's irate stance immediately unsettled the new generation witches and their allies. On a good day, Medea was not the most temperate or sympathetic of the Judiciary. On a bad day, she would smite men, women, and children arbitrarily and at her leisure.

Circe, however, believed in strict adherence to justice and fairness unless it came to matters associated with her love life. She was unpredictably predictable, and, in times where she aligned with Hecate, it was because there was an element of fairness to the decision. She voted with Hecate to initially allow Evie into the coven despite her mother's corpse but had agreed to the Draconian measures Medea demanded given the Council's decision to allow Evie in despite Medea's wishes. Circe herself was resting her hands on her hips, head canted at a disbelieving angle.

Hecate, however, drew all of the witches' eyes. Her violet eyes were glowing orbs of rage that illuminated the Judiciary members standing opposite her, throwing grotesque silhouettes on the wall behind them, magic and shadows swirling violently around her. Fists clenched, jaw tight, she was the epitome of barely contained fury.

The coven elders sat in uncomfortable, fearful silence while the three Judiciary members argued vehemently at the front. Hesteia and Thea sat among their sisters, hips pressed against each other and fingers intertwined for emotional support. Chloe's head was buried in her hands, her shoulders shaking. For all intents and purposes, Evie was her daughter; in the last twenty-four hours, Chloe's mental state had deteriorated rapidly, the Council discussion and any resulting decision tearing her apart more so than anyone else in the coven. None of this felt right. Or safe. None of them had prophetic abilities, either and, without Cassandra, they didn't know what to expect. All told, they were a bit blind here, but, even without their seer, not a single one of them felt comfortable sitting in a chamber filled with angry witches, many of whom—more than they had initially expected walking into the chambers—wanted to end the world in flames and magic.

Finally, after almost an hour, Hecate turned to the witches sitting before her. "We appreciate your patience, my daughters." Although the words were positive, her tone was terse. Furious. "We received all votes for the covens gathered here today, and the vote was tied. A dead heat." The three Judiciary members took their seat. Having concluded their argument, each of the witches at the high table was now concertedly ignoring the others, even though Medea had to pass Hecate to take her seat. "As you all know, in the event of a tied vote by the coven elders, the Judiciary members must vote on the issue. Only in the event of a unanimous vote by the Judiciary will the motion carry. At this time, we will take a poll of the Judiciary. In favor means that the member wishes to fulfill the prophecy. Opposed means that the member does not agree that the prophecy must be fulfilled. Circe?"

"In favor," the witch responded with a pointed glare at the goddess.

"Medea?"

"In favor," the golden-haired witch announced proudly.

"I am opposed," Hecate concluded. "As you can see, we do not have a unanimous vote. In the event of a tie between the covens and a non-unanimous vote by the Judiciary, all covens that voted in favor of a particular motion must nominate one representative to present their position to the Council. The selected representative will have up to one hour to present their best and last case to the chamber, after which time, the covens will vote once more." Hecate stood. "At this time, those who voted in favor of fulfilling the prophecy, please gather in the front of the chamber to discuss with Medea and Circe who will present your argument. Those who opposed fulfilling the prophecy, please gather at the back of the chambers where I will join you upon my return." Shadows surrounded her and, when they cleared, she was gone.

Whispers echoed, shock at Hecate's sudden disappearance rippling through the room. Those in favor of fulfilling the prophecy went to the front to join Medea and Circe. Those opposed went to the back of the chambers. As she walked to the back, Hesteia glanced over her shoulder at the traditionalists, fear skating along her skin at the zealous fervor she saw in their eyes.

Chapter 50

Cole

Garden District, New Orleans, Louisiana

After hours on the phone arranging travel and finalizing their Budapest housing arrangements, Cole threw his phone onto the nightstand with an aggravated groan. He pinched the bridge of his nose with one hand, accidentally smashing his glasses into his face. *Shit.* He had forgotten he put those on earlier in the evening.

As expected, getting to Budapest wasn't nearly as easy as it should have been. It got more difficult when you considered that Evie, currently tangled around him and completely passed out, didn't have a passport, a driver's license, or any form of identification besides a birth certificate and a cold case categorizing her as a missing person. A truly horrifying amount of his time had been spent on the phone with a close friend in the Department of State to see how exactly he could go about expediting a passport for Evie. After hours of discussion, which devolved into outright threatening, his friend finally said he could arrange for them to pick it up in five days from the nearest priority processing hub. Which just so happened to be in another state. Five days wasn't ideal, but they could deal with that to make sure everything was aboveboard. He let Charles, Hayden, and the Moirai know; only Essi responded, her message chilling.

> Hurry, Lord of the Underworld. You are running out of time.

Sighing, he shook his head and slid down the headboard, curling Evie into him and nuzzling his nose into her wild curls, taking a deep breath of her orange and cinnamon scent. His tension seeped out of him as she melted into him, a humming sound of satisfaction making its way to his ears. A sleepy smile spread across his face.

He was dozing off when he heard pounding from downstairs. His eyes popped open in confusion. The hammering noise continued. "What the fuck?" he muttered, bolting upright as the wards protecting the house pulsed violently.

Evie made a quiet sound, her body shifting against his. "Cole?" she murmured, lifting her head from his chest, her eyes still mostly closed.

"Someone's at the front door." He skimmed a kiss over her forehead before sliding out of bed and pulling on the sweatpants he had dropped to the floor earlier.

"What?" All sleep vanished from her eyes, and she threw the covers back, jumping from the bed. She raced towards the closet where they had finally set up her clothing.

"Nope," he snapped, catching her hand before she could get across the room. "I need you to stay in here."

A disgruntled look settled over her face. "Excuse you? I am *not* staying here while you confront somebody who's at our front door at—" Her eyes darted towards the clock. "—3:00 in the morning. Are you out of your mind?"

She tugged at her hand, but he held firm. "It could be dangerous," he argued. "Good news doesn't pound on the door at the witching hour. Ever. I need to be able to do what I need to do if it's a threat, and I won't be able to focus if you're in danger. Please, Angel."

"No." Her voice was firm, the word snapped. "Absolutely not, Cole. I'm not going to stay isolated in safety while you risk your life, whether it's right now or in the future." He opened his mouth to argue, but she ignored him. "We're a team. It's the two of us together. Always. Even in danger. Actually, you know what, especially in danger. I'm not some wilting flower that you have to hide and protect. I'm your equal in power and responsibility. If you have a problem with that, we're going to have to have a conversation about it that you will not enjoy."

Despite the pounding noise, now paired with aggressive shouting he could hear all the way upstairs, he found himself smiling at the powerful, commanding witch in front of him, demanding that he accept her as an equal. "Okay. Okay, *petite déesse*. We go down together or not at all. *Mais* yeah, you stay behind me, understand? And you best be drawing fully on your power the entire time." Even he could hear the thick accent coloring his words.

Evie nodded and followed him down the stairs, her palms lit with magic, her eyes glowing blue and gold in the darkness.

When he reached the bottom step, he turned, placing his palm against her chest to hold her on the stairs. Her head tilted to the side. "You're down here with me, *mon ange*, but please stay on the step. You can strike anybody from here. This has nothing to do with hiding you away and everything to do with making sure you have a fighting chance if somebody comes in hot through the door." He watched her process the thought, eyes begging her to agree.

"Fine," she agreed haltingly.

"That's my good girl," he responded without thought. In the dim light of their magic, her pulse thrumming in excitement at his praise was clear as day. With a tight squeeze of her hand and plenty of internal screaming that he might be placing her in danger, he turned and strode to the door, leaving the wards in place to ensure the person on the other side couldn't get in unless and until he lifted them. One last glance at Evie to make sure she was still on the stairs then he unlocked and opened the door.

Standing in front of him was the goddess of witches, disheveled and irate.

"Cate? What the fuck are you doing here? Do you know what time it is?" he snapped.

Evie's feet padded quietly across the wood floor until she stood behind him, one small hand resting on his back. Poking her head around him, she took in the goddess standing at the door. "What do you need?" Her tone was calmer than his own.

"I have news that both of you need to know." Overhead, the gas lamps flickered, but their yellow light couldn't pierce the darkness of the shadows gathered around Cate's slim frame. "May I come in?"

Evie nodded and stepped back. Cole didn't move, still glaring in suspicion at the goddess. He must have impersonated a statute for too long because, suddenly, there was a sharp jab to his shoulder blades. "Cole."

Cole sighed but listened to Evie, inverting the wards to allow Cate to cross the threshold. Once she was in, Cole slammed the door and drew the protections back in place. When he finally turned around, Evie already had Cate seated in the kitchen with a cup of tea in front of her.

"What is it, Cate?" Cole demanded, stepping behind Evie and drawing her against him.

"I don't have much time, but I'm here to share recent conversations that the Witches Council has had about the two of you." Cate lifted the cup of tea to her lips.

"The Witches Counc—" Cole froze as the conversation he and Evie had the night before made its way to the top of his adrenaline-soaked mind. "The Witches Council? The Council overseen by the Witches Council Judiciary?"

"Yes."

"The Judiciary upon which you sit as the primary member?"

Cate hesitated, her brow furrowing. "Yes?" The response was a question.

In front of him, Evie drew in a deep breath. Clever little witch figuring out where he was going with this. "Cole—" she started warningly.

But Cole ignored her interruption and went in for the cross-examination kill. "The same Judiciary that wouldn't allow a coven to rescue a toddler abandoned in the woods unless they agreed to require her to undergo annual memory reversions and suffer a forced sterilization when she was eighteen?" By the end, he was all but growling. "Sound familiar?"

Cate's face paled. "Cole—"

"You want to tell me why I shouldn't annihilate you in our fucking kitchen and watch your blood soak my tiles?"

"It was a matter of safety—"

He stepped out from behind Evie, a menacing snarl emerging from his mouth. "I don't want to hear about the safety of your precious covens, you traitorous piece of shit. You sacrificed your precious goddamn morals and values when you authorized the maiming of and dangerous experimentation on a child, Hecate."

Shoulders drawing back, Cate finally snapped. "I will not be spoken to in this way—"

Magic pulsing under his skin, Cole roared back, "*You'll be spoken to exactly this way when defending your despicable actions against my queen while sitting in our home.*" At a rush of unnatural wind, the back doors slammed open, crashing into the walls behind them. Cate jumped as the lights flickered overhead, and then her body was thrown across the room, slamming into the wall. Pinned like a butterfly as Cole stalked towards her, funneling the surplus of death magic required to bring her immortal life to an end. "You're not even worthy to breathe the same fucking air as her," he hissed, lifting his hand to bring her final blow. Her body would crumble to dust, scatter to the four winds, and he would keep her soul in a goddamn box on their mantle until they took their rightful seat in the Underworld and he could fling it into Tartarus.

Cate flinched then bowed as much as she was able while locked to the wall. "I understand, my lord."

Suddenly, a halo of auburn curls filled his vision, blocking the raven-haired goddess bent in front of him. "Cole, no." A weight settled against his chest, warmth radiating from the pressure. It felt like... his witch.

As quickly as it had raged, his magic calmed. He blinked against sudden exhaustion then looked down where Evie was standing in front of him, her hand pressed to his chest. "Angel," he rasped, his voice cracking.

"I know, love." Her arms went around his waist. "I know you want to destroy anyone who hurt me."

"I wish to assist you with that," Cate supplied from behind Evie where she was making being trapped against a wall look elegant. "I understand vengeance and pain all too well, and I want to make sure that you're able to face those who condoned the measures the Council forced upon you."

Cole's eyes met Cate's over the top of Evie's head, and he gave an abrupt nod. "You'll give us those names." With a wave of his hand, he let her fall to the ground.

"Yes," she said firmly, bracing her knees against the fall to the floor. "I will share those names with you, but, first, I have to make you both aware of a grave threat." At Cole's raised eyebrow, she continued. "After you attacked the Barataria Coven, the elders were understandably confused and reached out to other covens to determine whether you were the old gods returned that implicate our prophecy. One of the High Priestesses recognized the name Aidoneus as—"

"The original Hades' mortal name," Evie sighed.

"Yes. And they called the Council together to determine whether this, general human bullshit as it stands right now, and the devastation that they don't know is caused by shades require us to initiate the prophecy."

"And?" Cole ground his teeth at the idea that he had to accept assistance from a woman who sat on the Judiciary that ordered the maiming of his witch. No matter whether Cate actually supported it or not, he was still unable to separate her role from what happened in his mind.

"The Council voted that you are the old gods returned. For the last three days, the elders have been discussing whether the prophecy requires an apocalypse or if it's more metaphor than anything else. I was there when the original prophecy was recorded, and I know my interpretation of it. Unfortunately, mine is the only accurate recollection of the prophecy."

"Why can't you just make them listen?" Evie asked. "If your interpretation doesn't demand the witches bring an apocalypse, then why would you let them keep believing it?"

Cate shook her head. "It's not that easy. Much like the humans, witches have grown more isolated and more polarized as time goes by. With the covens largely decentralized, distrust of others grows until, eventually, it's just too much to overcome. Passion becomes zealotry and caution becomes exclusion until all you're left with is a broken connection that can't be remade." The Mother of Witches released a harsh breath and raised her eyes to Cole and Evie. "About an hour ago, the Council came back in a dead tie about what to do next. Half of the coven elders support bringing about the apocalypse; the other half are aggressively opposed to it. The Judiciary vote to break a Council tie must be unanimous. It wasn't."

"How did it shake out?" Cole asked.

"Medea and Circe in favor of following the prophecy. I was alone in opposing it." Cate took another sip of her now-cold tea and reclaimed her seat at the kitchen island. "The next step is for those opposed and those in favor to appoint a representative to put forth their best, most persuasive case in support of their position."

"So why are you here?"

"I'm here because I think it is now an urgent matter to install the two of you as the Underworld's regents." Cate shifted, raising her gaze to Cole. "I don't think we have all the time in the world anymore. You should move as quickly as possible no—" Without any preamble, her voice stopped. Confusion raced across her face. Then, just as suddenly as the conversation ended, Cate screamed. Loud, banshee-like wails shattered the glass in the kitchen windows, and shadows wrapped around the goddess as she sank to her knees on the floor, arms wrapped around her waist, tears pouring down her face.

"Cate?" Evie cried, pushing against Cole's arms, trying to cross the kitchen to the screaming goddess. He tightened his grasp around her, locking her in place. There was no way in hell his Evie was going anywhere near whatever the fuck was happening to Cate.

Cate's familiars leapt from her tattoo, landing silently on the floor next to her, circling her once before beginning throwing their wolf-like heads back and howling in agony. Their cries were perfectly pitched to Cate's own, a haunting chorus that filled the kitchen. The shadows surrounding her suddenly exploded outward, the tendrils wrapping around the edges of the room and blocking out all light in the kitchen. Then they vanished, revealing... nothing. Cate and her familiars had disappeared.

"What the fuck was that?" Evie's eyes were wide, her expression dazed as she glanced around their utterly destroyed kitchen disbelievingly.

"*Mais* I don't know, me," Cole responded, so shocked by the unexpected turn of events that the Cajun patois he hadn't used in decades slipped out of his mouth easily. "Whatever it is, though, it moves our timeline up by a lot. We don't got the time to wait for your passport to come through. We'll take the jet in the morning and wing it once we get there. Go make sure we're packed, Angel, while I get everything arranged for us to leave at sunup."

She had them packed in an hour, everything was arranged for their departure in less than two, and they were on the plane within three.

Interlude

Council of Witches

Megiddo National Park, Jezreel Valley, Megiddo, Israel

At the back of the cave, Hesteia stood close to Thea and Chloe, surrounded by the witches that opposed carrying out the prophecy.

"Where do you think she went?" Hesteia overheard a new Shenandoah elder ask; another member of her coven quickly shushed her.

Carys, a round, Welsh witch from the Gwydir Coven, finally spoke up. "Who should present our case?"

"Why would Hesteia not present it?" A Romani witch, Lavinia, turned to Hesteia. "She knows the issue better than anyone, given her closeness to Evie." Several of those gathered nodded in agreement, but far more shook their heads.

One of the latter group, a French witch with the Landes Coven whose name Hesteia thought might be Fleur, interrupted. "That is just it. She is, perhaps, too close to the situation."

A rumble of disagreement rose around them, but Hesteia shook her head, holding up her hand to stall any arguments. "She's right." Voice quiet, she let her concerns spill out to the elders surrounding her. "I've known Evie since she was a toddler. Helped Chloe raise her and saw her grow from a determined infant to a talented and caring adult in spite of everything this Council agreed to put her through. I love her as a daughter, and, unfortunately, I know I can't maintain a neutral viewpoint when it comes to her. It was bad enough that the initial edict allowing Evie to join the coven required measures that harmed her so very badly. The Barataria elders struggled with this every time we performed a memory reversion in accordance with the edict, knowing that if we didn't, Medea herself would rain fire down upon us." Pausing, she carefully considered her next words before continuing. "I'm not sure I can be civil when arguing against people who are trying to condemn not only Evie herself but a world full of Evies to death based upon a prophecy issued millennia ago that we no longer have any written record of." Thea wrapped Hesteia in her arms, rubbing her back in long soothing passes. On the other side of Thea, Chloe sat on the floor crying.

Before she could say anything else, a shout rose across the room. Hesteia stood on her tiptoes to see over the other's heads. The hair on the back of her neck lifted in unease just before the glowing orbs overhead flashed from glimmering white to a deep, bloody scarlet. Her eyes darted upwards, horror flaring through her at the color she knew the magical lights could emit but had never seen.

Lavinia glanced up, terrified face bathed in the grim lighting. When she spoke, only one word emerged: "War." If anyone would know what color the orbs took before war, it was the Romani witches. They were hunted, almost to the point of extinction, by the superstitious local villagers.

Another shout sounded by the Judiciary table. Hesteia pivoted sharply towards the sound.

Medea's hands were raised over her head, golden magic filtering through her fingers, sparkling in the light. Circe stood beside her, her appearance calm but for her eyes, which were roiling pools of ocean blue. Around them, witch elders crowded. Old, young with every color and ethnicity represented, different but for the singular, polarizing cause uniting them. They were chanting something that Hesteia couldn't hear. Discordant voices raised in ever-increasing volume.

The witches opposing the prophecy were now blatantly staring at those across the chamber. "What are they doing?" Carys breathed, eyes wide with concern.

Somebody whispered back, "I don't know," but it was drowned out by Medea's shouted, "Burn the opposition!" Plumes of fire rocketed into the air, and then the chambers exploded into action as the witches favoring the prophecy raced towards them, murder in their eyes and fervor splashed across their faces.

Hesteia gathered fire, drawing upon the magic contained in the glowing orbs surrounding the chamber, but she and the others were too late, too delayed, in their response to the unexpected charge. Curses were streaming around them, felling witches as they hit their targets, intended or not; fiery trails of flame plunging around them, setting ablaze the witches who couldn't escape from beneath them. To Hesteia's left, a witch fell to the ground, shriveling away as a curse struck her. Her mummified body fell to the ground before she could even cry out. Burning bodies surrounded her, the smell of flesh cloying in the space.

The chamber's only portal was in a recessed room behind the Judiciary high table so there was no use trying for it. Coven elders raced towards the only physical exit from the chambers, which sat behind them, but smoke and roaring flames obscured their escape.

Screams filled the chambers. Their attackers' faces were lit by the fluid glow of magic and fire and their own malice. They had taken up Medea's battle cry of, "Burn the opposition," their eyes maddened and fervent, their voices unified. The traditionalists were now close enough for hand-to-hand combat and, although the magical deaths were horrifying, watching a middle-aged witch from Florida plunge a machete into Chloe's chest was a special sort of torture. Hesteia drew upon the fire filling the air around her and forced it into a gale wind that swept the Everglades Coven member into one of the chamber walls. Her body fell to the floor, crumpled and broken; she lay still where she landed.

As if in slow motion, Chloe dropped to the ground, eyes gone dull staring at the machete hilt extending from her chest. Blood seeped out around the blade, but it was embedded too deeply for much to escape.

Hesteia choked back a cry, hopelessness weighing heavily on her chest as she ran to her sister's side. She was too late by seconds, Chloe's chest rising then falling on a final exhale just before Hesteia fell to her knees next to her. Chloe's eyes stared blankly at the ceiling. There was nothing Hesteia could do besides shut her sister's eyes with her fingertips and murmur, "Blessed be" to the lifeless corpse on the ground in front of her.

Struggling to her feet, gasping for air, she searched desperately for Thea's golden hair. Fire and spell work obscured any visual of the room. Terror filled her, her stomach weighed down by dread. The new generation of witches weren't fighters in the traditional sense, and they certainly weren't prepared for a war with their own kind. It appeared, though, that the traditionalists had been readying themselves for this as they launched attack after attack, executing coven elders ruthlessly and efficiently.

From behind her came a deep hissing sound. She frowned but was too busy lunging away from a witch swinging an athame with alarming precision. The sacrificial blade glanced off Hesteia's side, sending an arc of her blood to the ground, before Hesteia was able to funnel another plume of smoke, throwing the attacking witch away from her. She sank to her knees, exhausted from the near constant use of magic over the last several minutes, but her head raised once more at the sound of a loud scrape near her. Turning slowly, she scanned for the source of the noise but was completely unprepared for the sight that greeted her.

Two massive golden drakes, heads flared like cobras, slithered past her. They tore witches apart with their fangs on their journey, crushed them under their bodies as they moved quickly past the slowly dwindling number of coven members defending against the traditionalists. Gasping, Hesteia froze, convinced that if she didn't move, didn't draw attention to herself, she might be able to find Thea, Bernadette, and Adelaide—wherever they were—and get them away from here. The serpents were almost fully past her when a tail the size of a mature red oak smashed across her back, knocking her to the ground. Pain seared through her as her head smashed to the ground, and the world went black.

Chapter 51

Evie

Private Jet, Somewhere over the Atlantic Ocean

Their day started before the sun rose, although Cole did everything in his power not to wake her before he had to, even going so far as to carry her from the house to the car. She woke when they pulled into the private airfield, just in time to carry her own bag onto the plane and select her seat. The pilots had introduced themselves, a flight attendant gave them instructions on what to do in the case of an emergency, and, in no time at all, they were in the air. All fairly straightforward, except for Evie's descent into terror as the plane itself ascended.

Frankly, Evie blamed her takeoff-induced panic attack on the flight attendant's helpful speech on emergency protocol. She tried to hide it, but, of course, Cole noticed. Without any fuss, he informed her that one of the perks of owning your own jet was being able to sit anywhere and tugged her into his lap, his hand rubbing along her back while he told her stories about his childhood in the soothing baritone that had never once—not in over two decades—failed to calm her.

Eventually, the flight leveled out, and she found herself able to breathe normally again. Once that happened, Cole all but force fed her breakfast and made her drink water while she watched the sun rise through the window. Her head resting against Cole's shoulder, Evie simply observed the beauty of the sky surrounding the plane. She thought it would be terrifying this far away from the ground—and it was—but it was also magical. This high up, she could feel the moon in a way that she never did when she was on the ground.

Eventually, Cole got impatient answering emails, which was around the time when he unbuckled their seatbelts and laid her out on the table in front of their seats. The first leg of her first-ever flight was then spent moaning while Cole licked and fingered her like it was what he had been put on this earth to do and demanded that she, "Come all over my face like the dirty little witch you are." Which she had, screaming his name as her fingers tangled in his hair, until, with a growled "*fuck*," he flipped her onto her stomach, ripped down his pants, and drove her into a conscious-altering orgasm before he shouted a curse and came so hard that his cum was dripping down her thighs before he was done.

Cole slumped down and rested his weight along her back. His breath was ragged as he kissed her shoulder, palming her ass. "Angel, you are going to be the fucking death of me."

"Do you think they heard?" Evie glanced at the cockpit where the pilots and flight attendant were seated, giggling breathlessly at the thorn-riddled rosebush that had magically sprouted around the cockpit's door.

Cole aimed an amused glance at her over her shoulder. "I think they probably heard us all the way back in New Orleans."

Evie buried her head in her hands, feeling the blush spread across her cheekbones.

Before she could feel truly embarrassed, though, Cole had pulled out of her and rolled her onto her back, his piercing eyes staring down at her. "And I wouldn't have it any other way. Every sound you make, no matter what it's for, is my favorite. Like music to my ears, especially when you're screaming for me." He gave her an exaggerated wink. "So do I think they heard us? Fuck yeah. Do I give a shit? Not in the least."

Resting a palm against Cole's cheek, Evie tilted up and kissed him gently, pouring all of her love for him into the connection. Somehow, despite having spent as much time together as they had over the last several days, things only kept growing in intensity: the sex better than anything she could dream up, the relationship more loving than she ever imagined it could be. She loved him with all of her heart and never wanted to be without him. Fortunately, she would never have to be. Wriggling against Cole, she tried to raise herself from the table, but he was having none of it.

"You're gonna have to give me a few more minutes," he murmured, pinching her ass. Evie let loose a high-pitched squeal of pleasure at the pain. "But if you make that sound again, it won't even take that long."

With a laugh, Evie pushed him away and sat up. Cole had barely undressed her before pressing her back on to the dining table. As a result, her jeans were hanging from one ankle, her panties were a shredded bundle of lace on the floor across the way—she was almost certain he had ripped them off her with his teeth in his desperation to have his mouth on her—and her cozy off-the-shoulder sweater was drunkenly sloped to one side. "Excuse you, I need to breathe," she scolded him jokingly. "You're heavy!"

One dark eyebrow raised in response. "You've never complained about not breathing before." He chuckled, and, in spite of everything they had done and her comfort with her sexuality, Evie felt her cheeks flush both at the imagined visual and the raspy tone in which he said it.

"Damn, you're cute when you blush," he commented.

"You think I'm cute when I do anything so that's not exactly a novel concept." Evie sat up and set to rearranging her top before wiggling back into and buttoning up her pants. "You told me you thought it was cute that I couldn't drive in a straight line in—oh, what was that video game you showed me?" Playing the game had been one of Cole's late-night ideas. Once she had figured out how the controllers and the game worked and what she was supposed to be doing, it had been fun, if not a little chaotic. That wasn't to say she was any good at it because she most definitely wasn't.

"Mario Kart. And you were cute. You kept running into the walls and driving backwards, but you had this scrunchy, annoyed look on your face—yeah, that one you're wearing right now—that said you were either going to get it right or die trying." He tapped her on the nose. "It's a lot less endearing to have that irritated glare directed at me, though." She stuck her tongue out at him, and he gasped mockingly. "You make fun of me on my very own jet? How far I have fallen from my days of glory."

"Speaking of your private jet." Dropping into the seat next to him as he tucked himself back into his jeans, she swiveled towards him. Before she could get comfortable in the cushy chair, though, Cole had picked her up and situated her in his lap. At her lifted eyebrow, he shrugged and snuggled her further into him. "Uh-uh, no, my love, you do not get to get out of conversations by being cute." She pushed against his chest to straighten herself, but his arms tightened around her until she gave up and decided to have the conversation with her head nestled into his shoulder. "Private jets cause massive damage to the environment and are hardly ever actually necessary since you could easily fly a commercial airline instead. They certainly aren't all that much faster. So you're just creating a *huge* carbon footprint for something you don't actually need."

Cole's lips twitched. "I'm 6'5", Angel. Do you know how uncomfortable it is to fly commercial when you don't physically fit into the space?"

"I do not, no, nor do I particularly care." Her words would have been far more effective if she hadn't nuzzled into him and caught a whiff of his scent that knocked her breathless.

"Are you asking me to get rid of the jet, little witch?" His emerald green eyes, glinting in mischief, met hers.

"Yes. That's exactly what I'm asking."

"Well." His thumb rubbed her chin, and she practically melted against him. "I think I could be okay with that. But it isn't all bad," he continued just as she was about to jump on his agreement. "There are some good elements too."

"Oh, and what are tho—" Her squeak of surprise cut off the snarky reply when Cole stood with no warning, hoisting her in his arms and striding to the back of the jet.

"So I guess the private amenities, known staff, your spouse's ability to fit in a seat, none of that will convince you to keep the jet, hmm?"

"Nope." He was trying to prove a point. What point that was she couldn't say, but she wasn't going to bite. "Not at all."

"Well, then I guess this room won't matter, huh?" After balancing her on his hip, Cole reached out and swung open the door in front of them revealing a spacious room, a significant portion of which was taken up by a bed covered in plush, soft-looking bedding.

Evie hopped out of his arms and meandered into the room. The carpet was a brilliant snowy white, thick and sumptuous under her toes as she padded around the space in her bare feet. She skated her hand over the covers, biting back a moan at how decadent they felt.

Cole leaned against the doorframe, his dark hair mussed, an amused smirk gracing his face as he watched her roam.

Gods, he's too damn beautiful, she thought, coming around the bed to stand in front of it.

Her facial expression must have reflected the intensity of her emotions because his face lit up in a full smile, although his next words were teasing. "So I guess we can shut this room off then, hmm? Since there's nothing I can say or show you to change your mind?"

With a grumble, Evie grabbed his shirtfront and tugged him to the bed where he made an extremely compelling case as to why they should keep the jet. And when she nodded off after he made her scream for him—something he reminded her that he couldn't do if they flew commercial—and turned her brain into barely functional mush, her mind was empty of anything but Cole.

Chapter 52

A blade stuck through the center of Aidoneus' throat. Blood poured from the wound, dripped from the corner of his lips, and she could hear his gasping breaths through the hole. Kore shrieked in pain and fear and fury as her love crumbled to the ground, arms still wrapped around her.

Standing above her was a dark shadow. "Hello, goddess," someone sneered in a low, resonant voice. She squinted against the sunlight, the features of the person above her coming into view. A man with thick brown hair glowered down at her, whiskey-colored eyes filled with a killing rage, blood streaked down his throat, coating his hands. That one small detail, more than any of the sounds raging around her, brought her back to herself, jolting her out of her almost catatonic state.

Kore screamed, a wordless, throat-rending sound, releasing a blast of magic that threw him across the battlefield. Or that should have thrown him across the battlefield. Instead, the man—Aidoneus' murderer—merely stumbled back several feet before falling in an ungainly heap. But Kore paid him no mind, instead rolling Aidoneus to the ground and gathering him to her chest. "My love," she crooned, sweeping his coal-black hair back from his face. His eyes, beautiful emeralds that saw everything, were dull. Not lifeless yet but cloudy and unfocused. Tears fell down her face. He couldn't die. "It's alright, my love, we'll fix this."

Even aspirating on his own blood, Aidoneus was still somehow able to give her a dubious look. "I'm... sorry," he gasped out, blood bubbling from the gaping hole in his throat. "Love... "

"Don't you dare pretend like this is the bloody end," Kore swore at him. "You promised me lifetimes together, Aidoneus, and I want every single one of them. You're not allowed to leave me."

His lips turned up at the corners. "Not... even... you... cheat death." He could barely manage the air necessary to force the words out of his mouth. Cupping her cheek, Aidoneus pulled her close. "Love... you... " He barely managed to get the last word out before he wheezed, one final, rattling noise that was wet with his blood, and his hand fell limply to the ground.

"Aidoneus, no!" Kore wept, tears falling from her eyes so heavily that she could barely see him. Thorned plants sprang around them, clustered around the goddess of flowers and lady of the Underworld, as her tears struck the ground. He couldn't be dead. No. She wouldn't fucking let him die. What was the point of being the queen of the thrice-damned Underworld if she couldn't bring him back.

Gathering magic, she thought through the spells she could cast that would revive Aidoneus. If she knew where his soul was in the Underworld, she could retrieve it; these days, though, with the shades escaped, they were more focused on returning the escapees to the Underworld than actually organizing it.

Too busy cycling through the magic available to her, Kore didn't hear the near-silent footsteps behind her, the quiet ring of metal through the air, until it was too late. Until a scythe was protruding from her chest. She stared stupidly at it, barely able to comprehend what had happened, even as blood wept out around the steel. Her heart was stuttering in her chest, and she knew, with absolute certainty, that she was nearing her own death. No. This is ***not*** *how we end, Kore thought ferociously.*

Swiping her hand through Aidoneus' blood, knowing she had only seconds left, she drew a halfhearted binding spell around the two of them before placing her hand on her husband's chest, chanting ancient words, a legendary curse built on blood and magic that would strip them of their memories and magic, transitioning back to their native tongue when she felt the last of her strength draining from her. Thunder rattled and lightning struck around them as she murmured, "We will return, my love" and fell to Aidoneus' chest with a final gasp.

Evie

Private Jet, Somewhere over the Atlantic Ocean

Evie woke to deep gasping sobs. In that in-between state of waking and sleeping, it took her long enough to recognize that she was the one weeping for Cole to recognize what was happening, chuck his laptop to the floor, and pull her into his arms.

"Shh, Angel, it's okay," he murmured, rubbing his hands along her back. She inhaled deeply with each stroke of his palm, slowly calming as she breathed in his scent, all while Cole kept up a constant refrain of, "You're okay, you're safe," in her ear. Eventually, once her breathing had evened out, Cole leaned back against the headboard, peering down at her through... glasses?

"You wear glasses?" Evie blurted out, unable to stop herself.

At the unexpected questions, Cole's lips tilted into a subtle smile at odds with his furrowed brow. "Yep. That's what we gonna focus on then, huh, Angel?"

She wasn't aware that glasses were sexy until Cole was wearing them. "I... they look... I wasn't expecting them."

The slight smile had morphed into a full-fledged grin. "It's okay you think I'm hot. I would be worried if you didn't."

An inelegant snort escaped her. "Cute."

"I know I'm cute, sweetheart, and you definitely think so too if the way you were begging for me a few hours ago is any indication." That stupid blush crept back over her cheekbones, and Cole kissed her forehead gently. "Now. You ready to talk about why you woke up in tears?"

Evie shrugged, not wanting to be thrown back into the hellscape of her dream. "I had a nightmare, and it... " She bit down on her lower lip to avoid potentially crying again. In that sun-bleached reality, she felt so hopeless. Could do nothing as Aidoneus died in her arms. "It felt so real."

"Not to freak you out or anything, but it's possible it was real," Cole reminded her softly as he tugged her lip free from where she was worrying it between her teeth. "What was it about?"

"You were—no, that's not right—he was. He looks so much like you." Her voice broke on an errant sob, but she swallowed it down and continued. "I saw Aidoneus get stabbed. Felt him die in my arms."

"Angel, I don't want to minimize the experience because obviously it was traumatizing as fuck, but you were seeing through Kore's eyes." As her mouth opened to respond, he held up a hand to stall her. "I know because I had that same nightmare when I was about 15. When I woke up, I couldn't believe that I was still alive. I kept feeling for a stab wound in my throat. I could feel that sucking, gasping rattle whenever I tried to breathe. The only reasons I didn't go crazy were, first off, knowing it was Aidoneus who died and not me. Second off, this feisty, red-haired fantasy of mine kept showing up in my dreams and keeping me company."

In spite of the grim topic, Evie felt happiness teasing the corners of her lips up at the reminder that she had been with Cole for most of his life. Just like he had been with her. She was about to suggest they get dressed when she gasped suddenly. "Oh, but you wouldn't remember this!"

Cole's eyebrows popped up at her excitement.

"I saw who killed you. Him. Her. Them. Kore and Aidoneus. I saw who killed them." She was breathless at the realization. "Aidoneus never saw him because he was dead. But Kore saw him." Another gasp escaped her. "And I heard the curse. Your family never had that information, right?" At Cole's head shake, Evie bolted upright. "It was an accident."

"What?"

"The curse... it was technically an accident! She was just guessing when she cast it. She knew how to disembody memories and powers but was just guessing that she could push them through time to a future couple. Witches typically can't bend the future like that. Best bet is that she inadvertently put their memories and powers on ice for a little while. But she had no idea what she was doing plus she was, y'know, dying when she cast the spell so she couldn't force the future couple to actually *be* Kore and Aidoneus, even though that's what I think she wanted to do."

"So it's really just you and me with some long memories and crazy power," Cole finished, eyes lit with excitement and magic. In the darkness of the room, they were almost hypnotic. She couldn't tear her own gaze from them, even as she nodded back at him, confirming what the two of them already knew: their love was real and about them as Cole and Evie. Fated? Perhaps. But still separate and distinct from Kore and Aideoneus' own love story.

Cole tilted his head down. "I love you, Angel. For you and only you."

Evie swiveled in his lap, her knees landing on either side of his hips, and cupped her hands around his face. "I love you, Cole Aidoneus."

With an almost shy grin on his face, he kissed her insistently, tilting her head back so he could part her lips with his tongue and take what they both knew was his. Had known was his since they were young, since the moment they met in person, since the moment he abducted her, in a million moments over the course of *their* lives—not Aidoneus and Kore's—all of which proclaimed that they were meant for each other.

Seeing that they were still undressed from when Cole stripped them getting into bed, Evie was already able to grind down on him, her hips rocking desperately. "Please, Cole," she gasped.

"Fuck, Angel, I love it when you beg, but I've got something to ask you first."

"Does it have to be now?" She could hear the whiney note in her voice but didn't care. All she knew was that she needed him inside her. Now. Everything else could wait.

With a groan, Cole shifted her off his lap onto the unmade bed. She pouted at him when he stood, scowling when she heard the muffled laugh as he grabbed something off the floor. He finally turned, pants in hand.

She raised a skeptical eyebrow at his offering. "I was naked in your lap, and you needed pants?"

"Fuckin' brat," came his fond response before he crawled back into bed and situated her back onto his lap. "You gonna keep up the sass or you gonna let me ask my sweet witch to be my sweet wife?"

"I'm absolutely going to keep up th—" Evie's voice trailed off, her mouth dropping. "I'm sorry, what did you say?"

"There it is. I was wondering when you would catch up."

"Wait. Did you—"

"Ask you to marry me? Yeah, I did. Well, technically, I implied that I was about to. Haven't quite gotten around to asking yet, though."

Evie pursed her lips. "I've been led to understand that proposals involve getting down on one knee and a ring. Plus, y'know, actually asking me whether I'll marry you."

Cole tugged a small velvet box out of his pants pocket and tossed them back to the floor. "You mean like this ring?" Flipping open the box lid, he showed her the ring nestled into the lining: a beautiful purple-blue stone sat central in a dark gold band, bordered by tiny, metallic leaves with gems set along the veins. The beautiful jewels glittered, even in the dimness of the bedroom, and she gently touched the leaves before shifting her gaze back up to Cole. "It was my mother's ring. She and my dad... well, he would have destroyed the world for her, and she would have killed for him. When Charlie gave it to me, he told me that he promised my dad he would give it to me only when I found the person who makes me feel the same way Dad did about *Maman*."

"We've already figured out I'm a little bit willing to abduct you to keep you." At her giggle, he gave her a self-deprecating smirk. "And that I would happily burn the world for you." She gasped, but his face clouded in confusion at the sound. "We don't have to actually get married if you don't want to, but I—"

"Wait," Evie cut in, confused by the sudden hurt in his eyes. "You don't want to marry me?"

"Of course I want to fucking marry you. You seemed put off by the idea, though. Why else would you gasp like that? I want you to be happy, Angel, whatever it takes."

"You're an idiot, Cole Aidoneus. I gasped because I'm excited and happy." Her words were harsh, but her tone was fond. "Of course I want to marry you, you beautiful man. Now keep telling me how much you love me, or I'll think you forgot your words, which would be an absolute shame since that's what you do for a living."

Cole pinched her butt, smirking at her resulting yelp. "I love you so fucking much, Angel. You're everything good about me. I know I don't deserve you, but, selfishly, I need you to be with me. In my life, badgering me, bratting at me, making every day better just by being with me. You've been my everything since I was twelve, and I didn't even know you were real then. Now I have you for real, and I can't—I won't—let you go. Angel, *ma belle petite sorcière*, will you marry me?"

Tears were pouring down her face again, falling from her chin as she nodded. At least this time it was happy crying? She supposed that made it better. "Yeah. Yes, I'll be your wife, my love. You are my whole world, and I love you so much." Evie barely noticed him sliding the ring onto her finger because she was already wrapping herself around him, rocking against him hungrily.

As soon as the ring was settled on her finger, Cole was like a man possessed, rolling her to her back, one hand grasping her hair so he controlled every motion of her head. "Gods, I fucking love you, Angel," he snarled into her ear. Evie gasped, grinding against him, but he shifted away to kneel in front of her, lazily stroking his hard cock while his eyes glowed down at her. "Now show me how much my fiancée needs me to fuck her."

With a moan, Evie spread her legs open.

"Good girl," Cole purred, but his voice dropped an octave when she stroked her hand down her body to splay open her lips, revealing herself to be dripping for him. "Goddamn, that's my dirty little witch." His voice was a gravelly growl as she swiped a finger down across herself, sighing in pleasure as she did so. She was just about to drive two fingers into her pussy when Cole forced her hand to his mouth, licking her fingers. "You taste so fucking good, Angel, and, god, do I want to eat you until you're coming all over my fucking face, but I need to be inside you right now."

Evie was practically panting the word "yes" at him by the time Cole lined up at her entrance and thrust deep. She let out a small scream of joy.

"You feel so fucking good, *mon petit ange*." He lifted his head from where it had dropped against her shoulder then grabbed her hands and bracketed them in place against the pillow. With a quick grin, he drew a few symbols across the skin of her wrist before lifting his hands from her arms and drawing his hips back until he was only just inside her.

"Gods, no, please, Cole, please don't stop." Her words were high-pitched, her tone pleading. She was so empty and aching without him filling her with his thick cock, that piercing at the tip rubbing against her perfectly. Evie tried to reach out to stop him, to pull him back, but her hands wouldn't move. Glancing up, she tried again.

As her lust-soaked brain tried to make sense of it all, Cole slid out of her fully and bent her leg up and out to the side. This time, she felt the tingle of magic in the air as he drew a ward on her ankle and knee, locking her leg in place against the bed. "Are you *warding* me?"

"Yep." His response was quick, his expression gleeful. "You get one leg free to wrap around my waist while I fuck you until you come so hard you black out, but everything else is mine to move as I see fit. Do you understand, little witch?"

Her pussy clenched on air at the change in his tone. From boyish to dominant in seconds, and all she could do was get wetter with each order. "Yes, sir," she murmured.

"You're beautiful when you beg, but you're so fucking perfect when you submit to me." He was tracing his fingers over her body when his cell vibrated on the nightstand next to them. Cole ended the call without sparing a glance at his phone, taking her nipple into his mouth as he did so.

Cole was lining himself up with her entrance again, her free leg wrapped around his waist, when a quiet knock sounded at the door. Shaking his head, he pushed his hips forward, the tip of his hard length sliding into her.

A low moan slid out of her. Evie wriggled against him, trying to get him to go deeper. "Please, sir."

"I know how badly you want my—" His dark chuckle was cut off by a more insistent second knock.

"Mr. and Ms. Aidoneus?" The flight attendant's voice carried to them through the door.

"Ms. Aidoneus, hmm?" She glanced up at Cole through lowered eyelashes.

His shoulder lifted in a shrug. "It was gonna happen sooner or later. I wanted to hear it sooner rather than later."

"Gods, Cole." Sweet Selene, she loved the idea of having his last name. After a lifetime of feeling like she didn't belong anywhere, Cole made her feel like she was finally home. She lifted her hips into him again, this time managing to take him slightly deeper. Moaning, she pressed her leg against his back.

"Maybe if we ignore her, she'll leave?" Cole mused as he punched his hips forward, bottoming out inside of her. A low cry left her at the same time a feral groan emerged from him. "That's right, witchling, you take me so—"

A third knock—this time closer to a full knuckle strike against the door—sounded. When the flight attendant spoke again, her words were clipped and closer to an annoyed shout than the civilized tone she had used before. "We're preparing for landing now. The pilot has requested that the two of you take your seats." She paused a beat. "I know neither of you are interested in coming out now, but the pilot says we'll lose our landing slot if we wait, and we don't have enough fuel to keep circling until they have another space available."

Cole glared over his shoulder at the door.

"I'm sorry, Mr. and Ms. Aidoneus, I can't leave until this door opens."

With a groan from him and a grumpy whine from Evie, Cole dragged himself out of her and reached for his pants. "Fine," he snarled loudly enough that the flight attendant could hear him. More softly, he said to Evie as he inverted the wards, releasing her from the bed, "Time to get dressed, Angel." Lifting her to her feet, he dropped his mouth over hers, his kiss bruising in its intensity. "I'll make this up to you soon."

Interlude

Hesteia

Megiddo National Park, Jezreel Valley, Megiddo, Israel

Hesteia woke slowly. The world swam around her, slowly coming into focus. Gods, her head was pounding, and her face felt like it was on fire. *What happened?* she wondered sluggishly. *Why am I lying on the ground?* She tried to move, maybe raise her head, but dizziness pulsed through her. The little movement she had accomplished vanished as her body caved back to the floor, and she sank into darkness once more.

Voices filtered into Hesteia's consciousness, ringing in her ears, pounding through her head. After earlier, she knew not to try to get up so instead she just lay there, eyes closed. As awareness came back to her, so too did the events of the... however long before.

The traditionalists *attacked* them, killed so many of them. *Mother of witches, did they kill Thea too?* Thea was standing next to her before the attack, but they had been separated during it. *They murdered Chloe.* The memory of watching the machete tear through her sister's chest, the sound of her final shaking breath, tore through Hesteia, wrecking her. A tear snuck out from under her closed lids, but she kept them clamped shut as footsteps rang through the chamber.

She bit the inside of her cheek to avoid crying out in terror when an arrogant voice rang out across the chamber. "Where's the prophetess?"

Medea. Her brain placed a name to the voice, and she nearly flinched at the Judiciary member's betrayal. Medea had always been mercurial, violent to the point of unpredictability, and had been the Judiciary member who forced the issue of Evie's mandated sterilization at 18 and the annual memory reversions after the Council overruled her in their vote to include Evie as a coven member. But this? This was—emotionally, she shied away from the phrase, but her brain still supplied it—mass murder. The extermination of a group of people who didn't agree with the traditionalists' view. Genocide.

Dragging sounds carried to Hesteia followed by a loud thump. She dared a quick lift of her eyelids, just enough to get a peek of the room. Through that narrow slice of vision, she caught a glimpse of a small group of traditionalists and Medea and Circe gathered around the high table where a small body was huddled.

Her pulse thudded in fear, so loudly she was convinced they might hear it. She was closer to the front of the room than she remembered being but far enough away that they hadn't tracked the subtle movements of her eyes. What had happened between when the witch cut her side with the athame and now?

Circe's voice cut through Hesteia's racing thoughts. "Now, prophetess, get up." A small woman sat up, her back to Hesteia. "You're to scry for the location of the old gods for us."

The witch shook her head, whimpered a little, but Medea unsheathed her dagger, extending it so the golden blade pressed against the woman's throat.

"You'll either do as your Judiciary tells you or we *will* kill you. And once we've burned you at the pyre, we'll go to your coven and destroy them as well for the disloyal new generation cowards they are."

The witch turned slightly, barely enough to reveal her face, but it was enough. Hesteia couldn't help the soft intake of breath. Although they had never met, she knew Sibyl, the most revered prophetess in the covens, on sight. The witch had a narrow, almost pinched face and mousey brown hair cut close to her skull for reasons passing understanding. Some said it was because she had gone mad at the visions that plagued her and, in a fit of lunacy, cut off all of her hair; others said it was because she lived in Greece where it got alarmingly hot during the summers. Nobody could say with certainty, but it only added to her mystique. Most alarming of all, though, were her eyes. Practically black and wild in her too small face, they spoke of a life spent staring into the past and future with too little of it spent in the present.

"Bring me a map," Sibyl demanded in a deeply accented voice.

Medea gestured in front of Sibyl. "It's right in front of you." Voice pitched low but not enough to avoid Sibyl overhearing, she added, "Crazy witch."

Sibyl tilted her head sharply at the witch, saying softly, "You will be torn apart by fur and darkness and only the shadows will see it." Medea blanched, a look of fear flashing across her striking face, but Sybil had already turned to the map and picked up the scrying crystal next to it.

Magic poured through the cave as Sibyl rocked back and forth, the crystal swinging from the string in long arcs while she mumbled nonsensically over the map. Small words carried to Hesteia. *War. Blood. Throne. Death. Love.* Then the shout of a phrase with which she was intimately familiar. *Lovely death. Deathly love.* The same phrase that Cassandra repeated every time she tried to look into Evie's past or future. It took everything in Hesteia not to jerk in surprise, but she forced herself to remain still. Any movement would mean her own death

Finally, a jubilant cry filled the chamber as Hesteia heard the scrying crystal clank against the table.

A voice she didn't recognize read out, "Budapest?"

Silence before someone else asked in confusion, "The old gods are in Budapest? Wasn't the witch in Louisiana?"

Maia—*godsdamned Maia, if only Hecate had destroyed her when she had the chance*—interrupted them all. "We have their heading then. We must get there as quickly as possible."

"We'll use the Council's portal," Medea instructed. "It was created to support the Council's duties. Fulfilling the prophecy is the Councils' entire purpose, no matter what the new generation may say." Laughter filled the chambers. "Now, what to do with our traitorous seer who thinks she knows better than the prophecy that came before her?"

Several voices shouted, "Kill her," but Circe silenced them with a derisive laugh. "You all would cut off your nose to spite your face, wouldn't you?" A sneer colored her words. "What if we can't *find* them in Budapest? It's a large city and a haven for magical beings. It may not be that easy to locate them. We may still have a use for our darling sister here." With a wave of Circe's hand, Sibyl's body raised into the air, bound by unseen ties. "We'll bring her with us through the portal. Once we find them, we'll dump her somewhere. The Danube runs into the Black Sea. I'm sure my father would be only too pleased to take on a new pet once she makes her way to open water."

Although the solution was fair, it clearly didn't sate the traditionalist's bloodlust if the angry grumbling was any indication. Circe was a powerful sorceress, though, and no one was willing to confront her.

Feet pounded across the chambers to the recessed room housing the portal. In less than five minutes, the cavern was quiet, empty. Hesteia allowed a few more minutes to pass before she cracked open her eyes. A few more seconds after that to catch her breath then struggle to her feet, dizzy from what she could now identify was a swollen knot on the back of her head and a long burn lancing her left cheek. Offbalance and unsteady, she lurched forward, catching herself before she fell with a hand on... oh, gods, *that was a body!* Her stomach heaved as she surged backward, her hands scraping over the rough chamber floor as she scuttled away from the corpse in terror, only to back herself into another witch's body. She looked around wildly, only to see an almost perfect circle of dead women gathered around her. Black dots sparkled in the periphery of her vision, and nausea threatened. It was all she could do not to vomit—or faint—at the gruesome tableau in front of her.

Her mind rebelled in horror as she stared around her. Blood splattered the chamber walls in random, nonsensical designs; the stone and dirt were barely visible under the viscera covering the floor. Mangled bodies littered the room, and severed limbs were cast about, no doubt courtesy of Medea's heinous drakes. This wasn't an attack. It was a massacre.

Hesteia stood once more, legs shaky underneath her. Barely breathing, she scanned the room, searching desperately for Thea's long, golden hair. *Where is she? Is she dead?* Her thoughts were disorganized at best. Thea was her rock, one of her very reasons for living, not to mention a powerful witch and the incredible wife who kept Hesteia grounded. She couldn't be dead.

A low moan sounded near the Judiciary's table. Hesteia snapped her head in the direction it came from, wondering if, in her panicked state, she had imagined it. Then the sound carried again. Without a thought, she rushed towards it, taking care to pick around the bodies, her heart pounding with each step toward the front. She couldn't get her hopes up that it was Thea. It would only devastate her if it wasn't.

She cried out in disbelief as she rounded the table, catching sight of her wife, bloody but still very much alive, and flung herself to her knees at Thea's side. "I thought you were dead," she gasped, arms wrapped around Thea's neck. "I couldn't find you, and I thought you were dead!" Tears poured down her face, drenching Thea's bloody clothing.

Thea chuckled, a thin, reedy sound that wasn't nearly as powerful as it should be. But she was alive to make it, and that was all that mattered. "It will take more than a few bigots to kill me off." She clucked at Hesteia's distress as she wiped a tear from her wife's face. "Now help me up, my love."

Wavering, Hesteia rested a bracing hand on Thea's shoulder. "What if you shouldn't move, my darling? What if it injures you further?"

"Don't be silly," Thea scolded. "I'm just disoriented from that snake, Medea, choking me out. I passed out because I couldn't breathe. She must have thought

I died." Her lips pursed in an oddly judgmental expression, her tone thoughtful but dismissive. "She never was very smart." Looking back to Hesteia, she commanded authoritatively, "Now help me up, Hessie."

When her wife used that tone, who was she to argue? With a sigh that elicited a raised eyebrow from Thea, Hesteia grasped her wife's hand, placing the other hand on her back to raise Thea to her feet.

Thea's stance was tentative, but her eyes were fiery. "Who all is left alive?"

"I don't know," Hesteia admitted. "I just woke up, and I was too busy looking for you to pay much attention. But I know—" Her voice cracked. "I know Chloe is dead. I saw an Everglades witch kill her myself. She was gone so quickly. But there are so many of our sisters dead out there." Out of the corner of her eye, a small movement caught her attention. She whirled, drawing fire to her free palm before recognizing Akna.

"Akna," Thea exclaimed, pushing down Hesteia's raised palm and rushing to the Chugach High Priestess. "You're alright!"

Hesteia followed behind her, a firm hand resting on her wife's back to stabilize her.

"Yes. Somehow." Akna heaved a sigh. "I don't think Medea, Circe, and the traditionalists were sufficiently prepared to execute their little coup, and many of them have never killed so much as a bird, much less a fully-powered adult witch. So there's a small group of us—" She gestured behind her to a group of bloody and battered witches. "Who survived the slaughter." Her eyes grew hard. "We're prepared to wreak havoc on them for their bigotry."

Carys gasped. "But what about the creed? Witches are nonviolent."

Bernadette, Barataria's voodoo practitioner, stepped forward. "Kindly, Carys, and I mean this with all the love and respect in my heart, fuck the creed." Carys gasped at her coarse language, but Bernadette ignored it. "They acted first, and they executed us. Look around you! They murdered our sisters in cold blood! There is no world in which we cannot respond in kind. Their violence—the horror they want to unleash upon the world—can't be allowed to go unchecked."

A small witch with distraught eyes emerged from the group. When she spoke, her words bore a a heavy German accent. "They killed my family. There were only three of us in my coven, and they're all dead. Except me." Voice cracking, she broke down, crying so hard that there weren't even tears coming down her face.

Thea raced to the witch to bring her into a close hug, her eyes grim. "You are welcome with our coven, my dear—"

She was interrupted by a guttural shout.

The small gathering of remaining witches turned towards where Hecate and her familiars had arrived in a cloud of shadows. Her face was tight, violet eyes wild as she rushed toward them, taking in the carnage around her. "What the fuck happened?" Magic pulsed violently around her.

The small horde of survivors looked at one another in silent concern. Hecate was an extraordinarily powerful goddess and the likelihood that she would take this betrayal well was alarmingly slim. From her appearance, she already appeared borderline maniacal. Her clothes were torn, her hair disheveled, and deep scratches raked down her arms at an angle that made it look like they might be self-imposed.

"Well?" Hecate demanded. "Somebody, answer my question. *Now.*"

Akna was the first to speak. "After you left, the traditionalists gathered with Medea and Circe and then... well, they attacked those opposing the prophecy, Hecate. All of this," she gestured around the room. "All of this was at the traditionalists' hands."

Hecate's face crumpled in confusion. "What were Medea and Circe doing at the time of the attack?"

Akna tried to speak, but her voice caught in her throat.

When no one else stepped in to answer the question, Hesteia quietly supplied, "They led the attack."

"No. They wouldn't... they wouldn't dare." Hecate shook her head viciously, the bones tangled in her hair slapping against her cheeks.

"Yes," the German witch corrected. "They coordinated the charge, and Medea summoned her drakes to support them."

Silence settled over the chamber before Hecate screamed, a keening wail that practically tore out of her throat. Shadows exploded around her, wrapping long tendrils around her in what almost looked to be a seductive caress. Her familiars prowled around her, eyes alert as they protected their mistress. Almost as suddenly as her cry began, it ended. The chambers rang with its echo, but Hecate was silent. Her head tilted towards the floor. Eventually, she spoke again, her voice low. Distorted. "Where are they?"

"Hecate?" Hesteia approached the distraught goddess.

When Hecate raised her eyes towards them once more, the entire group took a unified step back. Her irises were purple fire, her raven hair blowing in a nonexistent breeze. The shadows that had simply surrounded her before were now wrapped tightly around her, draped like a lover's body around hers. Hecate tilted her head at the group. The movement was slow. Menacing. Eerie. "Where. Are. The. Traitors?"

It had never been clearer to them before just how foreign and powerful Hecate was. Sitting at the Judiciary table, she always appeared simply to be the Mother of Witches, a goddess in her own right, of course, but caring and compassionate. Standing before them now, however, she was wrath incarnate, sublime and terrifying in her rage.

"Where. Are. They?" She spoke quietly. The sound carried as if she had shouted.

"They're in Budapest, Hecate," a young witch from Croatia responded. "They scryed for the old gods and found them there. We believe they mean to kill them, so that they can't oppose the prophecy."

"Then we go to Hungary," Hecate announced. "You're not required to come with me. Know that if you do, this will end bloody, And I expect you to fight if you come with me. If you choose not to travel with me because you can't commit to violence, I will not hold it against you. But if you come with me to battle, and you hide or second guess your decision and one of this group is hurt because of it, there will be no rock under which you'll be able to hide, no end of this world or the next to which you can run where I will not find you and make you pay for your cowardice." Her piece said, she swept towards the portal, not even looking back to see if they followed her. "Follow me if you wish to avenge your sisters."

And, after a long look exchanged amongst themselves, every witch in the group followed Hecate to a war that they never asked for but would commit to for their fallen.

Chapter 53

Cole

Budapest, Hungary

By the time they finally touched down, it was ridiculously late—or absurdly early, Cole was too tired to figure out which—Evie was antsy, and he was prepared to do anything legal and many illegal things to get them to Hayden's flat.

The guard at the private airport boarded the jet, eyes darting around. His mouth opened, probably to ask for their passports, but then he caught sight of Evie, tousled and still aroused from the flight attendant's interruption half an hour before. Eyes bulging, he approached her, clipboard extended.

Cole growled, stepping in between them. "What do you need from us?" At almost six-and-a-half feet, he towered over the smaller man. Behind him, a small snicker emerged at what he was sure was an absurd sight. Tall man crowds Hungarian gnome away from the beautiful witch. Sounded like something out of a children's fairytale.

The guard swallowed nervously, his gaze tracking up Cole's chest, all the way to his furious glare and scowl. "I'll coordinate with your pilot for the flight plan and paperwork, sir. You, um, you may go. I do not require anything from you."

Fuck right, we can. Although he had expected a bigger—well, any, really—fight about passports, no chance he was looking that gift horse in the mouth. "C'mon, *mon ange, allons-y.*" He extended his hand to her. Her hand slid gently into his, fingers entangling with his own.

All told, it only took about 30 minutes from touchdown to step on to Hungarian soil, his Angel wrapped in his arms. Despite his past experiences in Budapest, it was much more tolerable with her.

Evie blinked up at him, eyes bleary with fatigue and banked desire. "Where are we staying?"

"A little place in the city. Hayden's home away from home away from home." Cole smiled gently down at her and bundled her closer, lifting her into a bridal carry. "It's okay, Angel, I'll carry you to the car."

"You just don't want anybody to see me walking around outside of your arms. I know your game, love." The retort was mumbled into the collar of his jacket.

"I don't think you mind my games, though." Cole crossed the parking lot to the hired car where the driver opened the door to admit them. He dropped slowly into the back seat, careful not to disturb Evie.

With one hand, he pulled up the messages that came in from Hayden while they were on the plane.

Did you know that there's a website dedicated to all of the weird and unexplained weather anomalies that have happened since you and Evie got together?

https://www.wtfisupwiththeweather.com

Maybe you two should stop fucking until you claim your throne so that you don't cause the universe to implode?

Wait, this all stops once you guys claim the Underworld right?

Then he sent the meme of Anakin and Padme. Cole snorted. His best friend was a child. His fingers flashed over the keyboard as he sent back a straight forward response:

Fuck. Off.

At his laugh, Evie glanced up at him from the book she was reading on the eReader application on her phone. She hated almost everything about the electronic device and seemed steadfast on either losing or destroying the thing, but her hatred for it had waned a bit once he showed her that she could read pretty much any book she wanted at any time. His witchling was a voracious bookworm who read everything she could get her hands on. "What?"

He tilted his phone towards her, letting her see the message chain. Even in the darkness of the car, he could see both the blush staining her cheeks paired with uncertainty at the destruction caused by their ravenous sexual appetites. He understood it, felt a bit of guilt about it too, but there was no way he could have gone cold turkey celibate with her near him. If he was this overly possessive of her with regular sex, he couldn't imagine what he would be like if they had waited.

Her attention shifted back to the book she was reading, a smutty one about rockstar vampires based on his quick scan of the page she was reading. With Evie distracted, he turned his focus back to his own phone, backing out of his message chain with Hayden and into the group chat between him, Charles, Hayden, and the Moirai.

Arrived safe and on our way to the flat. Will call in the morning.

Once it sent, he dumped his phone on the seat beside them, only too happy to disconnect from prophecy-related matters for a few seconds. Stunning, historic architecture blurred around them as the car made its way into the heart of Budapest, but Cole couldn't be bothered to pay any attention to it. Instead, he stared straight ahead, running his hand over Evie's hair thoughtlessly, thinking his way through the day ahead of them.

The car ride passed in blissful silence broken only by Evie's quiet taps against the screen to turn the page. They finally pulled up to a lightly-colored stone building discreetly tucked on a side street along the Danube in central Budapest. With a word of thanks to the driver, Cole gathered Evie from the car and strode towards the locked iron doors of the building.

"You know I can walk, right?" she commented mildly, tilting her phone down and glancing up at him.

"Yeah, I know you can walk." He smirked at her. "But I like carrying you so you're just gonna have to get used to it."

She wrinkled her nose at him, and he was pretty sure she mumbled the word, "bossy" under her breath.

The night guard buzzed them in through the locked doors into the lobby. The room was ornate but not ostentatious. Plush rugs covered marble flooring while, above them, a colorful trompe l'oeil ceiling drew the eye with its illusions of dimension. A large, white stone fireplace, lit with a blazing fire, graced one wall while, across from it, a guard in a pristine uniform that looked like it had never seen a wrinkle or speck of dust observed them warily.

Cole strode across the lobby to the guard, opening his mouth to introduce himself and Evie, but the guard stopped him. "Mr. Aidoneus?" he read from a small log sitting to his right where Cole could see a scribbled scrawl that looked like his name next to two small photos of him and Evie, respectively. The guard's gaze shifted to Evie. "And Ms. Dyeus?"

Cole nodded, thankful that Hayden had arranged everything before they got here since the pilot hadn't been able to collect the key in advance of their flight. "That's us. Mr. Sopor told me you would have the key for us when we arrived." Although he tried to sound civil, after Cate's alarming visit the night before, an almost 12 hour flight, and the interrupted celebration of Evie's agreeing to marry him, his voice was gravelly, and he knew his exhaustion and irritation were blazing from his face. It was pure dumb luck that his amped-up emotional state, arousal, and unbelievable sleep deprivation weren't forcing magic out of him like a bad battery.

Without any additional fanfare, the guard scanned Cole's passport and had him sign the log-in book before handing him an antique key. "Here is the key to flat 1007P where you and Ms. Dyeus will be staying. The only elevator bay that accesses the penthouse is down that hallway." He gestured towards a removed area of the lobby. "You'll need to scan your fingerprint through the elevator's biometric scanner to get to the flat, which is on the tenth floor. Mr. Sopor provided us with your fingerprints earlier today so the system is already set up for you and Ms. Dyeus."

For a split second, Cole briefly wondered how Hayden had gotten Evie's fingerprints but disregarded it just as quickly. *Too tired to care.* "Thank you," he said, taking the key from the guard and trudging over to the elevator bay. Their bags would be delivered in the morning since he had been too impatient to get them here to pay much attention to their luggage. Since neither he nor Evie had worn many, if any, clothes to sleep in the last several days, he wasn't particularly concerned about pajamas.

Fortunately, the biometrics worked perfectly, and the elevator delivered them to the penthouse with no stops along the way. The elevator slid open, revealing a small entryway and a singular door marked **1007P,** which he opened using the key provided by the guard. The dark space within was illuminated only by the lights of Budapest streaming in through the floor-to-ceiling windows across the room. The city's nightlife revealed tastefully-selected furniture, an open floor plan with a wrought iron staircase leading to an upper floor, and a far-removed, partially-open door on the other side of the room that he hoped against all hope was a bedroom.

Sometime during the elevator ride, Evie's eyes had slid shut. She murmured against his chest in her sleep. At the sound, he glanced down, sleep-deprived irritation almost completely forgotten as he walked them towards the open room. *Please let it be a bedroom.* He nearly moaned whe he saw the king-size bed visible from the door. A relieved sigh escaped him as he stripped them both of their flight-worn clothes and snuggled Evie and himself under the plush covers, her back pulled into his front.

As if she knew, even in her almost sleeping state, that he was relaxing, Evie made a satisfied sound and pushed further back into him. He kissed her gently before dropping his head to the pillow. Within seconds, his eyelids fluttered shut, and he slid into a deep sleep.

Chapter 54

Cole

District V, Budapest, Hungary

Cole woke to screaming. His entire nervous system flooded with adrenaline, and he lurched up, eyes searching for whatever was wrong. But all he could see was his Angel, high-pitched yelps spilling from her sleep-parted lips at whatever nightmare was haunting her. He unwound the sheets from around her with one hand, slipping the other beneath her head as he rested his body over top of hers to stop her from thrashing. Running his nose along her silky cheek, he murmured, "Angel, it's okay, but I need you to wake up."

Her screaming slowly tapered off. "Cole?" she asked, voice raspy from her screams.

"Yeah, sweetheart, it's me, you're safe." He could see her pulse pounding in her throat, feel her heart fluttering under his chest. "You had a nightmare. But your pulse is going way too fast, little witch, I need you to breathe for me." Her breaths were still emerging as gasps, consistent with her intaking far too little air. "Hey, hey, breathe with me." He modeled a breath for her, her wide, grey eyes staring at him. "C'mon, Angel, breathe with me."

Evie nodded, finally inhaling along with him. "That's right. That's my good little witch." She was settling down, her breaths coming far more evenly, and his body was now realizing that he was cradled right where he wanted to be. "Good girl."

She nodded, eyes still round but no longer filled with fear.

"Another memory?" he asked. Fuck, he needed to not be a creepy piece of shit.

"Not a different one," she responded. Her arms were still tight around him, but her fingers were slowly scraping along his spinal cord. "Same one. Aidoneus dying, although I did see his murderer's face more closely this time." She scraped her nails along his back, digging in slightly, and his hips rocked against her. "Aidoneus looks so much like you. When he's dying in her arms, all I can see is you dying in mine."

"Angel, it's not me. I'm still very much here and alive." Cole pulled one of her hands off his back, placed it on his cheek. "See? Still soft and warm and living."

"Not all that soft," his siren of a future wife cooed, wrapping her lithe legs around his waist and rocking herself against him.

Soft morning light poured in through the windows surrounding them. A full wall of windows to the left of the bed. A skylight almost the length of the ceiling over their heads. In the warm glow of the rising sun, Evie practically sparkled.

"Fucking hell," he grumbled down at her. With one large hand, he palmed her ass, forcing her against his rapidly-hardening dick. "You're insatiable."

"I don't think you mind it," she snarked back, eyes shimmering with mischief, sealing her fate.

"Bratty little witch, you think you would have learned." His voice was lower than he'd ever heard it, almost feral in its intensity. With a sudden move, he lifted off Evie, which was a monumental feat on its own, given the sad whimper she made when he pulled away. "On your hands and knees facing the headboard."

Evie followed his order quickly, her auburn hair sweeping down over her right shoulder as she glanced back over her left at him. The wrought iron rods of the antique bed sat right in front of her face.

"Now wrap those perfect hands around the headboard."

Once she followed his command, Cole leaned back, admiring the scene in front of him. Her body was laid out across the bed, a buffet stretched out for him alone, her ass raised at the perfect angle for his intended punishment. "Jesus wept, Angel, you're so perfect." Stroking a hand over her ass, he gave her a soft swat. Her resulting gasp nearly had him throwing his plans out the window and sinking into her immediately. He could see how wet she was from where he was kneeling behind her, knew that he could drive into her in a single thrust that would cause his world to tilt even further off its axis. But he wanted to see her ass jiggle under his palms, bring her pain tempered with pleasure that would have her shattering around him when he finally deigned to let her come on his cock.

The grin that spread over his face was probably more than a little deranged. "Little witch, you know what happens when you're a brat, don't you?"

Her responding smirk spiked his own body temperature. "No, sir."

Her and that smart mouth and brilliant brain of hers. "No, you don't know what happens when you're a brat? Or no, you're not a brat?"

"The second one, sir. I would never be a brat." Her tone was too light, the underlying giggle a little too innocent, for it to be believable.

"Of course not." Cole nodded as if he agreed. Right before he swatted her ass a bit harder, roughly enough that a red handprint appeared on her porcelain flesh as she moaned. Leaning down over her back, he summoned his magic, warding her hands to the bed.

Even that small bit of magic had the skin on her back exploding into goosebumps. Her hips shifted, desperately looking for him, while her breath emerged in small pants. Her own magic responded so sweetly to his, scraping along his skin erotically. Cole chuckled, traced his fingers down her spine, relishing the sight of her before him. "I think you're lying to me, though, *vilaine fille*," he said quietly, dropping back to his knees behind her. His hands fell away from her. "I think you know how much of a brat you've been, and you're desperate for me to punish you for it."

Evie shook her head swiftly, her mouth opening to respond, but she rocked forward as his hand landed hard on her ass. A small sound of pleasure rolled out of her open mouth instead of words.

"That's right, Angel." He slapped the other side of her ass. She tugged against the headboard, but his wards held her fast. "Don't get any ideas about escaping. The only way out of this is to safeword. Do you remember your safeword?" He dealt her a glancing slap, a tease more than anything else.

Her head bobbled forward in a nod.

"No, I need you to respond verbally, sweet girl." Cole seized a handful of her hair in his palm and tugged her head gently back. "Do you remember your safeword?"

"Yes, sir," came her throaty response.

"Say it for me now."

"Marshmallow. My safeword is marshmallow, sir."

He made an approving sound in the back of his throat. "And if you say that word for any reason, I stop immediately. It's the only word that will make me stop since 'no' is a natural response to pain, even pleasurable pain. So, if you want to stop for any reason, you just say your safeword. Do you understand?"

"Yes, sir."

"Such a good little witch when you know you're about to get punished." Cole smoothed a hand over her ass. "Now if only you behaved regularly, you wouldn't have to deal with the sore ass I'm about to give you."

Evie let out a high-pitched whine of frustration and rocked against the wards anchoring her hands to the headboard.

"Oh, sweetheart, flaunting that perfect ass isn't going to make me stop. In fact, it just makes me want to spank it red even more." Fuck, she was so tempting, served up for him like this, ready to accept every depraved fantasy he had. "You're gonna get twenty strikes, ten per side. Each time I spank you, you're gonna count. Do you understand?" She nodded again, and he pinched her ass. "No, baby, you're gonna speak for me now. Use that smart mouth of yours to tell me you understand."

Evie's mouth opened. "I understand, sir."

He growled, letting loose a slap at her right ass cheek. Evie yelped as his hand connected before gasping out, "One." "You're being such a good girl for me,

Angel. Don't forget to keep up your counts, though, or we'll have to start over again."

He alternated between sides of her ass, location of the hit on her cheeks, and the intensity of the slaps. His Angel kept up her count the entire time, even though her speech disintegrated into loud moans, gasping sobs, and open tears that were barely distinguishable as words by twenty. By the end, her skin was flaming red, and she was begging for him. "Have you learned your lesson, brat?" he asked, one hand gently stroking his length.

"Yes, sir. Gods, yes, I've learned my lesson, sir." She was rocking back and forth, the rhythmic flow of her body the most beautiful thing he had ever seen in his life. "Please."

"Please what?" The side of his lips tugged up in a slight smile.

"Please fuck me, sir. I need you inside me so badly." Her voice cracked. "*Please.*"

"Well, since you asked so sweetly." Cole dipped his free hand between her thighs, groaning at how wet she had gotten during her punishment. "God, Angel, you're soaked." And, suddenly, his original plans vanished because he knew with absolute certainty that, if he didn't get inside of her right now, he would lose his fucking mind.

Lining himself up with her entrance, he thrust into her, setting a punishing pace from the start.

"Fuck, Cole." Evie's voice was climbing in volume. "Oh my gods, yes, right there! Please, Cole, I'm so close."

Her throaty voice calling his name, begging for him, was going to be his absolute undoing. He could already feel himself unraveling, his balls drawing tight as she bore down on him. "Angel, fuck, baby, I need you to come for me." He dropped his fingers between her thighs once more, her clit raised under his fingers. At the smallest brush of his fingers over the bundle of nerves, Evie cried out, arching her back. The wards flared bright blue, clear evidence of the magic flowing through her finding its way out, even if it was only to dismantle his own wards holding her captive.

Magic roiled through the room, almost physical in its overwhelming presence. He could feel it running up his spine, stroking around him, little tangible touches and reminders that Evie and he were made for each other. A low, growling sound filled the room, and he realized it was emerging from his own chest as he thrust into his witch, hard enough that the headboard was slapping against the wall and her body shook under the intensity. The world was awash in the neon blue of his magic, dragged to the fore by her own.

Cole ran his fingers over her taut clit one last time. "Come for me, sweetheart," he ordered.

At his command, Evie came apart around his cock. Her screams filled the apartment, her inner walls clamping around him as she broke for him. Ultimately, it was her orgasm that dragged him under.

His punishing tempo faltered, and his back seized as he pumped into her, christening her pussy with his cum. "That's right, take my cum for me, sweetheart, feel it fill that desperate cunt of yours," he demanded, black dots sparking along the edges of his vision with each clench of her around his cock. His gaze narrowed to a tunnel where all he could see were Evie's own lust-drenched, magically-lit eyes peeking back at him through an auburn veil of curls. "You're so fucking perfect."

His little praise slut squeaked at his words, a happy shiver running along her body before she slumped to the bed. At some point, her hands had gotten free. He glanced at the headboard, lifting an eyebrow at the wrought iron rungs now melted by her magic. Hayden would probably bitch an annoying amount about the ruined antique, but that was an issue for another day.

Running one hand along Evie's back, Cole quickly checked her breathing and pulse rate with the other. "You good, Angel?"

She nodded lazily, arms stretched above her head as she lowered herself to the bed. "Um-hm." Her eyes were closed in bliss, one knee elevated up by her waist.

Cole's heart gave a slow pulse at the sight of his whole world lying in this bed, his mother's ring encircling her finger. His gaze tripped lower, catching sight of her ass, reddened with his hand prints. A smirk tugged at the corners of his mouth before he got out of bed to go search the bathroom for arnica cream. Since it was Hayden's place, he assumed there would be some readily available.

"Where you going?" Her voice trailed after him as he rummaged through the bathroom.

"Looking for some arnica cream so that pretty ass of yours doesn't bruise too badly." Ah, there it was. Snatching it out of the medicine cabinet, he turned back to the door, tube in hand. From his vantage point, he could see the whole of the bedroom including his naked witch propped up on her forearms, head swiveled towards him with a stunning smile on her face. He pressed a hand against his chest, hoping to calm his stuttering heart, before walking over to her. "It has anti-inflammatory properties so it'll help soothe... " Noticing the charmed expression on her face, he trailed off. "What?"

"Cole, my love, I'm a witch. I know the properties of arnica." Her eyes were merry. "Since we didn't have access to drug stores and pain medications in the forest, we made do with what we had." She gasped softly as he rubbed the lotion over her cheeks. "But the application was a lot less seductive than that."

With a chuckle, Cole swiped the remainder of the cream from his fingertips onto his upper thighs and quickly kissed Evie's shoulder. He stood up, catching a glimpse of the happiness on her face. If he could keep her smiling like that for the rest of their immortal lives, he would count that as an eternity well spent. "I'm gonna go grab some water for you and check if they dropped off our bags. Don't move, okay?"

Evie gave him a quick nod before snuggling down under the covers.

Their bags were sitting inside the front door, courtesy of the guard from downstairs per the note identifying the specific times when he had entered and left the flat. Cole tossed the piece of paper on the kitchen counter before seizing the bags and a bottle of water from the refrigerator and walking back into the bedroom.

Evie was still in bed but not where he had left her. Instead, she was seated on the edge, the blankets draped around her shoulders and a look of bewilderment on her face. "Do you hear that?"

Cole started to ask what he was supposed to be hearing, but the instant the apartment fell silent, he heard the roar from outside. "What the fuck?" Dropping their luggage, he strode to the window. Silently, Evie joined him, and they looked in horror through the window at a towering plume of lava in the distance.

"Does Hungary have volcanoes?" Evie asked. "I didn't think it did."

Cole shook his head. "I don't know of any. I know it's famed for its volcanic-region wines, but those were from the age of the dinosaurs." That random knowledge thanks to the labels on expensive bottles of wine from thankful clients.

"Cole." Evie's voice was low and urgent. "Did we do that?"

He wanted desperately to reassure her, tell her that it definitely wasn't them. But, although he wasn't sure they had caused the lava spraying in a country with no active or dormant volcanoes, it was a good bet they had. "Yeah, I... um, I think we did."

They stood in silence, staring at the still spewing column of lava, so far in the distance it was hazy and obscured behind clouds and mountains but still there. Down below, screams of panic and the ambient noise of sirens joined the unsettling soundtrack of the volcano's eruption.

Evie glanced up at him. "I'm pretty sure Hungary just told us where we're supposed to go, huh?" Her lips quivered a little bit, almost as if she was considering laughing but couldn't bring herself to do so. "Guess we don't need to call the Moirai for that answer then."

"Seems like it." Wrapping his arm around her waist, Cole hugged Evie into him, brushed a kiss over her temple. "I guess the Underworld awaits, my queen."

Chapter 55

Cole

Ciomadul, Carpathian Mountains, Romania

As it turned out, they did have to call the Moirai.

In a truly annoying turn of events, the lava they had seen from the window was not in Budapest. It wasn't even in fucking Hungary, a fact they discovered once he started surfing the web to figure out a heading more specific than "somewhere that way towards the blazing lava." "Hungary," an annoyed official informed him in a snide tone, "doesn't have volcanoes."

After some extensive searching on the web, they confirmed that, no, Hungary did not, in fact, have volcanoes. But its neighboring country, Romania, did have a 30,000 year dormant volcano, which, as of that morning at 6:42 A.M., according to social media, was now active. So, a long story short, the supposed entrance to the Underworld was in Romania, an almost ten hour drive from their flat.

He had already called and lectured the Moirai, who hung up on him a total of three times before Essi apologized for the wild goose chase to Budapest and confirmed the Romanian volcano was the entrance to the Underworld. Cleo told him to fuck off several times before Essi shooed her away, and Addy hadn't even been home.

After quick separate showers so they didn't get distracted, they got dressed, took one last look at the antique headboard Evie had melted and disregarded it as a lost cause, then called a cab to take them back to the airfield, from which they flew to a private airstrip just outside of Brasov in Romania. Once they landed, Evie agreed under protest that the jet was a convenient travel method.

The only positive of the whole mistaken location was that it made a compelling argument for Evie and him to keep the private jet, which reduced the nine hours of car time to just over an hour of flight time.

Hayden arranged for a rental car to be at the airfield since no company would willingly send one of their drivers to transport a couple to an active volcano site. Something about not putting their employees in danger. So now, they were well into an hour-and-a-half drive from Brasov to Ciomadual, the volcano that had erupted with no warning after 30,000 years of dormancy, only fifteen kilometers away from the airstrip. Unlike the rest of their trip, where there were cars on the road and evidence of life, the closer they got to Ciomadul, the more apocalyptic the environs surrounding them looked.

The road was coated in ash, the sky above it practically blotted out by smoke. Visibility was absolute shit, so bad that Cole couldn't see more than three feet in front of the car. At this point, he was using magic to guide them around the sharply curving roadways of the Carpathian Mountains because his eyes couldn't see far enough ahead to keep them safe. Out of the corner of his eye, he could see Evie chewing on her lower lip, concern splashed across her face. He reached out, running a hand across the top of her thigh. "We're gonna get there safely."

She huffed out a sigh. "It's not that."

"Then what's wrong, Angel?"

Evie's gaze was locked on the wilderness outside of the window. "I can feel it." When she turned back to him, her eyes were wide and unfocused. "I can feel something—I guess it's magic. Almost like a tugging sensation. Here."

Placing a hand over her chest, she continued, "It's like it's pulling me towards the eruption site."

"I know," he confirmed. The same feeling was gathering in his gut, more intense with each mile they passed. "It's getting stronger." Her nod confirmed his own experience.

They drove for a little while longer until Evie sat straight up in her seat and said urgently, "Cole, stop. Now."

Cole stepped on the brakes, bringing the car to a sudden stop. With a quick pop of his finger, he clicked the car's start button, the sound of the engine dwindling into nothingness. Without its noise, the world was deathly quiet. Small flakes of ash rained silently around them, making no sound as they struck the car's metal exterior.

"We're here." Evie's words were pitched low. Raising her hand to the door handle, she made to open it, but Cole lunged across, grabbing her wrist before she could.

At her raised eyebrows, he pulled two handkerchiefs out of the glove compartment. "That's a carcinogenic minefield out there, little witch. We might as well be sucking exhaust fumes out of a tailpipe."

An inelegant snort burst from her, breaking the tension in the car. "You do that often, love?" Evie giggled, poking Cole in the ribs. "Is sucking exhaust fumes out of tailpipes not something I should be doing?" Her laughter wrapped around him, comforting and warm.

"I can think of something better for you to suck on, sweetheart."

Evie's eyes jumped to his, her pupils dilating in lust, her lips parting on a gasp.

With a smirk, he nipped her lower lip, savoring her small moan, before he pulled back, tying one of the handkerchiefs to cover her mouth and nose as he did so. Her eyes stared accusingly at him over her makeshift mask. "No worries, Angel, we'll have plenty of time for that later," he teased.

Evie growled at him in frustration as he tied his own makeshift mask. "I have no worries, but you probably should," she threatened. "Maybe I take a page out of your book and ward you down."

Cole lifted an eyebrow at her. "Oh, sweetheart, you've got a smart mouth that's gonna be put to good use. You know I love putting my bratty little witch back in her place."

Evie clenched her thighs together. "How about we go retrieve our thrones before I climb into this backseat, strip off all my clothes, and see if you can resist me when I'm fingering myself a foot away from you?"

Chuckling, Cole nodded. "Let's go then." As he got out of the car, he thought back to two weeks prior. Back when sex was a meaningless release, he thought the red-haired woman in his dreams was a fantasy he had made up, and he believed he would have to wed a total stranger to fulfill his fated destiny. Now, he craved his fiancée—the fiery woman from his dreams—with a brutal desire he had never felt before in his life, and, in a short hike, they would be taking the throne together, fulfilling a curse millennia in the making, staving off an apocalyptic end to their world, and gaining immortality for their trouble.

With Evie's hand clutched in his, they started the long treacherous walk in the direction of the magical tug they both felt at their cores. The volcano was still shrieking overhead, flinging chunks of molten lava like they were grenades. Molten pools of magma, burning the brilliant reds, oranges, and yellows of a sunset, oozed towards and around them. It almost seemed to shy away from them as if even the lava flows recognized them and what they were doing there.

A faint whining, almost doglike, came from in front of them just as they emerged from the burning trees into an open, plain-like area bordering a lake. While the idea of a dog in the mountains was strange, Cole was distracted from the odd noise by the hellish lakefront in front of them. Although the water was probably serene, the area idyllic, on a normal day, now it was bubbling, smoke rising from it as it seemed to boil from underneath while flaming streaks of lava soared into it from above. A deep blue hue illuminated the water from beneath, giving it a sinister appearance.

Evie walked carefully towards the lake, Cole following closely behind. Without looking at him, she extended one foot towards the boiling lake, sending Cole scrambling to whisk her into his arms, staring down at her in disbelief once he was holding her. "Angel, just a question," he commented casually, doing his best to sound calm. "Um, what, what exactly was your plan here?"

Shifting in his arms enough to meet his eyes, she cast him a severe look. "The entry's under the volcano, Cole. I can feel it calling to me, and I, well, I can't explain it, but I need to go into the lake." She gave a little wiggle, almost as if she were testing the tightness of his hold,

He swatted her softly on the ass for it. "Just a thought." Despite her increasing struggles to get out of his arms, Cole held her easily. "Maybe skinny dipping in a boiling lake can be our plan B?"

"My love, don't be silly." She patted his cheek, somehow making the motion simultaneously reassuring and condescending. "I was going to keep my clothes on when I went into the lake."

Cole could hear grinding in his head; it took a moment for him to realize he was gritting his teeth hard enough to wear down enamel. "My absolute pardon, Angel. I can't believe I was concerned about the wrong part of this equation. Obviously, clothes are the biggest issue here, not the whole 'stepping into a lake of lava' thing."

"I'm glad you see where I'm coming from." Evie smirked at him. "Now put me down." In response to his head shake, she pursued her lips, narrowing her eyes at him. "Put me down, Cole. I know what I'm doing. You need to trust me on this."

Cole's heart stopped in his chest. Had she used any other tool in her arsenal—whether it be sensuality, magic, tears, whatever—he could have easily resisted it. But his witch was asking him to trust her. As her partner, he had to trust her decisions. As her spouse, he had to trust her with his heart. As her king, he had to trust his queen in all aspects of their domain. It all came down to trust, didn't it? "So my choice is to let the love of my life walk into a lake that may flash cook her or let her know I don't trust her." It wasn't a question.

Evie's responding smile was far too smug. "Pretty much."

On a deep sigh, he loosened his arms, letting his beloved witch slide to the ground at her own pace. Her feet finally landed on the soft earth, but she didn't walk into the water immediately. Instead, she rested her hand gently on his cheek, drawing him into her. "It's going to be alright, my love," she whispered to him. "This is what we're meant to do."

Cole nodded slightly, drinking in the sight of Evie standing before him as if it might be his last. A slight smile on her face, she turned, but before she could even step away, he hauled her back into his arms, crashing his lips down over hers. She gasped softly at the intensity, and, without a second thought, he slipped his tongue into her mouth, taking in the sweet taste of her. It was a rough, sloppy kiss, full of urgency and passion, and over far too soon.

He drew away, cupping the back of her neck tightly. "I love you, Angel, and I trust you with my life, but you better fucking be right about this. Because if I lose you, I will raze this goddamned earth to the ground to bring you back." He stared into her beautiful eyes, lit blazing blue and molten gold as she drew on both her magical sources.

"I'm right, my love." She drew away, turned back towards the lake, which had somehow only grown more intense in its rumbling and bubbling. "Let me prove it to you."

Cole was practically shaking, but Evie kept one hand in his, which calmed him. Somewhat. "*Ouais*," he heard himself say. "*Ouais*, let's do this, *ma petite sorcière*." He stepped next to her. "Together, though. "

Evie gave him a brilliant smile that practically stopped his heart before leading him towards the lake. A small step forward into the roiling, lava-riddled water sealed their fate. But while he expected the water to be liquid fire, it was lukewarm where it lapped around their ankles. Evie took another slow step forward, and he followed her.

A small splash drew their attention to the center of the lake. Nothing was there, though. Then another splash, larger this time. Cole raised an eyebrow in confusion, prepared to drag Evie from a new, potentially more dangerous situation, when a plume of water geysered uncontrollably out of the lake. Under their feet, the ground began rumbling. Cracks splintered around the grassy area surrounding the lake itself, steam exploding from the fissures.

"Good or bad sign?" he asked Evie.

Before she could answer, the earth around them emitted a massive crashing sound. The boiling waters split from where they were standing to the base of the volcano, revealing a dark muddy path with a steep incline that ran from the lake's edge to under the mountain itself and into the void beyond. The water parted around them was dark, practically black, but an inexplicable blue light shone along the pathway. It was the same blue currently lighting both their eyes; death magic powered this.

If he needed any further proof that this was the way, it was answered by the tendrils of magic currently threading themselves around him, through him. Even living across from a cemetery, he had never felt his source anywhere near this powerful. The hair stood along his neck, and goosebumps rose along his arms. He was also rapidly hardening under the onslaught of magic; his body didn't seem to understand that this intense full-body arousal wasn't sexual in nature.

Evie's jaw dropped in shock. "Cole?" Her voice was breathy. He imagined that she could feel the same unfiltered power coursing through her veins, the same overwhelming arousal causing her to soak the lace panties he had laid out for her before they left this morning.

Hell, he wanted to slip a hand under her jeans and see just how wet she was, would have happily dragged her down to the mud and fucked her while they were high on their magical source, if the rational part of his brain wasn't reminding him that time was definitely a factor. He shook his head unhappily, satisfying himself by running his thumb along her wrist and watching her shudder. "I'll make it up to you for leaving you unsatisfied later," he murmured into her ear.

Her eyes were hazy with lust, but her voice was crystal clear, her smile taunting when she looked up at him and responded, "You better."

Cole threw back his head and laughed, tugging Evie along with him down the exposed path.

A loud shout came from the bank. They both paused then shrugged, continuing down the path. The shout sounded again, this time clearer. "*Aidoneus*!"

Cole stopped, turning towards the shore. Who the fuck was calling his last name? His eyes raked along the lake edge, the open field, until his gaze came to a massive group of women gathered by the trees surrounding the clearing. Fury radiated from them, toxic even at this distance. A low murmur rose from the women, lulling, almost a chant.

"Mother of witches, no!" Evie cursed.

He was about to ask her what was going on when fire exploded around them. In seconds, his vision was obscured by a wall of fire, ears ringing, skin burning. Evie let out a shrill, fear-laced scream, and then her hand, held so tightly in his own, was gone. Roaring, mind blank with rage at the idea that someone would take *his fucking Angel*, he lunged for the last place he had seen her. A second scream pierced through the sound of blood rushing through his ears, and then his world went black.

Chapter 56

Cole

Ciomadul, Carpathian Mountains, Romania

His eyesight came back slowly. His hearing followed. Rational thought never returned. He couldn't remember his own fucking name, much less why he was here. The only thing he remembered was his Angel. His heart seized in pain and fury.

His witch was *fucking gone*. One minute she was holding his hand, the next the world burst into flames. *And then his Angel was gone*. He heard her scream, felt her hand rip from his. *They fucking took her from me*.

He was lying on the ground, a roaring in his ears, his vision lit with the familiar blue of his magic. Blood trailed down one of his arms, pooling along his fingers and into the dirt beneath him. His leg sat at an awkward angle with bone jutting out of a sharp gash. Broken? Perhaps. But he couldn't let that get in his way. The women who took his witch from him were going to pay for what they had done.

He didn't know whether his Angel was dead, but he couldn't detect the warm, comforting feeling of her existence in his heart. *They fucking took her*.

Rolling to his stomach, he tried to push himself to a stand, but his broken leg wouldn't support his weight, and he fell back to the ground just as quickly as he had risen. A furious growl rolled from his mouth.

Almost as if in response to the sound, magic surged from far down the pathway leading under the volcano bank, slamming into his chest. He couldn't help the snarl of pain that emerged from him as he watched his leg snap into its proper placement, the bone slipping back in through the gaping wound. All over his body, he could feel skin knitting together, soothing the burns out of his skin, repairing his broken leg as the magic smoothed along his body until it had put him back together again.

Standing up silently, he strode back along the muddy path between the parted waters. He curled his lips back, baring his teeth in a feral smile that shone through the sticky remains of the blood still coating his face. They would pay for this. *They will die bloody for this.*

From the field in front of him, he could sense human bodies, buried deep under the earth, some still in early decay, some long since rendered to just bone. Ah, it seemed this was a killing field, some sort of unsanctioned burial ground. His lips spread wider, his mind turning over the options available to him. He could work with this unusual cemetery.

A howl sounded behind him, and he heard loud pounding, but his focus, his entire self, was narrowed in on the women staring at him from the edge of the lake. *They took his fucking Angel.* He was almost off the pathway and past the parted waters when something barreled into him from behind, hard enough to make him stumble but not fall.

He whirled, hands raised in preparation for an attack, but the only thing behind him was a massive, black three-headed dog with six glowing ruby-red eyes all laser focused on him. A tongue lolled happily from each mouth. The dog chuffed at him, a blast of hot breath on his face, and then dropped its chest to the ground, wriggling its lifted backside and single tiny tail excitedly. *You came for me!*

He stared at the dog in confusion, his thoughts slowing to an almost controllable buzz at the sound of a voice that wasn't his in the mix.

You came home!!! I've missed you! The dog shoved one of its heads under his palm, one of the other heads swiveling excitedly while the third head had turned its attention to the women on the banks. *Where's Lady! I want to see Lady!*

Was this dog *talking* to him??? That, more than anything else, forced his focus because dogs didn't fucking speak. His response scraped out of his throat. "Lady? Who is... do you mean my Angel?" He could think again, breathe again through the uncontrollable fury.

Beautiful, red-headed Lady! Where is Lady!

"She's... " His breath caught in his throat and his heart shattered. *My witch is gone.* When the words poured out of him, his voice was brutal and dark, ending on a snarl. "*They fucking took her from me.*" His focus blurred as he said it out loud. *They'll die fucking bloody.*

The dog lifted from its sploot on the ground, its heads rising above his own as it raised to its full height. *They took Lady?* At his sharp nod, the dog's red eyes darkened to a bloody crimson, glowing like fire, and a threatening growl rumbled from deep in its barrel chest before it poured out through each set of bared teeth. The rough fur along its back bristled, standing on edge.

He placed a hand on the dog's neck, turning back to the women who were still standing at the water's edge. With absolute certainty, he knew that this dog would follow his lead. His voice was distorted when he whispered in one of the dog's ears, "Let's make them die bloody." The canine snarled in response.

Lifting his hands, he scattered his power across the field, digging it down into the dirt surrounding him. "Answer my call," he shouted to the bodies surrounding him. Magic crackled around him as corpses long buried crawled from their places deep under the grass to follow him into battle. Gnarled hands broke through the surface, their owners dragging themselves from the ground.

The ones still formed and capable of standing ranged around him and the dog. The others were crawling along the ground towards the women at the treeline.

"Destroy them," he ordered. The bodies silently followed his bidding, racing towards the group with bloody-minded intent.

Magic rolling through him, he followed his dead army into the fray. Ash exploded around him as he laid his hands on the first woman, the second, the third, over and over until he lost count, forcing decay to overtake them, dissolving them into nothing. Their screams of pain filled his ears, a symphony of death that brought glee to his racing mind. A dark smile rose to his grimy face as he watched the dog rip one of the women into shreds.

Through it all, only one thought echoed through his mind. *They will fucking pay for what they took from me.*

Chapter 57

Evie

Ciomadul, Carpathian Mountains, Romania

Evie moaned and rolled over, her back spasming at the movement. Long cuts lined her body, and claw marks pierced her torso. Hissing, Evie sat up slowly, trying to determine whether she had any other more significant wounds. From what she could tell, no breaks, just bruises, gashes, burns, and puncture marks. Godsdamned serpents.

She had seen the gilded drakes sweeping above them seconds before they spewed their flames all over her and Cole. She screamed in surprise and then in pain when one of the monsters snatched her from where she stood, ripping her hand from Cole's and sweeping her away over the trees. She had only escaped when, in a fit of rage, she loosed a stream of magic that struck the drake in the eye. Screaming in pain, the thing had dropped her; she had half a second to force the trees she was hurtling towards to lift their limbs to slow her descent. Fortunately, they did actually slow her enough that she didn't burst like a ripe watermelon when she hit the ground. Unfortunately, many of the branches broke, one of which was currently stabbing into her waist, and she had blacked out before her less-than-graceful landing.

Taking a deep breath, she tugged at the branch piercing her waist, a short yelp escaping her as she tore it from her flesh. Fucking nine realms, that hurt. Now that she no longer had plant life inside of her, though, she started panicking. Cole wasn't with her. She had no idea how far the drakes had taken her, had no clue how long she had been unconscious. What if Cole was... she shied away from completing the thought. No. She couldn't think about that right now. If she let herself anywhere near the idea that Cole might be gone, she would go mad sitting here on the forest floor in the middle of the Carpathian mountains.

Although why the devil snakes would attack them, she had no idea. Only a powerful witch could control drakes. Why would a witch of that caliber be interested in destroying her and Cole? But she had seen witches ranged along the tree line before the drakes showed up. She clenched her eyes shut, pressing her palms to them in an effort to make it make sense. She couldn't puzzle any of this out. At the end of the day, though, it didn't really matter why. All that mattered was that she get back to Cole.

Evie forced herself to her feet, slowly bringing herself to a full stand. The world spun around her, and she stumbled inelegantly, almost tumbling to the ground. Her fall was broken by a tree extending a willowy branch to wrap around her waist before she could drop. As she stayed put, standing but not moving, supported by the branch, her head slowly stopped spinning. "Thank you," she whispered to the tree limb as it slowly drew back from her.

The forest was deadly quiet, the ash providing an overwhelming barrier against all sound. Even her own hesitant steps were muffled. The only thing she could hear with clarity was the still-shrieking volcano. So those damn drakes hadn't dropped her in another country. A small victory. The thrumming from the Underworld entrance still pulsed through her like another heartbeat, guiding her steps towards the volcano.

The birds and other wildlife had been run out of the forest by the natural disaster. While many may have escaped, she could feel the corpses of those that hadn't moved quickly enough, burned and twisted beyond recognition by the lava flows still streaming steadily down the mountain.

Her steps were weak, each one leaving a small trail of blood behind her. From each blood speck, a new tree grew, increasing from the size of a sapling to a fully established tree to decay in just minutes. The full spectrum of life, all from a small drop of her blood. With each tree's death, though, she felt the magic seep from it into her, wound after wound knitting itself shut in this way until, after a few hundred steps, her injuries were completely healed. Her skin was still coated in blood, but she didn't care. There was no need for cleanliness. Once she returned to the crater site, to the witches who had endangered Cole, she would bathe in their blood.

To her right, a branch cracked loudly. She whirled towards the sound, already summoning trees to her aid but stared in confusion when she saw Hecate. "Cate?" Her voice faltered as the goddess she had met at Cole's uncle's house stepped towards her.

That day, Cate had been collected and cool. Now, though, she appeared unhinged. Her black hair was disheveled and tangled, falling unevenly around her shoulders, and her perfectly applied eyeliner was heavily smudged around her eyes, giving her a gaunt look. Shadows followed her every move, thick and heavy, cloaking her from head to toe. Most noticeable, though, were her eyes themselves, glowing violet in the ashen afternoon, a tangible madness festering within their depths.

For a moment, Evie forgot about everything that had happened: the attack, the witches at the lake's edge, all of it. "Cate!" she exclaimed, rushing towards the goddess. Halfway to her, Evie stopped, her mind catching up, flinching at the memory of plummeting to the earth after freeing herself from the drakes. Drakes that had to be controlled by a powerful witch. Cate was a member of the Witches Council Judiciary. The goddess of witches. Surely if a powerful witch were involved in a murder attempt involving the flying serpents from hell, she would know about it? Evie stood frozen, mere feet away from Cate, unsure. Could she trust her?

"They found you, didn't they?" The goddess' voice was throaty, a raspiness that spoke of screaming rather than sensuality.

Evie nodded. "They did." She hesitated for only a second before asking, "What happened? Why are there witches here?"

"After the Council vote that I warned you about, the traditionalists took matters into their own hands. They were led by Medea and Circe. They believed the only way to follow the prophecy to the letter was to kill you and Cole, so that the two of you couldn't interfere with the execution of their plan." As if to herself, Cate muttered, "Not that *killing* the old gods was ever part of the fucking prophecy."

Well, that would explain the gilded drakes. Legend had it that Medea controlled two of them, but those who knew they existed weren't exactly around to tell the tale. But both witches were members of the Judiciary with Cate. What if she was part of this? Evie drew her shoulders back. "Were you a part of their plans?"

"*Never.*" Hecate's eyes flashed, the shadows surrounding her flaring around her head like a viper's hood. "Those *cowards* waited to attack until I left to warn you and Cole of the Council's vote on the prophecy. I only discovered the slaughter when I was summoned back to the chambers and saw my beautiful daughters... " Her words trailed off, her eyes going blank.

"What slaughter?" The goddess remained silent. "What fucking slaughter, Cate?"

"Language, my dear girl," a familiar voice chastised from behind the catatonic goddess. Hesteia stepped out from around Cate, her face seeming older than it had the last time Evie saw her.

Evie choked out a sob and raced towards one of the constants in her life, throwing her arms around the elder's neck.

Running a hand down Evie's back, Hesteia answered her earlier question. "The Council was voting on whether you and your gentleman friend—" Evie tugged away to give Hesteia an appalled stare at her choice of words. "—were the old gods returned to initiate the witches' prophecy and, if so, whether we must adhere to the prophecy's requirements." Sighing, she continued. "The vote was tied, and the Judiciary didn't have a unanimous vote either way. Hecate left to warn you and Cole of the Council's actions, and, while she was gone, Medea and Circe led the traditionalists in a massacre of the elders who voted against them. We—" she gestured to the small group now surrounding them. "—are all that's left of the elders who opposed carrying out the prophecy."

"Where's Chloe?" Evie's eyes scanned the crowd. "Thea? Adelaide? Bernadette?"

"Evie, my love, I'm here." Thea sprinted towards her, grasping the younger witch's hands to draw her in to a firm hug. "And Ette is right over there."

"Thea, Ette, and I survived." Hesteia wrapped an arm around her wife. "But, Evie, gods, I'm so sorry, Evie. Chloe died in the massacre."

"What?" Evie shook her head. "No, that can't be right. Chloe was a powerful witch. She never would have... " Her eyes caught on Hesteia's broken expression. "No. You must be mistaken."

"I'm not, darling." Hesteia's response was heavy with emotion. "I saw it with my own eyes. I was there when she took her last breath. She's gone, Evie. I'm so sorry."

Evie's mouth trembled. No matter what had happened between them, no matter what Chloe had hidden, she wasn't ready for her adoptive mother to be dead. Not after they left their last conversation the way that they had. Tears pressed against the corners of her eyes. The closest thing she had to a mother was gone. At that realization, her tears fell, quick and heavy down her cheeks. Raising a shaking, bloody hand to her face, Evie swiped them away viciously. "And Adelaide?"

"Adelaide... she didn't make it, either. The small group of elders before you? We're all that's left. We may have all trained to fight, but we weren't prepared for this." One of the younger elders whimpered, a horrifying soundtrack to Hesteia's next statement. "The Council is now spearheaded by our most extreme bigots, and the more moderate covens are leaderless."

Evie's eyes hardened, her head tilting. "Let me get this straight," she began, disbelief dripping from every word. "You are allied with the goddess of witches who so aggressively opposes the outcome of the prophecy that she was willing to align herself with the 'returned old gods.'" Her hands flew up into scare quotes on those words before dropping back to her sides. "And you have the 'old gods' themselves on your side. But you think that the new generation covens are leaderless?" A harsh laugh echoed from her mouth, completely devoid of humor. "That's asinine."

Hesteia jerked backwards. "Evie, I don't think you under—"

"Don't coddle me, Hesteia, I understand far more than you think," Evie snapped, pursing her lips as realization dawned on her. "Including that I imagine these Council and Judiciary traditionalists, specifically Medea and Circe, were the ones who forced you all to sterilize and perform memory regressions on me."

Beside them, Cate finally moved, shocked out of her stupor. "Yes. After Cassandra had her vision when your elders found you, certain Council members were concerned about letting you join a coven. They were overruled by an overwhelming number, but Medea forced the Draconian measures you just mentioned to a vote by the Judiciary. Circe concurred."

"Well, you may want to steer clear of Cole once we get back to the lake. His feelings towards the Witches Council are still somewhat homicidal at the moment." Evie drew her shoulders back. "Wait, how did you find me?"

"The traditionalists scryed for you, and Hesteia overheard where you were."

"But we were in Budapest. We didn't get to Romania until... you know what? I don't care how you found us. I need to get back to Cole. Now." Evie strode in the direction of the magical tug from the Underworld. "Medea's drakes attacked us just when we found the path to the Underworld. Those golden flying assholes grabbed me right after they spewed fire on us, and I don't... " Her fire tapered off a bit, but she kept walking. "I don't know what happened to him." She couldn't lose Cole. Not only that, but she wouldn't lose him on the same day Chloe was taken from her. It wasn't happening. As she realized the depths of the anguish she felt at Chloe's loss, her choice to take the throne with Cole became even more clearly the right one. Death was a part of life, but she wouldn't be party to people's needless suffering at the witches' bloodthirsty interpretation of an ambiguous prophecy. That is if Cole was still alive. She stumbled as fear flooded her but caught her footing and sped up. Tears still rolled down her face, but her purpose was clear. Get back to Cole. Claim the Underworld. Destroy the traditionalist elders.

Sensing her panic at Cole's fate, Hesteia jogged to her. "It's alright, my darling," she murmured breathlessly as she tried to keep up with Evie's rapid pace. "You'll be back with him soon."

"And you've brought reinforcements." Cate's eyes were hard, glowing amethysts made more astonishing by the darkness surrounding her. "I have but one request, Queen of the Underworld."

Evie's eyes darted around before she realized Cate was referring to her. Trying to compose herself, she answered, "And that is?"

Cate's expression was mutinous. "I want to be the one to dispatch Medea and Circe. Let me be the one to destroy their bodies before you and Cole throw their souls into the depths of Tartarus."

Evie inclined her head in agreement then shouted to the rest of the group, "You heard her! Cate gets Medea and Circe. You may have any of the rest." Catching sight of open air past the trees, she raced to its edge only to stop in astonishment at the sight of a blood-drenched Cole wearing an evil smile and turning a witch into ash with a single touch, a massive three-headed dog with a woman's torso dangling from its mouth, and a sea of corpses attacking the mutinous elders.

Chapter 58

Cole

Ciomadul, Carpathian Mountains, Romania

He was covered in blood. Had ripped out more than one witch's heart with his bare hands. His hair and clothes were liberally coated in ash, thanks both to the cloud of volcanic ash overhead and the witches he was disintegrating with the death magic coursing through his blood. A feral grin extended across his face, a raucous laugh bursting from him, as he watched another witch splinter and shatter into dust in front of him. *They fucking took my Angel—*

His heartbeat slowed suddenly. He blinked. He could breathe fully again. The first full inhale he took brought with it orange and cinnamon with the faintest hint of fire.

Cole could think again, although he didn't know the cause. But he could smell his witch, that spice and citrus scent unique to her. His eyes scanned the blood-soaked field, passed over the witches still fighting corpses and a hooded figure that he didn't remember being there when all this started, the three-headed dog... where the fuck was she? He knew that he would descend into madness if she died, but he didn't expect mental clarity while he did so.

Finally, he turned, staring at the behind him. There, by the wilderness' edge, was another gathering of witches. Far out in front of them, tearing across the field in a full sprint, was a small blur, auburn curls streaming behind it. Evie.

She's a-fucking-live. In the time it took him to recognize what was happening, she had already crossed the battlefield. Before he could move, Evie had taken a flying leap, her face buried in his neck, legs wrapped around his waist, body shaking against his.

He plunged his hands into her hair, threading his fingers through her thick curls, relished that silky smoothness he thought he would never touch again. "Fuck, Angel, I thought you were dead," he whispered, voice cracking. "I can't fucking do that again, sweetheart, please don't ever leave me again." Tears were running down his face, drawing tracks through the filth coating his skin.

Evie was sobbing. "It w—w—w—wasn't intentional," she gasped out.

He snorted at her response, the sound a bit wetter than usual given his tears. "Ever a brat I see, *mon amour.*" Her lips tilted upward, not quite a full smile—there was too much anguish in her eyes for it to be that—but still enough to make his chest tighten at the familiarity of the expression.

"As sweet as it is to see the two of you together once more—" A voice floated up to him. He looked down to where a familiar looking witch, hands wreathed in fire. stared up at them in mild disapproval. "Maybe you should claim your throne before the dissenters take advantage of your distraction."

"Perhaps," Cate commented, calling her familiars to her side. "You could leave Cerberus with us to help take care of these murderers."

"He's all yours," Cole responded before glancing down at the precious package in his arms. "You gonna make me carry you to our throne or what?"

"Might as well." She sniffled, tears finally ebbing as he took a firm grip on her ass—for stability, obviously—and set off towards the pathway under the volcano. "Sets a good precedent that you're at my beck and call for the rest of our immortal lives."

"Sweetheart, I don't think there's any doubt that I'm going to be wrapped around your finger for the rest of eternity, but I'm still happy to carry you." The screams and sounds of battle fell away as they walked through the mud, finally crossing under the threshold of the volcanic bank. "Are you hurt?" His eyes scanned her face for injury.

"I... well, physically, I'm fine." Evie tightened her arms around his neck, bringing her body closer to his in a desperate hug. "But emotionally? That's another story." Her eyes glowed up at him. "The witches who attacked us—the traditionalist elders—they slaughtered the witches who opposed fulfilling the prophecy. So many of them." A lone sob escaped her.

Cole inhaled sharply. "What?"

Evie nodded, tears pouring down her face once more. Each one broke him a little bit. "They murdered Chloe."

"Sweetheart." He stopped, staring at her. "They killed your mother?"

"Yes. Hesteia saw it. She's gone, just like that, and the last things I ever said to her were accusations. And then they came to execute you. Us. So that we couldn't take the throne and stop their prophecy."

Standing in the middle of the path to the Underworld, he squeezed her to him hard, letting his witch sob every emotion, every trauma, every horror, into his chest. For all that he wanted to turn right back around and finish the annihilation he had started so he could make the Council pay for everything they had done to her, Evie needed him to be strong for her. To be *here* for her.

It seemed like hours in the dark tunnel before her tears dried, but he held her through all of it.

"Tell me what you need, Angel." He stroked a tear from her cheek. "Tell me whatever you need from me, and I'll make it happen."

Evie looked up at him, her eyes still glittering with despair but dry. "I need us—" Her voice hit hard in emphasis on that one word. "To go take our throne, my love. We need to seize our immortality and prove to these traditionalist assholes that their horrifying, murderous time is *done*."

Cole gazed down at his fierce witch. "You're amazing, *mon ange*." With that, he obeyed his queen's orders and kept walking.

The pathway had a sharp decline, descending further and further beneath the earth. Lights in varying shades of blue, ranging from a pale, almost white blue to the cobalt of their magic, floated along in front of them, providing barely enough illumination for him to see where he was walking.

They walked miles, so far that Evie finally dropped from his arms to walk next to him, before they came upon a river that stretched as far as the eye could see. The water was dark as night, small glimpses of starlight winking at them from its depths as it flowed gently downwards. At the water's edge sat a small wooden boat in alarming disrepair; in it sat a tall man, skin as dark as the river in which his boat sat. As he lifted his gaunt face towards them, eyes the color of molten gold settled upon them. His rough voice was warm when he spoke. "My lord? My lady? Is it really you? Have you returned after all these years?"

"In a way. We're Kore and Aidoneus' reincarnates, but we're distinct from them if that makes any sense. I'm Evie, and this—" Evie fluttered a hand at Cole, who seized it and drew his witch back into him. "—is Cole." She gave the man a small smile. "And you must be Charon?"

"I am." His thin lips stretched wide in happiness. "You look so like them but not. You, Queen Evie and King Cole, have lived much different lives than they did. It's all in the eyes." Charon stood, drawing to his full height—which stood well above Cole's own 6'5"—his long robes unfurling around him with the movement. "May I escort you to your throne, my lord and lady?"

Cole nodded. "Please. It's a matter of some urgency that we get there quickly."

Charon chortled as they settled into the boat. "I imagine it must be, given the urgency with which the young pup raced out of here." He withdrew a long pole from the interior of his cloak, digging it into the water to set them on their way. "He hasn't been that excitable in many years. Not since the last time he was summoned to protect the Underworld's royalty."

Evie looked up at him. "Do you know when that was?"

"Why, when you were just a small babe, my lady." Charon's movements were effortless, his pole lifting in and out of the water elegantly. The boat sped along, the rock face on either side of them a blur. Even with his attention on navigating them along the poorly-illuminated river, the boatman still noticed Evie's eyes widen in shock. "I have waited for your return for many millennia. With each new generation, I watched the five rivers for a sign that the rulers of the Underworld had been reborn. When your mother decided to abandon you and she died upon laying her hand on you, I saw it in the river's depths and knew who you were. It's my duty to protect you. So I sent Cerberus to care for you, watch over you, until you were safe." He smiled gently. "The young pup has loved you both from afar for many years since then, often—pardon my pun—hounding me to go to the surface to see you until you returned to claim your thrones."

Charon tapped his pole against the river's edge, slowing their speed enough for the boat to nose gently against the shoreline. "Here is your stop, your highnesses." He bowed reverently to them as they stepped out. "I am happy to see your safe return." When he stood, tears had formed at the edges of his arresting eyes. "I loved your predecessors as my own kin and have missed them dearly. I look forward to having a similar relationship with you both."

Cole nodded, arm wrapped around Evie, watching Charon disappear into the darkness before either of them could answer. Evie turned in his arms, raising her eyes to his. Even covered in blood, ash, and other unrecognizable substances, she was still the most stunning woman he had ever seen. More so for that glimpse aboveground, however brief, of what his life would be like without her. Tucking a stray curl behind her ear, he asked quietly, "Shall we?"

Her eyes sparkled up at him. "I think we shall."

And together, they turned to face the looming gates of the Underworld.

Chapter 59

Evie

The Gates of the Underworld

Evie wished her first response upon seeing the gates of the Underworld had been something other than a whispered, "Mother of fucking witches," but alas, it was not. To be fair, her response was more poetic than Cole's yelped, "Holy fuck, Gondor wants its statues back," which was something but not much.

The Underworld's entrance was blocked by a four-story high filigree city gate that spanned the entire width and height of the rocky chamber in which they stood. Directly to the left and right of the comparatively small wicket doors nestled inside the Underworld gates were two statues that closely resembled a modern-day Grim Reaper, cowl drawn over his features and scythe facing outward. The overall effect was unnerving to say the least.

The doors were thrown wide open. No surprise, given both the Underworld's closed-for-business status for the last several millennia and the mass exodus of all the souls in the Underworld save those in Tartarus. From where they were standing, she could see glimmers of light glinting from between the doors.

Seizing Cole's hand, she walked him towards the open doors. Her brain told her that, if they kept standing there, they might both run screaming down the tunnel out of sheer intimidation at the task before them. As they strolled through the gates, an air of false casualness about them, a wave of rightness swept through her just before magic crashed through her, piercing her, settling deep inside her. Her breath caught in her throat; her skin felt like it was two sizes too tight, an intense ache settling between her legs. Cole's muffled groan and tented jeans confirmed that he felt the same.

"Gods," she whispered. More than anything, she wanted to tackle Cole to the ground and ride him until they were both relieved of this ache, but they were on a time crunch. The battle to execute them and jumpstart the apocalypse, courtesy of an absurd, unrecorded ancient prophecy and lunatic witches, still raged miles above their heads. As long as their throne remained unclaimed, the more plausible it was that somebody could summon them away. As long as they remained mortal, any assassination attempt would most likely be extremely permanent. But she couldn't tear her eyes away from Cole.

"Angel." Her name was a growl. "We gotta get moving." She didn't move. Cole stepped towards her. "As much as I love it when you look at me like that, we have some things to take care of before I can take advantage of that eye fucking you're giving me."

Nodding, she bit down on her lip. Tore her gaze away from his and turned, finally taking in the sight before them.

The Underworld was mostly barren, a dark wasteland lit only by floating blue orbs. A slight breeze blew, teasing the black grass underfoot and lightly shifting her hair, but, in the gaping emptiness before them, the wind sounded more intense than it really was, its powerful song loud around them. She couldn't see any residences or souls or plant life. And yet, deep in her soul, she could sense a powerful tree, its roots sunk deep in the volcanic soil.

Without a word, Evie peeled off in the direction of the plant she had sensed. Its magical signature pounded in her head, blurring out all other thoughts and sounds. She knew Cole was behind her, could feel his hand still tight around hers, but she couldn't hear anything he was doing or saying. The one plant in a city of death owned her focus for the moment.

It wasn't long until they saw the building, a towering edifice built similarly to some of the Gothic cathedrals, that took them far longer to reach than to see it. When they finally arrived at its doors, Evie looked up. And up and up and up. What set the building apart wasn't its size or its existence as the only structure they had seen so far. What made it unique was the massive tree extending up through and far above where the roof should be, its thick limbs extending through the windows. The tree looked dead, but... that didn't make sense. She could *feel* it, living and breathing, as real as Cole beside her.

"Should we go in?" Cole asked hesitantly.

She understood his hesitation. Everything about the building was intimidating, especially now that they were standing only feet away from it. Was this how Kore and Aidoneus had ruled all those years ago? With intimidation and might? Somber gargoyles glowered down at them from their perches along the roofline, and she could see fragments of white that looked like bone baked into the black bricks that composed the building. She shivered, this time with alarm, and Cole drew her back into his chest, arm sliding around her waist. This building wasn't made for comfort or welcome. It was made for punishment.

"I don't kn—" She stopped as magic slithered across her skin. A compulsion. They needed to go in. This was a necessary step of their journey. "Yes. Yes, we need to go in."

Cole stepped out from behind her. "Let me go in first." At her incredulous expression and irritated grunt, he clicked his tongue. "We don't know what's in there. If there's something dangerous, I want to be its target, not you." Her eyebrows rose further at his response. "We're equals. I learned my lesson on that one after I tried to hide you in our bedroom when Cate came calling at the witchin' hour. Just play along with me, okay, Angel? I've already almost lost you once today, and it fucking broke me. I need to protect you. Please."

Her heart beat faster at the stark expression on his face. "You aren't the only one who thought they lost everything today. I actually did lose my adoptive mother and one of the other coven elders who raised me, in addition to thinking, for however brief a time, that I may have lost you. I had no idea whether you were still alive when I woke up after the drakes dropped me." She rested her hand on his forearm, stroking it gently. "Let's compromise. How about we go in together?"

His body tightened, but he nodded sharply. "Okay, let's... okay, we go in together. Same time." Before she could move, he grabbed the back of her shirt. "Same fuckin' time, Angel. We walk in that building at the same time or not at all."

"You're hot when you're bossy." Her response was intentionally bratty in an effort to relax him.

He chuffed out a laugh, the tension in his shoulders easing slightly. "Fucking hell, brat. Fine, let's go into this terrifying, probably deeply haunted building."

As one, they lifted their palms and pressed them to the doors. They opened evenly, unexpectedly silent as they swung inwards. They stepped over the threshold at the same time. Stepped slowly past where the doors ended.

As soon as they were in the building, a gust of wind blew through the large room, slamming the doors behind them. The sound of them crashing into place rattled the structure, the tree directly in front of them shaking with the force.

Evie could feel Cole tense with anxiety beside her, but the tree held her attention captive. In a blink, it had gone from decayed bleakness to sparkling with magic, the intense golds of her lunar magic and the neon blues of their shared death magic intertwining, skimming along the length of the trunk and up over the branches. Life followed the power, foliage and fruit blooming in its wake until the tree sat before them, alive and thriving.

A burst of color in the dark space, the tree now took up most of the center of the room. It was covered in lush, dark green leaves and, sprinkled throughout the new growth, were plump fruits with a scarlet skin.

"Pomegranates?" she asked just as Cole said wryly, "Seems a little on the nose."

Evie let out a short laugh. "I guess we eat the pomegranate seeds?"

Cole shrugged, snorting as he did so. "Makes as much sense as anything else we've done or seen today. Probably more so if we're supposed to tie our lives to the Underworld."

"And that's how Persephone did it in the lore, right?"

"Yeah. I mean... yeah?" Shoving a hand through his hair, he sighed. "But the family documents are annoyingly silent on what we have to do now. So it's all a guess. What if it's more Adam and Eve eat the apple than Persephone eats the pomegranate?"

"Well, then I guess we'll realize we're naked, cover ourselves in shame, and go back up to the earth where some of my sister witches will kill us so they can start an apocalypse without the old gods around to muck it up?" Evie snickered, ignoring his grumpy expression. "But we can't know if we don't try, right? We have to do *something*."

"Well, if eating this magically created fruit doesn't work, maybe we go find the thrones in this pile, instead, and I eat you out like you deserve." His voice dropped sensually.

"Oh, my love, that's still very much on the table." She blew a kiss at him, smiling as he retrieved one of the pomegranates from the tree and brought it back to her. With a quick punch of magic, he halved the fruit and split it open, brows wrinkling in confusion at its interior.

Instead of the garnet-colored arils that usually filled a pomegranate, they were a rich gold, glinting decadently in the ghostly light filling the building. Evie thumbed out a dozen of the seeds, passing six to Cole and keeping six for herself. He set the split pomegranate gently to the floor before taking them and glancing at her in a silent question.

She shrugged at his look over the amount. "It felt appropriate. Myth says that six pomegranate seeds kept Persephone here. Might as well keep up the tradition?"

A fond smile spread across Cole's face. "I fucking love you, Angel," he said, swooping in to give her a kiss that curled her toes and made her heart beat fast. He pulled away and glanced down at the seeds he held. "Bottoms up?"

"To eternity together, my love." She tilted her fist over her face, the golden arils sliding into her mouth at the same time that Cole ate his own. Sweet then tart flavors exploded in her mouth, richer than any pomegranate she had ever tasted before. A rush of wind blasted through the room but died down quickly. They chewed for a few seconds in silence before Evie spoke. "Is something supposed to happen then?" She glanced over, nearly choking at the sight of the crown, burnished silver in the shape of flames dotted with rich blue sapphires, that had appeared on Cole's head.

"I think it just did." He gestured to her own head.

Reaching up tentatively, her hands skimmed along a crown of her own, perched precariously atop her curly hair. She lifted it off her head, staring in amazement at the silver crown, more delicate than Cole's and inset with amber and sapphires. When she lifted her eyes back to Cole, he was holding his own crown, wearing a dubious expression.

"Feels a little pretentious, right? You think we have to wear these all the time?"

"I think we can rule however we want to, my love," Evie reassured him. "We can build an Underworld that makes sense to us. One of the many perks of having to start from the ground up." She glanced down at the crown in her hands in distaste. "And the trappings of royalty and the manipulations of power don't suit either of us so... we wear these things when we have to." A dark smile lit her face. "But we do need to check in on how Cate and the others are doing. Should we go above and show the traditionalists just how badly they've failed?"

"Just this once, I think I can wear a crown to make them feel inferior." Cole's smirk was as sinister as her own.

"I wonder if there's an easier way to get in and out?" Evie considered the glittering tree before them. "This tree has magical roots that run the entire length of the area we traveled. It's how I sensed it was here. I wonder if it has other abilities too?" She walked towards it, running her fingers along the bark of the trunk. "Do you have any other secrets to share, my darling?" she whispered. For a moment, her memory flashed to another time when she cooed to the Chanterelle mushrooms she had raised to feed her sisters. Then, she felt a whooshing of air next to her head. With a broad grin, she turned to what she knew instinctively was a portal out of the Underworld that had formed in the trunk of the tree. A quick glance through it revealed a field covered in blood.

Cole sauntered over, his crown perched back on his head, eyes sparkling with mischief and mayhem. Too devastating for his own good. Plucking her own crown out of her hands, he lowered it gently onto her curls, tilting it back so that it didn't hang over her forehead. "Hey, *belle petite déesse*," he said softly, running his hand down her arm to entwine his fingers with hers. "Are you ready to go make sure your good coven sisters dropped a metaphorical house on the bad ones?"

She squeezed his hand. "I think I just might be." And with that, the newly-crowned royals of the Underworld stepped through the portal.

Chapter 60

Evie

Ciomadul, Carpathian Mountains, Romania

The battle still raged around the crater lake when Evie and Cole stepped out of the portal. Now, however, Cate's forces far outnumbered Medea and Circe's. The volcano's shrill, piercing scream had also stopped, and the ash cloud had dispersed as if it never existed, although pools of lava were still cooling around the field. The grass was stained a shade of crimson that only came from massive bloodshed; bodies were strewn far and wide. Some of them Evie recognized as friends; many she didn't. Was it too much to hope that their supporters had stopped the traditionalists without further loss to themselves?

Her eyes darted around those still fighting, searching desperately for Cate, Hesteia, Thea, and Bernadette. If she knew those four were fine, she could breathe more easily.

Cate was the easiest to spot, surrounded as she was by shadows, cutting through opponents smoothly with a... was that a broadsword? Where had the mother of witches found a broadsword when she most certainly hadn't arrived with it? A second later, Evie realized that the weapon itself was made up of the nightmarish, opaque shadows that surrounded Cate. It soon became clear that wasn't the most powerful magic Cate was wielding, though. While Evie looked on, the shadows seized a traditionalist sneaking up behind Cate and flung the witch into a tree so hard she disintegrated into a fine red mist.

Evie barked out an astonished laugh before turning away to continue her search for Hesteia, Thea, and Bernadette. The three smaller witches didn't stand out quite as much as Cate, even with Thea's height, but she finally spotted Hesteia and Thea standing back to back, encircled in a protective round of Hesteia's fire. Any time someone tried to attack the pair by going through, above, or around the fire, it blazed into even more aggressive life, sending the attacker either rolling to the ground in panic to put themselves out or, if they didn't move quickly enough, immolating them where they stood, only a charred bone or two falling to the earth outside of the circle. Thea had raised a protective ward around the fire itself, redirecting all spells that struck it back upon the caster.

Not too far from them, Bernadette crouched, blood dripping from her open hand, encircled by small shadow figures who were lashing out at anyone who came near. A tall man wearing white face paint with black makeup encircling his eyes and slashing over his mouth stood near her. Although he seemed to be watching over Bernadette and controlling the shadow figures surrounding her, his eyes were narrowed on Cate, an unreadable expression on his intense face as he watched her cut her bloody way across the field. Almost as if he sensed Evie's eyes on him, the man glanced over at her, tipped his black hat at her in greeting, and then vanished as if he had never been there.

A shadow swept overhead; Evie looked up just in time to see one of Medea's gilded drakes angling down towards where she and Cole stood. Fury burned white hot through her veins at the memory of her last encounter with the serpentine beasts, and she narrowed eyes gone neon blue on the monster as she drew upon the abundance of death magic available to her now that they had claimed their thrones. No. She had lost too much today. This ghastly beast wouldn't take the love of her immortal life from her. This would be for Chloe. For Adelaide. For the hundreds of nameless coven elders who had lost their lives because they wouldn't support extremism. She knew this wouldn't stop the traditionalists, wouldn't undo everything they had done, or protect Sandrine and her other coven sisters should Medea and Circe and whoever else out there believed in the prophecy decide to go after them. But it was at least a start.

The drake opened its jaws wide, a stomach-turning shriek pouring from its mouth as it dove. It descended quickly, but it appeared in slow motion to Evie. She could see its metallic skin, impenetrable to almost everything. Its megalodon-like teeth, razor sharp and taller than she was. Its blackened tongue, slithering from its mouth, and the ignition of fire building quickly at the back of its throat. The beast shrieked another battle cry as Evie loosed a stream of magic at the drake.

Even with its gilded armor protecting it, the drake was no match for pure, unfiltered death magic. A grim smile overtook Evie's face as she watched the monster decay from the inside out, unseen at first before its flesh peeled away to reveal its ashen insides. Minute shards of bone fell to the earth along with small drops of acidic blood that bore into the earth, leaving only charred dirt and infant snakes in its wake.

With the drake's sudden death, the field fell quiet. Then a scream as Medea fell to her knees, manicured fingers driven into her hair, tears pouring down her face, shrieks pouring from her throat at the loss of one of her monstrous familiars. Circe turned at the sudden sound, but her gaze caught on Cole and Evie, crowned and glowing with the power of the Underworld, before it ever reached Medea.

From what Evie could see, there were few remaining traditionalists still in the field. The ones still alive were staring at them as if they had seen a ghost. And, realistically, it was almost like they had. Her and Cole's survival, their opening of the Underworld and all that entailed, meant the end of a millennia-old prophecy, passed down through generations of witches.

Evie tilted her head and spoke to the traditionalists. "You have fought hard," she started, her words carrying across the silent field. Beside her, she heard Cole add, "And fucking stupidly."

Raising an eyebrow at him, she tried to signal the seriousness of the moment, but her king was having none of it. She rolled her eyes at him before turning her attention back to those in the field. "We understand what led you to fight, but we can't support it. And—" Her voice turned cold as ice. "We will not forgive it. Those few surviving elders who were involved in the insurrection at the Witches Council chamber will be stripped of their magic and their memories." With a snap of her fingers, magical bonds appeared around their wrists. "The elders who opposed your treasonous activity will escort you to the Council chambers—" She shot a glance at Hesteia, who blew a kiss at her before nodding, gathering the unbound elders, and escorting them to collect the traitors. "Where you will await Hecate's judgment. Be thankful your punishment is not worse. If your covens try to avenge your death or pursue the defunct witches' prophecy, know that we will exterminate them like pests. I will lose no sleep over their deaths. Those who led the charge will be executed." She turned her gaze to where she had last seen Medea and Circe, who had been bound with the rest, but the two powerful witches had managed to vanish.

Cate strode over to her and Cole, a black look marring her face. "I'm happy to do as you've asked. But then I would request your leave to hunt Medea and Circe to the ends of the earth like the murderous snakes they are." A hiss left her as she added, "I will hand you their souls for Tartarus and dance to the sounds of their screams as they spend time with the Titans."

A bloodthirsty grin on his face, Cole nodded. "Seems fair. My queen?"

"That's fine." Evie smothered a smile at Cole's formality and commitment to their equality in ruling before summoning a sizable bone shard from the drake's carcass to her hands. "Cate, when you find them, will you please give this to Medea before you bring her to us? I want her to have a reminder of the excruciating pain and torment that we will put her through when she's a resident of Tartarus."

Cate nodded, taking the shard from Evie's hand. "I will be happy to, my queen. My king." Her shadows surrounded her, but, before she vanished among them, she added, "In case I didn't make it clear after Cole tried to kill me in your kitchen—" Beside her, Cole snorted audibly, not a hint of regret on his handsome face. "I hereby pledge my loyalty to you both."

Evie nodded. "We accept and look forward to you taking your role in our court once you take care of the treasonous elders and bring us Medea and Circe."

Evie turned to Cole, preparing to tell him to take them home. Before she could say the words, though, her gaze caught on a person approaching from behind Cole. They were wearing a black leather jacket over a zip-up sweatshirt, the hood raised, plunging their face into darkness.

Both Cate and Cole caught sight of her stare and swiveled towards the newcomer.

Cole's back tensed as he faced the stranger. "Who the fuck are you?"

The stranger lifted a tattooed hand and swiped back his hood. "A friend," he responded in a deep voice. As the fabric fell back, it revealed short thick brown hair, carelessly styled, sitting above whiskey-colored eyes staring cooly at them. "Feels like you could use one."

Evie stared at the man in confusion. She knew that face. She knew *those eyes.* She had seen them before. But where?

"My lord." The stranger turned his attention to Evie, a small smirk forming on his lips. "Hello, goddess."

And with those two words, the memory of a life long past that belonged only to a small part of her burst into full color behind Evie's eyes. *Standing above her was a dark shadow. "Hello, goddess," someone sneered in a low, resonant voice. Kore squinted against the sunlight, the features of the person above her coming into view. A man with thick brown hair glowered down at her, whiskey-colored eyes filled with a killing rage, blood streaked down his throat, coating his hands. That one small detail, more than any of the sounds raging around her, brought her back to herself, jolting her out of her almost catatonic state.*

"You," she snarled angrily. "You murderer!" Rage ran through her veins, and she bolted towards him, prepared to annihilate him.

"Whoa!" Her feet left the ground, Cole's arm wrapped around her waist as he snatched her up. Her foot connected with his knee, his resulting grunt of pain echoing in her ear. "Angel, what the hell?"

"He murdered them," she spat, a blue veil obscuring the world.

Cole rested his cheek against hers; his eyes remained on the man. "Murdered whom?" His voice was quiet, intimate, meant for her ears only.

His low tone and gentle touch did its job; her pulse stopped pounding. The magic buzzed slightly lower in her ears. She could breathe again. "He murdered Aidoneus. And Kore," she breathed.

Cole inhaled deeply behind her before raising his voice. "That so?"

The man nodded and shrugged. "Pretty much." His stance was nonchalant, his voice and words indicating just how little he cared about the execution. "They were trying to take me back to the Underworld, and I didn't want to go."

"You're a shade," Cole commented. The man tilted his head in confirmation. "Any reason why I shouldn't let my pretty little witch turn you into dust the way she's dying to do?" Evie could feel Cole's arm loosen around her waist as he asked the question.

"You need me." The man tilted his head. "You two are going to have to do a lot of unsavory things to fix this shit show. I've been following you, and, frankly, neither of you have the skills to reclaim the escaped shades currently littering this earth."

"And you do?"

"I know all of their hiding spots and have spent millennia snuffing them out so... " The man's eyes were dead. That, more so than the knowledge that he had killed Kore and Aidoneus millennia before, raised the hair along Evie's arms. "Yeah. Yeah, I can."

Evie shook her head against Cole's. "We don't know you," she hissed.

The man inclined his head. "True. I'm Than. And I know who you are, little Evie." His face shifted to the priest who had called the car to get her out of the forest. "And you, Cole Aidoneus, I know all about you." His face morphed into one she didn't recognize, but Cole's body went still against hers.

"Todd?" he yelped. "You're my asshole neighbor, Todd?"

Than's face shifted back to its original form. "I told you. I've been keeping an eye on you."

"And too many goddamn eyes on Evie." Cole's voice was menacing, deeper than usual, his arm banding tighter around her.

"Yeah, well, it's not my fault you were finger fucking your girl in the driveway." Than's eyes roved over Evie, but there was no heat or sex to it. Just pure, cold calculation. Even still, Cole growled at him from behind her. "The fuck was I supposed to do? Look away? You made the movie, man, I just watched it."

Despite her own anger, Evie still found herself suppressing a chuckle at Cole's possessiveness, rubbing her hand along his forearm reassuringly. She opened her mouth, but Cole was already talking. Well. Snarling, more like. "Keep talking about my witch at your own goddamn peril, *man*." He made an angry gesture, a plume of his magic surrounding Than.

The magic cleared revealing a bound and tied Than, who looked far too bored for his current situation. "This is your solution?" One dark-brown eyebrow raised, Than stared in amusement at Cole.

"Until we figure out what to do with you, we're gonna ward you into that house of yours," Cole sneered. "You'll get to go stir-crazy, and we'll get to do whatever we want. In the meantime, I don't want to see your face until we make up our minds about what to do with you, so... Cate!"

From next to them, her dry voice answered. "You shouted?"

"Can you take our friend here back to 1429 Seventh Street in New Orleans and make sure he's locked down until we can get back home?" Cole glanced at his longtime friend. "Then you can go on your revenge march."

Cate gave him a mocking curtsy. "By all means." With a lilting tone of mockery, she asked, "Is there anything else, my liege?"

Evie grimaced at Cole and shook her head. "Nope, I think we're good here."

With a shake of her head, Cate stomped over to Than and snatched his cuffed hands with her own. In a sudden rush of shadows, they vanished. Once Than was gone, Cole placed Evie carefully back on the ground, a hand still positioned on her waist.

With the elders escorting the war criminal witches back to the Council chambers, they were finally left alone to the barren field littered with bodies and stained with blood. However, there was an ecstatic three-headed dog racing towards her with glee in its eyes and skeletal remains around them. "What in the nine realms happened here, Cole?" she asked, eyes wide.

He at least had the good sense to look a little ashamed. "I thought you were dead. I figured I would take as many of them with me as possible before I joined you." A spray of mud splashed over them as the dog came to a screeching halt in front of them. "My buddy here decided to help me with that."

The three-headed dog barked in excitement at her, dropping to his belly and wriggling his stumpy tail in excitement. *Lady!*

"Is this—" Evie lifted a hand to pet one of the dog's heads.

"Cerberus." Cole stroked a hand over the head nearest him; the dog whimpered in happiness. "Charon made it sound like Cerbie here has been watching over us and keeping us safe for a long time."

"So I guess we have a dog now?" At Cole's bewildered shrug, she asked, "Do we have enough space for him?"

"In the Underworld? Sure. At home in New Orleans?" He drew his head back. "Um, maybe?"

To be fair, she was less concerned with where they were going to put their new family member than how they were going to tackle the massive shade problem multiple millennia in the making. Cerbie knocked against her when her hand paused in its scritches. She picked back up her petting but finally looked to Cole "What now, love? We did what we needed to do to stop the initial problem, but... what's next?"

A joking smile broke over his face. "Pretty sure there's plenty for us to do, Angel, so you shouldn't get bored with me too early." At her unamused frown, he continued, "First, I think we have to put these fucking skeletons back in the ground. They deserve a rest after all they've been through. Then we're going to pack us and this mongrel back into that terrible rented car, take it back to the company, and get ourselves home." He palmed the back of her head, drawing her into his chest, her hand falling limply from Cerbie's head as her body melted at his rumbling tone. "Then I'm going to make you my legal fucking wife and spend the next 24 - 48 hours making you scream so loudly that our asshole neighbor will wish he never moved in next door. Not necessarily in that order, though."

Her knees went weak as his eyes grew heated. "Then what?"

"Then we're going to put this Underworld back in order and restore the earth to its somewhat shade-free glory. We have a group of gods who have sworn fidelity to us, a pet guard dog apparently, and a ridiculous amount of power between us." His thumb rubbed along the slim column of her neck. "But, even without any of that, we would be fine. We may have been reincarnated for this, but we were always meant for each other so... we'll make all of this work."

The earth could have stopped turning around her, and she wouldn't have noticed as she stared into his eyes. "You're my whole world, Cole."

The look of love in his eyes melted her. "And you're my fucking everything, Angel."

Epilogue

A Month Later

Cole

Garden District, New Orleans, Louisiana

A lot had happened in thirty days. After a ridiculous hour-plus ride in a four-door sedan with a dog the size of the car itself stuffed into the backseat with all three heads sticking out one of the windows and a long-ass flight back to New Orleans—during which they discovered that Cerbie got airsick—he and Evie finally got home less than a day after the battle in the Carpathians. He had taken the world's quickest shower to wash the filth off him before setting off to check the wards surrounding Than's house, happy to see that not only had Cate over-warded against every deity—except for him and Evie—and beast entering or exiting the premise, but she had also put up several 'No Soliciting' and 'Trespassers will be shot' signs—so many, in fact, that even the tourists were avoiding the house. Once he let himself in, he was thrilled to find out that Cate had not only ripped out the phone system and taken away any form of more modern communication but, in a perfectly petty move, disconnected the Wi-Fi too. Than shared this fact with a furious glare only after he took a swing at Cole with a knife. Apparently, no work, no play, no internet, and no murder made Than a very homicidal boy.

Cole simply dodged, took the knife away from him with a laugh, and left the house with Than's spitted curses following him.

Once they were settled in, Evie had taken one look at their home's backyard and scoffed in his face at the incomplete look of it. At that point he reminded her that bachelors didn't really care about the appearance of their gardens and she was lucky he had a gardener coming in to do upkeep at all. His loving goddess then told him to get lost.

With a chuckle, he left her to her plants and went to Charles' house to catch his family up to speed on everything that happened in Romania, including their new feud with Medea and Circle. As if the mass murder wasn't bad enough, both had supported the harmful measures required of Evie before allowing her to enter the coven. Cole wasn't exactly calm when it came to people harming his Angel, and everyone already knew that fact. In theory. However, they developed practical knowledge of it after he nearly set Charles' kitchen table on fire when he lost his cool while sharing what the Council had done to her. There were now scorch marks on the table. Unfortunately, when he quipped to his uncle that it added character, Charles told him, in no uncertain terms, to get out and go home to the person actually willing to put up with him for her immortal life. As he left, he threw over his shoulder that he had proposed to Evie. Essi had cried, Charles had given him enough expensive booze to start his own bar in the Quarter, and Hayden just looked slightly lost. Hmm. A puzzle for another time.

When he got home that night, Evie, sitting calmly in the kitchen with Cerbie snoozing nearby, informed him that the garden was no longer a travesty. He made appropriate sounds of excitement then shooed Cerbie off his human-sized daybed into the backyard and bent his little witch over the nearest waist-high surface. With their claiming of the Underworld throne, their sex didn't cause cataclysmic world events anymore, but their home was still being overtaken by flora and fauna, thanks to Evie's uncontrolled release of magic whenever she came. He happily accepted that he now lived in a greenhouse. Hell, he would live in Tartarus itself if his Angel was with him.

Less than a week after they got home, he kept his promise to Evie and married her in an intimate ceremony in the backyard of their New Orleans home, surrounded by his family, the newly established pantheon of Underworld gods, Sandrine, Hesteia, Thea, Bernadette, and her other coven sisters. Frankly, once he saw Evie in her wedding dress, nobody else existed for him anyways. A fact that he now received endless ribbing about given that he had stolen her away to their bedroom during dinner and made her scream so loudly and pitch perfectly for him that she shattered three wine glasses. *Worth it.*

Evie steadfastly refused to move to Romania, saying flatly that she wouldn't live that far away from Sandrine, Hesteia, Thea, and Bernadette. With some assistance from Charlie and the witches—many of whom were now venturing further afield from the preserve—she dedicated herself to figuring out a magical method for travel. A week after their wedding, Evie proudly announced that they now had a portal from New Orleans to the Underworld by way of one of the historic trees in their backyard. He asked zero questions. Whatever made her happy.

Even with all of the progress they had made, though, they were still trying to figure out the best way both to collect the shades wrongfully in the human plane and carry the souls the Moirai pegged for death to the Underworld. The gods of their pantheon bore a significant amount of power between them, but none had the skills necessary for this particular task. Which was why, after weeks of nonstop discussions between him and Evie, he was now walking into Than's heavily-warded house a month after imprisoning him.

"What the fuck do you want?" Than glared at him from his spot at the table. A glass of what looked and smelled like whiskey sat in front of him, despite it only being—Cole checked his watch—barely 11:00 in the morning.

"Man, you look like shit," Cole responded cheerily, kicking a chair out from the table and taking a seat. In addition to everything else they had done in the last month, he had taken on a named partner-only status at the firm so anything he did for work was at his discretion. It meant an escape from the daily grind of the last ten years. It also meant that he could wake up late and spend as much of the morning as he wanted making his gorgeous wife come apart for him. "You ever hear of sleep and a shower?"

"I have some extremely rude neighbors." Than's terse reply only made Cole chuckle.

"I dunno what to tell you. May be time for you to move."

"Haven't you heard?" Eyes the same color as the whiskey in Than's glass fixed on his in a furious glare. "I'm a prisoner in my own fucking house."

"Well, that's not really true now, is it?" Cole pulled out a set of papers from the briefcase sitting next to him. "Technically, this house belongs to a Todd Waterson, born in Baton Rouge in 1981, gone missing in 2018. Family's still looking for him, even after all these years." The man across from him didn't so much as glance down at the papers that Cole slid across the table. "You murder Todd, Than?" he asked mildly.

Than shrugged carelessly. "More of a mercy killing, really."

Cole nodded, glad he had been correct in his assumption. "That's why I'm here, actually." At that statement, one of Than's dark brown brows shot up. "Not about Todd—I don't give a shit. Seems like the world's better off without him in it anyways, given the shit he was into. More about your illustrious career as the world's longest-running serial killer."

With a tug of his wrist, he pulled another envelope from the briefcase and splayed newspaper clippings, case summaries, and random notes across the table. "You didn't stop after Kore and Aidoneus. You spent the next several millennia popping up from place to place, murdering anyone you saw fit and then ducking your head back down until your next big exploit." The table was now covered in enough true crime materials to write a book. "You've had a lot of names over the years, buddy. Nero, Vlad the Impaler, Jack the Ripper, the Zodiac Killer. Any time something big and bloody happened, you were at the center of it, situated in just the right way to revel in it. Helluva career in killing right there, *couyon*."

Another shrug. "You here to lecture me on my past? Because, after what I saw you do in that field in Romania when you thought your girl was dead, I'm not really up for a showcase in hypocrisy."

"First off, that's my fucking wife so have some goddamn respect when you talk about her," Cole hissed before forcing himself to relax back into his chair. "And, second, I'm actually here to offer you a job."

Those cold eyes darted up to his, interest sparking for the first time since Cole had walked in unannounced. "What?"

"As it so happens, the Underworld is desperately in need of a god of death. Evie and I could collect shades to our heart's content, but a ton of our time has to be dedicated to building a structure in the Underworld or we're just going to have another mass exodus of souls." He tapped his finger on the newspaper clippings across the table. "As a shade, you've spent lifetimes spilling blood and murdering your way across the globe. During that time, I'm assuming you've amassed untold power from the people you've executed. Taking this role would just allow you to do that on... the company dime, let's call it. You would just have to collect all the outstanding shades and carry new souls to Charon when they die. And you could keep up the extracurricular of being everyone's favorite unsolved true crime monster."

"What's in it for me?" Than demanded.

"Well, for starters, it's either this or Evie comes over here and turns you into dust the way she's been begging me to let her do for the last month." Cole's mouth twisted fondly at the memory of his bloodthirsty goddess sitting naked in his lap, begging him to let her destroy Than. "All the other perks are fairly standard—real immortality rather than whatever half-life, shade-based bullshit you got goin' on now, ear of the royals, deity status, blah, blah, blah." Cole went in for the kill. "Plus you get to choose where you live. Can be in the Underworld or here."

Than's eyes flared at that.

Hell, he guessed Evie's voice carried more than he thought... or maybe it was that he sometimes made an extra effort to piss off their neighbor by fucking Evie outside or opening the windows when he took her inside the house. "You would trust me?"

"Well, to be fair, your entire life force would be tied to the Underworld so destroying you if you fucked around and we found out wouldn't be too difficult." Spreading his hands, Cole inclined his head. "Frankly, I can't hold Evie off much longer. She's been itching to execute you since Romania, and I'm running out of reasons to stop h—"

"I'm in." Than shoved his hand across the table. "So when do I start, boss?"

The Chthonians will return.

BILLIE NICKS

Acknowledgements

It has been a forever dream of mine to publish a novel, so I'm going to just thank until truth flows like a river.

Let's start with the big one: to Mr. Billie. Mr. Nicks? Y'all, I don't know what to call him, but let's just make it easy. To my spouse. He never once asked why I felt the overwhelming need to write well into the wee small hours of morning, drink enough caffeine to power a small nuclear reactor, or ever said anything about the feral raccoon I become when I'm in the writing/editing/formatting cave. He simply opens the door to make sure I'm still alive, ignores me when I hiss at him or read a snippet of what I just wrote like that answers the question he asked, and tosses food at me regularly enough that I don't starve. You are my everything, and there is no way for me to describe all the ways that Gold Dust Grimoire wouldn't exist without you. I love you with every fiber of my weird, little goth-girl heart forever and always. I'm so sorry that Cole has an alarming amount of qualities that are very similar to you. It was mostly an accident.

To Dawn Darling and Candice Clark. Without the two of you accidentally bec oming my author mentors and very intentionally becoming my dear friends, Gold Dust Grimoire never would have happened. It feels, somehow simultane- ously, like it was just yesterday and 300,000 light years ago that I was mumbling a storyline to myself and staring at a blank page. I wrote several chapters of the story that ultimately became the book in your hands then put the thing down for SIX FREAKING YEARS. The only reason I picked it back up after so much shaming of myself for setting it on the back burner was because of Candice who inspired me to get back on the writing horse by publishing her very own debut and the phenomenal Dawn who gave me the advice that totally changed my perspective: write the damn thing. You two changed my life.

To my glitter babies in the Dumpster—you are the best Glitterati a girl could ever ask for. Even when I stopped believing in myself—usually at 4:00 AM accompanied by terrified voice notes that y'all listened to when you woke up at hospitable human hours—you all never once stopped believing in me. Your unwavering love and support mean absolutely everything to me, even though I'm not wholly certain that I deserve them. And now because I promised that I would name check each and every one of you, you thought I was kidding (and in alphabetical order so nobody thinks I love them more):

- Black Widow Nat
- Bri Baby
- Brio
- Charliebird
- Elizabeth
- Er-Bear
- Faye Love
- Grace
- Hi It's Me Candice
- Joshy the Glitter Pup
- Jessica (aka Glitter Rawdog)

- Jules
- Kiki
- Kristal
- Leen
- Lise
- Lizzie
- Milady Kathy Baby
- NikNack
- Oblair
- Shrek Sugar Mama
- Sterlibird
- TayTay
- Tracy

I love you all so much—you're my rocks. I'm so honored to have a group of besties that have my back through everything and were willing to jump into my Greek mythology bullshit with pretty much zero questions asked. And to the honorary members of the Glitter Dumpster

To my amazing Glitter Trash Pandas. Y'all are the best, most feral street team an author could ever ask for. I know many of you took a chance, took a chance, took a chance on me before you ever read a lick of my writing. I'll never not be honored by that show of faith in me.

To the artists who brought Cole and Evie to life in no small part. Er-bear, you swept in with the most beautiful cover I could ever imagine, YOU GAVE GOLD DUST GRIMOIRE ITS DAMN TITLE, and both of these things happened "just for fun." Your brain is incredible, and I'm so damn thankful that I informed you that you were going to be my best friend after two weeks of knowing each other. Called that one, huh? Amanda Desilets (@art_by_adsilets), you absolute beauty—when I needed a digital portrayal of Evie and Cole for the cover and cold-contacted you because I was obsessed with your work, you created something beautiful that I'm so proud to include on the cover. And to my incredible Lilith Luxe . . . your character art for Evie and Cole is everything I could ever dream of. I'm grateful to call you my friend and so excited to see your star on the rise.

To Brandi, my PA, My Only Ho Smutty Yoda, the ADHD Saddie to my Anxiety Brain. I know you say I'm not nearly as feral or disorganized as I think I am, but your ability to motivate me and understand the hellaciously absurd voicenotes and messages I send you at all hours of the day and night, your dedication to marketing, branding (down, fellow dark romance girlies, I mean like marketing branding, get your mind out of the gutter wink), and organizing me have all been absolutely critical to any success I might have. I know this is absolutely brand new information, but I freaking love you!

To my author besties who supported me along the way. You know who you are, but I got to call some of them out specifically: Nova B. Quinn, Luna K. Wicked, the aforementioned Candice Clark and Dawn Darling, and my babes in the one-wo/man-show and SBB. Y'all inspire me and make me want to be a better writer. I love you all with every weird damn bone in my body.

To my Nana. You always encouraged my writing even when I was little and told me that I had a story to share with the world. While I don't really think that you expected that story to unhinged mythological smut, I still think you would have been bemused by it and proud of me. I wish you were still around to see my story finally get published for real.

To my parents and my in-laws. Although my mother hasn't read my writing since I was a kid and definitely hasn't read Gold Dust Grimoire yet, she is prepared to hard sell every book I ever write to her friends. As discussed, Maman, if you ever read this, please don't tell me. I don't need to be aware that you know some of the smutty tomfoolery that lives inside my brain. My father who makes sure I know that he's proud of me for writing a book, even though I suspect he would have preferred that it was nonfiction. Jokes on you, Papa, my love for Greek mythology and the epics came from watching you! To my father- and mother-in-law who are already trying to plan a release day party because they want to celebrate this milestone: you are both so wonderful, and I'm so lucky to be a part of your family.

And last but absolutely not least... to anyone who has read Gold Dust Grimoire. I'm so appreciative and honored that you took my debut journey with me in any part.

Made in the USA
Coppell, TX
22 February 2026

72083533R00321